# Road Closed

ALSO BY LEIGH RUSSELL
FROM CLIPPER LARGE PRINT

Cut Short

# Road Closed

## Leigh Russell

# W F HOWES LTD

This large print edition published in 2013 by
W F Howes Ltd
Unit 4, Rearsby Business Park, Gaddesby Lane,
Rearsby, Leicester LE7 4YH

1 3 5 7 9 10 8 6 4 2

First published in the United Kingdom in 2010
by No Exit Press

A CIP catalogue record for this book is available
from the British Library

ISBN 978 1 47122 773 8

Typeset by Palimpsest Book Production Limited,
Falkirk, Stirlingshire
Printed and bound in Great Britain
by MPG Books Ltd, Bodmin, Cornwall

*Dedication to*

*Michael, Jo and Phill*

# PART I

*'All things that we clasp and cherish,*
*Pass like dreams we may not keep.'*

Heinrich Heine

# CHAPTER 1

# INTRUDERS

The glass cutter made a soft scratching sound. Slowly Cal dislodged the panel with the tips of his gloved fingers and reached in to undo the window catch. His companion's lanky frame hovered awkwardly on the sill as he swung his legs over. A flash of torchlight revealed they were in a kitchen.

'Hungry?' Ray grinned and nodded at a packet of chocolate hobnobs beside the kettle. Cal put his finger to his lips. Ray instantly froze, his eyes wary. The distant hum of a car was carried in on the breeze from the open window. Inside the house all was quiet. They made their way into a broad hallway. Cal squinted up at his companion, then turned and led the way up the stairs.

Silence.

They went into a study. The beam from Cal's torch hovered over a desk. Ray seized a digital camera and shoved it into a khaki bag slung across his shoulder. The top drawer of the desk was locked. Cal bent down and picked at the catch with practised fingers. It slid open with a click.

'Jackpot,' he whispered with barely concealed

excitement. He drew out a leather jewellery case and opened the lid. They caught a glimpse of stones, glittering red and green and white.

'Is it the real thing?' Ray's hood had fallen back to reveal a mess of sandy coloured hair above bulging watery eyes.

'Let's get it home for a closer look.'

As they made their way back to the stairs, Ray grabbed Cal's arm.

'What?'

'Thought I heard footsteps.' They stared at one another, straining to hear. The house was quiet. They edged forwards. The bag jingled softly on Ray's back. They reached a bend on the landing, and a voice startled them.

'Elliot? Is that you, Elliot?'

At the same time, the overhead light flicked on, making them blink. An old lady was standing in front of them, her figure silhouetted in an open doorway. She gasped audibly as she took in the two figures staring at her across the landing. 'Who are you?' she rasped. Her eyes glared wildly at them. One hand was pressed against her chest, the other pushed at the door. Cal leapt forward and seized the old woman by the arm. 'I'm calling the police,' she faltered, but her legs buckled.

'Shit,' Ray cried out. 'She's seen us. Let's get out of here.'

'First things first.' Cal lifted the woman off her feet. Shouldering Ray to one side, he strode past, and hurled his burden with a grunt. They watched

4

her crumple and disappear backwards down the stairs.

A few muffled thumps.

Silence.

'What did you do that for?' Ray's face was rigid with terror.

'Stupid cow shouldn't have put the light on. Don't worry,' Cal grinned. 'She can't identify us now. Come on, retard, let's get out of here.'

A shudder ran through Ray's long frame. He leapt forward and bounded down the stairs. His boot accidentally kicked the woman who lay, motionless, at the foot of the stairs. Her body jolted at the impact. Charging down behind Ray, Cal almost tripped over her inert figure. Struggling to regain his balance, he knocked into Ray. The bag slipped from Ray's shoulder. It fell with a clatter that seemed to reverberate around the walls. Gold chains and coloured jewels spewed out of it.

Their feet thumped on the carpet. Ray reached the front door first. He twisted the handle. The door didn't budge. It was double locked. He kicked at it and swore aloud. They turned and ran back along the hall, across the kitchen and out of the open window into the cool of the night air.

When they reached home Brenda was awake, shaking, in her chair.

'Make us a mug of tea,' Cal grunted. Brenda scurried to the kitchen, head lowered, shoulders hunched. Cal turned to Ray and held out a hand. Cal's face darkened and seemed to swell.

5

'I don't know what happened, Cal. I was scared. It must've slipped off my shoulder back in the house, when we were doing a runner. I reckon I dropped it in the hall, when . . . the old woman . . .'

'You left it behind? All that gear?'

'I'd have gone back for it if I'd known.'

Cal's voice was low, measured. 'You retard,' he said. 'Was there anything in the bag could be traced back to you?'

'No.' Ray's face shone, sweaty. 'I swear it, Cal. I picked it up at the market like you said and I never touched it, only with gloves on. I did everything just like you said, Cal.'

'Like I said?' Cal was yelling now. 'If you'd listened to me, you wouldn't have just lost us a small bleeding fortune.'

Brenda came in and set two steaming mugs down on the table. 'Give it a rest, Cal,' she said.

Cal spun round. 'Or what?' he roared. Brenda cowered away and sat down. 'You still here?' Cal turned his attention back to Ray. 'We're finished.'

'Give us another chance,' Ray pleaded. 'Just one more chance.'

'Another chance?' Cal mimicked. 'He wants another chance, Bren.'

'He can piss off,' she replied. Ray's eyes met hers in a cold stare. Her head drooped. She stared down at her fingers, picking uncontrollably at her sleeves.

Cal turned back to Ray. 'You want another

chance,' he sneered. 'Who do you think you are? I'll tell you. You're a fucking retard. That's what you are. Ray the retard.'

Ray stepped forward, fists clenched, then subsided, muttering.

'What's that you said?' Cal asked.

'I said you can leave it out.' Ray flinched as Cal lit a cigarette.

'Supposing I was to give you another chance,' Cal said slowly. 'How do I know you're going to keep your head this time?' Ray kept his eyes fixed on Cal who flicked the lighted match at Ray's face. Ray jerked his head to one side. The match fell harmlessly to the floor. 'The thing is,' Cal went on, 'that was a balls up. What was it?'

'A balls up,' Ray repeated, scowling at the floor.

'Right. And do you know why?' Ray shrugged, staring at his large scuffed shoes. 'Panic,' Cal answered his own question. 'You panicked. You forgot the exit plan. The first rule. The first thing we do next time, soon as we're in, we find the back door. That was your job, retard.' He stood up and pointed his cigarette at Ray who took a step back. He stared at the dusting of dandruff on Cal's shoulders. 'First we unlock the back door, then we look about us and see what we can find. That way, we can split, no sweat. No flapping about. Next time we might not be so lucky. We've got to be careful. Got it?'

Ray nodded in relief. 'I'll make it up to you, Cal. I promise I'll make it up to you.'

'We were lucky to get out in time,' Cal went on.

'Yeah,' Ray agreed. 'We were lucky.'

'But we've been clever too,' Cal added.

'Yeah, we've been clever.'

'We're going to do one of the big properties up on the top of the hill,' Cal was suddenly brisk. 'You with me then, retard?' Ray nodded. 'Those big white houses at the top of the hill.'

'Must be loaded,' Ray said slowly. His bulging eyes lit up. 'Let's do it.'

'Do you think you ought?' Brenda asked. 'They might have a dog. What if they've got a dog, Cal?'

'What are you on about, you stupid cow? We're just going to relieve those rich bastards of some of their dosh. They're so loaded, they don't know what to spend it on next.' Cal laughed loudly. He turned on Brenda. 'Why don't you keep your nose out of this, you stupid bitch? Go to bed.' He cuffed her on the side of the head as she walked past. She stumbled at the blow but recovered her balance and continued on her way without demur.

Ray laughed nervously. 'What's she on about, what dogs?'

Cal turned. 'You got a problem?'

'No, nothing Cal,' Ray muttered. His ears went bright red. 'I wonder why she stays with you, that's all. You're a vicious bastard.' The words burst out of him. He stood, mouth slack, his long legs tensed for flight.

To Ray's relief, Cal sat down and took a long drag of his cigarette. 'I'll never understand it myself,' he agreed. He leaned back and blew ragged smoke rings at the ceiling. 'A looker like Bren. She could have anyone.' He squinted sourly up at Ray. 'Don't you go getting any funny ideas.' Ray shook his head. There was no need to explain what he thought of Brenda. He had seen the filthy smack head naked, walked in on her in the bathroom by mistake and recoiled at the sight of her scraggy tits and white belly. She hadn't even known he was there. Cal was barking if he thought Ray fancied Brenda. Might as well shag a dead fish.

'She's out of my league, Cal,' he lied with inspired cunning. 'Too good for me,' he added, making sure.

Cal grunted and tossed his cigarette on the floor. 'We're agreed then,' he said treading the stub into the carpet.

'It won't happen again. I won't let you down again,' Ray babbled. 'It was only a bag. I'll get another one.'

'It's only a bag,' Cal mimicked him. 'Retard.'

'I'll make it up to you,' Ray muttered, under his breath. He had a plan. He was going to surprise Cal by pulling off a job all by himself.

'What are you grinning at?'

'Nothing, Cal. I was just thinking about those houses on Harchester Hill.' Ray hung his head, hugging his secret to himself. He would show Cal. He could be clever too. He didn't know how he was going to do it, but he'd think of something.

★    ★    ★

9

Elliot Green checked on his mother three times a week. Mrs. Green was mobile, but it had become a major excursion for her to leave the house. Elliot tried to be a good son. He always brought her food and small toiletries so she didn't have to go out if she was feeling tired. It was heartbreaking when she was housebound, worse when she went out. Several times neighbours had found her wandering in the street, unable to remember where she lived. There wouldn't always be responsible people around when she got lost. But if Elliot was anxious about his mother going out, he was also concerned about her being alone in the house.

'It's a nightmare,' he confided in his business partner. 'I have to take care of everything. Pay the bills, the cleaner, the gardener, everything.'

'You ought to move her into a home.'

'I know. I've tried, but she refuses to leave the house. She's lived there over sixty years.'

His partner whistled. 'Bloody hell. Even so, you ought to move her. For her own good.'

Elliot sighed. 'I wish I could, but . . . you don't know my mother. You can't tell her anything. God knows, I've tried.'

On Friday morning, Elliot was late. He barely had time to call on his mother and almost gave it a miss. He cursed when she didn't answer the door. He had to fish in his wallet for the key. It turned stiffly in the lock.

His mother lay sprawled in a heap at the foot of the stairs. Strings of fake pearls and diamonds were tangled together across her torso, a gold chain straddled her face.

Elliot felt his legs trembling as he approached and stared down at her.

'Mother?' he whispered. 'Mother?' He crouched down. He didn't want to touch her. She lay, rigid, her legs splayed, her head twisted at an awkward angle so her glassy eyes appeared to be staring straight at him in blind accusation. There was nothing he could do. Nothing anyone could do. He reached out and touched his mother's eyelid. No response. He wondered if medical attention might help but sat on his heels for what felt like hours, unable to move.

When he finally stood up, he noticed a blood stain on the carpet. A wave of nausea hit him. He turned and hurried back down the hall, and threw up over the front step.

# CHAPTER 2

# FUNERAL

Geraldine glanced around the kitchen. Hannah bridled, misunderstanding the expression on her friend's face. 'There's no need to look so disapproving,' she snapped. 'Not everyone's as anal as you.' Geraldine smiled as Hannah seized a damp rag and swiped at a patch of butter on the table, smearing crumbs. 'Oh sod it. Let's go in the other room.' As though that would be any better.

Over the years Geraldine had grown used to the chaos that surrounded Hannah. Looking around at the jumble of clothes, children's books, toys and women's magazines, Geraldine remembered her surprise the first time she had walked into Hannah's bedroom after school.

'No wonder you keep losing your homework,' she had said, staring primly at the clutter that covered every surface of her friend's room.

'I know, I'm hopeless.' Hannah had shaken her head until her ponytail wiggled. 'My mum goes spare.' That was how their friendship had begun. Geraldine lost count of the number of times she saved Hannah from detention by lending her friend books, PE kit, or homework to copy.

'So what's the problem this time?' Hannah asked. She swept a pile of towels off a chair so Geraldine could sit down. 'I thought you were going to Dubrovnik with Craig. I thought you said it was all booked.'

'It was. It is.'

'So . . .?'

Geraldine shrugged. 'I'm not sure I want to go away right now.'

Her friend let out an exaggerated sigh. 'It's a bit late to be having second thoughts, isn't it? I thought you liked this boyfriend. Why did you agree to go away with him if you don't like him?'

'Of course I like him. I really like him. But—'

'But what?'

'I've already had to take time off—'

'For your mother's funeral. That's hardly a holiday. And in any case, one thing's got nothing to do with the other. If anything, it's even more reason for you to go away. Look, you've booked this trip to Dubrovnik, haven't you? You've paid for it. For goodness' sake, give yourself a break. You're entitled to a holiday. We're not getting any younger. And it's not healthy to be so obsessed with your work.'

'I'm not obsessed with my work. I happen to believe it's important, that's all.'

'Self-important more like.'

13

'That's not fair. Police murder enquiries protect everyone.'

'Oh cut the pompous crap. So you're a detective inspector. Well, good for you. You work on a Murder Investigation Team. You make a difference to people's lives and help to make society better for everyone. I'm not saying you don't. But what about *your* life? You've finally met someone you like. At least give him a chance. It'll be a break if nothing else. You need to get away. You look terrible. Understandably. You have just lost your mother.' She patted Geraldine's hand sympathetically and Geraldine sighed. She couldn't even tell her oldest friend how she felt about her mother's death.

From an early age Geraldine had been aware that her sister, Celia, was very close to their mother. As they grew up, her sister's life followed a similar pattern to their mother's. Geraldine, independent, ambitious, hadn't married or produced precious grandchildren. Her mother had never openly criticised the life choices Geraldine made, but nothing Geraldine achieved ever seemed to please her. Her mother had greeted the news of Geraldine's promotion to detective inspector with congratulations but she was more interested in hearing about her granddaughter.

'I'm a detective inspector, mum,' Geraldine had wanted to shout. 'I've worked hard for this. It means something. It matters.'

But her mother was speaking to Chloe. 'You're going to learn the flute? How wonderful!'

14

'How wonderful,' Geraldine had echoed, smiling at her young niece.

When Geraldine's mother died unexpectedly, Geraldine felt crushed by regret that she had never tried to improve their relationship. Now it was too late. The funeral passed in a blur. A chill wind gusted across the cemetery making Geraldine's eyes water. She glanced around the drab assembly of mourners. Celia, black coated, leaned on her husband, shaking with grief. Unmoved, Geraldine watched the wooden casket disappear from view. Her sadness had given way to a dull anger. Her mother had never really cared for her.

The ceremony over, the mourners went to Celia's house. Time gathered dust while Geraldine engaged in small talk with vaguely familiar relatives.

'You remember me, don't you, Geraldine?'

'Yes, of course,' Geraldine lied.

'Your poor mother.'

Geraldine circulated, clutching a glass of wine.

'Wasn't it a lovely funeral?'

'Didn't Celia do everything beautifully?'

'Those lilies.'

'You know she saw to everything herself?'

'Well, you couldn't expect Geraldine to—' Catching sight of Geraldine, the speaker pressed thin lips together. Geraldine turned away, pretending she hadn't heard.

'Thank God they've all gone,' Geraldine exclaimed when she finally fell into an armchair and kicked her shoes off.

Celia burst into tears. 'I'm sorry,' she mumbled, dropping her face into her hands. 'I miss her so much.'

Geraldine wondered if working with other people's anguish had dulled her capacity to experience it first hand. While Celia was inconsolable, Geraldine felt only a guilty impatience to return to work. 'When's Chloe coming back? I'm—' She almost said she was dying to see her niece. Celia had decided that her daughter was too young to attend the funeral. 'I can't wait to see her.'

Celia blew her nose. 'Yes, it's been a while since you were here. You won't believe how much she's grown. Seven going on seventeen. You will stay here tonight, won't you? I know you're busy, but it would be nice to see more of you, and I'm not saying it just for my sake. I know Chloe would like to spend more time with you. She's growing up so fast.'

'Yes, I'd like that. I know I've been preoccupied with work lately, but I will make more of an effort.' She studied her sister. Other than their pale complexions, they weren't alike. Geraldine had always envied Celia her ash blonde hair, fine and naturally wavy. Geraldine's hair was coarse and straight, so dark it was almost black.

'We've only got each other now,' Celia said.

'I'll change.' Geraldine promised out loud. 'I want to spend more time with you.'

'Yes, this makes you think, doesn't it? None of us know how much more time we've got.' Celia sniffed.

16

Chloe's return lightened the mood. She came running in, pigtails bouncing, and flung herself at Geraldine. 'Are we going shopping, Aunty Geraldine?'

Geraldine smiled. 'Not this time, Chloe. But soon, I promise.'

'Don't pester Aunty Geraldine or she won't buy you any more presents,' Celia scolded.

Chloe snuggled down on the sofa beside Geraldine and prattled about her best friend. She kept up her chatter throughout supper. When Chloe finally went to bed Celia broke down in tears again. Geraldine reached for another bottle of wine.

'You'll regret it in the morning,' her sister warned her. 'Haven't you had enough?'

'I'm not driving, and it's not as if I'm on duty.'

'Your all important duty.'

'Here, let me,' Geraldine's brother-in-law seized the corkscrew from Geraldine.

'You need some coffee,' Celia snapped. 'For God's sake, Geraldine, we buried our mother today. Show some respect.'

'Respect the dead.' For the first time that day, Geraldine felt like weeping. 'That's all I ever bloody do. I spend my whole life respecting the dead.'

'Coffee,' her brother-in-law said firmly. He stood up and took the bottle from Geraldine.

'You'll feel terrible in the morning,' Celia said. She was crying again.

'I feel terrible anyway.' Geraldine felt queasy, yearning for a grief she didn't feel.

'Your mother's dead, you unnatural bitch,' she muttered to herself as she climbed into bed. In her mind, a small voice answered. So what?

When Geraldine opened her eyes the next morning, her head felt as though someone was thumping it with a bottle. Groaning, she rolled out of bed and kept her eyes shut as she felt around for her clothes.

'So I did suffer when my mother died, after all,' she thought sourly.

# CHAPTER 3

## SOPHIE

'Slow down. You're making me nervous,' Tom said. Sophie jammed her foot on the accelerator. 'Slow down.' The car jerked forward. 'She can't even be civil,' Sophie fumed. 'From the first moment she set eyes on me, she's resented me. Well, the feeling's mutual.'

'It's me you married, not her. And I love you.'

'I've never been good enough for you, as far as she's concerned. Who does she think she is, speaking to me like that?'

'I appreciate your keeping your temper with her,' Tom said humbly. He stared at the streetlights zipping past and waited for his wife's temper to cool. Sophie was never angry for long.

'She's never liked me. I don't know why we have to go and see her every week. Every bloody Sunday. And she's still not satisfied. What more does she want?' They both knew the answer.

Whenever they visited her, Tom's mother harped on about how she had been twenty-one when her son was born. 'It doesn't do to leave it too late. It's not natural. It causes all sorts of problems. And I'm here to take care of the baby whenever

19

you want to go back to work. I know some women prefer not to look after their own children these days. Best leave the upbringing in capable hands. All these new ideas they have nowadays, they don't do a child any good. Look at how the youngsters behave these days. It's not surprising, left to train themselves. It's a wonder they're ever toilet trained. I had my Thomas on the potty at six months. More tea, Tom?'

Sophie wasn't thinking about starting a family. When she did, she would be back at work within six months, with a nanny at home. She would swing before she let her mother-in-law care for her children.

'She's on her own. She's lonely,' Tom murmured, lighting up a cigarette.

'That's no excuse for being rude.' Sophie eased her foot off the accelerator and glanced across at her husband. It wasn't his fault. 'It's hard for you, being stuck in the middle,' she apologised. 'She is your mother. I shouldn't go on about her like that.'

Tom shrugged. 'She brings it on herself. I'm with you now. If you want to stop going to see her . . . Well, you're the only one I want. You know that.'

Sophie smiled. 'And you're the only person who matters in my life,' she said fiercely, 'the only one.'

Absorbed in computers, Sophie had never considered herself lonely. When a girl at the office had issued a blanket invitation to a Christmas party,

Sophie hadn't even replied. Parties held no appeal for her. The other girl paused when she happened to walk past Sophie's workstation the afternoon of the party.

'You coming tonight?' she asked. Flattered by her colleague's interest, Sophie accepted the invitation.

She regretted her impulse as soon as she arrived. Everyone in the room seemed to be talking. No one acknowledged Sophie's arrival. She didn't understand why she had been invited. She stood in a corner, pressing her back against the wall, uncomfortable with the noise and smell of so many people crammed into one small room. It was a complete waste of her time. There was a new update waiting for her to install at the office, where she could have been working uninterrupted. She turned to leave, and bumped into a stranger.

'Sorry,' she muttered.

'I don't know anyone here,' he blurted out. She heard the panic in his voice and hesitated.

'I don't know why I came,' she replied.

He asked about her role in the company and they discussed work for a while. With music thumping, conversation was difficult. 'It's so stuffy in here,' she complained. She would have gone home but didn't want to be rude.

'We could go somewhere else?' he suggested. She felt an unfamiliar thrill and wondered if he was coming on to her. 'I mean, for a coffee or something. Or a drink. There's a pub round the corner.

21

I mean, if you don't mind. My name's Tom Cliff.'
He held out his hand, oddly formal. Over his
shoulder Sophie could see a couple in a passionate
clinch.

They left the party together and went for a drink
and discovered they worked for the same company.
'Funny we've never met before,' they agreed.

'I don't really leave my desk,' he admitted.

'Me neither.'

'We're there to work,' Tom said. Sophie nodded
seriously.

After a couple of months Tom took her home
to meet his widowed mother. Sophie wasn't clever
at reading people, but she recognised the other
woman's hostility straight away.

'You're imagining it,' Tom insisted. 'Mum's not
like that.'

'You're a substitute for your father,' Sophie told
him, with rare insight. 'You live in the same house,
you eat together every night, you even go on
holiday together. She'll never let you go.'

'That's nonsense,' he replied, 'because I intend
to live with you, as my wife.'

'Do I have a say in this?' Sophie asked, smiling.

When Sophie announced her promotion, Tom's
mother was shocked. 'What do you mean, you
might have to go to work on Sundays? You always
come and see me on Sundays. It's the weekend.
No one works on Sundays.'

'I'm only on call. Chances are they'll never need

me on a Sunday. I'm only on call every other night and it's only on alternate weekends.'

'Can't someone else do it?' her mother-in-law asked. Her grey curls bounced as she handed Tom a cup of tea. 'Tell them you're engaged on Sundays. I'm sure they can manage without you. It's not as if you're a brain surgeon, Sophie. It's hardly life and death, is it? It's only computers.'

Sophie explained that the printers had to be kept working round the clock churning out bank statements, pay slips and other essential documents.

'Nonsense,' her mother-in-law interrupted. 'It's nothing that can't wait till Monday morning. What if there was a power cut?' Her eyes gleamed as she slid a slice of pie on to her son's plate. He lit another cigarette and waved the glowing tip in the air in protest. 'You'll have to come here later on, when your office is closed.'

'I may be called out at night,' Sophie said, irritated by her mother-in-law's interference. 'I may have to work all night.'

Tom's mother stared at her, dumbstruck, cake slice in hand. 'You're a married woman.'

# CHAPTER 4

# DUBROVNIK

The heat in Dubrovnik was debilitating. Beneath the heavy scent of oleanders a stench of drains lingered. Pink flowering bushes and purple boughs of bougainvillea hung bright against white washed walls. Geraldine followed Craig gratefully into the shade of an arch at the side of a square where tourists gathered to drink from a central fountain. Geraldine screwed her eyes up against the glare of sunlight and watched pigeons perch on top of the fountain. She was aware of Craig's presence at her side. She could feel the warmth of his arm almost touching hers and breathed in the scent of his aftershave.

'I don't think I'll risk that,' she screwed her nose up at the fountain. 'Like drinking pigeon piss.' Tiny lines around his eyes crinkled as Craig smiled down at her. The heat of the day softened slightly as the afternoon strolled towards evening and they climbed up on to the ramparts to view the city of terracotta roofs spread out beneath them in the soft heat haze. Geraldine turned and gazed down at the sea. Flecks of sunlight flickered on the water like fairy lights, winking up at her.

'It's beautiful, Mark,' she murmured.

Words once spoken couldn't be unsaid.

'What?' She didn't answer. 'Did you just call me Mark?'

Geraldine hesitated. Craig knew that she had lived with someone for six years, but she couldn't remember if she had told him her ex was called Mark.

'A mark,' she stammered stupidly. 'There's a mark.' Flustered, she rubbed at Craig's shoulder. He shrugged and turned away from her feeble lie. The moment was tainted.

Staying in Dubrovnik felt like stepping back in time, a world away from the stresses of her normal day's work: studying crime scenes, reading post mortem reports, observing bodies laid on cold slabs, interviewing suspects, reading witness statements and the endless paperwork that accumulated at every step of the process. Geraldine revelled in the sense of purpose her job on the Murder Investigation Team gave her but, along with her colleagues, deplored the pointless paperwork demanded by bureaucrats who had probably never seen a cadaver, let alone felt a thrill of adrenaline at the start of a case. If they had, they wouldn't care whether officers filled in forms or not, only about putting the killers behind bars.

Geraldine smiled at the feel of Craig's hand on her shoulder. He had suggested a city break when her last case had finished and booked a flight as soon as she could escape.

'Surely you're entitled to a break before they throw you into your next case? You've been working twenty four seven for weeks.'

'It's not as simple as that.' Geraldine had tried to explain the importance of the paperwork that followed a successful arrest. 'We have to make sure he doesn't get off on a technicality.'

'How can he possibly get off? He's locked up. But you're not.' Eventually the case was tied up and they booked their holiday.

'You look better already,' Craig told her as she rolled out of bed after their first night in Dubrobnik.

'Better than what?' she asked, grinning. Craig was right. Three days in Dubrovnik with Craig was just the tonic she needed. She hoped it would give them a chance to establish the terms of their relationship, but they didn't seem to be making much progress with that. There never seemed to be time to broach the subject at home. They had been seeing each other on and off for a year, but she still wasn't sure how serious their relationship was. Going away together had offered them an opportunity to talk. She had ruined it by calling him Mark.

'You'll be home before it arrives,' Craig told her when she wrote a postcard to Hannah. He read it upside down. 'All well. Beautiful city. Lunch in restaurant overlooking bay. Hot enough. Flowers everywhere. Love Geraldine.' Craig gave a mock frown. 'No mention of the wonderful company?' Geraldine remembered to post the card at the hotel desk as they were leaving.

26

'Here's hoping you'll have a few days' grace before they whisk you off on another case,' Craig said on the flight home. He sounded tetchy.

Geraldine gave him a rueful smile and went back to studying her passport. 'You can hardly see it.' She pointed to a faint imprint of a stamp with the name 'Dubrovnik' barely legible.

'Write over it,' Craig suggested.

'I can't do that.'

'You can't, but I could,' he replied, laughing. 'All you need is a fine black biro.' He grabbed her passport. Geraldine snatched it back and turned away, irritated.

The next day she downloaded the photos from her phone and trawled through them with a smile that wavered only when her own face appeared. She studied her image on the screen and tried to be objective about her dark hair, unruly when it wasn't pinned back with slides, her large black eyes that always seemed to glow with health, and her small crooked nose that spoiled her looks.

The phone rang. Geraldine hung back for a moment before answering it. She didn't want Craig to think she had been waiting for his call.

'Well? How was it?' Hannah asked.

Geraldine swallowed her disappointment. 'Lovely,' she replied. She knew what her friend meant. 'It's a beautiful city. I'd recommend it. And the weather was perfect. Not too hot.'

'I'm not interested in Dubrovnik,' Hannah interrupted impatiently, 'How did it go with Craig?'

Geraldine hesitated. 'Probably too well,' she admitted.

'When are you seeing him again?'

'I don't know.'

'You don't know? How can you not know? You've been seeing each other for nearly a year, and you've just been on holiday together.'

Geraldine sighed. It was all right for Hannah. Married for eight years, she had no reason to feel insecure about her relationship. Geraldine felt like a love struck teenager waiting by the phone. She kept herself busy with chores, but the days passed and he didn't call. On Thursday evening she caved in and dialled his number.

'Craig Hudson.'

Geraldine felt her breath quicken at the sound of his voice. 'Don't make a fool of yourself,' she thought. 'Hi, it's me,' she answered breezily. 'Geraldine. I wondered if you'd like to come over for dinner one evening? If you're free, that is.' Intending to appear casual, she sounded apologetic.

To her relief Craig answered straight away. 'Sounds great. When did you have in mind?'

'How about Saturday? Around seven thirty?'

'Saturday? No, I can't make this Saturday. Tell you what, let's make it Sunday.'

'Fine. See you Sunday.'

Geraldine gazed round her tidy flat and wondered how Craig was planning to spend his Saturday evening – and whether he would be spending it alone. He was charming and attentive when they were together but then weeks would pass without her hearing from him. When he did want to see her, the chances were she would be preoccupied with a case. Her relationship with Mark had been straightforward. With Craig, everything was so complicated. But Mark had met someone else. Geraldine had no idea how long he had been seeing the other woman before he left. Perhaps life had only seemed simple then. She remembered how hot it had been in Dubrovnik and shivered.

# CHAPTER 5

# MARKET

'It's bloody hard work,' Alice said, 'and it's getting harder. I don't know how you manage, with your kids. You're a bloody marvel.'

'A martyr more like,' Maggie grunted.

'I mean,' Alice warmed to her protest, 'I suppose we do better than some I could mention, who haven't even got a licence. But even so, working the market all weathers, it's no picnic, is it?' She ran a hand through her iron grey hair before repeating, 'I don't know how you manage.'

Maggie grimaced. 'It's bloody hard work. You're right there. But needs must. No point complaining when we haven't got a choice.'

Friday was generally busy. Maggie liked to arrive early and set up without having to rush but she had to get the kids' breakfast ready before she set off. As her battered van rattled along the street, it began to rain. Maggie swore. Her windscreen wipers weren't aligned properly but she couldn't afford to get the van seen to. Worse, the market was always slow in wet weather. She drove carefully, screwing up her eyes to peer through the veil of fine rain, and screeched to a halt beside the inadequate parking area closest to her stall. A dirty black van was straddling two spaces, leaving no room for her. She had to park at the other end of the market, furthest from her pitch. Fuming, she hauled banana boxes out of the van and lugged them across to her stall. She set up as quickly as she could, unpacking her stock in the shelter of the tattered awning. New bags went up last, in the front.

'That's nice.' Alice pointed at a pink and purple bag as Maggie finished. 'Is it new?' Maggie shrugged. Her mind wasn't on the job that morning. It was a dull day. The rain cleared but there weren't many people around. Maggie stood idle, fretting. After a while she wandered over to Alice on the neighbouring stall.

'Keep an eye out, will you, Alice? I'm going to speak to Geoffrey.'

'What's the fat bastard done now?'

Maggie described how she had been unable to park near her stall because Geoffrey had blocked her space. 'Selfish bastard.' She tugged at the zip on her anorak, squared her shoulders, and strode off.

'Geoffrey!'

'Hello, Maggie. Take a look at this, will you? It's perfect for you.' He held up a small fake gold watch hanging from a thin black strap.

'I'm not looking for a watch. And if I was, this would be the last place I'd go. You know why I'm here.' Geoffrey leaned his hands flat on his trestle table and met her gaze, a smile on his rubbery lips. 'And you can take that bloody grin off your face.'

'No need to be abusive, Maggie.' He turned away and began fiddling with his stock.

'You did it again, you selfish bastard, parked right across two spaces,' Maggie burst out. Geoffrey appeared to ignore her, but she could see his fat lips twitch in annoyance. 'Just keep away from me, or I'll speak to the manager. You park anywhere near my stall again and you'll be—'

'Don't you stand there and tell me where I can and can't go,' he interrupted her, suddenly red-faced. Spittle flew from his lips. Maggie stared in disgust. 'I'll park where the hell I like. I didn't see your name written there. I was there first.'

With a curse, Maggie retreated. It was obvious she wasn't going to get anywhere with Geoffrey. At least he knew she was on to him, and she meant what she had said. She would go to the market manager and complain if Geoffrey took up two parking spaces again.

'How did you get on?' Alice asked.

'Was it busy?'

Alice shook her head. 'You didn't miss much.' She gazed around the damp empty market place, and pushed her hair out of her eyes with the back of a gloved hand. 'Some bloke took a bag, one of those khaki ones with the shoulder strap. Stupid sod tried to give me some cock and bull story about how he'd bought one off you and the strap broke. Tried telling me I should give him one for free. As if. Weird looking bloke, funny eyes.'

Maggie was still thinking about Geoffrey. 'Bastard.'

'What's that?'

'Nothing.' Geoffrey had rattled her, but she wasn't going to be intimidated. She knew why Geoffrey had it in for her. Maggie's stall was in a prime position, on the corner opposite the station. A wintry sun broke through the clouds and she smiled. From now on, she would make sure she was in early enough to park where she wanted. Let that Geoffrey leave his van round the other side. 'Serve him right,' she said. 'Stupid sod, thinks he can get one over on me, just because I wasn't there. I'll show him.'

'Exactly,' Alice agreed companionably, 'but don't worry. I made him pay for it, full price.'

# CHAPTER 6

## BRENDA

It was dark when Brenda woke up. She didn't know what time it was. A streetlamp cast a dim light into the room. Although the television had been switched off she stared at the screen for a few moments. In the silence the house was making strange noises. She hauled herself stiffly out of her chair and made her way quietly upstairs. Cal didn't like it when she woke him up.

She stole into the bedroom. The bed was empty. She patted the covers tentatively to make sure. If she woke him up, he'd be angry, but at least she wouldn't be alone with the noises and the darkness. He wasn't there. She turned the light on. A naked bulb threw stark shadows round the room. Her own face stared at her from the mirror, white and misty. She fumbled for a cigarette. It took several attempts to light a match; she was shaking by the time she finally inhaled.

The door to Ray's bedroom creaked. Brenda peered inside. His bed was empty too. She took a few steps into the room and dropped ash on to the pillow. Serve him right. Before Ray came to live in the house, Cal used to take her out with

34

him. Now it was all Ray, Ray, Ray. She dragged frantically at her cigarette and flicked more ash on to Ray's pillow. She hoped it would choke him.

A blade of pain sliced through her head. Her legs shook. Her heart was pounding. Alone in the house, she heard footsteps coming up the stairs. She stood very still, not daring to breathe. The house was silent.

'Silly,' she mouthed. If she showed she didn't care, the footsteps would go away.

Cal would have laughed at her. 'There's nothing there,' he'd say. Brenda waited. It was all right for Cal, but you couldn't be too careful when you were in the house on your own. Anything could happen. They came in through the walls.

'Go away!' she shouted suddenly, surprising herself. 'I'm not frightened!' They knew she was lying. Aching all over, she went back downstairs and fell into her chair. She couldn't settle. Cal and Ray had gone out on a job. She hoped Cal wouldn't come home in a temper again.

Brenda trembled as she thought of his rage. But if he was angry with Ray, that was good. She gave a wary smile.

Pressing herself into the safety of her chair she screwed up her eyes and looked round the room. A strand of dry hair clung to her face, scratching at her eye. That wasn't what made her flinch. Something was lurking in the shadows. A voice whimpered nearby. Brenda pulled herself to her feet and limped over to Cal's chair for a light. A moment later a flame shot from her fingers. She fought for control of her body. Her legs kept jerking which made it difficult to light her spliff.

At last she leaned back in her chair and watched as a thin trail of white smoke trickled out of her nose. It didn't help. Dope might soften the pain but it couldn't stop her shaking. Feeling nauseous she sat up without moving from her chair. When she threw up, Cal made her scrub the carpet until the stink of dettol made her sick all over again. Experience had taught her to know when she was only going to retch.

Craving wrenched at her guts but Cal had gone out. He never left anything in the house. Said he couldn't trust her. Viciously she stubbed her spliff on the arm of the chair and watched it singe a ragged hole in the fabric. Glowing threads faded into grey.

With a soft fizzle, the naked light bulb above her head went out. The whimpering began again.

'I know you're there,' she whispered. Her eyes flicked round the corners of the room. In the darkness, something stirred.

Cal dismissed her night terrors. 'There's nothing here.' He would stamp his foot in the corner of the room. 'So much for your snake. I've squashed it. Flat.' Then he would throw his head back and laugh. Nothing frightened Cal. But Cal had gone out. She was alone in the darkness.

'He'll be back soon,' she whispered, glaring into the darkness. Her voice was feeble. In the corner,

36

the snake hissed. Brenda whimpered. She lit a cigarette and forced herself to think about Cal.

He had been complaining again. 'If it weren't for you, we'd be fine. As if I haven't got enough to worry about with the rent due and the fucking TV, you're always going on, never bloody satisfied.' His face had been red and sweaty. She had waited, trembling. But afterwards he'd brought out the skag and everything had been all right. 'You're a lucky girl,' he told her as he wiped a dribble of blood off her chin. 'Don't say I don't take care of you.' Brenda had nodded, too far gone to speak.

She trembled in the darkness. Salty tears stung her split lip. 'Bastard,' she muttered. She would never dare speak to him like that to his face. If only he had left her a fix. 'It's not so much to ask,' she whined. She began to cry in earnest and the whimpering fell silent. As long as she was crying she was safe from the voices. Her eyes throbbed. They felt as though they would burst, but she couldn't stop crying. 'Let me sleep,' she pleaded with the silence. 'I want to sleep.' Her eyes were sore. They hurt when she shut them. With shaking fingers she clutched at her cigarette and leaned back in her chair, inhaling deeply. She didn't know when Cal would be back.

Cal took care of her. She pressed herself against the back of her chair, clutching a cushion to her chest. Cal put on a front, but Brenda knew better. He wasn't so tough. When it came to it Cal was no worse than all the other men. Better, because he looked after her.

'If it wasn't for me, where would you be now?' he asked her. 'How would you live? And where? On the street, that's where.'

'Yes, Cal.'

'Where would you be?'

'On the street, Cal.'

'Bronxy's had enough of you.'

'Yes, Cal.'

'But I look after you.'

'Yes, Cal. You look after me.'

Brenda had been happy at first, working for Bronxy. Bronxy was tough with the girls but fair. She looked after them.

'We're a team, girls,' she used to say. 'I make sure the punters are comfortable but you're the ones who keep them happy.' The trouble was, Brenda wasn't keeping men happy any more. She still danced, but none of the customers wanted to pay to spend time with her. It wasn't as if she was old. When Bronxy took her off the podium, Brenda was shocked.

'What am I supposed to do for tips now?' she complained to the other girls. They didn't care.

'All the more for us,' one of them pointed out.

'What can I do?' she asked Bronxy in desperation.

'Clean yourself up for fuck's sake,' Bronxy snapped. 'You're a disgrace.'

When Cal took her to live with him, Brenda couldn't believe her luck.

Bronxy seemed pleased with the arrangement too. 'He'll put a roof over your head and take care of you. Don't mess it up, Bren. And get yourself off the smack for fuck's sake, before he gets tired of you. You're being given a chance here. Don't screw it up.'

Brenda tried to explain that the smack wasn't the problem but Bronxy wasn't listening. No one understood, except Cal. She wondered where he was. He could be gone for hours. She closed her eyes.

In the darkness a snake uncoiled, hissing.

# CHAPTER 7

# SECOND ATTEMPT

They waited until the road was clear. Cal turned the van lights out and was careful not to rev the engine as they crawled slowly up Harchester Hill. He parked in a side street. No one saw them hurry on foot past houses set back from the pavement behind tall bushes. Without a word, Cal vanished through a gap in a hedge. Ray followed close on his heels. They crept along under cover of evergreen shrubs. Somewhere a dog barked. Cal paused, one hand raised above his shoulder. Ray almost barged into him. He stopped himself just in time and hung his head, waiting for Cal to move. They listened. The dog went on yelping. It was nowhere near them. Cal tapped Ray on the arm. They resumed their cautious progress towards the house. In the darkness they made their way silently down the side of the front garden, trampling late autumn flowers into the earth.

'Quick, make a dash for it,' Cal whispered in Ray's ear. They sprinted across a narrow strip of grass. Security lights came on. They reached the house and flattened themselves against the wall.

'They'll think it's foxes,' Cal whispered to Ray who nodded, hunching his shoulders and holding his breath. His heart was pounding beneath his jacket. He hoped Cal couldn't hear it. They waited. As soon as the lights clicked off, Cal gave Ray a shove and a leg up over the side gate. Ray slid the bolt across. They were inside. The security lights came on again. No one looking out of the window would have seen two figures pressed against the side wall of the house in the shadow of the gate. After a moment the lights went out. They manoeuvred their way along the wall, avoiding setting off the lights, until they reached a low window.

Ray glanced around nervously while Cal worked. It was awkward cutting the glass while keeping himself pressed against the wall. The faint scratching seemed to go on forever. At one point, Ray sidled up and put his hand on the window.

Cal paused in his task. 'What?' he snarled under his breath.

'Thought I heard a phone ring.' They stood listening. There was no sound from inside the house. Cal shrugged and carried on, muttering softly.

'It's taking too long,' Ray whispered. The security lights had made him nervous.

'Nearly done,' Cal insisted. He pressed harder against the glass. The cut out panel broke away with a soft snap. He reached in to release the window catch.

Cal and Ray were in a large kitchen. The wall

to their right was covered in pristine white cupboards, a gleaming glass fronted oven stood in the corner, and in the middle of the floor stood a central island with a stainless steel gas hob. On the far side of the room an open door led into a dining area. They could dimly make out a table and chairs through the opening. To their left a back door led out on to the garden. Cal crossed the room and closed the door to the dining room. Then he tried the door to the garden. It was locked.

Ray put his bag down on the hob and waited as Cal picked at the lock, his eyes screwed up in concentration. There was a click when he gave the door handle a wrench and it responded. He straightened up with a grin. 'Come on, let's see what we can find.' Their exit secure, they were ready to explore the house. Ray reached for his bag. Cal crossed the kitchen. He opened the door to the dining room.

And heard footsteps.

He closed the door.

In the light of his torch, Ray saw Cal's eyes, white and angry. 'What now?' Ray whispered hoarsely.

'Go!'

Ray grabbed his bag from the hob. There was nothing in it, but Ray wasn't going to leave his bag behind again. He grabbed at the strap. It had caught on something. He jerked it free. There was a soft click and a faint hissing. Cal had disappeared.

Ray ran after him, closing the back door behind him as he escaped into the night. They sped down the side passage, careless of the security lights. Cal forced his way through the hedge on to the next door drive and sprinted down on to the road. Ray raced across the front of the house and made for the safety of the street down the drive of the property they had just broken into. A car shot out of the driveway behind him just before he reached the pavement. He spun round, startled. For a second its lights shone straight at him before he slipped round the hedge and away.

'Bugger!' Cal snarled as the van started up. 'Bloody waste of time.'

'At least we got away,' Ray mumbled. He was still shaking. 'We're safe and no harm done. And I got the bag, Cal.' He held it up. The strap was broken. Cal scowled. He slammed his foot on the accelerator and they roared away into the night.

# CHAPTER 8

# NIGHT

The telephone shook Sophie awake. It was nearly two thirty in the morning. For a second, she was confused. She had been running along an empty beach, searching for Tom. Through a slit in the bedroom curtains a splinter of moonlight shone into the room. Beside her, Tom rolled over on to his side and groaned in his sleep. She reached for the handset.

'Yes?' She listened. 'I'll be there in half an hour.' Some technical problems could be resolved remotely from her laptop at home. On this occasion she knew she would have to go in. She hung up and wriggled round to look at Tom. He was still asleep, peaceful as a child. Sophie smiled. After two years of marriage, she still couldn't believe her luck.

'Are you sure he's not just after your money?' her mother had asked with a quizzical smile when Sophie had announced she was getting married. 'You're a relatively wealthy woman, Sophie, and you've only known him for a few months.'

Sophie hadn't admitted that she had no idea how much Tom earned. It wasn't something she could explain to her mother. Her parents were dutiful but distant. Until she met Tom all her passion had been channelled into her studies and her work. Tom had transformed life into something miraculous. She had never realised how lonely she was until she met him.

Sophie would have liked to speak openly to Tom about her feelings, but was afraid he would laugh at her for being sentimental. In any case, she wouldn't be able to find the right words. She settled for an inadequate 'I love you,' which she whispered repeatedly to him as he slept beside her. Sometimes the intensity of her feelings brought tears to her eyes when she watched him as he slept. All the love she was capable of feeling had been stored up for this man sleeping beside her. He stirred. She slipped out of bed, careful not to wake him. She could have lain awake watching him all night, but she had to go to work.

Sophie felt for her clothes in the dark and crept downstairs. She hesitated in the hall but decided not to stop for coffee. The sooner she reached the office, the sooner she could get started. She was keen to get the system up and running again, to minimise the backlog. It wasn't ideal, driving when she felt groggy, but the roads would be empty at that time of night. She could have plenty of strong coffee when she reached the office. She thought of her husband, sleeping soundly upstairs and her face softened into a smile. He wouldn't need to get up for another five hours. She blew a kiss at the stairs before she set off, closing the front door softly behind her.

The freezing air shocked her fully awake. Overhead, stars shone brightly in a clear sky. Sophie felt a dreamlike alertness as she hurried over to her car. The revving of her engine broke the silence. As she accelerated out of the drive, a figure suddenly darted in front of her. Sophie slammed her foot on the brake and swerved. Her car door came to rest against the hedge. Leaves and twigs scratched at the window. In the orange glow of a street lamp bulging eyes stared wildly at her before the figure dashed away into the darkness. Sophie reversed away from the hedge and drove off, shaken by the near miss.

It was gone half past six by the time she left work. Pumped up with caffeine, she knew her restlessness masked an underlying exhaustion and her reactions might be sluggish so she drove slowly back through the centre of town, past closed up shops and out towards Harchester Hill. The streets were deserted at that time of morning. Soon, houses would light up as people dragged themselves out of bed. Two hours later, the centre of town would be crammed with cars idling in queues. She passed a police car cruising the streets. Apart from that, all was quiet. At this rate, she would easily be home before Tom left for work. She accelerated involuntarily at the prospect of seeing him. The engine whined.

Sophie was on her way to Harchester Hill when she heard a muffled boom. For an instant the air in front of her windscreen quivered. As she

46

approached the bottom of the hill, a siren pierced the hum of her engine. In her rear mirror she saw a fire engine race towards her, police cars on its tail. She pulled over to allow the emergency vehicles to pass before pulling out to accelerate behind them up the hill. Ahead of the flashing lights a column of black smoke hovered above the rooftops like a medieval angel of death. The emergency vehicles swung off the main road, leading her in the direction of her home. She followed. Turning the final corner of her journey, she found her way blocked by a police car. Fear struck her like a punch in the guts. She scrambled out of the car. Leaving the engine running and the door open she ran along the street. Her legs felt weak. She battled for breath. It was an effort to keep moving. Her heart was thumping painfully as she pushed through the watching crowd. Some of them recognised her and fell back.

A man shouted crossly. 'We're all trying to see here—' His voice stopped abruptly when he caught sight of Sophie, as though someone had switched off the radio.

'Keep back there please,' a police constable called out.

'Tom!' Sophie gasped. None of the uniformed figures took any notice of her. She seized a fireman, clung to the coarse fabric of his sleeve. 'My husband! Tom!' Her voice rose to a shriek. A tall man in a helmet advanced towards her.

'Mrs Cliff? I'm very sorry.' He shook his head.

Sophie stared at his blackened face. 'No!' She gazed around, stupefied. Over the fireman's shoulder she could see her smouldering house. Men in uniform were moving around, silhouetted against the red glow. The line of onlookers behind her was being pushed back. A man with a megaphone was shouting at them.

'We're evacuating the neighbouring houses,' a voice called out.

'We need to move all those cars, now,' another voice barked.

A movement nearby caught Sophie's attention. Two men were carrying a stretcher, its small load covered. Sophie stumbled over to it. The stretcher bearers paused. She raised the blanket. Tom was sleeping, his face smudgy and grey. Soon he would open his eyes and scold her for leaving home without waking him to say goodbye. She reached out. Gently she stroked his cheek, ran her finger along his bottom lip, round his chin. Her eyes filled with tears and her head sank forward on to his body. She would have stayed there forever – she had nowhere else to go – but someone pulled her away. A hand pulled the blanket over Tom's face as he was carried into the van.

'Where are they taking him?' she asked. Her voice juddered as though she was sobbing but her eyes were dry. No one answered her. A siren rang out. Sophie watched the mortuary van disappear in the smoke-filled air.

# CHAPTER 9

# SUMMONS

Geraldine was up early on Saturday morning. Over a breakfast of coffee and wholemeal toast, she studied a well thumbed cookery book. Craig was visiting his sister at the weekend but would be back home by Sunday evening. It was going to be the first time she cooked for him. Before their holiday in Dubrovnik, he had always insisted on taking her out to eat.

'You work hard enough,' he would say. Geraldine had smiled, conscious that his refusal to stay at her flat gave their relationship a temporary feel. Now she was determined to impress him. She considered just about every recipe in the book before finally settling on an old favourite. Best to play it safe. She was queuing in the supermarket when her mobile rang.

'How soon do you want me there?' she asked, eyeing the stationary queue in front of her. The girl at the till was chatting to a woman at the front of the line.

'I need a price' the cashier called out.

'I'm on my way,' Geraldine sighed into the

phone. Abandoning her trolley, she hurried home, changed into a work suit, and set off.

Her destination was the nearby historic town of Harchester. Originally a popular stopping place for pilgrims travelling to Canterbury, it had grown into a thriving market town on the main route from a busy sea port to the city of London. It was said that Geoffrey Chaucer himself had spent the night at the Hawtree Inn in Harchester. The inn had long since disappeared but Geraldine had read somewhere that Chaucer's visit was commemorated by a plaque in the shopping mall, ironically placed between WH Smith's and Starbucks.

Geraldine pulled into the police station car park with less than an hour to spare, tugged a comb through her hair, pinned it back off her face, and went into the station. Her day took an unexpected turn for the better when she caught sight of a familiar face on her way to the Incident Room. She had worked with Detective Sergeant Ian Peterson on an earlier case when his quick thinking had saved her life.

'Gov!' Peterson's handsome features relaxed into an infectious grin which quickly faded. 'I heard about your mother . . .' He paused, struggling for the right words, an awkward giant of a man. He ran one large hand through neatly combed hair which leapt into spikey disarray.

'We deal with it all the time, but it's different when it happens to you.' Geraldine gave a rueful grin. It wasn't easy to talk in the corridor. They were constantly interrupted. Several uniformed officers overtook them, they had to stand aside for people carrying computers, and a few women marched past wielding files. The corridor grew more congested as they neared the Incident Room.

'At least we know which direction to go in,' Peterson said with a cheery smile as he stepped aside for two men manoeuvring their way along the corridor with a desk. He was on his way to the canteen but Geraldine wanted to get her bearings before the briefing began so she went directly to the Incident Room. Her spirits lifted at the familiar bustle.

'DI Steel?' the duty sergeant repeated, checking her list. 'Yours is the second door along.'

'Sorry?'

'Your office, ma'am. Second door along.' She pointed to a series of doors leading off the Incident Room.

'Thank you.'

Geraldine was pleased to discover she had her own tiny office, partitioned off from the main Incident Room by a flimsy internal wall. She tapped her keyboard and was relieved to find her computer had been set up. After checking her emails she scanned through several reports. A man had died in a gas explosion possibly under suspicious circumstances. Geraldine finished her reading and went back into the Incident Room.

The atmosphere was brisk. Officers were scurrying around, greeting one another, dodging people carrying computers and files, and questioning the harassed duty sergeant. Geraldine couldn't see Peterson and didn't recognise anyone else. She returned to her office and sat for a moment, wedged behind her desk, listening to the bustle on the other side of the partition wall. She was pleased to be back in the only environment where she felt at home. Deferring her paperwork, she manoeuvred her way back across the Incident Room. There was still time for a quiet coffee before the briefing. She needed to clear her head.

Glancing around the canteen, she spotted Peterson and was pleased when the detective sergeant's face lit up on seeing her. Even in rest he exuded energy. Geraldine paused to return his grin before joining the short queue for coffee, their mutual pleasure at working together again expressed only in an exchange of smiles and a quick nod. It was enough.

As Geraldine sat down at Peterson's table an older man came over to introduce himself as a local detective inspector, nearing retirement. He was investigating a spate of robberies in the area.

'DI Steel?' He looked down at her with a slow smile and Geraldine gestured for him to join them. Thin and leathery, he looked as though his life had been spent working outdoors.

As they sipped canteen coffee, Bennett told her about his case. 'We've been on the trail of a gang of thieves for a few months and now we've had what looks like a case of aggravated burglary.'

'Any leads?' Peterson asked, his enthusiasm a stark contrast to the older officer's indifference.

Bennett shook his head. 'It's been a case of one step forwards, two steps back, I'm afraid.' Geraldine liked him, but couldn't help wondering how effective he would be. Born out of his time, she imagined him content to pound the beat in a village, a friend to the local residents. 'Until now, it's been a few stolen antiques, watches, cash, fifty quid and such, small change really. Things they could pocket easily and fence without suspicion, all of which has made them difficult to trace. They've not been exactly a priority. You know how it is, so much time given over to drunken brawls. I've hardly had any uniform support at all. The death of the old woman changes things.' He sighed wistfully. 'I'm due for retirement soon. I could do without all this. A string of break-ins is trouble enough.' Geraldine nodded sympathetically, hoping she would never lose her sense of excitement at the start of a new investigation. 'I hear you've got Kathryn Gordon on the fire case,' Bennett added.

'Do you know her?' Geraldine asked. Peterson smiled. Gordon was a sharp senior officer. Geraldine was in two minds about working with her again. Professionally, she would be the first to admit Gordon was first rate. On a personal level, Geraldine was anxious. She'd had a few run-ins with the detective chief inspector on their previous case.

'If her reputation's anything to go by, she's a

force to be reckoned with. You haven't come across her?' Bennett was asking. 'Has the DIs quaking in their boots, I've heard,' he added, with a rapid glance over his shoulder. Geraldine sipped her coffee. 'But it's only hearsay. I haven't worked with her before.'

'She's the dog's bollocks,' Peterson said fervently.

Geraldine grunted and rose to her feet. 'Best get there before the briefing begins,' she said.

'Plenty of time,' Bennett replied, looking at his watch. Geraldine didn't want to be late so Bennett obligingly led the way back to the Incident Room. Built like a runner, he was wiry rather than thin, his movements fluid.

They reached the Incident Room just as the briefing was about to begin. Geraldine studied the Incident Board. The faces of the victim and his widow looked back at her: a fair haired man with pinched features and a woman who stared intensely at the camera through thick lenses. Some DCIs preferred not to display pictures of murder victims after they had been killed. Such images were considered bad for morale. But Geraldine was more disturbed by photos of the victims before they died. 'Look at me,' the dead man's face seemed to say. 'You can see how contented I am with my life.' A life that had come to an abrupt end. And it was Geraldine's job to find out how that had happened.

# CHAPTER 10

## DCI

The detective chief inspector rapped on the board for silence. She was wearing a pale green jacket that seemed to drain her face of colour, heightening the clown-like effect of her flushed cheeks, but any impression of frailty was eclipsed by her blazing eyes. She wore no make up and her greying hair was cut in a practical bob along her jaw line.

'Good morning, everyone,' she said. The room was instantly silent. A female police constable dropped her pen and retrieved it, red-faced. 'I'm your Senior Investigating Officer DCI Kathryn Gordon. Thomas Cliff died early this morning in an explosion at his home, 17 Harchester Close. A gas ring had been left on in the kitchen. Gas was leaking overnight. Mr Cliff entered the kitchen at approximately seven. The gas air mix had reached a critical level when it seems he lit a cigarette, causing an explosion.' Gordon moved her arm further along. Her fingers trembled, almost imperceptibly, as they touched the board. 'This is his widow, Sophie Cliff. She wasn't home when the explosion occurred. She was called away at two

55

twenty in the morning – this wasn't unusual – but it was just about the time the Fire Investigation Team suspect the gas was turned on. She returned home shortly after the emergency vehicles arrived on the scene.'

Geraldine stared at Sophie Cliff's photo as the DCI ran through details that confirmed Mrs Cliff had been called to work in the early hours of the morning.

'Would she have known in advance when she might be called out in the night?' someone asked.

The DCI nodded at a sergeant who had been on the phone to Sophie Cliff's line manager.

'She'd have known in advance which nights she'd be on call,' the sergeant explained, 'but not if she was going to be called out. If she was needed, she didn't always have to go into work. Sometimes she could work on the system remotely from home. Some nights she wasn't called on at all, so she couldn't possibly have known beforehand if she was going to be called out of the house on any particular night.'

'But if the gas leak started around the time she went out—' Geraldine began.

The DCI finished her thought. 'She could have left the gas on deliberately once she knew she'd be out of the house all night.'

'But how could she have predicted an explosion? It takes a critical amount of gas in the air,' someone pointed out.

'She knew he smoked. It was a fair bet.'

A number of officers broke into scattered discussions with their immediate neighbours about the feasibility of predicting a gas explosion.

'It seems unlikely,' the DCI held up her hand for silence. 'But the victim smoked so a gas leak would certainly be high risk. It all hinges on what time the gas leak started. We know what time Sophie Cliff arrived at work. Now we need to wait for the full Fire Investigation Team's report.'

'He might've gone down and heated something up after she'd gone out,' someone suggested, 'and left the gas on himself.'

'Enough speculation. We'll have to wait for Scene of Crime officers and the FIT to finish. In the meantime, the adjoining properties have been evacuated while the gas supply's being checked just in case, though there's no reason to suspect a leak was caused by anything other than the tap left on in the Cliffs' house,' the DCI concluded. 'Now let's get going and see what else we can find.'

Back at her desk, Geraldine scanned the Fire Investigation Team's initial findings which confirmed the fire had been caused by gas leaking from an open tap. They were still at the scene. It had taken time to control the blaze and the property had sustained substantial damage. After talking to neighbours, they had been able to pinpoint the time of the explosion: just before six in the morning. Thomas Cliff had been in the kitchen when the gas had ignited. He had been thrown to the floor, probably stunned, where he died of smoke inhalation. Sophie Cliff had been on her way home at the time.

Geraldine sat in the privacy of her office and sighed. Having an office to herself wasn't as satisfying as she had expected. She missed the bustle of the Incident Room. She grabbed her jacket from the back of her chair and went to check her schedule for the day. The list was ready. She was assigned to work with Detective Sergeant Ian Peterson.

'Excellent,' she muttered under her breath. Peterson was a reliable officer. She had appreciated his steady good sense on their last case together.

Geraldine found him perched on a desk chatting to a young blonde detective constable. Sprightly and well turned out, his hair combed flat once more, Peterson looked out of place in the dingy Incident Room. His shirt was pressed and his shoes polished. He looked more like a TV sports presenter than a detective.

'Let's go, Sergeant.'

He slipped smoothly to his feet. 'Yes, gov.' Geraldine wasn't sure, but she thought he winked at the seated constable and felt irritated. The sergeant grinned at her and she thought, with a pang, how young he looked.

'Gordon again,' he said as they left the station.

'Better the devil you know.'

Peterson nodded. 'Just what I was thinking, gov.'

He grinned as he emphasized the last word. Geraldine pursed her lips.

She ran through the gist of the report with Peterson as he drove. From its origins in the Middle Ages, Harchester had evolved into a sprawling jumble of incompatible styles of architecture. Still, in some sense, a market town, the heart of the place was its brand new shopping mall. Radiating out from the main shopping centre were streets of dilapidated Victorian properties, multiple bells indicating that they had been divided into apartments. Most of the buildings looked as though they were in urgent need of renovation. An occasional purpose built block of flats from the sixties added to the pervading air of neglect. As they drove further away from the centre of town, the tall properties gave way to smaller houses opening straight on to the pavement. Still further out, the streets were lined with conventional suburban semi-detached brick houses. These sported front gardens, wrought iron or wooden gates, and low picket fences or evergreen hedges separating them from the street. Geraldine had heard about an old part of Harchester, with buildings that were said to be genuine Tudor, but there was no sign of it as they drove through the town.

Finally they climbed Harchester Hill. Here the houses were larger, detached, and concealed from the road by tall bushes.

'Let's hope there's not going to be another explosion,' Peterson said as they negotiated the road block and approached the damaged house.

'They're still investigating. They've cleared the neighbouring houses to avoid any danger of contamination but it's quite safe.' Geraldine hoped she sounded confident.

The Chief Officer of the Fire Investigation Team was expecting them. A constable led them along a dark hallway into the burnt out shell of a kitchen. The place stank.

'One of the gas taps was turned on,' the fire officer explained. His eyes sparkled at them from a sooty face, like a Hollywood version of a Victorian chimney sweep. He indicated a mangled twist of metal, and pointed at fire damaged plaster on the ceiling. 'At the rate the gas was escaping, it must have been leaking for several hours to reach a flammable mixture in the atmosphere. The explosion occurred here.' He touched a crusty central hob surrounded by a blackened worktop. 'We're still looking at it. From the direction of damage to the plasterwork and flooring, it looks as though the victim entered the room there, went to turn on the light . . .' He nodded at a burnt out electric switch by the door.

'You mean it wasn't a cigarette that caused the explosion?'

The fire officer frowned. 'Looks like he switched the light on and sparked it, but it could have been a cigarette. We haven't found evidence he was smoking when it started, but that's hardly surprising.' He glanced around the burnt out kitchen and shrugged.

'Would switching a light on be enough to cause an explosion?'

'Given the right fuel oxygen mix in the air, yes. That's all it takes. It happens.'

'Jesus,' Peterson muttered under his breath, gazing round. 'Just from switching on the light.'

The fireman nodded. 'You'd hardly credit it, would you?'

'Makes you think twice about turning the lights on.' Geraldine frowned at the sergeant's flippant tone.

The fireman smiled. 'There's really nothing to worry about, as long as you don't have a gas leak.' He turned back to his exploration of the ruined kitchen, picking his way carefully through the debris.

'If the kitchen's like that, I dread to think what the victim must look like,' Peterson said as they left.

'We'll find out soon enough,' Geraldine replied briskly, doing her best to conceal her own dismay.

# CHAPTER 11

# MORTUARY

That afternoon, Geraldine and Peterson met at the mortuary.

'George Talbot,' the pathologist introduced himself.

'DI Steel and this is DS Peterson.'

They were about to follow Dr Talbot through the swing doors when Kathryn Gordon arrived.

'Not much mess,' the doctor announced cheerfully. 'No spilt blood and guts with this one. Other than from my intervention,' he added. Above his mask, Geraldine thought his blue eyes were smiling. No one smiled back.

Apart from the long, neatly sewn up incision across his chest, and the horribly white flesh, Thomas Cliff could have been asleep.

'His face was black with soot but he's cleaned up nicely. The widow's coming in soon to identify him,' the doctor explained. 'You can see he's hardly burnt at all. Just the palms of the hands, here, and again on the knees and shins. He managed to crawl out of the kitchen into the next room but that's as far as he got.' He indicated the charred palms of the dead man's hands and the burn marks on

62

his legs. 'He pulled a rug over his head, but didn't manage to keep his hands inside it. He was holding on to it.'

'The rug didn't save him,' the DCI said.

'It probably protected him from the flames on the back of his head and across his shoulders, but it was the smoke that got him. If the fire service had got to him sooner, it's possible he might have survived, but he was trapped for too long before they found him.'

'If the door from the next room into wherever – was it the hall? – had been open, could he have got out?' Peterson wanted to know.

'I'm not sure,' the doctor replied. 'The dining room might've reached flashover if it was ventilated by an open door.'

'Wouldn't an open door have lowered the temperature?' the sergeant asked. The doctor shrugged. 'And why the hell didn't anyone hear the explosion?' Peterson went on. He sounded angry.

'They did,' the DCI answered, 'a neighbour called up almost immediately, which is probably why the victim escaped being burnt. But it was still too late. They didn't get to him in time.'

'What about the windows?'

The doctor shrugged. 'The smoke must have overcome him too quickly. The presence of cyanide in his blood was already nearing potentially lethal levels—'

'Cyanide?' Geraldine interrupted. 'Are you saying he was poisoned?'

'And the fire was started to cover it up,' Peterson added.

'No, no, that's not what I meant,' the doctor answered. 'You'll have to ask the fire investigation officers for the specific source but cyanide can derive from any number of burning substances, wool, cotton, paper, plastics and other polymers, for example, any number of which might've been present in the kitchen, and cyanide poisoning, even before it reached such a dangerous level, would have incapacitated him. It prevents the body from carrying oxygen. He managed to crawl as far as the adjoining room before he lost consciousness. The cyanide might've prevented him from even attempting to escape. At the very least it would've contributed to his difficulties, and prolonged his exposure to fatal concentrations of carbon monoxide which killed him.' He sighed. 'In any event, he didn't make it. The combination of cyanide and carbon monoxide did for him.'

'So he died from smoke inhalation?'

'Yes. That's basically it.' The doctor tapped the neat incision across Thomas Cliff's chest as he listed the symptoms it concealed. 'He died from respiratory failure although there's significant pulmonary injury evident, which is hardly surprising. There's swelling of the airways, and soot evident in the nostrils and throat. The respiratory tract is full of black mucus, also present in the trachea and lungs. Oxygen levels are low in the blood, and cyanide and carbon monoxide present, as I mentioned, in lethal levels. He died of asphyxiation from the smoke. There's no question about that.'

Geraldine gazed down at the corpse. Thomas Cliff looked so peaceful. It was strange to think of all the internal damage concealed beneath the neat bloodless scar. The sergeant and the DCI left straight away. Geraldine waited for the widow who was expected shortly. She watched as the body was wrapped in sheets, only the face showing white above a sheet tucked up to the chin.

Sophie Cliff arrived ten minutes early, wearing a grey coat, her hair concealed beneath a navy scarf. She was very thin.

She peered nervously at Geraldine through thick lensed spectacles, her magnified eyes bloodshot from weeping. 'Are you the doctor?' Geraldine held up her identity card and introduced herself. 'A police inspector? Where is he? Can I see him?'

'This way, Mrs Cliff.' Geraldine gave the widow a sympathetic smile before leading the way, her heels tapping out a subdued rhythm on the floor. At her side, Sophie Cliff padded noiselessly.

Thomas Cliff had been laid out in readiness. Geraldine glanced at Mrs Cliff and looked away. There was something shocking about the dead man's composure beside his wife's anguish. Geraldine wondered if Thomas Cliff had been as serene in life; certainly not in his final moments, the skin from his hands and shins clawed away by unbearable heat.

The widow didn't move. Tears glistened on her pale cheeks as she stood crying silently.

'Mrs Cliff, is this your husband? You can indicate your answer with a nod.' Sophie Cliff didn't respond. She didn't need to. Geraldine lowered her voice. 'Would you like to be left alone with him for a minute?'

Sophie Cliff looked up. Geraldine was startled by the sudden harshness in her eyes. 'A minute?' Geraldine felt embarrassed by her clumsy offer of a moment alone with the dead man when Sophie Cliff had lost her whole future with him. There was a rustle of movement as the widow walked out of the room.

'I'm sorry, Mrs Cliff,' Geraldine said, catching up with her in the corridor. 'We're doing everything we can to find out what happened.'

Sophie Cliff spoke in a furious whisper. 'I want to know who did this to my husband.'

'I'm not sure we can say anyone's to blame—'

'I want to know who's responsible. Tell me when you find him.'

Geraldine frowned. 'We're doing what we can,' she repeated helplessly. Sophie Cliff turned and strode away down the corridor, her feet falling silently on the scrubbed floor.

Geraldine sighed and made her way back to the police station to type up her report but she found it hard to settle. She kept thinking about the widow's eyes glaring wildly in her pale face, like the eyes of a trapped animal. That was what grief looked like, Geraldine thought with a guilty pang; she hadn't even cried at her own mother's funeral.

# CHAPTER 12

# WIDOW

'You've all read the Fire Investigation Team's initial findings on the damage at 17 Harchester Close. The gas leak wasn't caused by defective equipment.' The DCI flipped through the report. 'The kitchen was almost new, but not new enough to have teething problems. The appliances were installed by an accredited experienced gas fitter ten months ago. DC Hargreaves spoke to him and the fitter was adamant he followed correct procedures and the paperwork was in order to show everything had been properly fitted and tested. There was no evidence of any fault. The gas tap had been functioning fine since the kitchen was installed. There's no reason for it to suddenly malfunction and the FIT have found nothing to suggest it did. They're positive we're looking at human error. Which opens up the possibility that we're dealing with a crime scene, if the gas was left on deliberately, a possibility the FIT raised from the start. Polly.' She nodded at the detective constable who had been talking to Ian Peterson that morning.

'The victim took out a life insurance policy ten

months ago,' the constable said. 'His life was insured for a million pounds.'

'There's nothing remarkable in that,' the DCI took over again, 'considering the victim got married two years ago, and they bought their house three months later. The property is currently valued at nearly a million pounds, and they're making substantial mortgage repayments. It's quite in order for him to have insured the house against his death. It was insured against his life only, not hers. That's not unusual except that she was earning more than her husband which makes it slightly odd that they took out insurance on his life and not hers.'

'Perhaps they were thinking of starting a family and she planned to give up work?' someone suggested.

'Yes, they might've been thinking of starting a family. The widow's not that young. Late thirties.' Geraldine felt herself blush and looked down. The room suddenly felt hot and stuffy.

'So now the house is paid off.' Peterson said. 'She could sell up and walk away with millions.'

'A million,' Geraldine corrected him.

'Let's not get sidetracked into speculation,' the DCI snapped.

'It's motive, not speculation,' the sergeant mumbled audibly.

Gordon ignored him. She turned and tapped at a photograph on the Board before looking round the room again. 'The victim's wife.' She didn't say

68

anything else but a question hung in the air. Geraldine studied the picture of the woman she had met in the mortuary the previous day. Sophie Cliff's straight mousey coloured hair grew in a long fringe over her forehead. Her eyes looked unnaturally large behind her glasses.

'Now let's get going,' the DCI said briskly and the team stirred. There was a general air of activity and purpose. Geraldine checked the schedule and found she was working with DS Peterson again. She found him talking to DC Polly Hargreaves.

'Let's hope she doesn't find herself having to give chase in that skirt,' Geraldine muttered as they walked away.

'More likely find herself being chased.' Peterson laughed. Geraldine forced a smile. She hoped the sergeant wasn't going to allow himself to be distracted from the case. They were both excited to discover they had been assigned to interview Sophie Cliff and her neighbours, and pleased to be working side by side again.

They drew into the kerb alongside a screen of tall laurel bushes. On one side of the Cliffs' house cast iron numerals displayed the house number on a white fence post at the end of the hedge, beyond which a wide driveway led to a double garage. The house itself was concealed from the road.

'Nice,' Peterson murmured as he followed Geraldine through the gate and caught sight of a large double fronted house. Matching waist high fir trees grew in terracotta pots on either side of the front door which opened as soon as the bell chimed. A plump middle-aged woman stood framed in the doorway, arms crossed, face slightly belligerent. 'Whatever you want, the answer's no.' Geraldine held out her identity card and the woman's expression softened.

'You'd better come in,' she said, glancing up the path behind them. 'We've had reporters knocking since early morning.'

For all her willingness to help, the neighbour was unable to tell them anything new. 'We didn't see much of them,' she admitted apologetically. 'They only moved in about a year ago. We invited them in for drinks at Christmas but they never came. She was very polite. Said they were busy. They seem – seemed a nice young couple but they kept themselves to themselves. She works of course, so it's not as if she's around much during the day. She's a doctor, I think. She goes out at all times. We hear her car coming and going at night.'

'She works in IT,' Peterson said and the neighbour frowned.

'Did they seem happy together?' Geraldine asked.

The neighbour just shrugged. 'You know.'

'That was a waste of time,' the sergeant grumbled as they made their way back to the road.

'At least she didn't let her imagination run away with her,' Geraldine replied. 'Come on, let's see if the other side have more to say.' She tried to control the impatience in her voice.

'She's just here till she gets herself sorted,' Jane Pettifer explained as she led the way across a wide hallway. 'She didn't seem to have anywhere else to go. My husband brought her in,' she added over her shoulder as though Sophie Cliff was an abandoned kitten they had found on their doorstep. 'She's in the TV room.'

Jane Pettifer ushered them into a sumptuously furnished living room. Sophie Cliff was leaning forward in an armchair, head down, her thin arms wrapped around her chest. She looked very different to the passionate woman Geraldine had seen at the morgue.

'Mrs Cliff?' Geraldine said gently. 'Sophie?' The other woman raised her head. Her eyes barely registered Geraldine. Her lips, prim in the photo, hung slack. She looked like a stroke victim. Grief or guilt, Geraldine wondered.

'She won't speak. We've called the doctor,' Mrs Pettifer said. 'He should be here soon.'

Geraldine tried not to frown. Once the doctor arrived, he would probably prescribe a sedative and the opportunity to question Sophie Cliff would be snatched away for another day. There was no time for sympathy.

Geraldine sat down opposite Sophie Cliff. Behind her the sergeant spoke softly to Mrs Pettifer. Geraldine waited. A large flat screen television hung on the wall to one side. It had been muted.

71

The screen was flashing with advertisements on the periphery of Geraldine's vision. Beside it on a low table, a huge vase of lilies filled the air with their heavy scent. Geraldine fiercely dismissed the memory of her mother's funeral.

Three large armchairs and a matching settee covered in a velvety red fabric stood in a semi-circle around the television. This probably wasn't even the main living room. Geraldine recalled the Cliffs' skeletal black kitchen, metal shreds of an extractor fan hanging from the scorched ceiling, the air choking with sooty dust and the foul stench of smoke. It was hard to imagine Sophie Cliff and the figure in the mortuary sitting together in a well furnished living room of their own, relaxing in front of the television.

Mrs Pettifer was hesitating. 'I called the doctor. He's on his way.' She looked from Geraldine to the sergeant who was holding the door open for her. Peterson ushered her from the room and closed the door.

Geraldine waited for the sergeant to sit down and take out his note book before she leaned forward and spoke gently. 'Mrs Cliff?' No response. 'Sophie? I'm sorry about Tom.' Hearing her husband's name, Sophie Cliff raised her eyes to look straight at Geraldine through the thick lenses of her glasses. Having caught her attention, Geraldine tried a direct question. 'Mrs Cliff, do you know who left the gas on in your house last night?' Sophie Cliff didn't answer. Geraldine took a different tack. 'Mrs Cliff, Sophie, your husband died in a fire caused by a gas explosion. We want to find out how it happened. We want to know why Tom died.' Sophie Cliff moaned softly. She began to rock backwards and forwards on the armchair. 'For the record, can you tell me if you turned the gas on in your kitchen last night, for any reason?' Geraldine insisted. Sophie Cliff didn't answer.

'You work in IT?' Geraldine asked. Silence. 'Can you tell me why you were called out last night?' Sophie Cliff looked blankly at Geraldine. 'Were you called out to work last night?' Geraldine asked. Silence. Geraldine adopted a conversational tone. She leaned back slightly in her chair. 'We know it's nothing unusual for you to be called out at night. It must be very difficult for you. I sympathise. I know it's hard driving when you've just woken up. Do you have a routine on such occasions? I know I do. I expect you make yourself a cup of coffee before you go out, to wake yourself up before driving?'

'Where's Tom?' Sophie Cliff's voice was barely louder than a whisper.

Geraldine sighed. Dealing with grieving people was the worst part of her job. 'I'm sorry, Sophie, your husband died in the fire.'

'He wasn't burned.'

'No. He was overcome by smoke. He's dead, Sophie. Tom's dead.'

'Where is he?' Her voice rose in panic. 'What are they doing to him?'

'He's still in the mortuary. Do you remember? You saw him there. You identified him. You'll be able to make the funeral arrangements as soon as we know what happened.'

'I want to see him. I want him back.'

'Yes, you'll be able to see him. You'll have him back soon, Mrs Cliff.'

'I want him to come home.' The last word drew out into a wail. Sophie Cliff started shaking. Geraldine struggled against feeling pity for her. Time was pressing. The first few hours in any investigation were crucial. She had to consider the possibility that Thomas Cliff had been murdered.

'Sophie, please concentrate. This could be important. We know the explosion was caused by a gas tap left on in your kitchen overnight. We need to find out how that happened. Did you go in your kitchen before you went out last night? Think carefully.' She paused. Surely the woman wasn't too far gone to realise the significance of what Geraldine was saying.

'I went out. I didn't want to wake Tom. I had to get to work as quickly as possible. I drove . . .' Sophie Cliff gave a start and turned to Geraldine, her face suddenly alive. 'I know who did it. I saw him.'

'Was your husband up in the night?'

'No. I was quiet. I never woke him up.' Her features changed, suffused with tenderness. She was almost attractive. 'He was sleeping like a baby. But I saw someone.' Her face grew taut again. 'As I was leaving last night.'

'Who?'

'I don't know who he was. But I'd recognise him anywhere. I'd know his eyes.'

'Who are you talking about?' Geraldine was aware of the sergeant, pen poised, staring at Sophie Cliff. 'Who did you see? Where was he?' Geraldine felt an impulse to seize the dazed woman by the shoulders and shake her. She gave what she hoped was an encouraging smile.

'As I was driving out of the house, I saw a man. I don't know who he was. I'd never seen him before. I'd know if I had. I'd recognise that face. He just appeared from nowhere in front of the car. I could see him clearly in the headlights. I nearly ran him over. He just appeared from nowhere and ran right across the drive in front of me. He had horrible eyes, kind of bursting out of his face. I had to swerve to avoid him. I slammed my foot on the brake and skidded into the hedge.' She stood up, suddenly agitated. If she was fabricating the story to protect herself, it was a convincing act. 'It was him, wasn't it? He started the fire.' She was trembling and her voice rose.

'Sit down, Mrs Cliff. We've found nothing to suggest a third party was involved.' Geraldine glanced at the sergeant who was busy taking notes. 'Can you think of anyone with a grudge against you or your husband?'

'No. There was no one. Only us. There was only us.'

'The fire started inside the house, in your kitchen.

There's no evidence of arson, nothing to suggest a third party was involved.' Watching the widow's face, Geraldine felt uneasy. There was something odd about Sophie Cliff's reluctance to look at her directly, as though afraid her eyes might reveal too much. And people had been murdered for a lot less than a million pounds.

# CHAPTER 13

## INTERVIEWS

On the way to Sophie Cliff's workplace, Geraldine and Peterson went over what they knew about Sophie. They agreed there was something strange about her, but there was nothing to implicate her in her husband's death.

'She never once looked at me, not directly,' Geraldine remarked. 'She could be painfully shy. It might've been the shock. But she made me feel as though I wasn't there. She looked right past me. Never once engaged with me while we were talking. It was the same when she went to view the body. I felt . . .' she struggled to find the right word. 'There's something – cold – about her. Detached. Like she's living on the other side of a glass wall.'

'It could be grief shutting her off.'

'It's not just now. They didn't socialise with the neighbours,' Geraldine pointed out.

'Perhaps she's one of those people who isn't comfortable around people?'

'Maybe.'

'She inherits the house,' Peterson added after a pause.

'But if that's what she wanted, why would she risk destroying the property in the process of getting her hands on it?'

'Insurance?' The sergeant shook his head. 'Unless she's totally insane – which we can't rule out – however you look at it, setting up a gas explosion has to be a very dodgy way to plan a murder. It's dangerous and unpredictable. There's so much could go wrong, and the chances of success are slim. And she would have been risking her own life too. I can't believe this was a deliberate murder. Arson maybe, but it can't be a premeditated murder. Can it? It doesn't make any sense, gov.'

'There's no rule book where murder's concerned.'

It took them just over half an hour to reach Sophie Cliff's work place. At night the journey would have taken about twenty minutes. She worked in an unprepossessing building on an industrial estate on the East side of the town. From outside it resembled an airport hangar. The interior was smart and conventional, with light powder blue walls and floor covered in matching carpet tiles. A young woman sat behind a curved pine desk, studying her computer screen.

She looked up as they entered. 'Can I help you?'

Geraldine held out her warrant card. 'We'd like to speak to your IT manager, please.'

'Certainly, madam. Would you like to take a seat, while I give him a call?' She flicked a button on her switchboard. 'Mr Corrigan, can you come to reception, please?' A moment later, she picked up her phone. Her finger nails gleamed scarlet in the halogen lighting. 'Yes sir. But there are two visitors to see you, sir . . . Yes, sir . . . But sir . . . It's the police, sir . . . Yes, sir.' She hung up and turned to Geraldine. 'Mr Corrigan will be with you directly, madam.'

The manager arrived after about ten minutes. 'I'm so sorry to keep you waiting. We're desperately short staffed and my back up operator has gone down with the flu. Would you believe it? Typical. How can I help you?'

Geraldine stood up. 'We'd like a word with you in private.' Mr Corrigan hesitated. 'If it's not convenient to talk here, you can accompany us back to Harchester police station. It's only about half an hour's drive from here. But we're as keen as you are not to waste any time. We'd appreciate your co-operation.' Without a word, Mr Corrigan turned and led the way through two sets of swing doors and along a hushed powder blue corridor.

'We can talk in my office,' he explained over his shoulder as they followed him to a door labelled Edward Corrigan. 'Please, take a seat.' He sat behind a large wooden desk, where he swivelled gently from side to side on a leather chair as Geraldine spoke.

'Mr Corrigan, we'd like to begin by confirming Sophie Cliff's movements last night.'

He nodded. 'I heard about the fire. Terrible, just terrible. Is her husband going to be all right? He was in the house, wasn't he, when it happened?'

'Mr Cliff died in the fire. Did you know him?'

'Never met him, I'm afraid.'

'He worked here.'

'A lot of people work here, Inspector. He worked on the admin side, I think. Our paths don't often cross. I may have been in the same room as him, but I wouldn't recognise him. We're a large organisation . . . But this is simply terrible. What a horrible way to go. And they'd not been married long.' He glanced at his watch. 'I'm sorry to hurry you, Inspector, but our systems operation has to be my top priority. We have banks dependent on our print runs, and hospitals. The penalties are prohibitive if we overrun. So I'd be grateful if we could keep this brief, with minimum disruption to my staff. We've already lost Sophie – I don't suppose you have any idea when she might be able to come back to work?'

Mr Corrigan confirmed that Sophie had been called into work on Friday night. She had been contacted at two twenty, and had arrived at the office at two fifty-five.

'Would it have taken her thirty five minutes to get to work at that time of night?' Peterson asked.

'She had to get dressed,' Geraldine pointed out. Sophie's phone had registered an incoming call at two twenty from a withheld number. Corrigan's confirmation saved them having to trace the call. He told them it was a regular occurrence but there was no way Sophie could have known in advance if she was going to be summoned on any particular

80

night. Her contract stated how often she had to be on call but often she could fix problems remotely without leaving home. She had to go into the office about once a month, on average.

Corrigan was unable to give a view on whether the Cliff's marriage was a happy one.

'I assume they were happy,' he said. 'They'd only been married about a year or maybe two. But it's not something I discuss with my colleagues. We don't have time to sit around gossiping, even if we wanted to.'

'Did you ever see her looking miserable?'

'Only when the system crashed.'

Geraldine spent the rest of the afternoon ploughing through reports, but they had been given the gist of the case at the morning briefing. Her afternoon reading material merely corroborated what she already knew. She read through it conscientiously, alert for some detail that didn't fit, but nothing struck her as out of place.

It was dark outside by the time she left. A heavy rain was falling as she crossed the car park. She shivered and walked faster. Damp and disgruntled, she pulled out into the street and caught sight of Peterson disappearing into the pub across the road. She was tempted to join him but was suddenly too tired to make the effort.

It was half past eight by the time she reached home. She threw her coat on the hall chair, shuffled into her slippers and hurried into the bedroom where the light on her answer phone was flashing.

Her spirits lifted when she heard Craig's voice but he was calling to cancel their date for Sunday. 'I don't think I can make it back in time tomorrow after all. Can we make it Monday instead? I'll assume that's all right unless you call.'

Geraldine wandered into the kitchen and poured herself a small glass of red wine. Then she sat down by the phone in her living room and hesitated. There was no reason for her to ring Craig. If he didn't answer and she left a message he might see the missed call and think she couldn't see him on Monday. She glanced at her watch. It was twenty to nine. She went back to the kitchen and refreshed her glass.

Tired, and with no immediate task to distract her, Geraldine thought about her mother. When their parents divorced, Celia had been the one to comfort her, leaving Geraldine feeling excluded, as usual, from the family circle. When Celia had married and given birth to a daughter of her own, she had grown even closer to her mother. Geraldine meanwhile, single and childless, had thrown herself into her career. On occasional visits home, she had been faintly shocked to observe the intimacy that had developed between her mother and her sister, and had felt even more isolated from them. With her mother's death, Geraldine wondered if she and Celia might forge a stronger relationship. She hoped her sister would want that too. She picked up the phone.

'Who's calling?'

'It's Geraldine. Celia's sister. Who's that?'

'Babysitter.'

Geraldine went in the kitchen and poured herself another glass of wine. Glancing at her reflection in the mirror above the fireplace, she was startled to see how haggard she looked: beneath straggly black hair her eyes were like empty holes, bored into a pallid face. She had spent so long around corpses she was beginning to look like one. An uncharacteristic wave of self-pity threatened to overwhelm her. Resolutely, she set her wine glass down on the table, opened her briefcase, and pulled out her laptop. At least she had her work.

# CHAPTER 14

# PLAN

When Cal had offered to put him up, Ray had jumped at the opportunity. It was better than staying at the hostel. He could learn a lot from Cal. There wasn't a lock Cal couldn't open. He could tell if a house was worth breaking into just by looking at it. He only had to walk past and he'd know. He was clever like that.

'How'd you do it, Cal? How do you know?'

'See what wheels are in the drive,' Cal answered, as though it was obvious. 'And watch the people when they go in and out. Check out what they're wearing, especially their shoes. Shoes are a dead giveaway. And whatever you do, don't touch a house with kids. Chances are a lot of equipment's stashed in the kids' bedroom where, let's face it, the brat's only got to wake up and you've landed yourself right in it. Mate of mine was sent down as a nonce for being picked up in some kid's room. Gadgets, that's what he was after, not some poxy kid.' He spat on the pavement. 'Kid wakes up and there's Donny, in his bedroom. What a carry on that was. Mother screaming, father yelling, and the kid was only waving a cricket bat in Donny's face. That bloody kid damn near had his eye out and for that the poor sod was put on the sex register before he could open his gob.' He heaved a deep sigh. 'Once they've got hold of you, no one listens.'

Ray nodded his head wisely. 'Ain't that the truth.'

'Steer clear of kids,' Cal repeated. 'They're the devil.'

Cal knew everything there was to know. 'Done more jobs than you had hot dinners,' he liked to boast, 'and never been caught, not since I was a teenager.' He had done a stretch inside before he reached twenty, same as Ray. It gave them something in common.

'Wasn't called a young offenders' institution in those days,' Cal told him. 'But it was the same in all but name. Bloody hole.' Ray nodded. They went to the pub where they passed a comfortable evening exchanging experiences. 'Makes you grow up fast, doing time,' Cal said. That was when he had offered to put Ray up.

'Stick with me and you'll be all right, kid,' he told Ray. 'Two pairs of hands are better than one, and you look like you learn fast.' Ray grinned.

Cal's previous partner was inside. 'He was careless,' Cal explained. 'I got away, I'm quick like that, but he was too slow. Shame. We'd done a lot of jobs together, but you got to move on. You stick with me and you'll be all right.'

'What happens when he comes out?'

85

'Who?'

'What happens when your old mate gets out? What happens to me then? To us?'

'He won't be out for years. Don't worry about him. Now, your round I think?'

Thanks to Cal, Ray knew how to open security doors and how to get through closed windows. He was learning how to cut glass in the overgrown bushes beside the canal path. It was the perfect place to practise. No one else ever went down there. Cal had a stash of glass cutters. He had given one to Ray and made him promise not to bring it in the house or carry it around with him.

'I know it looks like a pen, but it isn't a pen,' Cal explained. 'It's a giveaway.' Ray kept it in a hole in the trunk of an overgrown tree beside the canal. 'We're going to be rich one day, you and me,' Cal boasted, 'thanks to these little beauties.' He nodded at the glass cutter in Ray's gloved hand.

It had all been going so well. Now Ray was worried. Cal had set up a job and Ray had blown it. He didn't care so much about losing the stuff. Of course he was gutted about the dosh but Cal would find them another job. Cal was clever like that. They had already broken into lots of houses. It wasn't difficult. But Ray had let him down.

'These people are all idiots,' Cal said. 'All that fancy gear in big houses, they're asking for it to be lifted. All we've got to do is keep at it till we hit the jackpot.'

The first few jobs had been disappointing. Then

they had found something really worth nicking – and Ray had left the loot behind. As long as they kept going they would be lucky again, sooner or later, but Ray was afraid Cal wouldn't want him tagging along any more. If Cal had done that last job on his own he might have had enough to retire on by now. But Ray wouldn't know what to do without Cal. He had to do something to prove himself before Cal gave him the push.

The idea came to Ray when he was standing at a bus stop in the rain. He studied the houses across the road and thought about everything Cal had taught him. That was when he had his brainwave. It was so simple. He was going to pull off a job all by himself. Then Cal would take him seriously. He could stop calling him 'retard' as well. Retard Ray never remonstrated at the nickname, but it rankled. Cal showed him no respect.

No one had ever taken Ray seriously. He had always been an also ran. Even as a kid, he had been a hanger on, drifting about on the fringes of other kids' gangs. Finally he had ended up in Stan's outfit. Stan's boys spent their time on the streets, mugging kids and turning over small time corner shops.

'That's peanuts, that is,' Cal had sneered when Ray had boasted he was a member of Stan's gang. 'Nicking pennies from the sweet shop. Don't know why you bother. I wouldn't waste my time on a loser like Stan.'

'I'm in a gang,' Ray protested. That counted for something.

'That's your first mistake,' Cal replied. He launched into a rant against gangs in general, and losers like Stan in particular. 'Calls himself a gang leader, huh. He couldn't lead a bunch of geese. Listen.' He leaned across the table and pushed his empty glass towards Ray. 'No point working in a gang. That way, you've got to share it all out, see? You stick with me. I'll see you all right. And there'll be just the two of us to share out the dosh.' Ray was listening so intently, he picked up Cal's glass without realising it. 'Mine's a pint,' Cal said. Ray nodded. Somehow, Cal was always telling him what to do. Ray couldn't seem to refuse him anything.

Working with Cal was a step up from being in Stan's gang. Everyone knew not to mess with Cal. Ray was a nobody, but he was learning fast. Once he started to organise his own jobs, everything would change. He would still work with Cal, from time to time, but as an equal. Because he wouldn't need Cal any more. He would be number one with his own second-in-command, some young lad grateful to learn the ropes from him.

The bus came. Ray hopped on board, humming. He wasn't going to say anything to Cal about his plans. He wouldn't let on until afterwards. He imagined Cal's face when he came home one night with his haul.

'Where have you been?' Cal would ask, suspicious.

'Just done a little job.' Ray would casually empty his pockets on to the table, gems and gold jingling and sparkling. 'Here you go, Cal. Take that to

88

make up for the job we bungled the other night, the one where we left the loot behind because you panicked. Here, take this.' He pictured himself handing a diamond encrusted watch to Cal. His eyes would light up with excitement while Ray watched, cool yet sharp.

'You're a genius,' Cal would say. 'This little beauty must be worth at least . . .'

'A quid,' the bus driver's voice cut into Ray's daydream. Ray sighed and handed over his fare.

# CHAPTER 15

# HANGOVER

Geraldine woke late on Sunday with a pounding headache. She felt as though she was starting a cold. Her throat felt tight and her eyes were watery.

'Serves you right,' she muttered at her pasty reflection. Not yet forty, and successful in her career, she had been drinking alone at night. She resolved to take herself in hand. But first she had to hurry or she would be late for work. She left as soon as she had dressed, intending to grab a quick breakfast at the station canteen, but was held up by roadworks. She strode into the police station, ignoring her headache with a determined smile.

The desk sergeant returned her grin. 'Someone got lucky last night,' he said and her spirits dropped. Lucky with a bottle of cheap red wine. She was too late to run to the canteen for a hurried breakfast. The briefing was about to begin.

'You all right, gov?' Peterson muttered under his breath as she stood beside him. 'You look . . .' He stared at her eyes with genuine concern.

'Hung over?' she whispered. Peterson was about to reply when Kathryn Gordon marched in. The

DCI glanced round the assembled officers. Then she turned to the Incident Board. A picture of an old woman had been added, linked to Thomas Cliff by a large question mark.

'This,' she pointed at the picture of the old woman, 'is Evelyn Green who died on Thursday night during the course of a break-in. Death appears to have occurred from natural causes – but it seems there may be a connection between these two deaths.' She tapped the picture of Thomas Cliff. 'DI Bennett has been heading up the team looking into a spate of burglaries on the Harchester Estate. Without much success.' There was a shrill edge to her voice and Geraldine wondered if Kathryn Gordon was feeling out of sorts. She looked even paler than usual and her eyes seemed to burn with an unhealthy glare. It crossed Geraldine's mind that the DCI looked as though she had a hangover too.

'Evelyn Green died in the early hours of Friday morning. She was ninety, living alone in a large house on the Harchester Hill Estate. On Friday morning her son, Elliot Green, found his mother lying at the foot of the stairs.' Gordon glanced at her notes. 'The MO estimated the time of death at around two thirty on Friday morning.' She gave Bennett a curt nod.

The DI cleared his throat. 'On Thursday night, Evelyn Green's house was broken into. We're looking for a local gang who've carried out a series of burglaries on the Harchester Hill Estate. We think they could be responsible for this break-in. Only this time something went wrong. Evelyn Green seems to have disturbed them. The following morning her son called on his mother on his way to work and found her dead at the bottom of the stairs. A bag stuffed with her valuables was also discovered. It appears to have been dropped down the stairs after she fell. The bag was lying beside her at the foot of the stairs, and several chains and various items of jewellery had fallen out on top of her and beside her.' He lifted up a khaki haversack in a plastic evidence bag, put it down again, and counted theories off on his fingers. 'One, she heard the intruders, packed all her valuables in a bag and was trying to escape, or two, the bag belonged to the intruders. They'd filled the bag with the victim's jewellery, and were making their escape, when she disturbed them and fell – or was pushed – down the stairs, and they dropped the bag and ran.'

'Were they likely to run off without taking the jewellery if they'd already collected it in a bag?' someone asked.

'Five things,' the old DI replied, counting on his fingers again. 'One, we found a desk drawer had been broken into. It looks like a pro. In his statement, the victim's son told us she kept her jewellery locked in that drawer. She seemed to think it was a kind of safe, because it locked. Two, he didn't recognise the bag as belonging to his mother and three, some of the jewellery was found on top of her body suggesting it was dropped on her from above, after she'd fallen. The post mortem report's not back, but the medical officer thinks she was unconscious as she fell down the stairs, most likely dead before she reached the bottom.' He paused to check his notes. 'Four, a chain scratched the vic's face after she was dead which means the jewellery fell on her after she died. And five, she's got bruises on her upper arms which look like someone was holding her tightly, or at least grabbed hold of her, not long before she died.'

'If the jewellery was dropped after she died, someone was there when she fell down the stairs,' the DCI said. 'Which means they must have realised she might die, and they just ran off.'

'They could've panicked,' Peterson said, 'and not stopped to find out.'

'Or realised it was too late?' someone added. 'If she was already dead.'

'Or they pushed her down the stairs and didn't care if she was dead.'

'Or wanted her dead so she couldn't identify them.'

'If they'd summoned an ambulance . . .' The DCI didn't finish her sentence.

'So it's aggravated burglary?' a constable asked.

The DCI shook her head. 'There's nothing to indicate the intruders were carrying weapons, so we can't treat this as aggravated burglary. But we could certainly be trying for a prosecution for manslaughter.'

'She was ninety,' a young police constable said.

'Yes,' Kathryn Gordon sounded tired. 'The

medical officer at the scene thought it was a heart attack that killed her, which fits her medical records. She might have had a heart attack and fallen down the stairs. It may be that we'll never discover exactly what happened. But even if the post mortem confirms death from natural causes, as seems likely, she died during the course of a break-in so the impact of the burglary will be taken into consideration. But before we argue about the charges, we need to find these burglars. They're dangerous men, out there on the rampage, and we seem to know very little about them.' She turned to Bennett with an impatient gesture.

The DI nodded. 'There's a pattern. It's been going on for a number of weeks, the same burglars. They've broken into five properties, all on the Harchester Hill Estate.' Several local officers nodded. Geraldine knew the estate was in the expensive part of town. The houses were large and detached, many of them bordering on Harchester Hill Park.

'Do we have any idea how many of them are in this gang?' the DCI asked.

'We think two from the footprints. They wear trainers, two different sizes. No distinguishing features.'

'How do you know it's always the same two? Do they leave their footprints every time?' a voice called out.

'We suspect the break-ins are connected to a robbery at a framing warehouse last month, just north of town. Two men were caught on CCTV but they're impossible to identify. Several items were stolen, including a handful of glass cutting tools. Each one is the size of a pen and contains a diamond chip. At the time the loss was reported the investigating officer assumed the cutters were stolen for the value of the diamond chips, which isn't much. But each of these properties has been entered by cutting a section of glass out of a window to make the window catch accessible. The glass cutting is fairly neat. It's reasonably skilled, but anyone with a steady hand could learn to do it. We've taken statements from all the victims, and checked the neighbours. No one has seen anything. There's not a lot more we can do beyond advising the public on their security systems.' Bennett shrugged uncomfortably.

The DCI tapped the photo of the fire victim. 'Thomas Cliff died in a fire at his house on Saturday morning, after the gas had been left on overnight.' She turned and faced the assembled team. 'SOCOs have found evidence of a break-in at the Cliff household, similar to the other break-ins on the estate. All the windows in the Cliff kitchen were blown right out, so no one spotted it at first, but the fire boys discovered a small square of glass propped against the side wall of the house. Although it's not been confirmed, I think we can assume it'll match the samples of glass cut from windows where this gang have previously broken in. So it's looking as though the same burglars effected an entry at both properties. Five break-ins. Two suspicious deaths.'

She paused. 'We've not yet spoken to Sophie Cliff about the glass found on her property but we've had no report of a break-in at the house so we can assume the gang broke in some time during Friday night or the early hours of Saturday morning. We know how the gas explosion occurred but we don't yet know why. We've been assuming either Mr or Mrs Cliff left the gas on, perhaps by mistake, possibly not. If the presence of intruders in the house that night is confirmed, another possibility opens up.'

There was silence for a few seconds. 'Whatever happens,' the DCI concluded, 'we have to track down these burglars. Check your schedules with the duty manager.' With a final nod at the assembled team, she swept across the floor and out of the room. Geraldine had a clear impression the DCI was in a hurry to return to her office. Les Bennett raised his eyebrows at Geraldine and mimed drinking.

She responded with a very brief nod before turning to Peterson. 'Let's check out Evelyn Green's house.'

They reached the Harchester Hill Estate and made their way along wide tree lined avenues. As gateways flashed past her window, Geraldine glimpsed house fronts behind high hedges, and cars gleaming on drives. They drew up outside a large white house. Behind a tall hedge lay a beautifully landscaped garden with a series of small terraces, rock gardens and tiny lawns, and a fish pond. Stone steps led down to a wide house front, brilliant white in the morning sunlight.

'Must be a nightmare cutting those minute patches of grass,' Peterson said as Geraldine led the way to the back of the house. One of the windows had been boarded up, a temporary arrangement of card and gaffer tape. The lock on the back door had been tampered with but the burglars had evidently been in too much of a hurry to open it. Instead they had left as they had entered, through the window. SOCOs had photographed footprints on the mud of the flower beds which matched the prints found at the scenes of several other burglaries nearby.

Geraldine gazed around the garden, enchanted. Turning her attention back to the house, she could see where a square of glass had been cut out of the boarded up window. It was large enough for someone to put his arm through. The piece of glass was being scrutinised by forensics who would doubtless confirm that the cutter was the same as that used in other recent break-ins.

Geraldine led the sergeant into the house. At the foot of the stairs they studied the marked place on the carpet where Evelyn Green's body had been found.

'They must have watched her fall from the top of the stairs, dropped their bag and scarpered,' Geraldine said.

'Or they pushed her,' Peterson suggested.

'She must've seen them,' Geraldine added. They considered the implications in silence before making their way upstairs.

In a small study they found the desk where Evelyn Green had kept her valuables. Her son had confirmed that the items found with his mother's body were those she kept locked in the desk.

'She never takes it all out at once,' he had insisted. 'Maybe one piece, if she's getting dressed up for something, but the rest stay locked away.'

'I don't understand why they ran back to the kitchen,' Geraldine mused as they went downstairs. 'Why didn't they go out through the front door? They were already in the hall. Why run all the way back to the kitchen?'

'It's a security door,' the sergeant replied. 'Double locked. They couldn't open it without a key or a blow torch or something to cut through metal bolts. They must've been panicking or they wouldn't have left the valuables behind. We know they went along the length of the hall from the stairs. They probably tried the door, couldn't open it, and ran back to the window they'd left open.'

Geraldine gazed around, picturing two burglars entering the house. In her mind she retraced where they had gone, and how they had dropped their loot and made off in a hurry. But the actors in her film were anonymous. Faceless. She could have passed them on the street, or paid one of them for groceries, or petrol.

'They're dangerous men,' the DCI had said. Geraldine hoped they would manage to track the gang down before they killed again.

# PART II

*'There is always some madness in love'*

Friedrich Nietzsche

# CHAPTER 16

## SECURITY

Debbie patted her hair in place and keyed in her security code. She double locked the front door and felt a fleeting panic as the burglar alarm beeped. It would continue for exactly one minute. When she'd first had it installed, she would stand on the doorstep and listen whenever she went out, afraid it wouldn't stop. It always did.

The burglar alarm had been her mother's idea. Debbie's brother-in-law worked for a company that supplied and installed alarms. 'It's a sensible precaution for a young girl living on her own,' her mother had said. 'You never know who might be hanging around outside when you're home all alone.'

'Yes, mum. You've made your point. I've already said I'll get on to it.' Debbie had refrained from adding that, at thirty-five, she was hardly a young girl.

That afternoon Debbie didn't wait for the alarm to stop sounding. She didn't want to be late for her nephew's first birthday party. Her sister was making a huge fuss about it. She had been annoyed at Debbie for her lack of enthusiasm.

'What do you mean you might not be able to make it? It's Jamie's birthday. You have to come. You're his aunt. His only aunt. I'm not taking no for an answer.'

Debbie had scowled at her sister down the phone. 'I do have a life, Jen. I can't drop everything at the drop of a hat just because you want me to.'

'It's not a question of what I want. It's Jamie's birthday. His first birthday. Come on, Debs.' Her tone changed. 'We can't have his first birthday party without you. It wouldn't be the same.'

Debbie felt her indignation waver. 'All right, all right. But it is short notice. I do have a life.' They both knew Debbie was being stubborn to hide the fact that she had nothing else to do.

The conversation moved on. Debbie listened patiently as her sister grumbled about teething, nappy rash and doctors. It was a long time since they had compared notes about boyfriend troubles. Debbie was reluctant to discuss her problems with Jennifer. Her sister had changed so much since she had married and had a baby.

Debbie steered the conversation back to the birthday celebrations. 'Can I bring anything with me on Sunday?'

'You mean anyone?' her sister teased.

Debbie felt herself blush and was glad they were talking on the phone. 'No,' she hesitated. She tried to sound light hearted. 'He's not going to be around this weekend.' She hadn't mentioned to

Jennifer that it was all over with Bryan. As per usual. Debbie was nothing to look at, skinny and flat chested. Blokes always let her down.

'So it's family on Sunday,' Jennifer was saying, 'and Jamie's friends are coming round for tea on Saturday. It's not his actual birthday, but I can't manage everyone at once, and he's quite happy to have two parties.'

'He doesn't know it's his birthday on Thursday.' Debbie knew she sounded petulant. 'And the other babies are hardly his friends. He doesn't know who they are.'

'Of course he does. He understands everything, don't you, Jamie?'

When she passed the letter box Debbie remembered her electricity bill. She needed to post it urgently if it was to arrive before the end of the month. She glanced at her watch wondering whether to post the letter on her way into work the following day. There was no post on Sunday anyway. But if she forgot again on Monday, the cheque would arrive late, and if she hurried, she could easily run back for it and still arrive at Jennifer's on time for high tea at six o'clock. Swearing under her breath she scuttled back home, flung her umbrella on the doorstep, and unlocked the front door. Pausing only to key her code into the alarm, she ran into her tiny bedroom and fished the envelope out of her drawer.

As she straightened up, she glanced in the mirror. A flushed gaunt face stared back at her, framed by dark hair frizzy from her recent exertion. She grimaced. There was no time to try and smooth her hair down. She opened her wardrobe, grabbed a scarf, tied it round her head, and hurried from the room. As she closed her bedroom door behind her and walked towards the front door, she halted in surprise.

A man was standing in the hall with his back to her. He must have heard her bedroom door shut because he looked round. He was tall with long arms and legs that gave him a spidery appearance. Beneath his hood, a sandy coloured fringe hung down over pale watery eyes that seemed to pop out at her. As he turned Debbie saw the glint of a blade in his gloved left hand. A bolt of adrenaline shot through her. She spun round and fled back into her bedroom.

Shaking uncontrollably, she leaned against the door with all her weight. Fighting her growing panic she forced herself to push back against the door as she fumbled in her bag for her mobile phone. 'Please, please let it be here,' she prayed. Her hand closed around the phone. She moaned aloud in relief. As she pulled the phone out, her bag slipped from her shoulder. Make-up, keys, purse and diary spilled out at her feet in a jumble. She took no notice. She dialled 999 and lifted the phone up. It felt cold against her ear. She waited. Silence. Trembling, she hit the keys again and stared at the screen. Her battery was dead.

# CHAPTER 17

# MARKET TRADER

Most of Evelyn Green's treasures turned out to be costume jewellery, but there were a few valuable pieces.

'That's the ring my father bought her for their ruby anniversary,' Elliot Green told a constable. 'Those are the pearls he bought for her in Florida, must be thirty years ago.' When they had finished checking through it, he was dismayed to learn that he couldn't take his mother's jewellery home with him. 'It's the sentimental value,' he kept saying. He demanded to speak to a senior officer.

'It's evidence, Mr Green,' Geraldine explained patiently. 'We need to hand it all to forensics. Don't worry. You'll get it all back in time. I assure you your mother's belongings are perfectly safe with us. You can collect a receipt for them on your way out.'

It was relatively calm in Geraldine's little office when she returned there. After the bustle of the Incident Room, and Mr Green's agitation, she felt tired. She leaned back in her chair and closed her eyes. She barely had time to regain her composure when she heard a knock on her door. It was Ian

Peterson. Pleased to see him, Geraldine returned his smile.

'I know Elliot Green identified all the jewellery. Polly told me,' he said as he stepped into her office, twisting sideways to close the door. One day into the investigation Peterson was already on first name terms with the other young officers.

'Let's crack on then, sergeant.' The source of the canvas bag had been traced to a manufacturer in Asia. There was only one local outlet: a stall in the market. 'It's possible the bag was bought recently, because the price tag's still on it. The vendor might remember who bought it, might even be able to give us a description. Let's check with the market manager,' Geraldine suggested. Peterson grinned. They were both controlling their excitement. It was a promising lead.

Peterson was in high spirits. 'If the trader remembers who bought that bag, and can identify him, we could crack this gang of burglars just like that.' He snapped his fingers. 'The old DI's been after them for months.'

The market manager's office was hidden in a corner of the square. Peterson pressed the entry bell and a voice answered. The sergeant introduced himself. A buzzer sounded straight away. Geraldine followed Peterson up a cramped staircase that turned round on itself and led to a door with a dingy sign: Market Manager, Please Knock and Wait.

The market manager was a stout man with a

ruddy complexion. He bit his lip when Peterson explained the reason for their visit and began shuffling papers on his desk.

'I'm only the assistant manager. The manager's not in on Sundays. I can't promise our details for casual traders are always up-to-date. We do our best to keep track.' He lightened up straight away when Peterson told him they were looking for a trader who sold bags. 'That'll be Maggie,' he said, clearly relieved. 'She's the only one sells bags for us. Always here, Maggie, regular as clockwork, never misses a market day, never takes a holiday.' He paused for a cough that rattled in his chest. 'Hang about, I've got her details somewhere.' He tapped at his keyboard, shook his head, glanced anxiously up at a shelf of dusty grey box files, then tried his database again. 'Here it is.' He grinned in surprise. 'I am allowed to give out her address, aren't I?' he asked, anxious again.

'We're the police,' Geraldine reminded him gently. 'We could find out anyway.'

'Yes. 27 Maple Court.' He fished an envelope out of the bin and sketched a hurried map on the back which they didn't need, indicating a recently introduced one way system that he claimed interfered with the market traffic. He seemed to think they might have some influence over it. They took their leave as he was warming to his argument about the council's attitude to the market. 'They're happy enough to take our money,' he called after them as the door to the office closed.

Maggie Palmer lived in a rundown terraced property on the East side of town, not far from the market. To one side of the door an overflowing dustbin stood against a low fence beside a strip of grass. The other half of the front garden was littered with cans and bottles, damp cardboard boxes and dirty plastic bags. A battered white van was parked outside. They picked their way carefully over the cracks in a crooked concrete path. The sound of a wailing baby reached them from next door as Peterson rang the bell. A worn-looking woman in her late twenties came to the door. She looked disappointed, and gazed at them suspiciously. A small child with a snotty nose wound himself round her legs and peered up at them from the folds of her skirt. Next door the baby continued to cry. A girl of about nine or ten materialised in the narrow hallway behind Maggie Palmer, wearing a dress several sizes too large for her thin frame.

'Is it Aunty Alice, ma?' the girl asked.

'No, it's not.' The girl vanished. The woman leaned forward and squinted at Geraldine's warrant card. She straightened up, pushed a strand of hair behind one ear, and folded her arms across her chest. 'Well, what do you want then?'

'Maggie Palmer?' The woman nodded and her hair fell over her face again. 'We'd like to ask you a few questions about one of your customers.' Maggie gestured for them to enter and they followed her into a sitting room where there was barely enough space for them all to sit down. A table stood in one corner, covered in packets of toilet rolls. At the other end of the room, beneath a bay window, banana boxes were stacked knee deep. The sergeant held up the canvas bag that had been found beside Evelyn Green's body. Maggie examined it inside the evidence bag and confirmed it was one of hers. She didn't think they were available anywhere else locally.

'I've got my licence,' she burst out suddenly, rubbing her top lip with a hand that trembled. 'It's up to date and fully paid, which is more than I can say for some. I never cause any trouble. You can ask the market manager. I know what this is about,' she added darkly. Geraldine raised an eyebrow and waited. 'It's Geoffrey. He's gone and complained about me, hasn't he? But you'll find nothing on me. I import my bags directly and I can show you the orders and invoices to prove it. I don't owe anything.'

'We're not here to examine your stock,' Geraldine reassured her. 'We need to trace a man who we believe may have bought this bag from you last week.'

'What's he look like then, this man?'

'We were hoping you could tell us. We appreciate you must be busy, in the market—'

Maggie gave a snort of laughter. 'I wish,' she said. 'Not exactly queuing up. It's mostly young girls want the bags for a fiver. But I can't remember a man buying a bag last week. I would've remembered a man. I don't get many men coming to the stall.'

'Have any bags like this been stolen?' Peterson asked.

'No.'

Maggie promised to let them know if she recalled anything that might help them. Geraldine thanked her and stood up. Peterson put his note book away. The visit had merely borne out what they already suspected, that the bag used in the robbery had probably come from Maggie Palmer's market stall originally. They were no closer to finding out who had left it in Evelyn Green's house on Thursday night.

Back at her desk, Geraldine swore under her breath. She had been hoping the market trader would be able to give them a description of one of the burglars. For all their running around, they still had nothing to go on. She thought of Bennett, months into the investigation, and still nowhere. She forced herself to concentrate on typing up her report. They were only two days into the investigation but the pressure was already mounting. Apart from demands from the Superintendent, the newspapers had reacted to the gas explosion with predictable hysteria. They hadn't yet discovered the explosion might be linked to the spate of burglaries they had been reporting. Once they cottoned on to that, they would go wild. The police would probably be blamed for the gas explosion, as though failing to apprehend a gang of burglars was as good as lighting the gas themselves.

# CHAPTER 18

# PRETENCE

'Police! Police!' Debbie shrieked at her phone. She gabbled her address at the top of her voice. 'No, 16A,' she repeated as loudly as she could, as though someone on the line hadn't heard the number. She hoped the intruder wouldn't realise she was shouting into a dead phone. 'You've got a patrol car round the corner,' she yelled, making an effort to slow her voice down and speak clearly. 'That's great! You're bound to catch him unless he leaves straight away.' She paused, afraid she was being too obvious.

Footsteps pounded across the hall and a second later the front door slammed.

Debbie sank to her knees. A few minutes passed before she managed to clamber to her feet. Trembling, she pushed the door open and peeped out into the corridor. It was empty. She crept along to the hall. The man had gone. The front door was closed. She turned back and checked her kitchen and living room, even though she knew there was no one there. She was alone in her flat. Crying uncontrollably now, she stumbled into the bedroom and fell on the bed. She was still crying when her phone rang.

'Hi this is Debbie. I'm not here but please leave a message and I'll call you back as soon as I can.'

The phone beeped and her sister's voice came on the line. 'Debbie, where are you? Can't you be on time, for once? We're all waiting for you. You haven't forgotten have you?' She sounded irritated. There was a buzz of voices in the background and then her sister resumed. 'Call and let me know if you're not coming, OK? Otherwise we'll assume you're on your way and we'll wait. Hope everything's all right. See you soon. Bye.'

Debbie sat up, wiped her eyes and blew her nose fiercely. Then she phoned her sister back. 'Hi, it's me.'

'Deb? Is that you? You sound awful.'

'I'm fine,' she lied. If she told her sister what had happened, Jennifer was bound to tell their mother and then Debbie would never hear the end of it. 'Just a bit of a cold.'

'Perhaps you'd better stay at home?'

'No, really, I'm fine. I'm just about to leave.'

'It's gone six. You're supposed to be here already.'

'I know, I just had a problem at home, but it's sorted now. I'm on my way.'

'Debs, what's going on? Are you sure you're all right?'

'Nothing's going on.' She felt her resolve waver. 'Look, I'm on my way, OK?' She hung up. 'Bugger,' she muttered. Jennifer always knew when she was lying. She should have said she felt too ill to go round to her sister's for a family gathering, but it was too late to back out now. And it wasn't as if anything had actually happened. She climbed off the bed, splashed cold water on her swollen and weepy eyes, and made a stab at calming her wild hair. Despite her efforts, she looked awful.

'I've got a bit of a cold,' she told her reflection firmly and tried to smile.

Jennifer knew straight away something was wrong. 'Tell me when mum's gone,' she muttered. Preoccupied with her grandson, Debbie's mother accepted her daughter had a slight cold without interest. Debbie was relieved, but slightly disconcerted by her mother's indifference.

'You look like you could do with a few early nights,' was all her mother said before she turned her attention back to the baby. 'And whose birthday is it? Who's the birthday boy? Yes, it's your birthday.'

After their mother had gone, Debbie and Jennifer sat down at the kitchen table.

'We never really had a chance to talk earlier,' Jennifer began as she gave Debbie a mug of tea. The baby was asleep upstairs. His father was watching football on the television in the front room. They could hear the distant excited shouting of a commentator accompanied by gentle snoring. 'So what's up?' Jennifer leaned forward on the table and scrutinised Debbie's face. 'You look like shit.'

'Thanks.' They both smiled. 'It's nothing really,' Debbie went on. Gazing into her tea, she related what had happened earlier that evening.

113

'My God, Debbie! That's awful! Have you reported it?'

'What do you mean, reported it?'

'To the police. Have you reported it to the police?'

Debbie shrugged. 'Nothing happened.'

'He had a knife, Debbie. He could've used it. You could've been hurt.'

'Well I wasn't.'

'That's not the point. He could do it again. Next time you might not escape so lightly. You were lucky—'

'Lucky?' Debbie interrupted, her voice rising in agitation. She stopped and took a deep breath.

'You don't know what he might be capable of. He could be dangerous. What if he comes back? I'm worried about you, Debs. You have to go to the police.'

'And say what, exactly?' Debbie hedged. She knew her sister was right. She could identify her intruder. She had seen his bulbous eyes and hair the colour of wet sand. 'Jen,' she admitted, 'I'm scared. I don't know what to do.'

'Go to the police, Debs. You can't pretend it didn't happen.' She paused. 'Do you want me to come with you?'

'No, thanks. I'm not totally incapable.' Jennifer opened her mouth to protest but at that moment the baby began to wail. 'Time I was going anyway,' Debbie said, with a tired smile. She made no move to leave.

'You're sure you're OK?'

'I'm fine. And you're right. I'll go to the police.'

The baby's cries were growing louder. Jennifer stood up and went to the door. 'I'd better see to Jamie. Why don't you stay for a bit? There's no need to rush off. Stay and have another cup of tea before you go.'

'No, thanks. I couldn't. I'm absolutely stuffed, and I'm tired. I want to get home.'

'You sure you're OK? Do you want Bob to drop you back?'

'Don't be silly. Nothing happened. I'm fine, really.' She looked round. Her sister had already left the room.

# CHAPTER 19

# PAPERS

Geraldine went to bed early on Sunday and arrived at work early on Monday morning feeling invigorated. She fretted at her desk, impatient for the morning briefing to be over so she could start work in earnest. Several times she was tempted to make her way up to the canteen and see if Ian Peterson was there, but she forced herself to check her emails and scan her notes in preparation for the day. At last it was time to go through to the Incident Room for the briefing.

Kathryn Gordon's eyes scoured the team. A subdued muttering fell silent when she spoke. Her presence dominated the room but her voice seemed to have lost its power.

'We need to be aware of local feeling about these burglaries. Bear in mind the editor of the local paper lives on the Harchester Hill Estate. So the break-ins on the estate are all over the front page this week.' She spoke with reserved anger. 'Now there's been a second fatality. We need to step up the pressure. I've requested more uniform to help with the door to door, and additional clerical staff to cover the phones. We can expect more calls.' She brandished a newspaper above her head. 'You've all seen this? This morning's Harchester Herald.'

## LOCAL GANG MURDER TWICE

On Thursday night a woman was murdered in her own home on the Harchester Hill Estate by a gang of burglars who are terrorising the area.

## RESIDENTS PROTECT THEMSELVES

Police are advising residents to increase their home security. Detective Inspector Leslie Bennett said: 'We are advising residents to take common sense precautions to protect their property. We are following several lines of enquiry which we expect to lead to arrests very soon.'

## GANG TRIGGER GAS EXPLOSION

A local resident died in a blaze at his home in Harchester Hill in the early hours of Saturday morning.

## EXPLOSION

The fire was caused by a gas explosion. The area around the fire was evacuated until late yesterday afternoon, but has now been declared safe.

## BURGLARS

A police spokesman has confirmed that a gang of burglars broke into the house during the night. Police suspect they were responsible for leaving the gas on. Was this, as seems likely, the same gang that killed Evelyn Green? Detective Inspector Leslie Bennett said: 'We are asking members of the public to help us identify the members of this dangerous gang. Any information, however small, may be vital to our investigation so please come forward if you can help.'

## SAFETY MEASURES

'We want to reassure the public that gas poses a danger only when it leaks over a period of several hours,' a spokesman for the Fire Investigation Team said. 'Under normal circumstances, the domestic gas supply is perfectly safe. But this tragic event emphasises the need for care within the home. Gas must be properly switched off when not in use. A suspected leak should be reported immediately.'

The DCI glared round the room, but she spoke quietly. 'The local paper is agitating for an arrest but, as we all know, these investigations take time. I'm confident you're being vigilant and thorough. But we have to be seen to be doing everything possible to reach a quick result. Until this case is over, all leave is cancelled. We can anticipate interesting headlines in next week's paper.' She tossed an irate glance in Bennett's direction. Out of the corner of her eye Geraldine could see the top of the old detective's lowered white head. All this action on his patch was unfortunate timing for him, just as he was winding down for retirement.

'Who cares, what the papers say?' Polly asked.

The DCI frowned. 'It's a question of public confidence,' she answered, surprisingly gently. 'Our best source of information is going to be the people who know these villains, the people who live with them. They don't exist in a vacuum. The less confidence the public have in us, the less likely they are to come forward. So far we haven't been able to find out who they are. They're building a reputation as invincible among their associates, their neighbours, their family members. People around them may well be scared of them, or regard them as heroes.' She paused. 'We can't afford to be dismissed as impotent. We need to flip that around. Once it seems inevitable they're going to be caught, there's less incentive for those around them to conceal their identity. That's the message we need to send out. And the local paper isn't helping.'

'Why don't we get the paper on our side?' another young constable asked. 'At least tell them what to say, even if they don't agree.'

Kathryn Gordon frowned again. 'Because despite

what some of the media suggest, we don't live in a police state, and we do have a free press. Now check your schedules with the duty sergeant. Enough talk,' she concluded, suddenly brusque. 'We've got work to do.'

They were waiting for the day's schedule when the DCI summoned Geraldine. She straightened her skirt and took a deep breath before knocking on the door and was relieved to discover the DCI wasn't complaining about her sketchy report. There was no need to explain she'd had a bad day on Sunday, she would do better next time, it wouldn't happen again, ma'am.

Gordon pushed the local newspaper across the desk at her. Geraldine frowned as she leaned over the desk and skimmed the front page.

'The bloody newspaper knows as much as we do,' the DCI fumed. 'If not more. Where the hell did they pick this up? And why the hell are the fire boys talking to a reporter?' Geraldine's head was beginning to ache again. 'I don't want the papers better informed than we are,' the DCI concluded as she dismissed Geraldine. 'Make sure your report is thorough, Geraldine. Don't leave anything out.'

'We should be out there conducting door to door enquiries and questioning everyone who knew the victim, not wasting time changing our reports by adding in what we've read in the papers,' she grumbled to Peterson when she passed him in the corridor. He shrugged, sharing her frustration.

'Coffee?' she jerked her head in the direction of the canteen and he nodded. In the bright lights of the canteen, Geraldine noticed his pallor, and unhealthy pouches under his eyes. 'What's up?' she asked. 'You look worn out.' The sergeant's shoulders slumped forward. Geraldine waited. She hoped he wasn't sickening for something. A murder enquiry that threatened to consume their lives for the weeks ahead needed stamina. They had hardly started, and he looked exhausted.

'It's Bev,' he mumbled. Geraldine waited. The sergeant had mentioned his girlfriend before. 'She says she can't take it any more. Says she wants a normal life with a normal nine-to-five partner.'

'Do you want to talk about it?' Geraldine asked after a pause. She was surprised when he confided easily in her. 'But she knew you were a police officer before you got together?'

'She says it's different when you live with a detective. She thought she'd be fine with it, but when it comes down to it, she isn't.' Geraldine thought of Craig and gave the sergeant a sympathetic smile. Peterson took a gulp of coffee and grimaced in disgust. 'I'm sorry, gov, I shouldn't be taking up your time like this.'

'We should be getting back to work,' she agreed with a worried frown. She hoped Ian Peterson wasn't going to lose his focus on the case. Her concern wasn't purely professional. She was fond of the sergeant and dismayed to see him looking so upset. She didn't know what to say, aware that

121

the phrases she would have used with a member of the public were empty clichés. She fell back on discussing the investigation. 'I'm going through all the reports from the break-ins again. I suggest you do the same. We should finish by lunch time. Once we've got the background, we'll speak to the Cliff family, check out what was going on between Thomas Cliff and his wife.'

'Widow,' Peterson corrected her. 'Thanks for listening, gov,' he added awkwardly as she stood up.

'Work, that's the best thing for you right now,' she said briskly.

The sergeant gave her a quizzical look as he rose to his feet. 'Work always comes first, is that it then?'

'I mean it'll help to take your mind off – other things.' They exchanged a brief glance, a flicker of understanding, before they turned away.

# CHAPTER 20

# CANDLE STICKS

Geraldine spent the rest of the morning reading through statements. In five reported break-ins the burglars had stolen just under £2,000 worth of valuables and cash. No doubt they were congratulating themselves and laughing at police incompetence. Geraldine tried to ignore her irritation with Bennett. Half-hearted officers made life more difficult for everyone.

'How goes it, gov?' Peterson asked as she emerged from her office. Geraldine pulled a face. He glanced down at the report she was holding. 'Busy, aren't they?'

'Not as busy as we're going to be.'

'Now why don't I like the sound of that?' he smiled. He seemed to have regained his usual good spirits. 'Come on, then, gov, let's go get 'em.'

'If only,' she said, looking down at the list in her hand. 'No luck tracing any of the stolen property I suppose?'

'Now that's where you're wrong.' The sergeant had been on his way to tell her that the owner of a local junk shop had called in. 'He saw the pictures in the paper and thinks he's got the silver candle sticks from the first break-in. We've got to go and check it out.' He grinned and Geraldine felt her bad mood lift. Keeping on top of the paperwork was vital but, like the sergeant, she was happiest when she was out and about and doing something.

The name of the High Street changed to Lower Lane as they reached the East side of town where the streets narrowed and house fronts opened straight on to the road. An occasional tree drooped over the pavement. Starbucks in the centre of town gave way to JOE'S CAFE, Marks and Spencer changed to BEE'S BOUTIQUE with a handwritten sign in the window: EVRYTHING UNDER £5.

They drew up in a narrow side street, outside ALFIE'S ANTIQUES. The dimly lit interior was crammed with junk: tall lamps, ornate carriage clocks, chipped vases and glass ornaments, lone teapots and jugs, a wooden coat stand and a large black and gold china spaniel. A white haired man emerged soundlessly from the shadows. He wore a threadbare cardigan patched at the elbows, and corduroy trousers. Shrewd eyes sized them up over the top of rimless glasses.

'Police?'

Geraldine held out her identity card, and asked to see the candle sticks. The shopkeeper shuffled forwards, rubbing his hands together. He mumbled something incoherent about a reward. A retort about fencing stolen goods sent him scurrying to the back of the shop.

He returned with a pair of wrought silver candle sticks which he held up, turning them to catch the light. 'Beauties,' he said. 'Worth a bob or two.' He handed them over with an air of regret. 'I get nothing for them, then? Is that right? Nothing at all? I mean, I could've kept them, couldn't I? Kept shtum.'

'Stolen property,' Peterson reminded him and the shopkeeper sighed.

Geraldine promised the owners would learn how their property had been recovered. 'I'm sure they'll want to show their appreciation.'

The shopkeeper raised his shoulders in resignation. 'Archie. Tell them to ask for Archie.'

The candle sticks secure, Geraldine quizzed the old man about how they had come into his possession. He said a man had brought them in.

'Can you describe him?' The sergeant squinted at his notebook in the poor light.

The junk dealer told them a young man in a grey hoodie had brought the silver candle sticks in about a week before. 'Seemed like he was in a hurry.' Archie paused to cough. Phlegm rattled in his throat. 'Of course I asked him where he got them,' the old man went on. 'I don't deal in stolen gear, I told him straight, but he said the candle sticks belonged to his grandmother.' Geraldine nodded impatiently. They all knew his lies fooled no one.

Archie told them he had offered the man fifty pounds for the pair. 'He tried to haggle. Said the

125

candle sticks were worth more. He wanted two hundred pounds.' The sergeant snorted. Archie ignored the interruption and described how he had laughed in the young man's face and stood firm when the young man grew angry. 'You can't browbeat me, I've been at this game too long.'

Geraldine asked him to describe the man.

'Tall, ugly looking bloke, wearing black gloves. He was a big guy, a real bruiser, built like a boxer. There's many would be intimidated by a big bloke like that, but I'm no patsy. I may look like I've seen better days, but no one pushes me around.' He gave a hollow laugh that degenerated into another bout of coughing. 'It's fifty quid or nothing,' he resumed hoarsely. 'I told him. Take it or leave it.'

'So he took it?'

Archie shrugged. 'He didn't worry me but even so, in the end, I gave him what he wanted, he was making such a song and dance over it. He was getting impatient, I could tell. Kept looking over his shoulder like he was nervous.' He paused to spit phlegm into a filthy handkerchief. 'It was still a bargain. I did all right on the deal, or I would've done.'

Geraldine and Peterson exchanged a disappointed glance, frustrated that Archie couldn't describe the man in more detail.

The sergeant read out his notes as Geraldine drove them back through town.

'Wearing a grey hoodie, like a tracksuit top,

youngish, built like a tank.' He looked up. 'Anyone would look well built next to Archie.'

'And young.'

Peterson continued reading. 'Tall, ugly looking bloke, wearing black gloves. He was a big guy, built like a boxer. He seemed to be in a hurry and looked nervous. Not much to go on, is it?'

It was unlikely forensics would find anything useful on the candlesticks. The owners would be pleased to recover them, but the visit to Archie's Antiques had brought them no closer to identifying the gang of thieves.

'We'll find them,' Geraldine said, noticing Peterson's miserable expression. 'Sooner or later, we have to find them.'

'Let's hope no one else gets on the wrong side of them before we do,' the sergeant answered, with unusual pessimism.

# CHAPTER 21

# MOTHER-IN-LAW

Their next visit was to Thomas Cliff's mother. Mrs Cliff had called the station to say she had information for them, but wasn't prepared to speak to the police over the phone.

'Paranoid,' the constable who had taken the call told Geraldine. 'Said she didn't trust the phone.' Geraldine didn't mind going to see her. Statements from family members warranted close scrutiny.

Mrs Cliff senior lived in a village not far from Harchester.

'Pretty,' Peterson remarked as they cruised past a village green. White yellow-beaked ducks scudded among rushes at the side of a pond. Geraldine grunted, remembering a victim who had been discovered naked in a pond on a previous case.

They found Mrs Cliff's house easily enough, a few doors along from the village shop and past Ye Olde Bakery, a modern tea shop complete with mock tudor beams. Although she had requested a visit, Mrs Cliff kept them waiting. They understood why when she finally opened the door. She could scarcely walk on thin legs encased in elastic support tights.

'Come in,' she quavered, without waiting to see their identity cards. 'I've got information for you.' She tottered along the hallway assisted by a crutch.

They sat down in a living room furnished with chintz covered arm chairs and a glowing gas fire and waited while Mrs Cliff settled herself. Finally the old woman's eyes glittered at Geraldine, sharp above raffish pink lipstick, an incongruous splash of colour in an otherwise dowdy outfit: grey skirt and cardy, brown slippers. Geraldine hoped the old woman's information would prove worth the wait. The tape was set up, the sergeant poised, pen in hand. Geraldine had her own note book open ready. After a while she put her pen down and listened, watching Mrs Cliff's face closely.

'It was her, all right,' the old woman insisted, banging her crutch on the floor. 'I always knew she was a bad one. I told him so, but he wouldn't listen. She's no good, I told him. She's a bad lot.'

'A bad lot?' Geraldine repeated patiently.

'My husband used to look after things. When he died, Tom was only young, but he understood things even then. He was a clever boy. Clever about some things. He knew how to deal with the bills: the rates, the electric, the phone. It was all too much for me. I never could understand how people manage. 'Leave it to me mum,' he used to say. 'I don't want you to worry about a thing. I'm here to look after you.' And he did look after me. He was a good boy. So it made sense to put everything in his name. We talked about it, and we agreed it was best. It made life easier for both of us. He could sort everything out. He settled all the bills and paid off the mortgage, and I didn't have to worry about a thing. So we put it all in his name, the house, the savings, even the pension. He took care of everything. I had my allowance, like before. It was as though my husband had never gone. I never thought Tom would leave me too.' Her voice rose to a shrill whine. 'And he never would've gone, not like that, if it hadn't been for her. And now look what's happened. She's an evil woman.' Her eyes shone with malice. 'It was wicked, what she did. Now she'll be after evicting me from my own home, and where am I supposed to go? It was an evil thing she did.'

'Do you mean when she married your son?' Geraldine enquired.

'As soon as she had his ring on her finger she made him change his will. He did whatever she wanted. Had him right where she wanted him. She could trick him into saying night was day. You tell me if it's natural for a woman to control a man like that. He stopped listening to me. It was like I didn't exist any more, he was so blinded by her. And he did it, too. Changed his will, leaving everything to her. Everything my husband worked for, he signed it all over to her, the house, all our savings. It would all be hers if anything happened to him. 'Don't you worry, mum,' he said. 'By the time she inherits we'll both be gone.' It wasn't much of a comfort, knowing she'd get her hands

130

on my house, but it never crossed my mind I'd be alive to see it, so I put it out of my mind, like he told me. 'It's not going to affect you,' he said. I knew she was a nasty piece of work, but I never thought she'd finish him off like that. And now he's gone and it's all hers. That's why she did it.'

'She did what? What are you accusing your daughter-in-law of doing, Mrs Cliff?'

The old lady looked surprised. 'Haven't you been listening to a word I've said? She killed him, to get her hands on my house. Now she'll sell it and I'll be left homeless and penniless. Look at her, Inspector. Those cold eyes. I knew she was an adulteress, but I never thought she'd go this far to get her hands on what's mine.'

'Are you saying your daughter-in-law was seeing another man?'

'She had other men.'

Geraldine picked up her pen, interested at last. It seemed the old lady might have some explicit information for them. 'What can you tell us about the man she was involved with?'

'Men,' Mrs Cliff corrected her. 'It's obvious, isn't it? Ask anyone. She went out at nights. Stayed out all night. He was too naïve to believe what was going on right under his nose, but I could tell right enough. She's a whore. She'd do anything for money, that one. She'd stop at nothing. Only I never thought she'd resort to killing him to get her hands on what's mine. I knew there was something odd about her. I spotted it straight away.'

Geraldine put her pen down. 'Odd?'

'She's got no friends. None. And she never talks about her family. Not a word.' She sat back, triumphant, as though Sophie Cliff's social isolation was conclusive. Geraldine had never felt close to her own family, and never talked about them. Apart from Hannah, Ian Peterson was probably the closest she had to a friend, and he was really just a colleague. She felt a stab of sympathy for Sophie Cliff.

'So – she's a shy person?' Peterson asked.

'No.' The old lady gave an impatient shake of her head. 'I'm telling you, she was odd. Tom was the only person she spoke to. If I asked her anything, she'd look straight at him when she answered. Never at me. Shifty. I told him, but he wouldn't listen.'

'Do you think there's any truth in her allegations, gov?' Peterson asked Geraldine on their way back to the station.

'She couldn't give us a shred of evidence to back up her claims. Chances are it was spite talking. Her daughter-in-law took away her son, and now the old woman thinks she wants to take everything else that's hers. But Sophie Cliff was already comfortably off and she'd not long been married. She couldn't have known for certain her husband would alter his will in her favour once they were married. Did he do that at her instigation, I wonder? Had she planned it all?'

'No, because if it was all so carefully worked out

132

in advance, persuading him to change his will and so on, she would have used a more reliable means of killing him.'

'Yes, that really doesn't stack up, does it? But we need to make sure she wasn't having an affair, or had any financial problems we don't know about. She's a very wealthy woman now. People have committed murder for a lot less than she stands to inherit. Plus she now has a hold over the mother-in-law who's no doubt been giving her hell for the past year or so. I don't suppose Thomas Cliff's mother handed over control of her son without a fight.'

'Sophie Cliff's certainly a rich woman now.'

'Yes. There's no denying that.' She thought of the young widow, sitting alone in her magnificent house, bitter and isolated. Like her mother-in-law. 'But why would she want to kill her husband and have it all on her own, unless there was another man involved.'

'Problems between her and her husband? Or just greed?'

Geraldine frowned. Sophie Cliff didn't strike her as a woman who was interested in money.

'Something isn't right,' she said. 'And I can't work out what it is.'

133

# CHAPTER 22

## SON

Back at the station, Geraldine was soon engrossed in reading the detailed report on the explosion. By early evening she had almost finished when she was interrupted by a constable knocking at her door.

'There's a man making a bit of a scene, ma'am.' Geraldine looked up. 'He wants to see someone about Evelyn Green's case.'

'Evelyn Green? The woman who died during the break-in on Thursday night? Shouldn't you be speaking to DI Bennett?'

'He's off duty, ma'am. Gone home.'

'Thank you, constable,' Geraldine wriggled out from behind her desk and made her way along the corridor to the entrance.

The desk sergeant nodded towards the interview rooms. 'He was kicking up a bit of a fuss, ma'am, so I put him in there to cool off.' Geraldine read the sergeant's book upside down: Elliot Green.

'Evelyn Green's son,' she sighed. 'That's all I need.' She squared her shoulders and went in.

Elliot Green was thickset. His grey hair and tired eyes made him look older than his sixty-five years but he leapt to his feet with the vigour of youth.

'Well?' he demanded. 'Where is he? I want to see him now. I've been waiting here for—'

'Please take a seat, Mr Green. Who do you want to speak to?'

'The inspector. I want, I demand to speak to whoever's in charge of this enquiry. My mother's dead, her house broken into, I've been told nothing, all her valuables have been confiscated—'

'Please take a seat,' Geraldine repeated quietly. The man glared but sat down as Geraldine introduced herself.

'I'm sorry, Inspector,' he said. 'It's just . . . my mother . . .' He held out his hands in a gesture of helplessness. 'This should never have happened. I should have insisted but she kept refusing.' Geraldine waited. Elliot Green explained that he had tried to persuade his mother to move into a retirement block. 'Somewhere with a warden, you know, and those emergency cords to pull for help. She kept saying she wasn't ready, but she was ninety. When will you be ready, mum? I asked her. She was a wonderful woman, Inspector, but stubborn. She wouldn't listen. She was like a two-year-old. I should have insisted.' His shoulders stirred with a deep sigh.

'You can't hold yourself responsible for what happened, Mr Green. But we hope you can help us find out who broke into her house on Thursday night.'

'Yes. I'd like to help.' He was subdued now. 'It was horrible. I found her, you know.'

Geraldine nodded. She had read the notes on Evelyn Green's case. 'The police are taking this very seriously, Mr Green. We're doing everything we can to track down whoever's responsible.' She thought of Bennett, under pressure to find the culprits, and fought against a feeling of hopelessness.

'You can't let them get away with it,' Elliot said, his voice rising again.

'We're doing everything we can, Sir.'

'I know she was old—' he began.

'She was the victim of a serious crime,' Geraldine said firmly. 'We're going to find out who broke into her house that night, and see to it that they're prosecuted.' She didn't add, 'if we can.'

'Thank you, Inspector. I'm sure you're doing everything possible. It's just so frustrating, when all you can do is wait. She was a wonderful woman, my mother.' Studying his face closely, Geraldine realised she envied his grief.

The Incident Room was quiet as Geraldine returned to her office to study Evelyn Green's case. The full post mortem report confirmed the victim had died as a result of brain injuries sustained during a fall down the stairs. Bruising of her upper arms indicated she had been gripped tightly before her fall. The force of the impact, and the depressed fracture on the back of her skull, supported the theory that she had not died as a result of a simple face down fall. Evelyn Green had been thrown violently down the stairs. Geraldine stared at the report which confirmed they were dealing with a gang of burglars prepared to kill at will.

After a while there was another tap at her door. Geraldine glanced at her watch. It was twenty past seven. With a horrible lurch in her guts, she realised she had forgotten her dinner arrangement with Craig. She would never make it home in time. She hadn't even done the shopping. At the best of times her tiny kitchen was hardly well stocked. She dialled his number but there was no reply. As she was hanging on to leave a message, another voice interrupted.

'Is something wrong?' She was startled to see Peterson put his head round the door of her office.

'Nothing. I just remembered I'd invited someone over for dinner.' She hung up. 'Just a friend,' she added unnecessarily. 'I forgot to phone and cancel, that's all.'

'Call now,' Peterson suggested. Geraldine shook her head. Craig was probably waiting impatiently on her doorstep. He wasn't answering his phone so she had no way of contacting him. He would realise she had been held up at work, but that didn't explain why she hadn't let him know.

'It's not important,' she lied. As if the sergeant was interested.

'I'm off across the road for a drink,' he told her. She shook her head. She wasn't in the mood for socialising. With the briefest of nods, he vanished.

Geraldine cleared up her outstanding paperwork

and went home. As soon as she reached her flat she called Craig. It was half past eight. He still wasn't answering his phone. She left an apologetic message and called Hannah.

'And now he's not answering my calls,' she finished. 'What shall I do?'

Hannah was uncharacteristically dismissive of Geraldine's problem. 'What's so special about Craig? It's not as if you were even sure you wanted to go on holiday with him, so you can't turn round now and tell me he's Mr Right. As though anyone could be.'

'Hannah, what's wrong?'

'Nothing. Why should anything be wrong with me? You're the one with the problem, not me.'

'Why are you being like this?'

'Like what?'

'So—' Geraldine hesitated, 'so hostile.'

'I'm not being hostile. I'm just saying, Craig can't be anything special or you wouldn't have forgotten he was coming over.'

'I was tied up at work.'

'You always are.'

'What's that supposed to mean?'

'Just that you're always so wrapped up in your work, you never have time for anyone else.' Geraldine was taken aback. That was the accusation her ex-boyfriend, Mark, had thrown at her before he had packed his bags and walked out.

'Just tell me what you think I should do, Hannah. I really like him.'

'Forget about him.'

'I can't.'

'Then if you really want to see him, go round there and apologise in person. He might relent if he sees you looking all contrite. He must like you. You did go away for a week together.'

'It was three nights,' Geraldine corrected her.

'Don't be so bloody pedantic.'

'Can't have a slapdash DI.'

'You're not my inspector, you're my friend. You are a person as well as a police officer, or had you forgotten?'

'You really think I should just go round there?'

'Why not?'

It was getting late by the time Geraldine decided to follow Hannah's advice and apologise to Craig in person. If she turned up on his doorstep, he would have to listen to her. It was even later by the time she had showered and changed. She chose her outfit with care. She wanted to look attractive without making it obvious she had made a special effort. She settled for jeans and a cashmere jumper.

'What the hell am I doing?' she asked herself as she drove her car out of the garage, but it was better than spending another evening sitting alone.

She was irritated but relieved when Craig didn't come to the door. He still wasn't answering his phone. She wondered if he might be ill, but she couldn't stand on his doorstep indefinitely, listening to the wind rattling around the trees. It was beginning to rain, a fine rain that fell so lightly she barely noticed it until the damp began to seep through her jumper. She shivered.

In the car she fished in her bag and tore a page out of her note book. She scribbled a message, tore it up, started the engine, switched it off, wrote another note, hesitated for a moment, ran up the path, and dropped the scrap of paper through Craig's letter box. She regretted her impulse at once, but it was too late to retrieve the note. She drove home determined to put Craig out of her mind. It was a humiliating waste of time to chase him like that. He clearly wasn't interested. The time they had spent in Dubrovnik had been an enjoyable end to their affair, and it was best to leave it at that. She was probably better off on her own. She had an interesting job and a flat of her own, and wasn't sure that she wanted to share her life with anyone. At least she knew where she was from day to day.

Back at her flat, Geraldine ignored the half bottle of wine in the fridge and brewed a pot of coffee. It was past eleven o'clock when the phone rang. She let it ring three times before she picked up. She didn't want Craig to think she had been sitting by the phone waiting for him to call.

But it wasn't Craig.

'I need to talk,' Celia said.

'Not now. I'm waiting for a call.'

'You can answer when they call. I can talk to you while you're waiting. This isn't your work line.'

'No,' Geraldine explained impatiently, 'it's not work—'

'That's a first.'

Geraldine ignored the jibe. 'Go on then, what's up?' She drank her way through a large glass of wine as she listened.

'I miss her so much,' Celia kept repeating.

Geraldine offered what comfort she could, but she felt awkward. She had the impression there was something else Celia wanted to talk about. 'I'll speak to you tomorrow,' she promised at last, 'but I've got to go now.' Her sister's grief was a painful reminder of Geraldine's own guilty indifference.

'You know we really need to talk,' Celia insisted. 'I know it's different for you, but we need to talk.'

'Tomorrow.'

Midnight came and went. Geraldine poured herself one last glass of wine. Craig hadn't called. Miserably, she went to bed.

Unable to sleep, she found her thoughts drifting to Evelyn Green. The old lady had been disturbed by a noise in the night and gone to investigate. If she had slept through the burglary, she might still be alive. Elliot Green suspected the police wouldn't care about his ninety-year-old mother's death, but her age was irrelevant. The law was there to protect everyone. It was a terrible way for anyone to die, hurled down the stairs in her own home, in the dark. Whatever else happened, the gang of burglars had to be stopped before any more innocent victims died.

# CHAPTER 23

## GLASS CUTTER

The next day started badly. Geraldine had intended to arrive at her desk early to reread some reports, but she overslept. She could feel a headache threatening on the top of her head as she walked into the station. Instead of his usual cheery nod, the desk sergeant glared wanly at her approach.

'What's up, sarge?'

'Haven't you heard?'

'I've only just come back on. What's happened?' Bracing herself to hear that another victim had been found she was surprised when the sergeant replied.

'It's the DCI.'

'What about her?'

The sergeant hesitated, his plump features drawn. 'She's just been rushed to hospital. Suspected heart attack.'

Geraldine stared at him for a second, shocked into incomprehension, before she hurried inside. The Incident Room was buzzing with subdued panic. Geraldine made her way over to Peterson. He was perched on the edge of a desk piled high with files, chatting to Polly. Peterson sprang to his feet as Geraldine approached. He towered over her and the constable. Before any of them could speak, the duty sergeant announced that the briefing would be delayed.

'Back here in half an hour,' she said. 'The new senior investigating officer's on his way over.'

'How's the DCI?' Bennett asked. Everyone turned to stare at the duty sergeant who shrugged. There was no news.

'She's probably only just reached the hospital,' Peterson said.

'Suspected heart attack,' Polly added.

Geraldine went to the canteen but she had no appetite. As she waited, she thought about Kathryn Gordon. Dour and demanding, the DCI got the job done. For all their differences, Geraldine respected her and was beginning to enjoy working with her. You knew where you were with Kathryn Gordon. Now they were going to be starting all over again. She sat gloomily over a mug of coffee and was startled when Peterson called her name.

'What do you want?'

'It's half past, gov. Briefing's due to begin.'

'Oh shit.' Geraldine leapt to her feet and upset her coffee. It wasn't very hot, but the front of her skirt was drenched. 'Great, now I'm bound to make a good impression.' She glanced up. Peterson was already hurrying out of the room. 'First impressions,' Geraldine muttered to herself as she hurried after him. She made a mental note to thank him. If Peterson hadn't come looking for her she would still have been sitting in the canteen when the new DCI met the team.

Geraldine reached the Incident Room seconds before the new detective chief inspector arrived. Tall and slim he approached the Incident Board, turned and threw a bright smile around the room, exhibiting the confidence of a successful man in his prime. Geraldine wondered how old he was. She wished her skirt wasn't soaked in coffee. Their eyes met for an instant and she felt herself blushing, like a teenager.

'Good morning, everyone,' he said. He smiled easily round the room like a host welcoming guests to a party. 'I'm James Ryder, your new Senior Investigating Officer. I'm deeply sorry to be taking on this investigation under such circumstances but I understand DCI Gordon is expected to make a full recovery. Despite this change of SIO it's vital the investigation proceeds uninterrupted which means more pressure on everyone, I'm afraid. I'm as up to speed as I can be, but I'll be spending the rest of the day catching up with the background to what's been going on. In the meantime, we need to press on.' He spun lightly on his heel and moved his arm across the board. His sleeve inched back to reveal an expensive watch. Geraldine noticed he wasn't wearing a wedding ring.

'The square of glass found by SOCOs at the back of the Cliffs' house has been examined by forensics. They've confirmed it was removed by the glass cutter used at the other recent burglaries. So there's no doubt the same gang were at the Cliff house. They were presumably there on Friday night, as no break-in was reported before then.' He looked around, like a popular lecturer in front of a class of students, and caught Geraldine's eye. She gave a weak smile. 'Why would the burglars have turned the gas on?' the DCI went on without acknowledging her. 'Could one of them have knocked it accidentally?'

'It's feasible,' Geraldine answered his question. 'The hob's right in the centre of the room.'

'And if the leak wasn't caused by these intruders,' the DCI went on, 'I don't need to spell out that we may be looking at a suspicious death. Mrs Cliff received a call at two twenty and went out soon after. She arrived at work within half an hour. At that time of night, it's about a twenty minute drive away.'

'She could've turned the gas on as she was leaving, and left it on by mistake,' a sergeant suggested.

'Is it possible she knocked the gas tap without realising?' someone else asked.

Ryder looked at Geraldine who replied without looking at her notes. 'She said she went straight out, through the front door. She didn't go in the kitchen. She was in a hurry to get to work.'

The DCI nodded. 'That fits with her timings, but it's not conclusive. It would only have taken a few seconds to run into the kitchen. And she stood to inherit a million—'

'More,' Geraldine interrupted. She told the assembled team about old Mrs Cliff's accusations. She glanced at her note book and read aloud. 'She killed him to get her hands on my house.'

James Ryder listened, frowning. It was a different story from Sophie Cliff's parents. The local CID had sent a sergeant round to question them.

'How long had your daughter been married to Thomas Cliff?'

Sophie's father answered. 'Two years ago last August.'

'They got married in the summer. It was a lovely wedding,' her mother added. 'We never thought we'd see her settle down.'

'How would you describe the relationship?'

'I'm sorry?'

'Would you say it was a happy marriage?'

'Oh yes. They worshipped each other,' Sophie's mother said.

'It's true. They could've been made for each other,' her husband agreed. 'And they'd moved into a beautiful house.'

'We think they were planning to start a family.'

'So there were no problems in the marriage that you were aware of?'

'Quite the opposite, Sergeant,' Sophie's father said.

'We never thought we'd see Sophie so settled and happy. She was a very shy girl, never had any significant relationships before Thomas. He was her first serious boyfriend.'

146

'Her first friend, really.'

There followed a brief discussion between Sophie's parents about how shy she had been while she was growing up.

'It was all about computers with her, until she met Thomas,' her father said.

'How did they meet?'

Sophie and Thomas Cliff had met at work and, according to her mother, Sophie had fallen for him straight away. 'They decided to get married after less than a month,' she said. 'We were amazed at first, but they were right for each other, and there was no reason to wait. They weren't teenagers.'

'You approved of the marriage then?'

'Oh yes. We were pleased to see her settled and happy. And we hoped they might have a family. She's our only child.'

'And he was a very nice chap. Quiet, like her,' Sophie's father said.

'What about his mother? Did she share your feelings?'

'We only met her once, at the wedding.'

'She was a sour faced woman,' Sophie's mother added. 'But I suppose she was pleased for him. Why wouldn't she be? He was as happy as Sophie.'

James Ryder was pacing up and down in front of the Incident Board. 'Sophie Cliff certainly had motive, and opportunity,' he said, 'but it seems a ridiculous way to commit a murder, and she's no fool. Why would she plan such a hit and miss affair?

The gas air mix needs to reach a critical point for an explosion to occur. That might have happened after she returned home, because she did go back home, arriving not long after the explosion.'

'But we don't know she would've gone in if the explosion hadn't already happened,' Bennett pointed out. 'She could have been cruising by to check if her husband had been blown up yet.'

'It's an unreliable way of killing someone,' Geraldine agreed with the DCI. 'There might not have been an explosion at all. Thomas Cliff could just as well have come down in the morning, noticed the gas was on, turned it off and opened all the windows. He might even have called the gas board to report a leak. He wasn't necessarily going to die because of the leak.'

'More insurance if the explosion took place,' a female constable commented. 'Not only does she get rid of the husband and come into her considerable inheritance, she can claim a new kitchen on the insurance as a bonus.'

'A new kitchen? You think she might have wanted a new kitchen?' the DCI repeated in surprise. The constable looked down, embarrassed. 'It could've been a spur of the moment decision, a chance she saw and took, without really thinking it through,' he went on, but he didn't sound convinced.

'Maybe something just snapped, she walked past the hob, the idea struck her, and she acted almost without thinking,' Geraldine pursued his idea. 'If she was desperate to be rid of him, that is.'

'Or desperate to get her hands on his money,' Peterson added. 'But she didn't go in the kitchen.'

'So she said.'

'Enough speculation,' the DCI interrupted, suddenly firm. 'Lots of possibilities, but we're short on facts.'

A description of the stolen goods had been circulated to police stations nationwide. Sketches were being published on the front page of the local paper.

'Someone's got to come up with something tangible,' Ryder said, a hint of petulance in his voice. Geraldine wondered if James Ryder was as easy going as he appeared. No doubt he was being badgered for a quick result. 'The victims of the first break-in have confirmed the candlesticks are theirs, so we need to follow that up urgently, bring the junk dealer in to look at mug shots, see if he recognises anyone, as he couldn't provide a good enough description for an Efit. And I want all witness statements reviewed. Remember, we're looking at two suspicious deaths now. We don't want any more. We've taken statements from all the households burgled. We need to visit them all again, check nothing's been overlooked. We're going to spread the net, interview Cliff's work colleagues, and Sophie Cliff's colleagues and family. So let's get on with it.'

He paused and glanced down at his list. 'I'm holding a press conference tomorrow morning.' His blue eyes slid past Bennett and rested on

Geraldine. 'I'd like you there, Geraldine.' Out of the corner of her eye, Geraldine thought she saw Bennett's lips narrow faintly. Was he peeved, she wondered, or relieved.

'Yes sir.'

'Has anyone got anything else to add?' the DCI asked, gazing round the assembled team. No one answered. 'Let's find these characters before there are any further incidents.'

# CHAPTER 24

# ALIBI

'What the hell do you think you're doing, shoving the paper in my face like that? And what are you so jumpy about? You're driving me nuts.'

'Read it,' Ray answered. 'The front page. It's about us.' Cal glanced down at the paper and gave a bark of laughter. Brenda was curled up beside him on the sofa, clutching her bony knees to her chest. Cal pinched her cheek until she squealed.

'See that, Bren? We've made the front page, me and Ray. We're celebrities. We're up there with the greats. Butch Cassidy and the other one. The Kray brothers. Bonnie and what's-his-face.'

'Bonnie and Clyde,' Brenda said. 'One of them was a woman. Are you the woman, then, Ray?' She laughed.

'What are you on about, stupid bitch?' Cal pinched her cheek harder, until her eyes watered.

'Just read it!' Ray shouted, his pale eyes bulging.

Cal turned slowly and looked up at him. 'Why don't you read it to us,' he suggested lazily. 'And move over while you're at it, retard. I can't see the telly.'

Ray stepped aside and read aloud in a monotone. 'Gang trigger gas explodes. Local resi – resident died in a blaze at his home in Harchester Hill early on Saturday morning it explodes the fire was caused by a gas explosion the area round the fire was vacant until late yesterday afternoon but has not been decided safe a police spokesman has conferred that a gang of burglars broke into the house in the night police say they were responsible for leaving the gas on.'

Ray lowered the paper and stared at Cal. 'It's about this geezer who died in a fire. They think it was us, turned the gas on. It's on the front page. That was us, the burglars. We're the gang of burglars.' His face was white. Cal laughed at something on the television. 'That was us,' Ray insisted, his voice rising. 'It was us caused the fire that killed that geezer. It says it was a gang of burglars but it was us.' Time was, Ray would have been overjoyed with a mention in the paper like that. He would probably have crowed with triumph. But now a stranger had died in a fire. Gang member or not, Ray was a murderer. And he hadn't even known about it.

Cal turned to look up at Ray. 'And how are we supposed to have done that, then? Killed some bloke without knowing anything about it? We never even saw anyone.'

'The gas. The paper says we put the gas on. It was on all night.'

'Was it you turned on the gas?' Brenda asked.

152

'Why did you do that then? You don't want to go messing about with the gas.'

'Shut up you stupid cow.' Cal turned back to Ray. 'I never turned the gas on. Did you turn the gas on, retard?'

'No,' Ray answered quickly. He looked away. He was thinking about the handle of his bag catching on something. 'No,' he said, more firmly. 'It wasn't me. I never touched the fucking gas. Why would I?'

'There you are then,' Cal said. His eyes were glued to the television again. 'It wasn't you and it wasn't me. So what the hell are you on about? Like a bleeding old woman, you are. Worse than her with all your fuss. Maybe we were there, maybe we weren't. Maybe we turned the gas on, maybe we didn't. It's a load of bollocks, them trying to make out it was us. If you ask me,' he sat up suddenly, 'we had a lucky escape. It could have been us, going up in flames on account of some careless bugger leaving their gas on. If you ask me, it's us who are the injured parties. Just look at him,' he told Brenda. 'You've only got to look at him to see how shocked he is. That's trauma, that is. We ought to sue them.'

'Who you going to sue, you daft bugger?' Brenda asked. She sniggered. Cal slapped the arm of the sofa and laughed.

'And what about the old woman?' Ray burst out. 'What did you go and do that for, Cal?'

'She got in the way.'

Ray forced a grin, wondering what Cal might do to him if he got in the way. He looked at the paper and felt sick. He was quick fingered, always had been. When you had nothing, it was the only way. He had to survive. He had been in a few brawls on a Saturday night, had given his share of split lips and black eyes, and learned how to defend himself against all comers, but nothing like this. If anyone found out, he would be done for murder. He glanced at Cal, smiling and relaxed, and felt a thread of hatred. Cal was all right. He didn't care. Ray took a deep breath. 'You leave the clever stuff to me,' Cal would say, giving Ray a sharp slap for being stupid. And he was right. It was stupid to worry. They would never be found out.

Adverts came on the TV and Cal looked round. 'Make us a cup of tea, Bren.'

'Make it yourself. I'm not your slave.'

'That's what she thinks,' Cal laughed. 'Come on, slave girl, give us a kiss.'

Ray tapped the newspaper against Cal's knee. 'What if they find out?'

'What's the old woman on about?' Cal asked Brenda. She giggled.

'It's one thing if they get us for thieving,' Ray went on.

'They won't,' Cal bristled.

'I know. But what I'm saying is, it's one thing to be done for thieving. But this is murder, Cal. If they find out it was us, we're going down for murder. Who's going to believe it was an accident? It was different with the old woman. She was old.'

'Who are you calling an old woman?' Bren frowned.

'Oh shut up, will you. Old, young—' Cal waved his thick fingers in the air. 'No one knows we were there. You don't even know it's the same house. What makes you so sure that's the house we were in? Could be any house on the estate.'

'We could go and see,' Ray suggested, suddenly alert. Cal was right. It might not have been the same house. He could be fretting for nothing.

'We're not going anywhere near the place,' Cal told him. 'Once they see us hanging around, we might as well ask to be picked up. They can prove what the hell they like, once they get hold of us.'

'It'll be like CSI,' Brenda chipped in suddenly. 'You didn't drop anything there did you? Any hair or skin? Anything with DNA?'

'No we bloody didn't. And in any case, it would've got burned in the fire wouldn't it, stupid?' Cal said. 'Now shut it, will you? I'm trying to listen.' The football commentary droned on. Brenda sat back and closed her eyes. 'And what about that tea?' Cal slapped her leg.

She yelped and scrambled off the sofa. 'I'll make a cup for you but I'm not making one for him,' she said as she scuttled into the kitchen.

'You'll do as you're damn well told,' Cal answered. He leaned back in his chair and stretched out his short legs. He wasn't bothered either way.

'I don't want any bloody tea,' Ray muttered.

Cal caught sight of Ray's expression. 'And what's wrong with you?'

'What if they find out it was us, Cal?'

'Shut it. We've got an alibi. Soon as the footy's done I'll go and sort it. Just remember we were at the Blue Lagoon on Friday night. Right? Now shut the fuck up, will you? Because I'm telling you, there's nothing to worry about.'

# CHAPTER 25

# WITNESS

The canteen was empty apart from a couple of female constables sitting at a corner table, clutching mugs of coffee, deep in conversation. Geraldine approached their table but they didn't invite her to join them. She hesitated then moved away. As she sat down, she saw their heads were nearly touching as they chatted in subdued tones. Geraldine felt slightly better after her first shot of caffeine of the day and her headache eased. The two constables went soon after, leaving Geraldine alone in the canteen.

She was on her way back to her office when a young female constable accosted her in the corridor.

'DCI sent me to look for you, ma'am. There's a young woman come in to report an intruder.'

Geraldine smiled wearily at her. 'Go on.'

'She's called Deborah Mainwaring. Calls herself Debbie.' The constable checked her note book. 'She claims an intruder entered her property on Sunday around five thirty. She said she'd gone home to fetch something. She must've left her front door ajar behind her because when she looked round, there was a man in her flat.'

157

'Someone wandered in off the street? No forced entry?'

'She says he had a knife.'

Geraldine frowned. 'When did you say it happened?'

'Sunday, late afternoon.'

'That's four days ago. Why didn't she report it before now?'

The constable shrugged. 'I don't know, ma'am.'

Geraldine glanced at her watch, annoyed that she had to conduct the interview. As an inspector on the murder team she shouldn't be dealing with random minor reports of intruders. 'I'll be there in a minute.'

'Yes ma'am.'

Geraldine went and checked her emails before grabbing her bag and hurrying to the entrance hall where a young woman was sitting fiddling with the strap of her bag. She leapt to her feet when her name was called. Geraldine saw dark eyes gazing anxiously at her from beneath a fuzzy mop of dark hair. Geraldine led her into a small interview room and invited her to take a seat.

'You reported an intruder, Miss Mainwaring?'

The young woman nodded. Nervously she explained how she had been on her way out on Sunday. It was her nephew's birthday. 'I had to go out about half past five. I was in a bit of a rush.' She explained she hadn't wanted to be late for the birthday tea at her sister's. 'She only lives fifteen minutes away.' After setting out, she had returned home in a hurry to pick up a bill. 'I had to get it in the post,' she explained, 'so it wouldn't be late.'

Geraldine nodded, smiling to mask her impatience. 'Go on.' Coming out of her bedroom, Deborah Mainwaring had been shocked to see a man standing in her flat. 'Did you recognise him?' She shook her head and her hair flapped around her face. 'What happened next?'

'He saw me looking at him so I ran back into the bedroom and tried to phone the police but my phone was dead.' She paused, flustered by the memory.

'What did you do then?'

'I pretended.' She blushed.

'Pretended?'

'Yes. I didn't dare go over to the phone by my bed. There's no lock on my bedroom door so I was leaning against it, to stop him opening it. I pretended I'd got through on my mobile and was speaking to the emergency services and I shouted out my address and said how pleased I was that there was a patrol car round the corner. I said they'd catch him if he didn't leave straight away. And then I heard the front door slam.' She shrugged. 'And that was that.'

'Quick thinking,' Geraldine said in genuine admiration. Deborah Mainwaring's face turned a deeper red. 'Was anything missing from your flat?' Deborah shook her head. Geraldine glanced down at her note book. 'You mentioned something to my colleague about the intruder having a weapon?'

'Yes. He was holding a knife in his left hand. He was wearing black gloves and a grey tracksuit top with the hood up.'

Geraldine felt pointlessly pleased that the witness had noticed so much. It wasn't going to be any help. A man in a grey hoodie. 'Did you get a look at his face? Can you tell me how tall he was?'

Deborah Mainwaring nodded uncertainly. 'He was very tall,' she said, her head on one side. 'Over six foot, I'd say. His fringe was quite long and kind of light gingery, no, not gingery exactly, more light brown. It looked as though it could do with a wash. And he had horrible eyes.'

'How old would you say he was?'

Deborah Mainwaring shrugged again. 'About eighteen, maybe twenty?' she hazarded. 'No older than twenty, I'd say, or maybe early twenties. It's difficult to say. He could've been younger.'

'Thank you. Now, Miss Mainwaring, if we show you a selection of pictures of local burglars, do you think you'd be able to recognise him? I'm not sure we'll have anything to charge him with, but we can give him a severe warning and see what he has to say for himself.' Most probably a flat denial that he had been anywhere near Debbie Mainwaring's flat, carrying a knife. They wouldn't be able to charge him, but they would certainly pay the young chancer a visit, if Deborah Mainwaring was able to make a positive identification. If nothing else, they could at least give him a scare. It occasionally influenced youngsters, especially those starting out on a criminal path. They might have enough to caution him which would go on his record.

'You've been very helpful in coming forward,' Geraldine went on. 'If you'd like to wait here, I'll send a constable to show you some mug shots of likely local felons.'

'He won't know, will he? I mean, if he finds out I told you—'

Geraldine reassured her. 'Don't worry, Miss Mainwaring, if we find your intruder, we'll be keeping a close eye on him for a while, and he certainly won't know you came forward. In the meantime, you can speak to a crime prevention officer about security measures.'

'I've got a burglar alarm . . .' Deborah Mainwaring replied, blushing.

# CHAPTER 26

# SUSPECT

Only half an hour later, the WPC knocked on Geraldine's door again.

'Deborah Mainwaring's recognised her intruder, ma'am,' she announced, 'a Raymond Barker. I've got his details for you, ma'am.' The young constable stepped forward and handed Geraldine a print out. Geraldine could quite easily have looked Barker up herself. She smiled at her young colleague's eagerness.

'Thank you, constable. That's very thorough.'

At twenty years old Barker already had a string of petty convictions: shoplifting, being drunk and disorderly, disturbing the peace, possession of cannabis – run-of-the-mill antisocial conduct for which he had eventually spent six months in Castle Hill Young Offenders Institution. Geraldine slipped the report into her drawer and went to find Peterson.

They had traced Barker to a terraced house in Garden Street.

'Not much in the way of gardens,' Peterson remarked as they cruised along searching for a space. They had to park in a parallel road and walk back round the block. An assortment of rusting cars crowded the kerb on either side of the road, allowing room for one car to pass. Geraldine studied the old bangers, occasionally interspersed with newer cars. They turned into Garden Street and she shifted her attention to the houses, looking for number 17.

Apart from an old motorbike propped up beside a cracked path, there was little to see in any of the front gardens beyond a profusion of household detritus: empty cartons and crisp packets, bottles and cans, flapping plastic bags, mushy newspapers, soggy cigarette butts, broken crockery, bicycle parts, smashed bricks and a discarded pram without wheels.

'Not quite the Harchester Hill Estate, gov,' Peterson muttered.

The bell rang.

'Cal forgot his key.' Brenda hurried to let him in. A few seconds later, Ray heard the front door slam. Brenda reappeared and slumped down in her chair. 'It wasn't Cal.'

'Who was it?' Ray asked. The bell rang again and this time the caller knocked loudly. Brenda shook her head, muttering incoherently. 'Who is it, Bren? Who's at the door?'

The bell rang for a third time.

Ray leapt to his feet. 'Bloody hell. Do I have to do everything round here? Useless bloody cow.'

A slim, dark haired woman was waiting patiently,

163

as though she was used to standing on doorsteps. A sharp looking geezer stood at her side, tapping his fingers on his jacket. Spiritual nuts, Jehovah's Witnesses, collecting for something, Ray wasn't sure.

'Piss off.'

'Raymond Barker?' Something in the woman's voice made him pause as he was about to close the door. He swore under his breath. Filth.

'Who wants to know?'

'Detective Inspector Steel. This is Detective Sergeant Peterson. We'd like a word with you, Mr Barker.'

'Sorry about Brenda. She doesn't like strangers.'

'None of us like strangers walking into our homes uninvited, Mr Barker.' So that was it, he thought, relieved. The visit had nothing to do with Cal. He rubbed his sweaty palms on his trousers and thought quickly. He had found the door open. He hadn't taken anything. They had nothing on him. But Cal could be back at any time. He wouldn't be pleased to find Ray had brought the filth to the house.

'What's this about then?' he blustered. He had to get rid of them before Cal came back.

'Shall we come in? Or would you prefer to answer a few questions at the police station?'

Ray nodded quickly. 'I'll just get my keys.'

The woman narrowed her eyes. 'We'll come in with you.' She thought he was going to slip out the back. The thought had crossed his mind.

'Better not,' Ray remonstrated. 'Brenda won't like it. She panics if she sees anyone she doesn't know.'

Ignoring his protest, the two detectives followed Ray into the back room. Brenda was fidgeting in her chair, her legs tucked up beneath scraggy thighs.

'I'm just nipping out,' Ray told her. 'Listen.' He bent over her and lowered his voice. 'You don't want to mention this to Cal, right?' She stared blankly at the wall. Then, without moving her head, she swivelled her eyes to glance slyly up at Ray. 'I'll make it worth your while,' he promised.

'You ready?' The woman asked impatiently.

Brenda's eyes widened in surprise. She seemed to notice the detectives for the first time. 'Who's she then?' She drew her knees up to her chin and stared at the visitors with rheumy eyes. 'What's she want with Cal? Does Cal know she's here?'

'Just a mate.' Ray's false assurance didn't fool anyone but Brenda dropped her gaze. She had lost interest. 'I'm off then. If Cal asks, tell him I'm gone to see a mate.'

'Who's Cal?' the woman asked. Ray bit his lip in annoyance.

'Cal,' the girl said.

'That'll be Callum Martin,' the sergeant chipped in. 'The tenant.'

'Who?' Brenda asked. No one answered.

Ray tried to hide his unease under a cheery grin. 'We all live here,' he said loudly. 'But my business is my business. This is nothing to do with Cal. It's

165

none of his business. He doesn't need to know.' He glanced nervously towards the door. The woman pursed her lips thoughtfully.

'Cal always knows,' Brenda said. 'He always finds out, and when he does, you'll be for it, all of you.' She laughed then hung her head and began picking at the dry skin on her bare knees.

'Ready?' the sergeant repeated.

At the door, Ray turned and put his finger to his lips. Brenda didn't respond. She was staring at the wall. Her lips moved soundlessly.

When the questioning began, Ray relaxed because it had nothing to do with the fire. He licked his lips nervously, but he kept his head. Cal thought he was stupid. That's where Cal was wrong. Ray could handle himself in a tight spot. Shame he wouldn't be able to tell Cal how well he had dealt with the police. The thought of Cal finding out what he had done made him feel cold. That bloody girl must have recognised his face. He should have worn a mask.

'Raymond Barker?' the sergeant prompted him. 'Can you tell us what you were doing at five thirty on Sunday afternoon? Because we have a witness who claims she saw you at around that time.' Ray frowned as though trying to remember. 'In a property in Wilson Street.'

'I was just being helpful.' Ray blinked at the sergeant, his thoughts full of hatred for the smug git. But Ray hid his feelings well. He wasn't stupid, whatever Cal might think.

'You were being helpful?'

'Yes. I happened to be walking past and saw the front door was wide open.' He knew to keep to the truth as far as possible. 'I was concerned.'

'Concerned?'

'I thought, maybe an old lady was ill in there.' The detective stared at him. Ray carried on. He was getting into his stride. 'Like my granny. She had a stroke and no one found her for hours.' Should he have said days? 'For a day,' he amended it and then wished he hadn't. The policeman's eyes flickered at his hesitation. It wasn't true about Ray's gran, but they would never check. 'So I went in to see if everything was all right. I called out, and this girl appeared. She freaked out when she saw me, so I left.'

'Without any explanation?'

Ray shrugged. He had worked out his story. It didn't sound too bad. 'I panicked,' he admitted with a grin. 'I could see there was nothing wrong with her. So I left. I was being a concerned citizen, Sergeant.'

When the detective challenged him about a knife he had been brandishing, Ray acted surprised.

'Knife?' he repeated. 'I wasn't carrying a knife!' It was his word against hers and she had been in a fright. He was all right. Funny, he thought, how Cal was so much scarier than the filth. But they wouldn't let him go home when they finished. Instead Ray was taken down to a holding cell where he sat, head down, staring at his large feet and wondering what the hell they were playing at.

'You've got nothing on me!' he yelled out, angry and afraid. 'I haven't been arrested. You can't keep me here. Let me out, you fucking bastards.' His earlier bravado had evaporated. The police didn't worry him, not really; but he knew he could be in serious trouble if Cal ever found out about it. Whatever happened, Ray had to make sure Brenda kept her mouth shut.

# CHAPTER 27

# NEWS

Nearly a week had passed since the fire. Sophie Cliff had been staying at her neighbour's house. At first Jane Pettifer had enjoyed fussing over her, but she soon tired of a guest indifferent to her many kindnesses.

'Of course she's in shock,' Jane told her friends when they phoned to ask after the poor widow.

'You're a saint, Jane,' her friends assured her. 'We don't know how you cope.'

'I have to be patient with her but I'm bringing her out of herself. It just takes time.' Jane held back from admitting the truth. She wasn't bringing the bereaved woman out of anything. Sophie Cliff sat in a chair and didn't speak. She picked at the food Jane put in front of her and slept most of the time. After five days, Jane was at her wits' end.

'How long is she going to stay?' Gerald Pettifer asked his wife one evening. She shrugged. 'Well, you'd better find out. I'm sorry for the poor woman, who wouldn't be? That's why I brought her in. But we can't put her up indefinitely. How long did you invite her to stay?'

'It wasn't that specific. She'd just lost her

169

husband. She was hardly in a fit state to be making plans.'

'Well I think it's time you found out.'

'Of course you're welcome to stay.' Jane smiled brightly at Sophie across the breakfast table the following morning. She poured Sophie a cup of coffee. Gerald rustled his paper. 'But . . .' She hesitated. 'Would you like some muesli?' Sophie toyed with her cereal.

Gerald finished his coffee and left the table and Jane followed him into the hall.

'You said you'd ask her when she's leaving,' he reminded his wife, a touch of irritation in his voice.

'I tried . . . it's hard to know what to say. I can't just come out with it and ask her when she's leaving.'

'I don't see why not,' he said.

'You ask her then,' Jane countered irritably.

'Me? It's better coming from you. You're a woman.'

'But—'

'You'll speak to her then.'

'Oh, very well, leave it to me.' She muttered something that her husband didn't catch.

'Just sort it out, will you?' he called over his shoulder from the front door. 'Give me a ring at the golf club and let me know how it goes. Leave a message if I'm out on the course.'

Jane returned to the kitchen and sat down opposite Sophie. 'Right,' she said firmly. She didn't meet Sophie's eye. 'We need to talk. You've been here five nights now. Of course we've been very happy to help out. We, Gerald and I, we love having you here. But . . .' She paused and poured herself some coffee. 'Gerald wants to know . . . we want to know . . . that is, we'd like to know what your plans are. How long do you intend to stay here? We'd just like to know, that's all,' she ended lamely. A hot flush spread down her neck and across her chest.

'It's been very kind of you to let me stay.' The voice was flat and distant. Sophie's mouth seemed to move independently in a face otherwise immobile. 'I'll move out today.'

'Oh don't feel you have to go . . . not just yet . . .'

Sophie went upstairs and locked herself in the bathroom. From the landing, Jane could hear the tap running. With a sigh she went back into the kitchen and began to clear the table.

Sophie sat down on the side of the bath. The simplest of actions took careful planning. It was hard to think. First she would go back to the house and pack a small bag. She wouldn't go into the damaged part of the house, where it had happened. Once she had a few belongings, she would find somewhere to stay. After a while she might go to her parents' house. But not yet. One day she might go back to work, but not yet. Right now all she wanted to do was sleep.

She washed her face, brushed her hair, and went downstairs to find Mrs Pettifer. 'I'll be off then,'

171

she announced. Her voice sounded cheerful. Forced.

'Where will you go?' As if Jane Pettifer cared. No one cared. Not now.

'I'm going to visit my parents,' she lied. She needed to go away, somewhere she wouldn't see pitying looks, hear hushed voices. If only she could find her way out of this horror, find her way back to Tom.

'Will you have a cup of coffee before you go?' Sophie shook her head and her eyes fell on the local paper, lying on the kitchen table.

## GANG TRIGGER GAS EXPLOSION

Sophie snatched up the paper and read the article. Until that moment, she hadn't understood what had happened. She had assumed the fire had been sparked by a fault. If the report in the paper was true, the man she had seen running away that night had broken into her house and left the gas on, killing Tom as surely as if he had stuck a knife in his chest. Sophie put the paper down. With her eyes closed she could picture his face, glaring wildly: the face of the intruder who had caused Tom's death. Tom's killer. She should have run him over, and left him to die.

'Are you all right?' Mrs Pettifer asked. Sophie didn't answer. It was a stupid question. She hurried out of the kitchen and ran from the house without a word of thanks.

'Well, of all the ungrateful . . .' Jane Pettifer muttered under her breath, her indignation over-shadowed by relief. Smiling, she picked up the telephone to tell her husband the good news.

It was growing late and Geraldine's mind wasn't focused on work. She had another visit to pay before the day was over.

A door swung open silently and she entered the coronary unit. The nurse on the desk didn't even glance up as she approached.

'I've come to visit DCI Gordon.'

'Pardon?'

'The patient's name is Gordon. Kathryn Gordon.'

'Oh yes, the police woman.' Geraldine nodded. Illness cared nothing for rank. 'Second room along on your left. Don't stay long.' The nurse looked up with a weary frown. 'Are you a relative?'

'I'm her niece.' The pointless lie slipped out on the spur of the moment. It was too late to retract it. Geraldine hurried away along the hushed corridor. The hospital atmosphere brought a rush of memory that caught her unawares. She had to stop and catch her breath. She blinked, fighting the image of her mother lying in a hospital bed; her sister weeping noisily, eyes and nose streaming, clutching a sodden tissue, looking up as Geraldine entered the room . . . and Geraldine swamped by guilt, because by the time she arrived at the hospital, her mother was already dead.

'Are you all right?' A young nurse had stopped.

Geraldine forced a smile. 'I'm fine, thank you. It's just . . . hospitals . . .' She turned and made her way along the corridor to the room where Kathryn Gordon lay shored up on pillows.

Geraldine was shocked at how the DCI had aged overnight. Her cheeks had lost their usual ruddy flush and seemed to have collapsed inwards beneath bones that jutted out. Her lips were taut in a sour expression as though someone had removed her teeth. Geraldine stepped into the room and hesitated. Kathryn Gordon appeared to be sleeping. She was attached to a drip and a monitor that displayed her heart rate electronically in a fine green line that flickered disconcertingly at the periphery of Geraldine's vision. She looked like a frail old woman, clinging on to life by a fine green thread which moved inexorably up and down on the screen; it could stop at any moment.

Geraldine turned away, guilty at her intense relief that she wouldn't have to struggle with expressions of sympathy. She wasn't sure how Kathryn Gordon would react. Reaching the door, she glanced behind her. Kathryn Gordon's eyes were open now, staring straight at her. Geraldine hesitated, but she couldn't leave now that the DCI had seen her. She turned back into the room and approached the bed.

'How are you feeling?' she asked. Clumsily.

'How's the investigation going?'

'Don't worry about that. You need to concentrate on getting yourself fit.' How many more foolish platitudes were going to slip out of her mouth? Kathryn Gordon glared, faintly belligerent. 'Don't worry about the case,' Geraldine repeated. She was caught completely off guard, shocked at seeing the formidable Kathryn Gordon reduced to a feeble old woman. It was unbearably sad. Geraldine hadn't come to the hospital with the conscious intention of discussing the case, but standing helpless by the DCI's bedside, Geraldine realised that was what she had been hoping to do.

Kathryn Gordon began to speak but her voice failed. Geraldine had to bend forward to distinguish the words. 'Who . . . senior . . .'

'James Ryder.' She thought she saw a gleam in the older woman's eyes and wondered if it signified anger or approval, before she realised Kathryn Gordon's eyes were filling with tears. Geraldine had to look away.

Kathryn Gordon was the first to regain her composure. 'Geraldine,' she rasped softly. 'I'm not going to die. Don't think . . .'

The door opened and a nurse bustled in. 'Time for your niece to leave, Kathryn.'

Kathryn Gordon's eyes widened in surprise. Geraldine shrugged, and turned away to hide her embarrassment. She couldn't think of anything to say. When she glanced over her shoulder, she realised that words were unnecessary. Kathryn Gordon was smiling at her.

# CHAPTER 28

# RECOGNITION

As soon as the local paper had come out, members of the public had started phoning in. Every call had to be taken seriously, but most were from people concerned about the safety of their gas appliances. The staff on the switchboard were soon fed up of giving out the phone number of the gas board.

'Good news for gas service engineers,' a constable remarked.

Geraldine had to step out of her office to find out how the calls were progressing. On her previous case the police station had been too small for her to have her own office. She had preferred working at a desk in the Incident Room. Now, she could hear a buzz of activity through the flimsy partition wall without being able to distinguish words. It was distracting as she found herself listening, trying to make out what was being said. Even when she managed to block out the hum of voices, it was impossible to ignore the shrilling of phones.

Raymond Barker had been taken down to the cells to kick his heels overnight. They were getting nowhere with him. They would have to let him go before long. In the interim, he was kicking up an appalling fuss. Fed up, Geraldine wandered off to the canteen. A constable found her there, staring moodily into her coffee.

'Sophie Cliff's been found, ma'am.'

'Where is she?'

'She's been brought in. She'd left her neighbours and was picked up driving around. Seems she wasn't sure where she was headed. She seems a bit confused.'

'Sounds like it. All right. I'll see her now.' Geraldine took a deep breath and ran over a few platitudes in her mind as she walked along the corridor.

Bloodshot eyes looked up at her from a grey face. If she hadn't known better, Geraldine would have thought Sophie Cliff was suffering from a terminal sickness. Her hair was sticking up in wild clumps, her blouse was crumpled, her eyes crazed.

'I read the paper,' Sophie Cliff said hoarsely. Geraldine sat down. 'There were intruders in my house?' Geraldine waited. She wasn't sure where this was heading. 'They left the gas on, didn't they? It wasn't an accident. Those burglars. They killed my husband.' Geraldine would have felt more comfortable with anger or grief; there was a steely quality in Sophie's stilted voice that was unnerving. The other woman's grief felt like an accusation to Geraldine, unable to mourn for her own mother. Perhaps, when the case was over, suppressed emotion would surface and she would

177

weep for her mother. 'Who are they?' the widow was asking, her voice strident. 'I want you to tell me who killed my husband.'

'We're following several leads, Mrs Cliff – Sophie.'

'What leads? I have a right to know.' She was shaking now, her flat voice belied by her zealous eyes.

Geraldine explained that they had recovered some of the goods stolen by the burglars; candle sticks and other valuables. Officers were interviewing all the victims and neighbours again. 'I assure you, Mrs Cliff, we're doing everything we can to find these men. I'll let you know as soon as there are any further developments.'

Sophie Cliff took a deep breath and launched into a description of the face she had seen, illuminated under a street lamp, as she had driven off to work on Friday night. Geraldine nodded. Sophie Cliff's workplace had confirmed that she would have left her house shortly after two thirty. She had tried to leave quietly, she said, so as not to wake her husband. 'He was sleeping,' she explained, as though it mattered now. 'I didn't want to disturb him.' Geraldine sat and listened while Sophie Cliff talked.

It seemed that Sophie Cliff must have disturbed the intruders when she left the house. One of them had tried to run past her car. Sophie had nearly knocked him down. 'I didn't know,' she said. 'If I'd known, I wouldn't have braked.'

'You said earlier you thought you might recognise this man if you saw him again.'

'I'd know him anywhere.'

Geraldine studied the desperation in the pale face opposite. 'Are you sure, Mrs Cliff?'

'He was standing right under the street lamp.' She blinked at Geraldine through her glasses. 'I don't think he could see my face, in the car. He probably didn't know I could see him. But I saw him. I saw him as clearly as I can see you now.'

'Mrs Cliff—' Geraldine sighed. Sophie Cliff was in a state of extreme emotional disturbance. Geraldine could imagine a defence counsel coldly deconstructing a case built around her conviction. 'Mrs Cliff,' she began again. 'If you're feeling strong enough, we'd like you to describe this man you saw to an E-fit officer who will produce an image of his face. Do you think you could do that?'

Sophie stopped abruptly and gripped Geraldine by the arm. 'What will happen to him? He'll go to prison, won't he? He'll get life if I tell you what he looks like. He'll never get away, will he?'

'You have my word for it that we'll do our best to see justice done.' Geraldine hoped that her words wouldn't turn out to be a hollow promise.

Half an hour passed before Geraldine's phone rang. It was the desk sergeant. With a sigh, Geraldine made her way to the entrance. Sophie Cliff was sitting on a chair in the lobby, staring straight ahead. With a shrug at the sergeant, Geraldine sat down beside her.

'Thank you for your information, Mrs Cliff. Is there anything else you want to tell us?'

'You'll get him now, won't you?' Sophie Cliff was animated, her hair splayed out wildly around her thin face.

'We'll keep you fully informed. Where will you be?'

'I'll go to my parents.'

'We'll be in touch, I promise.'

As she pushed open the internal door, Geraldine glanced over her shoulder. Sophie Cliff hadn't moved.

On her way back to her office, Geraldine passed Barker being escorted along the corridor. A sudden shriek floated through the door to the entrance hall. Geraldine turned and hurried back along the corridor. Sophie Cliff was on her feet jabbing her finger at Barker. Her eyes blazed and her arm trembled wildly, like a child waving a sparkler.

'Murderer!' she screeched. 'You'll burn in hell for what you did!'

'Tell her to shut it, for fuck's sake. She's off her trolley' Rattled, Barker turned to the constable.

'That's him,' Sophie gabbled. 'It's him.' She seized Geraldine's arm and shook her. 'That's the man I saw outside the house. It's him!'

'I'm the innocent party here. It's slander, that's what this is. You need to do something to shut her up,' Barker blustered.

'Come along, sir,' the constable replied, unperturbed. He escorted Barker to the door.

180

Sophie ran out. Geraldine retired to her office but couldn't settle. She returned to the lobby which was now empty.

'She went quietly,' the desk sergeant told her, before she had a chance to ask. 'Left as soon as Barker had gone. Never a dull moment, eh?'

# CHAPTER 29

## BRONXY

**B**arker swore when he saw Geraldine and Peterson on his doorstep. He ran large hands through his dishevelled hair. 'I already told you I was there. I saw the door open. I only went in to see that everything was all right. Jesus, you try to be a good citizen, and end up being treated like a bloody criminal.' He glared. 'You've got nothing on me.'

'Mr Barker, this isn't about your trespass.'

'I keep telling you, it wasn't trespass. The door was wide open. I just walked in.'

'Where were you on Friday night?'

'What?' His mouth hung slack but his eyes were suddenly sharp.

'Where were you on Friday night?'

'Friday night?' He blinked, uncertain. Geraldine waited. 'How the fuck should I know?' He folded his arms and leaned back.

'Not great, as alibis go,' Peterson remarked conversationally. He too leaned back, mirroring Barker's posture.

'Alibi?' Barker spluttered. 'What are you talking about, alibi? I've done nothing wrong. This is

182

fucking insane. I act like a responsible citizen and you lot turn it into some kind of crime.' He paused. They waited. 'I need to check,' he said. 'I'm entitled.' Geraldine nodded and Barker slammed the door. A few seconds later they heard raised voices. Peterson hammered on the door. Barker opened it again.

'You can come to the station and wait for a duty solicitor—' Geraldine began.

'I don't need a fucking lawyer. I've done nothing wrong.'

Geraldine and Peterson exchanged annoyed glances and she resumed. 'Where were you on Friday night?'

This time, Barker had an answer. 'Bronxy's,' he replied.

'Bronxy's?'

'Yeah. That's right. I spent the night at Bronxy's. With a mate.'

'Where is Bronxy's?'

'The club. The Blue Lagoon. You can ask anyone there. They'll tell you. I was there.' He slammed the door.

'He's agitated,' Geraldine said.

'He's not just angry. He's scared,' Peterson agreed.

'But not of us.'

Bennett gave Geraldine and Peterson the background to Barker's alibi. 'Bronxy runs the Blue Lagoon. It's a strip joint posing as a night club, behind the scenes a knocking shop posing as a strip joint. It's a nasty dive. A real cess pit. It all goes on there. The owner was prosecuted for profiting from human trafficking a couple of years back. All came to nothing, more's the pity. Prosecution couldn't make it stick.'

'No convictions?' Peterson asked.

Bennett shook his head. 'Bronxy's a slippery customer with a finger in every stinking pie.' He shrugged. 'Best of luck. I hope you shut the place down and throw away the key.'

'Bronxy?' Geraldine repeated thoughtfully as they settled in the car. 'What do we know about Bronxy?'

Peterson shrugged. 'He isn't running a bridge club, gov.' He spun the wheel and drove off away from the centre of town to a rundown district on the east side of the town.

The nature of the Blue Lagoon was apparent as soon as they drew up in a narrow street of seedy pubs interspersed with strip joints and night clubs. A neon sign announced the name in bright pink letters: 'Blue Lagoon'.

'Should be blue lettering,' Geraldine remarked, as they approached the narrow poorly lit entrance.

A bouncer on the door sized them up straight away. 'Evening, officers,' he greeted them before they had shown any ID. 'Here for the evening's entertainment?' He ran watery eyes up and down Geraldine's body, and winked suggestively at Peterson. 'Nice.'

'We're here to see Bronxy,' Peterson replied sharply.

184

The man touched his cap. 'You're in luck then, gov'nor. Bronxy's in tonight. Bronxy's in every night.' He laughed. 'Back office. But you'd best let me—' Peterson pushed past the security guard without waiting to hear any more.

Geraldine followed the sergeant across a dimly lit foyer, through a thick dark curtain, into a stuffy room.

'Hey, where do you think you're going?' a heavily made up girl called after them, long red nails fluttering. On a podium, a scantily clad woman was gyrating to music so loud it made Geraldine's head pound.

One or two men complained as they pushed their way through the hot and smoky room. 'Watch where you put your feet, wanker.'

The stripper turned her back and ripped off her bra. Someone jeered. The sweet scent of cannabis floated on the air as they threaded their way to a door labelled STAFF ONLY. Peterson rapped on the door. He marched in without waiting for a response, ignoring a shrill female voice protesting behind them. Geraldine followed him, relieved when the door closed behind her, reducing the blaring music to a dull thump.

They were in a well furnished office. Halogen lighting made Geraldine blink. A woman was sitting at a desk. Short and muscular, she rose to her feet in one swift movement. Shrewd black rimmed eyes flicked over them. Highlighted hair had been swept back off her face in curls that swooped to her shoulders. There was something fake about her high cheek bones, pouting lips and smooth complexion. In her youthful face, shrewd eyes contemplated them with the scepticism of old age.

'We're looking for Bronxy.' Geraldine sat down without waiting for an invitation.

The woman's dark eyes flashed. 'Bronxy?' Her voice was husky.

'We're looking for Bronxy,' Peterson repeated. The woman sat down behind the desk and spread her hands on either side of her body, palms upward, in a gesture of submission.

'I'm all yours, Sergeant,' she drawled. Her eyes moved slowly down and lingered below Peterson's waistband. She licked her lips and laughed under her breath before turning to Geraldine. 'You must be Geraldine Steel. Should I congratulate you on your promotion, or has the moment passed?'

Someone had warned Bronxy they were coming. 'We'd like a list of your guests last Friday night,' Geraldine said.

'Condolences on the loss of your mother,' Bronxy continued in the same lazy drawl.

Geraldine wondered how Bronxy knew about her mother's death. The woman was playing mind games, trying to unsettle her. 'Your guests on Friday,' she repeated in a level tone, her face impassive.

'But at least your mother knew about your promotion before she passed away,' Bronxy continued. 'That must be a comfort.'

'Your guests on Friday,' Geraldine insisted in a quiet voice.

Bronxy screwed up her eyes. 'Let me see,' she said with exaggerated slowness. She lit a cigarette. Peterson reminded her sharply of the law prohibiting smoking in public venues. Bronxy inhaled deeply. It wasn't clear if she was playing for time or trying to rile them. 'Friday night,' she repeated. 'Friday night's always busy. We had a few regulars in. Cal Martin was in.' She was offhand, as though picking a name at random.

'Callum Martin?'

'Yes. He was here. All night.' She glanced up through heavy lashes. 'Ray Barker was with him.' She took a long drag of her cigarette and balanced it on the rim of an ashtray, a fierce smudge of scarlet lipstick on the stub. A wisp of smoke rose curling in the air.

'Callum Martin and Ray Barker were here on Friday night?'

'That's what I said, officer.'

'What time did they leave?'

'They were here all night.'

'So what time did they leave?'

'We closed at three.' Bronxy smiled, unruffled. They all knew she was lying. She swivelled round, opened a safe in the wall behind her and pulled out a handful of cheques held together with a large clip. Leafing through them she selected one and handed it to Geraldine. It was drawn on Callum Martin's account and dated Friday.

Geraldine returned it. 'Thank you, but that's not helpful.'

Bronxy turned to Peterson. 'Perhaps you'd like to question my girls, Sergeant? They're always happy to help out a policeman.' She smiled. 'And they all remember Cal's visit.'

'You know that, do you?'

'All the girls know Cal.' She laughed out loud, a coarse laugh that jarred with her carefully arranged features and immaculate hair. 'I haven't fallen out with him, even if he did take my girl.'

'Your girl?'

'Brenda.'

'What do you mean, your girl?' Geraldine asked. Bronxy puffed at her cigarette, considering the question. She didn't answer. 'Where does she come from?' Geraldine pressed her.

'Same place they all come from. I take them off the streets, put a roof over their heads. I do my bit same as you, officer. Most of my girls wouldn't have survived the winter if I hadn't taken them in.'

'Why would she lie to protect Martin and Barker?' Peterson asked when they were back in the car.

'Just what I was wondering.' Geraldine stared out of the window thoughtfully. The more information they unearthed, the less clear it all became.

# CHAPTER 30

# CARELESS TALK

As long as the rain held off, Maggie did all right on a Friday. In the run up to Christmas she added to her usual stock with bags that did well as gifts. Some pretty beaded ones were proving popular. The market had been more crowded than usual in November. The stallholders reckoned they could thank the recession. Stores were advertising sales all along the High Street, more shops than usual stood empty, but the market, with its bargains and cheap products, was surviving.

Maggie and Alice worked neighbouring stalls and covered for each other on and off throughout the morning. Brenda worked erratic hours, helping out at different stalls. For a short time she had a regular pitch of her own selling birthday cards, notepads that fell apart and cheap biros. Unable to keep it together, she haunted the market place earning a few quid standing in for other stall holders when they went for a break. It was charity really. The stall holders could cover for one another. Brenda was busiest in the cold weather when the traders took refuge in the café or queued at the coffee stall to warm their hands round polystyrene cups.

Maggie met her friends for a drink every Friday. She made a point of keeping back a few quid for these outings. It wasn't much of a social life but it made a change from sitting at home with the kids. She longed for more exciting company. Alice was nice but she was old, over sixty and not much fun. Brenda was a smack head and weird. What Maggie really wanted was to meet a man with some dosh, and that wasn't going to happen sitting with Alice and Brenda over a drink round the corner from the market.

'Maybe we should go for a proper evening out,' Maggie suggested. 'Go into town. We don't have to stick to Friday.' She didn't need to stay in on Saturday nights now Chloe was ten and old enough to be left in charge of her brother.

'We always meet on Friday,' Brenda whined. She glanced around anxiously.

'We always meet here Fridays,' Alice agreed. 'It's a tradition.'

Maggie shrugged. 'Whatever.' Alice was past caring about going into town for the night life and Brenda would never dare go out for a whole evening. She was scared in case her boyfriend found out she had been for a drink when the market closed, and knocked her about for it.

Maggie and Alice agreed Brenda was pathetic.

'Why does she stay with him? It's obvious what's

going on. Did you see those blisters on her neck? Cigarette burns. On her neck!'

'And her legs. She said she fell over.'

'Yeah right. And then she walked into a door. Pull the other one.'

'He's going to finish her off one of these days.'

'Like Lily,' they agreed.

Four of them used to meet in the pub until Lily had been the victim of a fatal mugging. Her attacker was never caught. Maggie and Alice suspected Lily's boyfriend was responsible. They used to speculate about it constantly until Brenda had moved in with Lily's ex.

'Best not to interfere,' Alice had said at the time, and Maggie agreed with her.

They were reminiscing about Lily while Brenda was in the loo because Alice, who had once met Lily's ex, had spotted him at the bus stop that morning. 'Whistling he was, happy as Larry. Vicious bastard. It gave me quite a turn, seeing him there.'

'We know what he did to poor Lily,' Maggie muttered, hoping she would never meet him.

'Sod all we can do about it,' Alice said, not for the first time. She had been around the market for years. 'If I've learned anything, it's not to trust anyone in uniform. Start with the pigs and before you can say jack shit they're crawling all over you. They'll take your kids away too. You wouldn't want to lose Chloe, would you? They don't care.' She took a swig of her pint. 'Take away your licence for no reason, if they feel like it. Remember what happened to Barney and his fish stall?'

Maggie stared at Brenda staggering across to the bar and wished she could do something to help her but Alice was right. You couldn't trust anyone.

'Pigs,' Maggie grumbled. She took a pull of her pint, before adding, 'They were round this week.'

'Who?'

'The filth. Came to see me.' Alice and Brenda stared at her.

Alice's lined face grew tense. 'What did they want? Don't tell me that arsehole Geoffrey's been at it again? You ought to make a formal complaint. Bastard's been after your pitch for years.'

Maggie shook her head. 'It wasn't about my pitch.'

'What then?'

'They were asking about a bag.'

'A bag? They knocked on your door for a bag?' Alice was indignant. 'You should've told them go to the market like everyone else. Bloody cheek. Think they own the place.'

'They didn't come round to buy a bag,' Maggie laughed. 'They wanted to know about some bloke. They reckon he bought a bag off me last week. One of those canvas bags. A khaki one.'

Brenda spilt her drink all over her jeans and swore. 'What did you tell them?' she asked. Her fingers wriggled in her lap like worms.

Maggie shrugged. 'I told them I couldn't remember

192

any bloke buying a bag from me.' She stared at Brenda. 'You all right, Bren? You look awful. Perhaps you'd better get off home and change out of those wet jeans before you catch a chill up your minge.' Alice sniggered. Brenda nodded uncertainly before clambering to her feet. The other two women watched her stumble to the door. 'What's got into her?' Maggie asked. 'She looks like shit.'

Alice scowled at Brenda's retreating back, narrow shoulders hunched beneath her dry blonde hair. 'She's beginning to really piss me off,' she said as the pub door swung shut. 'She keeps telling us she's all right, but if you ask me she's getting worse.'

Maggie nodded. 'She looks like the walking dead. Off her face more often than not.'

'She's going to end up like Lily if she's not careful.'

Maggie went up to the bar for another round. Two drinks were cheaper than three. She would stay on for a bit, what the hell.

'Tell you what,' Alice said when Maggie returned. 'I reckon it was me.'

'What's that?'

'Sold a khaki bag to a bloke last Friday, while I was minding the stall for you. And I'll tell you how I remember. He came back this week, when you were off seeing Geoffrey. That's when I saw him again. I remembered his funny eyes.'

'That's weird.'

'Yeah. So why did they want to know?'

'How would I know? They didn't exactly take me into their confidence. Who was he anyway?'

'Seen him around, but I don't know his name. Don't know and don't care.' She grinned at Maggie and lifted her glass. 'Cheers.'

# CHAPTER 31

# DISAPPOINTMENT

It was late by the time they returned to the station. Geraldine was dismayed to see Sophie Cliff sitting on a chair in the entrance lobby. She was staring straight ahead, fingers interlaced round a polystyrene cup of coffee. With a shrug at Peterson, Geraldine ushered her into an interview room.

'You need to go home, Mrs Cliff.'

'It was him, wasn't it?'

'Mrs Cliff – Sophie – Mr Barker has an alibi. We've checked it out and he has a witness. It couldn't have been him, the man you saw in your headlights on Friday night.' Sophie Cliff watched Geraldine's mouth, as though lip reading. 'We've checked it out very carefully,' Geraldine repeated gently. She spoke slowly. 'Mr Barker has witnesses who can vouch for his being with them throughout Friday evening, until the early hours of Saturday morning.' She paused. Silence. Sophie sat quite still. 'I'm sorry, Mrs Cliff, but I'm afraid you must've been mistaken. It wasn't Mr Barker you saw on Friday night. Mrs Cliff?' Geraldine had dealt with families of victims of violent death before, people for whom the case never closed. A spasm of pity threatened her composure but it crossed her mind that Sophie Cliff could have been responsible for her husband's murder. She was certainly unstable. Geraldine had encountered less likely murderers.

'Alibi?' Sophie Cliff repeated, as though she didn't recognise the word. Patiently Geraldine went over it again. Suddenly Sophie Cliff leaned forward in her chair. She was shaking. The cup she was clutching tipped precariously. She didn't respond as a trickle of coffee dribbled into her lap. Geraldine reached forward and took the cup from her grasp. 'You mustn't believe them,' Sophie Cliff hissed. 'They're lying. I saw him.'

'Mrs Cliff, we have witnesses who claim Raymond Barker was with them on Friday night at the time you thought you saw him outside your house. We have no case against him. He was somewhere else at the time.'

'I'm not mistaken. He's lying. Don't believe him.' Her eyes glistened with tears.

'We have witnesses, Mrs Cliff.'

'They're lying. I saw him.'

'You saw a figure for an instant, in the dark.'

'I saw him. They're lying.' Her voice rose to a hoarse shriek.

Geraldine considered. Sophie Cliff might have identified her intruder correctly, but her evidence was flimsy. She would be an unreliable witness. Raymond Barker had witnesses prepared to swear in court that he had been in the Blue Lagoon on

Friday night. A prosecution wouldn't reach court. 'I'm sorry, Mrs Cliff. My hands are tied.' Their eyes met just long enough for Geraldine to feel a faint unease before Sophie Cliff dropped her gaze. 'I'm sorry, Mrs Cliff.' Geraldine led Sophie Cliff out to the entrance lobby, where she slumped down on the bench. 'Where are you going now? Do you have somewhere to go? We could arrange—'

'I'll go to my parents.'

Geraldine watched Sophie Cliff leave the station. She glanced around the deserted lobby and exchanged a few words with the desk sergeant before returning to her desk to research the woman known as Bronxy.

The Blue Lagoon had opened in the nineteen sixties, one of the first clubs to appear in the neighbourhood. At that time, Eastglade had been a residential area with a small shopping centre. Within six weeks, a petition calling for the club to be closed down was presented to the Council. A copy had found its way on to the police file:

We, the undersigned, call on Harchester Council to close the brothel called The Blue Lagoon, which has recently opened in a residential district of East Harchester, in the vicinity of local schools and shops.

In 2004 the ownership had passed from Mr Derek Brooks to Mrs Susan Brooks. A list of employees included several girls with exotic names: Lulu, Renee, Foxy, Tallulah. There was no mention of anyone called Brenda. Geraldine read about

Eastglade's development into the centre of tawdry night life in Harchester. A filthy kebab shop had been unsuccessfully prosecuted, unlicensed cabs prowled the streets and there were unsubstantiated allegations of child prostitution. It made for unsavoury reading. But she found nothing to undermine Barker's alibi.

By early evening Geraldine was home and lonely. She had bought a flat when her partner, Mark, had walked out on their relationship after six years. Geraldine was pleased with the security of owning her own home but a new flat, however smart, couldn't fill her hours of solitude. She went out to her car and called Craig. He didn't answer his landline. His mobile went straight to voicemail. On an impulse, she drove to the small town where he lived. She hoped he would be pleased to see her.

'Sorry to turn up like this,' she imagined the conversation. 'I felt like company tonight.'

'That's great.' She pictured Craig's face lighting up in a smile that crinkled the little lines around his eyes. 'I was just about to call you.' Then he would kiss her and pull her into the bedroom. Afterwards they would curl up on the sofa, limbs entwined, and share a bottle of soft red wine. Geraldine smiled at the image she had conjured up.

She parked opposite his building and sat for a while, touching up her make up. She couldn't see his car. She checked her face in the mirror one last time before setting off but Craig didn't answer the door. She thought she might as well wait for him to come home, now she was there. He might be back soon. She waited about twenty minutes and was on the point of leaving when Craig's car drew up.

She glanced in the mirror and paused, lip gloss in hand, as Craig emerged, followed by a tall slim woman in a long dark coat. Craig half turned and waited for the woman. She slipped her arm through his. They were laughing. Geraldine slouched in her seat and stared at their disappearing figures. Her face was burning. She hoped Craig wouldn't look round and recognise her car, but he was too engrossed in his companion to glance back. Geraldine bit her lip. 'That's that, then,' she said aloud. One less problem to worry about. The woman might be his sister, or a work colleague. But she saw the intimacy between the two figures as they walked, arm in arm, along the path and out of sight. Craig didn't look back as Geraldine's engine growled into life and she pulled away from the kerb. Tears of disappointment slid down her face and dripped off her chin. Her nose began to run. She was surprised that she felt so distraught. Vexed, she wiped her face with the back of her hand, telling herself she didn't care. She had been on her own before. And right now she had more important things to worry about, with two unsolved murders on her caseload.

# PART III

*'It is a man's own mind, not his enemy
or foe, that lures him to evil ways'*

Siddharta

# CHAPTER 32

## UPDATE

When the DCI summoned all the officers involved in the investigation to a briefing on Saturday morning, most of them weren't pleased.

'It's Saturday,' Peterson muttered as they gathered in the Incident Room. He glanced at his watch.

'At least you can claim overtime,' Bennett grumbled. Geraldine pulled a face. As an inspector she was no longer eligible to claim overtime for additional hours worked.

'It's gone nine,' Polly complained to the room in general after they had been waiting ten minutes. A few voices chimed in. Geraldine wasn't too bothered. She had nothing to do that weekend.

'My daughter's coming round,' Bennett said looking wretchedly at the door. There was no sign of the DCI.

They were all feeling irritated by the time James Ryder finally turned up. It was past ten but he didn't apologise for keeping them waiting. Geraldine assumed he had been reporting to the Superintendent about the investigation. He was looking particularly well turned out in an expensive looking three piece suit. Even his shirt collar looked starched, in contrast to the rest of the team who all looked like they could do with a lie in at the end of a frenetic week. Geraldine felt sweaty and crumpled. Beside her, Peterson was tightening the knot on his tie, his shirt was wrinkled and his good looking face had lost its characteristic exuberance.

The atmosphere in the room was tense as though the DCI was no longer leading the team, but inspecting them. Glancing round, Geraldine saw her own tension reflected in other faces. She took a deep breath and tried to focus on what the DCI was saying. Ryder himself seemed edgy. Geraldine guessed he had been given a bollocking of some sort. He had only been on the case for four days, but the pressure for results was never far beneath the surface, from the Super, the press and anyone who had been involved with the victims.

'Right, I was tied up most of yesterday, as you know,' he opened the meeting. 'I'd rather have been here, I can tell you. So bring me up to speed. What's been happening in my absence? Have we cracked it?' He spoke with forced enthusiasm. 'Any progress?' He sighed. He was going through the motions. He ran his hand through his light brown hair which flopped forward over his forehead, his elegant guise wrecked with that one movement. 'I take it we're no further on then?' The atmosphere changed. He was back on the team.

Geraldine broke the silence by telling him about Deborah Mainwaring's intruder. 'She picked him out at once, sir. She was sure it was him.'

Ryder waved his hand dismissively. 'Let's stick to the burglaries, shall we?' he said. 'I'm not concerned about some minor trespass – it's not even a break-in. The woman left her front door wide open, for Christ's sake. Is there anything to link this to the case?' Geraldine bristled but was mollified by Ryder's reaction when he learned that Sophie Cliff had identified Barker as the man she had seen in her headlights on Friday night. They discussed Sophie Cliff's statement in some detail.

'She's hardly in a stable condition,' someone pointed out.

'Is she on any medication?' Ryder asked.

'No.'

'Bloody well ought to be,' the sergeant who had been on the desk said. He described Sophie Cliff's reaction after she had been told that Barker had an alibi. 'If you ask me, the woman's cracking up.'

'She's in shock,' Geraldine protested. 'She's just lost her husband in an arson attack. And they'd not been married for long,' she added, as though that made a difference.

'Whatever the reason, I wouldn't want to have to rely on her as a witness in court,' the sergeant replied.

'Still, she picked him out,' Ryder mused. 'It's an odd coincidence.'

'He might've reminded her of the person she saw,' someone suggested.

'If she really saw anyone,' another voice added. 'Perhaps she's trying to shift the blame, to make herself feel better.'

'She might've been mistaken, but she was genuinely convinced it was him, sir,' Geraldine said. 'And what's interesting is that her description matched Barker before she saw him here. She must've seen him, or someone very like him, before she came into the station. She gave a detailed description of this man she saw on the street outside her house.' She flicked through her note book and read out Sophie Cliff's description of the face in the headlights. 'I think he was tall. He was all arms and legs when he ran. And he had huge eyes, no not huge, but protruding, like marbles. He was pale and his hair looked like straw, like a scarecrow.'

Ryder studied the mug shot of Barker and nodded thoughtfully. He was interested. 'It certainly sounds like Barker.'

'The problem is, Barker's got an alibi.' As briefly as she could, Geraldine told them about her visit to the Blue Lagoon.

'Blue Lagoon?' Ryder repeated.

'It's a seedy local strip joint,' Geraldine explained.

'A knocking shop,' a local officer added.

'A bunch of old slappers,' Peterson pulled a face. 'Enough to put anyone off. You wouldn't want to take your worst enemy there on his stag night.'

'Not unless you want to give him something he hadn't bargained for,' another local officer called out with a laugh.

'I get the picture,' Ryder interrupted impatiently. 'So Barker was conveniently at the Blue Lagoon club with Bronxy on Friday night?' Geraldine nodded. 'Any CCTV?'

'No, sir. Just the word of the madam.'

'Together with a whole host of people on her payroll,' Bennett added. 'The doorman, the slapper who takes the coats, dancers, hookers you name it, they all dance to Bronxy's tune. If she tells us Barker was there, they'll all swear blind he was there. Check the records, sir. She's given out more alibis than you've had hot dinners, and they're always backed up by her team. Believe me, it's not just her, sir. She'll have a whole gang of them prepared to back her story, and there's more than a few court officials who know her from more than her court appearances.' He shrugged and an uneasy silence fell. Ryder looked worried. Geraldine felt a burgeoning sympathy for Bennett.

'That stinks,' Peterson broke the silence. No one else spoke. Bennett threw a sneaky glance at his watch.

# CHAPTER 33

# SHOCK

Geraldine was off duty on Saturday. Normally she would have gone in to work for the whole day anyway, but she was due at her sister's house later that morning. She was already going to be late, thanks to the briefing.

Celia had called Geraldine during the week. 'We've been putting off going through mum's things for long enough,' she had said firmly. Geraldine was relieved to hear Celia sounding like her normal bossy self, but her spirits sank at the thought of spending a day with her sister, clearing out their mother's belongings.

'Are you sure you want . . .' Geraldine broke off, ashamed to confess her reluctance. 'Are you sure you're ready for this?'

'Got to be done,' Celia answered stiffly. Geraldine wondered if she realised her sister wanted to duck out of her filial duty.

Celia was on her knees rummaging in the bottom of their mother's wardrobe among a clutter of shoes, bags and belts when Geraldine arrived. Geraldine tried not to glance inside the wardrobe: it felt like an intrusion. She stood with her back to Celia, rolling sheets and stuffing them into black bin bags.

Celia wanted to donate their mother's shoes to a local charity shop. She was stacking them in pairs in a cardboard box when she broke the silence. 'I thought you'd have this.' Geraldine squinted down at a faded grey box file and read her own name, handwritten on a peeling yellow label. 'I would've thought you'd have wanted it.'

'What is it?'

'Your papers.' Celia lifted the box and thrust it at her sister.

'What papers?'

'I thought you'd have wanted them. I mean I thought she'd have given them . . .' Celia sat back on her heels and stared up at Geraldine. 'She never told you, did she? She said she'd tell you. I can't believe she never told you.'

Geraldine put down the sheet she was folding and turned to her sister. 'Told me what?'

Celia looked down at the carpet. Ash blonde hair slipped forward and concealed her features. Geraldine could hear tension in her voice, sullen like a child. 'She said she'd tell you.'

'Celia, I don't know what you're talking about. What's in the box? What papers?'

'Your papers. Birth certificate, adoption papers . . .'

Geraldine sat down on the bed and stared at her sister's fine hair. 'You're telling me we're adopted?'

Celia's blonde head bobbed a nod. She didn't look up. 'Not us, you,' she mumbled.

'What do you mean? Celia?' Geraldine was on her feet. She felt her legs shaking and sat down again.

'You're adopted. Not me. You. She said she'd tell you. She was going to tell you . . .'

'I don't get it. How could . . .' Geraldine shook her head. This made no sense. Yet, with a visceral thrill, she knew it was true. So many things suddenly made sense.

Celia drew in a deep breath, and began to explain in a rapid undertone. Geraldine wanted to ask her to slow down but couldn't trust herself to speak. 'After I was born, mum had problems. Down there. Gynae problems, you know. It meant she couldn't have any more children.'

'But—'

'Just listen, will you? This isn't exactly easy for me. I'll tell you everything I know. It's not much.'

Their eyes met briefly. Celia looked away. Geraldine blinked. Tears spilled from her eyes but she didn't bother to wipe her face. Celia was speaking again, her voice stilted. 'She had a hyster-ectomy. She was only twenty six. So she couldn't have any more children. But they didn't want me to be – they didn't want an only child, so . . .'

'So they adopted . . .'

'You.' Celia thrust the box file at her again. 'Geraldine, I'm so sorry. I thought you knew. Take it. I'm sure it's all in there. I don't understand why she never told you.'

'You knew.' The accusation was unspoken.

'She said she'd tell you. I thought you knew. I never realised you didn't know.'

Geraldine was shaking so violently she couldn't stand up. 'Who else knew?'

Celia shrugged. 'How am I supposed to know? And don't shout at me. This isn't easy for me, you know. She wasn't exactly honest with me either. She promised me she'd tell you.'

'I wasn't shouting.' Geraldine snatched up the box, and strode from the room.

Driving home, she felt perfectly calm. The tears on her cheeks had dried. It made no difference now that her whole past had been constructed on a falsehood. She thought about murder victims' next of kin hearing that their loved ones were dead. Some of them reacted hysterically; others stood stock still, uncomprehending. She might have given them the terrible news in a foreign language. That was how she felt now, slightly light-headed and outwardly calm while inwardly she struggled against a growing sense of panic. She had no idea who she was.

It began to rain. A light drizzle hit the windscreen on and off, never releasing enough water to clear the screen. She set the wipers to intermittent. Her view was alternately smeared and clear. Doubting her own composure, she drove slowly. On the other side of the road, cars moved past in their own clouds of spray.

When the reaction came, the emotion hit her with such force that she had to pull off the road.

Her hands were trembling on the wheel. It wasn't the fact that she had been adopted that upset her. Not yet. She would face those feelings later. First she had to deal with her fury at the deception that had been practised for so long. It wasn't only her mother. She hadn't seen her father since he had gone to live in Ireland with his second wife. He hadn't even had the decency to attend his ex-wife's funeral. And Celia had been taken into her mother's confidence when Geraldine had been excluded. For nearly forty years they had kept her identity a secret from the one person who had a right to know.

She had no idea how long she sat there, trembling and alone in the world. The finality was intolerable. In the end her mother had been too cowardly to speak to Geraldine. But she hadn't taken her secret to her grave. More cruel than that, she must have known Geraldine would discover the truth.

'Why did you hide it from me all that time?' Geraldine asked out loud, knowing she would never hear the answer.

Celia's protestations had only made Geraldine feel worse. Celia had known. Celia the biological child. The true daughter. Geraldine was shivering with cold and shock. There was no one to comfort her. A rage of tears overwhelmed her. She sat in the car, sobbing wildly. But the heat of her tears would pass. Beneath the frenzy, a cold anger was growing.

She had no idea how she got home. The phone was shrilling as she opened her front door. She didn't answer. It rang again and went to voice mail. 'Geraldine, it's me, Celia. Please call me when you get this. We need to talk.' Geraldine ignored it. Almost immediately the phone rang again. This time there was no message. The phone rang for the fourth time. Another message. 'Geraldine, we need to talk about this. I'm as devastated as you are. I thought you knew. But nothing's changed. It doesn't make any difference. You're still my sister.' Geraldine reached down and unplugged the cord. Celia was wrong. Everything had changed. She had no sister.

As far as she knew.

# CHAPTER 34

# SATURDAY NIGHT

Geraldine opened her eyes. She lay in semi-darkness, sprawled on the carpet. She must have slipped off the sofa in a drunken torpor. An empty wine bottle stood on the table. No glass. She had a vague recollection of swigging from the bottle. She sat up cautiously, scrambled to her feet and staggered to the bathroom. Too late. She gazed in dismay at a thin splodge of vomit oozing across the floor. For a moment she seemed paralysed, then she set to work, cleaning up the mess. The stench of bleach made her gag. This time she was in place, arms around the toilet bowl, head lowered, before she threw up again. After that, she felt a little better, although her head ached horribly.

She showered and forced herself to eat some dry toast. Relieved when she kept it down, she drank two cups of tea and had another slice of toast. She felt much better. It was nearly six o'clock. The phone rang soon after she reconnected it. She didn't check the screen and was surprised to hear Craig's voice.

'Hi, sorry I couldn't get back to you yesterday. Are you free this evening?' he asked.

214

Geraldine snatched at the distraction. 'I've been wondering why you didn't call,' she lied. 'What happened? Is everything all right?' And by the way, who was the woman I saw you with when I just happened to be driving past your flat late last night, she thought.

And you'll be pleased to know my mother hasn't just died after all.

False alarm.

I never had a mother.

'Everything's fine,' Craig told her. 'My sister turned up.'

'Your sister?' She wanted to believe him.

'Yes. She lives in Brussels. She sometimes calls in on her way back from London, and she doesn't always give me much notice.'

'Brussels?' she repeated stupidly.

'Yes, Brussels. Look, are you free this evening? I can tell you all about my sister, if you're that interested. Give you her life story.'

Geraldine laughed. 'I'm more interested in her brother.'

'Great. I'll pick you up at eight?'

Craig had booked a table at a local restaurant. 'You OK with Chinese?'

'Fine.' Another lie. Eating was the last thing she felt like doing.

Sitting opposite the inevitable tank, Geraldine studied trailing fish tails while Craig studied the wine menu. They hadn't seen each other for over a week but slipped back into the easy familiarity

215

they had achieved on holiday. Geraldine apologised again for letting him down on Thursday and was relieved when he shrugged it off.

'I can drop you home if you like,' Craig said at the end of the evening.

'What if I don't like?' Geraldine asked, smiling. She had the rest of the weekend off.

'Have you got any plans for tomorrow?' Craig asked as they drove back to his flat. Geraldine couldn't think of a better way to keep her mind off her mother. Her so-called mother.

They woke late on Sunday morning and had a leisurely breakfast. Craig lived in a typical bachelor flat, neat and clinical, with white walls and ceiling, grey carpets, and chrome and black leather furnishings. Only the curtains offered an incongruous splash of colour. The first time she saw them, Geraldine wondered if a woman had chosen the long peach coloured velvet drapes. She noticed several cobwebs on the ceiling, and dust along the skirting boards, but the narrow kitchenette looked new and unused. She suspected Craig ate out a lot. Smiling, he produced a cafetiere of fresh coffee and two warm croissants. Geraldine watched him across the table, appreciating his lean good looks, and the boldness and intensity of his gaze that had first attracted her.

Far from being put off by her bungled invitation, Craig seemed as keen on her as before. It was a long time since her painful break up with her ex, Mark, time to move on with someone else, and

Geraldine was beginning to admit the possibility that she and Craig might have a future together. She certainly hoped so, and wondered if he felt the same. At least he was keeping her mind off the stranger who, for so long, had played the part of her mother. Geraldine wasn't ready to think about that yet. She smiled at Craig, contentedly buttering his croissant, and wondered if she had found somewhere she could belong.

It was a sunny day, if cold, and they decided to go for a walk, ending with lunch in a pub Craig knew.

'I'll have to go home first,' Geraldine pointed out. She was hardly dressed for a country walk, in velvet trousers and heels. Craig dropped her home and waited in the living room while she changed into jeans and trainers. They had a brisk walk, up and down hill, marvelling at the views across the landscape. It was a beautiful time of year. After a long wet summer the trees had not yet lost their autumn colours beneath a clear sky. After their walk, they went to a traditional country pub Craig knew where the fire was real, and the food excellent. He chose a bottle of mellow red wine and Geraldine felt more relaxed than she had done for a long time.

'You're very good for me, you know,' she told Craig, aware that she was feeling slightly tipsy.

After lunch, they took a stroll down the lane to the woods. Twigs cracked underfoot as they walked, a few birds sang as the daylight began to fade, and they caught sight of an old fox trotting casually through the tree trunks.

'Magic,' Geraldine whispered.

'It's only an old fox,' Craig laughed. He put his arm round her shoulders and kissed her.

'Can I take you out for tea?' Craig asked when they returned to the car. 'I know a nice little tea shop only a few miles further on.' He seemed to know a lot of places to eat.

'Depends,' she replied. 'What do you fancy doing this evening?' She was still feeling quite full up from lunch. If they were going to eat out again in the evening, she thought she might pass on tea. 'We could go out for tea and have an evening in, or maybe see a film?'

Craig frowned. 'Sorry, didn't I mention? I have to go out.'

'Out?'

'Yes, I'm sorry. I thought I told you. I agreed to see my sister again before she goes back. She's leaving soon. Maybe tomorrow.' He sounded vague.

'Oh.' Geraldine attempted a nonchalant shrug. 'Perhaps you should just drop me home?'

In the end they went out for tea. Craig was right, the tea shop was lovely. Geraldine admired the tiny porcelain tea sets on display, and praised the home made cakes, but the joy had gone out of the afternoon for her.

'Call me,' she said, when Craig dropped her home. But she had a sinking feeling in her stomach. She knew so little about him.

She phoned Hannah when she arrived home and left a message. 'Han, I need to talk. Call me when you get this.' She had a shower, pulled on her pyjamas, and settled down to watch the news. She expected to hear back from Hannah but the news ended and the phone still hadn't rung. Even her friend was too busy to return her call.

Only Celia had left a message. 'Geraldine, please, call me.'

'I'll call you when I'm ready,' Geraldine thought. She didn't touch the phone. Before she contacted Celia she wanted to study the contents of the battered shoe box. It lay on the top shelf of her wardrobe, concealed behind a stack of folded towels. But she wasn't ready to face her unknown past. Not while her future remained so uncertain.

# CHAPTER 35

# ATTACK

Of course Brenda couldn't keep her stupid trap shut.

'What do you mean by bringing the filth here?' Callum roared.

'It was nothing,' Ray stammered. 'Just some silly girl recognised me. They've got nothing.' He jerked away, too slow to avoid a slap on the ear.

Ray didn't mean to admit what had happened but Cal had a way of making people talk. 'Show me where this bitch lives,' he growled.

Brenda opened her eyes. 'What do you want another girl for, Cal? You don't need another girl.'

'Shut it.' Cal slapped her. He was wound up with rage. Dangerous.

'Think about it,' Ray spoke up. 'If anything happens to her, they're going to suspect me.'

'You'll just have to make sure they think it's an accident then.'

'Me? I'm not touching her.'

A slow smile spread across Cal's face. 'We'll see about that,' he said.

It was Cal's idea to go for a drink. Relief flooded through Ray but, although Cal had recovered his temper, Ray was wary of his good humour. You never knew when Cal might explode in a rage.

'No point in falling out over nothing,' Cal said cheerfully. Ray wisely kept his mouth shut. 'Come on, then. You coming or what?'

'Yes, Cal.'

Brenda stirred and opened puffy eyes, red rimmed in her bloodless face. 'Where are you going, Cal?' Her hands fluttered nervously in her lap.

'We're going down the pub.'

'Can I come?'

'No, you can't. We're going for a pint and we're leaving now. Look at yourself.' Ray was still sitting down flicking through channels on the television. 'Come on then!' Cal kicked Ray sharply on the shin. Ray jumped to his feet.

'Why can't I come?' Brenda whined.

'We're only going to the corner for a pint. You're not even dressed. You look like shit.'

'You're taking him,' Brenda called anxiously after them. 'It's always him. Why is it always him?' Cal ignored her. Ray turned round and pulled a horrible face.

The interior of the pub was barely brighter than the street outside, but warmer. Cracked and grimy ornaments gathered dust on high narrow shelves: chipped mugs interspersed with a motley assortment of china plates.

Cal made his way over to a table and waited, while Ray went up to the bar.

'The usual?' the landlord asked, throwing a

glance in Cal's direction. He pulled out a couple of pint glasses with a flourish, like a conjurer. The pub was nearly empty. In one corner two young women were nattering in low voices, their heads bobbing up and down as they spoke. An elderly man sat muttering to himself in another corner, his gnarled fingers clasped round a pint.

'Evening Bert,' Ray called out as he carried the drinks over to Cal who sat drumming his stubby fingers on the table. The old man didn't look up. 'Fancy a game of darts?' Ray asked without taking a seat. Cal shook his head. Ray set the glasses carefully on the table.

'I'll give you a game,' the old man wheezed.

Ray hovered, uncertainly. 'You're all right, mate,' he said and sat down opposite Cal, his back to the old man.

Cal slapped his knee and laughed. The old man scowled, mumbling into his pint. 'You?' Cal spluttered. He pointed at the old man, put his pint down and wiped his mouth on the back of his hand. 'You? Not bloody likely.' The old man sat motionless.

'Why don't you give it a rest?' Ray burst out. 'What's eating you?'

'It's just there's no need to be rude to everyone all the time.'

Cal raised his voice suddenly, and thumped on the table. 'Don't talk so bloody daft. Give that old git a dart, he'd have your eye out. He's half blind. Four-eyed old git. Look at him. Those aren't hands.

222

They're claws. Why don't you cut your nails, you filthy bastard? Use *them* as darts!' He laughed loudly. 'What's it to you anyway? He's nothing but a useless bag of shit.' Ray glared at him, one hand clasping his pint. On the table, Cal's fists clenched. The buzz of conversation from the two women continued uninterrupted.

After a second, Ray dropped his gaze. Cal's hands relaxed. 'I just think you should give it a rest, that's all,' Ray muttered. Cal looked at him through half closed eyes. 'That's what I thought, anyway,' Ray added lamely. He sat perfectly still, staring at the table.

'Don't try to think,' Cal retorted. They drank in bad tempered silence for a while.

'I've had enough.' Cal stood up suddenly. Ray didn't move. 'You coming then, or what?'

Ray shrugged. 'In a while. I can't see the rush. No point wasting good beer. You go on home. Don't mind me. I can please myself.' He wished he had the guts to tell Cal exactly what he thought of him, but Cal was a vicious bastard. Ray was relieved when the door closed behind him. He despised himself for being scared, but he had seen Cal's temper. He drank slowly, hoping Cal wouldn't take it out on Brenda. Not that Ray would give the spaced out cow the time of day, but Cal was brutal. One of these days he was going to kill Brenda.

'Sadist,' Ray grumbled into his pint.

'What's that you say, mate?' the old man in the far corner called out.

'Nothing. You're all right,' Ray answered. The old man sat back, still mumbling to himself.

Ray looked up and caught the landlord watching him curiously. He felt uncomfortable. He drained his glass and decided against staying for another one. It was dull sitting by himself. He could go home and drink in comfort in front of the telly. He wasn't going to stay just to prove a point.

Outside, he turned his collar up and thrust his hands into his pockets. He strode along the pavement, breathing heavily in the freezing air.

# CHAPTER 36

## PASSERBY

'Always knew you'd do well for yourself,' John told his old friend, Nigel. John wouldn't fancy living in New York himself, but he couldn't help feeling envious of his friend's glamorous life style, flying business class, and staying in a hotel, all expenses paid. They took the bus into the centre of Harchester but there was nothing much to do there.

'I remember the town centre being so exciting when we were teenagers,' Nigel said. He spoke with a faint American accent. 'It's not New York, that's for sure,' he added with a laugh. They wandered into a pub they used to frequent when they were younger. It looked the same from outside, but the décor was completely different, with loud music blaring out and the bar bustling with teenagers. They sat in a corner over a pint complaining about how times had changed.

'How can they call this racket music?' John asked. Nigel shook his head. They left after one pint and went for a curry.

'I've missed the food,' Nigel admitted.

'You must be able to get a decent curry in New

York,' John said as he ordered another pint of lager.

'Yes, you can get anything in New York. It's not the same, though.'

At the end of the evening John insisted on paying for dinner. They phoned for a cab to take Nigel to the station and arranged to drop John off on the way.

'It's all on expenses,' John's friend said, waving away John's offered cash.

'This'll do,' John said as they approached his turning. 'I could do with a breath of air.' He was beginning to feel a bit sick. He had lost count of the number of pints he had drunk that night. Climbing out of the cab he slipped on the uneven pavement and fell against a gatepost, scraping his knuckles and grazing his cheek. Swearing softly, he turned to wave but the cab had already disappeared down the road. Cheerfully drunk and comfortably full, John rounded the corner and almost tripped over a figure lying prone on the pavement.

'Stupid bloody place to sleep,' he cried out, startled. A car drove past. In the sudden glare of headlights, John saw it was a man, his head lying at a peculiar angle. He crouched down unsteadily to take a closer look. There was something odd about the figure on the ground. 'You're going to freeze to death if you stay there all night,' John told him. The man didn't move. John leaned forward, wobbled on his heels, and put his hand out to stop himself falling. The pavement felt sticky. 'Did you hear me? I said you'll freeze your bollocks off lying there.' The man didn't respond. 'Damned if I care.' John clambered to his feet and lit a cigarette, cupping his hand round the flickering match. His head was fuddled, but he recognised blood on his fingers.

'Jesus,' he whispered. He lowered the match and studied the prone figure. The man's face was concealed beneath a mop of untidy hair. He was a big bloke, broad shouldered, with large hands and feet, wearing a dark anorak and dirty trainers. Even in his confused state John was frightened. The man could be dying. He could be dead. John fumbled in his pocket with shaking fingers and dialled. 'Ambulance,' he gabbled.

It felt like an eternity before the emergency services arrived. John waited at the kerbside and waved at an approaching police car. A few seconds later an ambulance drew up, light flashing and siren wailing.

'He's over here,' John called. Paramedics leapt from the ambulance. 'Is he dead?' John asked, but he no longer cared. He just wanted to go home and lie down. He was freezing cold and shaking with shock.

'He's still breathing,' a voice replied. 'Who is he?'

John shook his head. 'I don't know. I just found him like that. I was going home.'

A policeman came up and started questioning him. 'Are you the gentleman who reported the incident?' It sounded like an accusation. John nodded. 'Who is he?'

'I told you, I don't know. I was on my way home and I almost fell over him.'

'Have you ever seen the injured man before?'

'Never.'

The policeman stared at John. 'That's a nasty bruise you've got on your cheek, sir,' he said slowly. 'How did you come by it? It's quite recent, by the look of it, I'd say. Still bleeding.'

John put his hand to his cheek, suddenly aware of a sharp stinging. 'I fell over,' he said.

'I see, sir.' The policeman raised an eyebrow.

John realised the policeman didn't believe him. He took an involuntary step back. 'I fell over,' he said. 'I scratched my face when I fell over.'

'And where was that, sir?' The policeman glanced down at the pavement. John wondered if forensic officers would find his own blood on the ground, mingled with the blood of the stranger he had stumbled across.

'Ask Nigel,' John blurted out, afraid and at the same time angry at the implication. 'I was with my friend when I fell over. He'll tell you . . .'

'You were with Nigel and you think he saw you fall over. I see, sir.' John wished the policeman would stop saying that. 'And where can we find Nigel?'

John frowned and stammered out his old friend's name.

The policeman stood, pen poised, waiting.

'And the address, sir?' he prompted John after a pause.

'I've only got his email address. He lives in the States.'

'Nigel lives in America? I see, sir. Have you been drinking, sir?'

John tried to explain about meeting his friend, going to the pub, the curry and finally the cab home. Suddenly it all seemed very complicated.

The policeman took his name and address. 'Just in case, sir.' In case what, John wondered, but before he could ask, the policeman directed him to go home. John turned and staggered away, relieved it was all over. So much for being a good citizen, he thought angrily.

# CHAPTER 37

# BRIEFING

Geraldine's night was troubled. She had stayed up late on Sunday rereading reports. Focusing on work kept her mind occupied, but when she finally went to bed, she slept uneasily . . . .

Craig was standing on a bridge laughing. He was watching Celia struggle in the river far below. Geraldine knew her sister was being swept away on the current towards treacherous rapids but could only watch, horrified. She wanted to scream out to Craig to save Celia, but she couldn't utter a sound.

. . . Geraldine woke, sweating. It was five o'clock on Monday morning.

'You look rough, ma'am.' The desk sergeant's face twisted in a sympathetic grimace.

'You're no picture yourself,' she replied. The sergeant laughed.

The Incident Room was buzzing when she walked in. A sense of isolation flooded through her. Relief at returning to the distraction of work slipped away. She glanced around the Incident Room feeling as though the truth hadn't only cut her off from Celia. She was alienated from everyone she had ever known. Every officer there had grown up in a family, of sorts. They all knew where they came from. Every one of them had childhood memories, even if they were miserable ones. They knew where they came from. None of them knew that Geraldine had been abruptly excluded from that basic human right to her own history. It felt strange to watch them carrying on with their daily tasks, as though nothing had changed. She wondered if she looked different, but even Ian Peterson didn't register surprise as she entered. Geraldine felt reassured. Perhaps life could continue as before. In work she could find her normality.

'Your suspect's been assaulted, ma'am,' the duty sergeant told her.

'What?'

Peterson joined them. 'Raymond Barker,' he said. 'Assaulted on the street on Saturday night. He's been in A & E.'

'Assaulted or brawling?' Without waiting for an answer, Geraldine made her way to her office. Annoyed with herself for not checking her emails before coming in to work, she glanced quickly through a report on the incident. At least she could be up to speed before the briefing began.

Raymond Barker had been admitted to A & E on Saturday night. Geraldine read through the injuries: temporary chemical blinding, broken nose, concussion probably caused by a fall, and broken ankle. Someone had been angry. She pushed her keyboard aside and read through the report again slowly.

Raymond Barker had visited his local pub on Saturday evening with his housemate, Callum Martin. Martin had left early. Barker had stayed on, drinking alone. On his short walk home, Barker had been violently assaulted. He had regained consciousness but wasn't yet able to make a statement. All he could remember was pain before he passed out. Luckily for him, a passer by had called an ambulance.

Geraldine read the witness statement. The injured man had been discovered just after eleven o'clock. The paramedics said Barker wouldn't have lasted the whole night in the freezing cold, with his injuries.

Geraldine frowned. Barker's wallet was visible in his back pocket. His mobile phone was in his jacket pocket. This was an odd mugging. She wandered thoughtfully back into the Incident Room.

Peterson interrupted her thoughts. 'Serves him right. He had it coming,' he muttered as the briefing began.

'No one deserves that,' Geraldine replied.

The DCI looked around for silence. 'We still need to establish if there's a connection between the burglaries and this Raymond Barker,' he said, tapping at Barker's picture on the board. His eyes were red and swollen, his nose bloody. 'Deborah Mainwaring picked him out as her intruder. Barker gave an account of his presence in her house, but . . .' he shrugged. 'He's got an alibi for the nights both burglaries were committed.'

'An alibi that's a tissue of lies,' Bennett muttered and the DCI frowned.

'Sophie Cliff claims she saw Barker running away from her house the night of the gas explosion,' Geraldine said.

'It was a bit of a coincidence her seeing him here,' someone pointed out.

'She could've been mistaken,' the DCI added. 'She could only have seen him for about a second, at night.'

'In her headlights,' Peterson said.

The DCI tapped at Barker's picture again. 'The assault on Barker doesn't appear to have been a mugging. The victim had his wallet and his phone clearly in view. Neither were taken. He had nearly fifty quid on him. He wasn't mugged for his cash. Which all suggests this could have been personal. It was certainly a vicious assault. His eyes were sprayed with a fluid containing butane, propane,' he glanced at his notes, 'ethanediol – all the components of a common brand of deicer.'

'So his attacker could have been a woman,' Geraldine said. 'Do we know Sophie Cliff's where-abouts last night? When I told her Raymond Barker had an alibi for the explosion, she refused to accept he wasn't guilty. She seems convinced Barker was responsible for her husband's death and was furious when we let him go. She said he should be punished.'

'She wants someone to blame for her husband's death,' Bennett agreed.

'Someone other than herself,' Peterson muttered. 'Never the woman's fault.' He sounded so bitter that Geraldine glanced at him in surprise before turning her attention back to the discussion.

'And next thing,' the DCI was saying, 'Barker's attacked.'

'Is it possible Sophie Cliff assaulted him?' Geraldine asked.

'It was a vicious attack,' the DCI replied. 'Violent. Probably took some physical power. My money's on Martin. Barker's a big chap. Could a woman have done that?'

'If she'd taken him by surprise.'

'What about this character John Squires? We've got him at the scene. Who is he? Did he just happen to be passing by? We need to eliminate him or find out if there's any connection between him and Barker.'

'There's something else in the report,' Geraldine said. 'When Barker was found by the paramedics . . .' she hesitated. 'The paramedic said someone had dropped a lighted match on Barker's back. It must have flared up and gone out. A dead match on a patch of singed fabric.'

'Perhaps he lit a cigarette when he'd finished,' Peterson suggested. Geraldine frowned.

After the briefing, Geraldine and Peterson were scheduled to interview Raymond Barker again, this time as the victim of an assault. He had been kept in hospital for observation over the weekend. That morning the doctors had checked him over and sent him home, his leg in plaster. Before calling on Raymond Barker, they went to his local pub to question the landlord.

Ian Peterson speculated as they drove off. 'It's funny, if you think about it. There wasn't enough time to rob the victim – fifty quid's worth having even if the motive for the attack was personal – but there was time to light up without worrying about being seen. If it was a personal attack, why stop to light a cigarette?' The DI didn't answer. 'Am I boring you?' Still no reply. He lapsed into uneasy silence wondering if he had upset her. He was concerned about the DI. She seemed distracted. He knew she was dedicated to the job; it was one of the qualities he admired in her. But she didn't seem to have her mind on work that morning.

'Everything OK, gov?' he hazarded as he drew up at the lights. He was startled when she snapped at him. He took both hands off the wheel and held them up in mock self defence. 'I was only asking.'

'Well don't.' After they had worked together so closely in the past, it was a curt reminder to know his place. He couldn't call it a friendship, but he thought they had built a sense of trust. He thought he knew Geraldine, but right now she seemed edgy. Distracted.

The lights changed and they drove on in silence. Arriving in Garden Street, Ian leapt out of the car and slammed the door confused, disappointed, but above all furious. You just never knew with women. One moment everything was going swimmingly, the next he was made to feel like an idiot. For no reason.

He had worked hard to become a detective sergeant at thirty four, and was hoping for promotion to inspector by the time he was forty. Anyone would be proud of his achievement. Anyone but Bev. He earned good money, and could expect a decent pension at the end of it. He loved his job. Trouble was, he loved Bev too. She had always been the girl for him, ever since they met at school, although he hadn't realised it back then. He had fancied her, of course. All the boys did. Love had taken longer. They had been seeing each other for years, on and off, before she agreed to move in with him. Ian thought life couldn't get any better. But once she had moved in, things had gone from bad to worse. He had never known such disappointment. It gnawed at him like a permanent toothache.

'I wouldn't mind if I knew,' she had complained that morning, 'but I can never tell when you'll be home.'

Ian had turned away frowning. He could easily be more regular in his hours but, when he was on a case, he couldn't focus on anything else. Overtime became routine. It wasn't about the money. He earned well enough, more than a lot of his mates, and job security was worth a lot in times when so many people were coping with redundancy.

He had done his best to explain. 'If I don't throw myself into it a hundred per cent, I might as well not do the job at all. I don't want to lie awake at night thinking that, if only I'd done more, we could've nailed some bastard sooner. You could try to understand, Bev. It's not an easy job at the best of times.' He had struggled to find the right words. 'It's more than a job. It's a commitment.'

'What about your commitment to me?'

'That's not an easy job either,' Ian had thought. Usually he caved in at the sight of her in tears. This time he was irritated. 'If you cared about me, you wouldn't do this. You'd at least try to understand.'

'I understand you care more about your bloody job than you do about me. You've made that clear.'

'It's not a competition,' he had answered wearily. She ought to find herself a bank manager if she wanted someone with set hours. 'I can't be what you want me to be.' He had turned away, fiercely sad.

'Where are you going? We're not finished,' Bev had called after him. He hadn't turned back. If Bev wanted to leave him, there was nothing he could do to stop her. He loved her, but it would be a relief to put an end to her nagging.

# CHAPTER 38

# RAY

'Wonder if they do food?' Peterson said as they went in, but it wasn't that sort of pub. Dimly lit and smelling of sour beer and sweat, the bar was unpleasantly warm after the brisk air outside. It was almost deserted. One old man sat in a corner nursing an empty pint glass.

'What can I get you?' The landlord didn't look surprised when Geraldine held out her identity card.

'Detective Inspector Steel, and this is Detective Sergeant Peterson.' The landlord leaned his elbows on the bar and waited. 'We'd like to ask you a few questions about yesterday evening.'

'Oh yes.'

Peterson showed him a photo of Raymond Barker. 'Do you recognise this man?'

'Should do,' the barman replied. 'That's Ray. He's in here most nights, him and his mate. Sometimes there's a woman with them. I don't know what it is, but . . .' He shook his head. 'She doesn't look right, if you know what I mean.' He made a gesture, rotating one finger by his temple. 'More than a bit cuckoo, if you ask me.'

'Is this the friend?' Peterson slapped a picture of Callum Martin on the bar.

'Yes, that's the one. They were in here last night. The short bloke left early – Colin, is it? Ray stayed on for a bit.'

'What time did Ray leave?'

'It must've been about ten. I gave it another half hour then closed up at ten thirty.'

'Did they usually leave separately?'

'No, but it sounded to me as though they were having words last night.'

'Words?'

'I couldn't hear what they were saying. They just looked like they were . . .' The landlord glanced round the room as though casting about for inspiration. 'The short bloke seemed pretty angry, anyway.'

'Was that unusual?' Geraldine asked. 'Did they often argue?'

The landlord shrugged. 'They drink together. I don't hear much, standing here. You could ask Bert Cartwright. He might have something to say.'

Geraldine turned to glance at the old man in the corner. 'Was he here yesterday evening?'

'Bert's always here.'

Bowed over the table, mumbling into his glass, the old man didn't stir when Geraldine sat down.

'Bert, I need your help.' He nodded without raising his eyes. 'Bert?' She waved her warrant card in front of his face.

He muttered something. It sounded like 'Not any more.'

She nodded at Peterson who went up to the bar for a half. He put it down in front of Bert who lifted the drink in an arthritic hand. He looked at Geraldine over his dirty glasses. She stared back at his filmy eyes and felt a jab of pity. Everything about him spoke of a lack of care, from his long fingernails to his unwashed hair. Close up she could see he was very old. He took a long draught, smacked his loose lips together and grinned, displaying a few yellow teeth.

His voice grated as though he wasn't used to talking. 'Hello, darling.'

Geraldine pushed two pictures across the sticky table: Raymond Barker and Callum Martin. 'Do you recognise either of these two men?' she asked. Bert glanced down at the table before raising the glass again. She waited while he drank.

'That's Ray,' he said. 'He's all right, is Ray. Stands me a pint, sometimes.'

'What about this one?'

Bert scowled at Cal's picture. 'He's a mean bastard, that one,' he said. Geraldine waited but he didn't say anything else.

'Were they in here yesterday evening?' she asked eventually.

The old man inclined his head. 'That one didn't stay long,' he said, tapping Cal's picture with a long dirty finger nail. 'Left before he finished his pint.' He drank again.

'Why do you think that was?' The old man shrugged. 'Did you notice anything unusual about the way he was behaving before he left?'

'Not unusual, no. He's always a stroppy little sod. And he's a bastard to the girl.' He closed his eyes and threw his head back, thinking. 'She wasn't here yesterday, so he had a go at Ray instead. They were having a bit of a barney.' He grinned suddenly. 'I thought the little swine was going to hit him.' He cackled and rocked in his seat. 'Ray's twice his size. Ought to punch his lights out. Serve him right.' He turned his attention to his glass. 'A half doesn't go far, does it?'

'What were they arguing about?' No answer. The old man raised his empty glass and gazed at her mournfully. She nodded at Peterson who brought another half over. The old man smacked his lips.

'Ray was assaulted on his way home—' Geraldine began.

'Vicious little swine,' Bert interrupted her. 'You lot going to lock him up then?' His eyes gleamed wetly at her across the table. It was Geraldine's turn to shrug. 'He's a nasty little sod, that one.' He tapped Cal's picture again. 'You've got to do something about him before he kills someone.'

Geraldine stared into the old man's eyes. 'If you have any information on Callum Martin, you need to tell us.' The old man was silent. Geraldine stood up. 'We'll talk to you again, Bert,' she said.

They walked back down Garden Street, past houses uniformly grey in the fading daylight.

Streetlamps were already on, casting a dim orange glow. A car rattled past, along an otherwise deserted street.

'Time was there would've been children playing out in the street,' Geraldine remarked. 'Kicking a football, riding their bikes.'

'And women sitting on doorsteps.'

'Bit cold for that.'

Brenda opened the door. She started when she saw Geraldine and Peterson and closed her mouth tightly, compressing a cold sore at the corner of her bottom lip. She didn't speak. As she made to close the door, Peterson stepped forward.

'Let's not make this any more difficult than it has to be,' he said, pushing past her into the hall. Brenda backed away from him, still holding on to the edge of the door. The skin on the back of her hand was chapped, her nails bitten to the quick.

'Is Raymond Barker here?' Geraldine asked. Before the frightened woman could reply, Callum Martin appeared at the far end of the hall. Brenda ducked her head and darted up the stairs without looking round.

'She's got nothing to say to you,' Martin told them as the sound of her footsteps faded. 'You've got no business coming round here bothering her. Now you've gone and upset her. So why don't you just—'

'We're here to see Mr Barker,' Peterson interrupted him. 'We don't want to talk to Brenda. Or you. For the moment.'

'What do you want with him?'

'That's not really your business, is it?'

The two men glared at one another. Martin's unshaven chin jutted forward. He clenched his fists. For a second he looked as though he was going to hit the sergeant. Instead he turned and led the way along the narrow hallway into the front room where Barker sat hunched in an armchair. One leg was in plaster. His eyes were bandaged.

Martin spun round to face the sergeant, blocking the doorway. 'You can see for yourself he's in no state to talk to anyone.'

Peterson met Martin's gaze. 'We won't keep you, Mr Martin. We're here to speak to Mr Barker. Alone.'

'I can't go anywhere. Can't walk. Can't see.'

'You heard what he said.' Martin made no move to leave.

'I heard what he said, and you heard what I said,' Peterson replied evenly. He stepped to one side and held the door open for Martin who left the room, swearing loudly.

Barker groaned when Geraldine began to speak. Note book in hand, Peterson closed the door and stood with his back against it as Geraldine questioned Barker.

'Don't know,' was his dogged reply to every question. Geraldine strode across the room and turned the television off. 'Let's start again, Mr Barker,' she said quietly.

'Jumped me from behind.' His voice was slurred.

'Didn't know what hit me. Never had a chance. Put the telly back on. I'm in agony here. I need another pain killer. Get Cal. He knows where they are.'

'You weren't robbed during the course of the attack, Mr Barker.'

'Yeah. That's something at least.' The injured man tried to nod and groaned again.

'Let's go through your movements yesterday evening. You went to the pub.'

'I need a pain killer.'

'Last night, Mr Barker,' Geraldine persisted. 'We know you went to the pub.'

'Me and Cal. We went down there together.'

'What time was that?'

'After tea.'

'Which was what time?'

'Dunno.'

'So you and Callum Martin went for a drink,' Geraldine paused, waiting for a response. Barker sat silent. 'And then he left the pub before you did.'

'He left when he was ready.'

'But you stayed on by yourself.'

'I hadn't finished my drink.'

'What did you argue about?' Geraldine asked suddenly.

'We never argued.' Barker growled.

'We have a witness who says you did.'

'What witness?' Geraldine didn't answer. 'Maybe a few words, that's all.' Barker was struggling to keep his temper. Or perhaps he was afraid. His voice quivered. 'Nothing out of the ordinary.'

'Were you and Mr Martin in the habit of quarrelling then?'

Barker began to shake his head and flinched. 'I'm telling you, we never quarrelled. We were – We're mates.'

'We have a witness who says you and Martin had an argument just before Martin left.'

'We never quarrelled.' Peterson held up his hand. Geraldine paused. With a swift movement, the sergeant flung the door open. The dimly lit hallway was empty.

'Thought I heard something,' he said as he closed the door. Geraldine resumed. 'Now why don't you tell us what happened last night on your way home from the pub.'

'Some bastard jumped on me. Took me by surprise.'

'Was it Callum Martin?'

'No. It wasn't him.'

'It was Martin, wasn't it? What did you argue about, at the pub? About your share of the proceeds from stolen goods, was it? Or did you have a row about Brenda?' Barker's hands twitched but he didn't say anything. 'Or perhaps you've been ripping him off. So you had a row and he decided to teach you a lesson.'

'No. It wasn't like that. It wasn't Cal. I know it wasn't him.'

'If you didn't see your attacker, you couldn't know that, could you?'

'I know it wasn't him,' he insisted. 'I know it wasn't Cal because it was a woman. I was beaten up by a woman. Are you happy now?'

# CHAPTER 39

# VICTIMS

Cal paced up and down the bedroom, rubbing his hand over his stubbly cheeks while downstairs the police questioned Ray. It seemed to be taking forever.

'Why the fuck is it taking so long?' Cal frowned down at Brenda who lay fidgeting on the bed. He resumed his pacing. 'Why are they taking so long?' He spun round. 'And what're you so jittery for?' Her hands fluttered restlessly at her sides, her legs refused to stay still. 'What are you jumpy about? Don't I look after you?'

Brenda stared up at him, trembling more violently. 'I know you look after me, Cal,' she wheedled. 'It's good gear.'

'Only the best for my girl.'

Brenda nodded with sudden energy. 'That's what I said, Cal.'

'What's wrong then? You've been like a cat on heat for days.'

'Nothing.' She shrugged one shoulder, unable to meet his eye.

'Well stop your bloody twitching,' he snapped suddenly. Brenda rolled to one side. Not fast enough. He didn't hit hard – he only used force when he was angry. He looked at her lying on the bed, and clenched his fists again.

'You go around provoking people, you're going to end up with a fist in your face, stands to reason. Put a smile on your face, you miserable bitch.'

'I'm not miserable. Not miserable with you, Cal.' She pulled herself into a sitting position and smiled at him.

'Should think not, stupid cow. What have you got to be miserable about?'

'I'm not miserable, Cal. I'm scared.'

'You scared of me?' He started forward.

'No! Not scared of you,' she stuttered rapidly. 'You look after me, Cal.' She hovered on her knees on the bed, uncertain whether to scramble out of his way.

'What then?' he asked.

'Was it you?'

'What are you on about?'

'Was it you did that to Ray? Someone did.' She looked slyly at him. 'I don't mind if it was you, Cal. He deserves it. We don't need him here. If he gets hurt badly enough, maybe he'll go away and it'll be just you and me again. I'd like that Cal, wouldn't you?'

Scowling, Cal seized her by the arm and flung her back on the bed. She hit her head on the wall. For a second she was dazed. A sharp ache began pounding inside her skull.

'You're not still on about Ray, you stupid cow?' He leaned over her, red-faced.

'You and me, Cal,' she repeated, over and over. Cal smacked her once, hard.

Brenda bit her lip. 'I'm not scared of you,' she whined. 'You take care of me. I'm not scared of you. It's them.'

Cal sat down on the bed. Brenda sat up and shuffled back until she was propped up against her pillow, ready to slip off the bed and out of reach of his fists. 'What's on your mind, Bren? You got nothing to be scared of. What's bothering you?' He turned and studied her face closely, her swollen brow, the bruise emerging under her pale skin. 'Don't I take care of you?'

Brenda nodded, staring at him. 'You take care of me.'

They heard a distant hum of voices. Cal leaped to his feet and ran lightly downstairs. Brenda waited. A few moments later he reappeared and began pacing the narrow room. Brenda sat on the bed, watching him. At last they heard footsteps. The front door closed. Cal looked out of the window. He turned and gave Brenda one last shove on the shoulder before he stormed out of the room. Brenda lay completely still. All she wanted was to hide away in darkness, under the bed covers.

Ray was snoring. Lazy sod.

'Oy,' Cal called to him. Ray groaned.

'What did they want?'

'Dunno.'

'What did they ask you?'

'Dunno. I wasn't listening.'

Cal leaned forward, put one hand on Ray's injured leg and squeezed. 'What did you tell them, retard?'

'Nothing. I didn't say anything.'

Cal grunted. 'I'm going for a drink.'

'Where's Brenda?' Ray asked.

'Upstairs.'

'Do us a favour, take her with you. She's getting on my nerves. The doctor said I need to rest after what I've been through but how can I rest with her mumbling and crying all the time?' Cal leaned over Ray and began rummaging through his pockets. 'Here, what are you doing?'

Cal pulled out a worn leather wallet with a flourish. 'Your round.'

'You put that back.'

Cal laughed. 'I'll have one for you,' he grinned.

Ray swore. Cal shrugged indifferently. He stuffed Ray's cash into his own pocket and dropped the empty wallet on the floor. 'See you later.'

Brenda heard the front door slam. She buried her bruised cheek in the duvet and began to cry. Her biggest fear was that Cal would go away and never return. She stuffed the corner of the duvet between her teeth. It tasted salty. She spat it out and pressed her lips together trying to think, but she couldn't stop crying.

★　　★　　★

It was cold outside. Cal strode swiftly along the street to the pub on the corner. It was usually quiet on a Monday evening. The bar was almost empty. The only other customer was the old git who was always in there, hunched over a pint. Occasionally Ray took pity on the old bloke and bought him a half. Cal wasn't a soft touch.

The old man touched his cap as Cal strode in. 'Evening, gov.' Cal walked straight past him to the bar without acknowledging the greeting.

The landlord didn't lift his eyes from his paper. 'Cold out there,' he said without looking up. 'What'll you have?'

'Pint.' Cal paid for his drink out of Ray's money, and sat down. He swore softly when the old man shuffled over to his table a few moments later.

'Much obliged, gov,' the old man said. His old eyes were rheumy with age, his skin drooped repulsively under his chin. Cal turned away. The old man stood his ground. 'Stand us a pint, gov,' he begged. He leaned forward supporting himself on the edge of the table. 'I'm skint, see.'

'Jesus,' Cal fumed. 'It makes me sick to look at you.'

Catching sight of Cal's face, the old man scuttled back to his corner.

Bert hadn't been exaggerating when he said he was broke. It wasn't even nine o'clock but he knew he couldn't coax another drink from the landlord. He certainly wasn't going to get anything out of

Ray's mate. Bert had come across his type before. Nasty little sod made Bert feel uneasy. He decided not to hang around.

It was cold outside. Bert walked as quickly as he could. He didn't have far to go. Without his glasses the air around the street lamps looked misty. A car drove past. As the whine of its engine faded, he heard footsteps. Bert hobbled faster.

A hand gripped him by the shoulder. Breath tickled his ear. 'Keep walking.'

'What do you want?'

'We're going for a walk. Just the two of us.'

With a thrill of fear, Bert recognised the voice. 'What do you want with me?' he quavered. No answer. 'That's my house.' Holding Bert firmly by the arm, Cal shoved him forward, propelling him in the direction of the canal. 'Where are you taking me?' Bert swivelled his head round. Under the street lamp he could see Cal grinning.

'A little bird told me you've got a big mouth, old son.'

'What are you talking about?'

'You've been opening your gobshite mouth to the filth.'

'Not me. I never.' They had reached the narrow strip of woods that sloped down to the canal. 'My shoes are getting wet,' Bert grumbled. Cal laughed. His grip on Bert's arm tightened as they reached the canal path.

'See this?' Cal held up a carrier bag. 'Guess what's inside.'

'Don't tell me, we're going on a picnic.'

Cal laughed again. 'Bricks.'

'Bricks?'

'What I can't decide is, shall I swing it at your head before I tie it round your neck, or are you going to go quietly?'

Bert ducked his head. Adrenaline jolted through his aching limbs. He squirmed out of Cal's grasp. Panting with fear, he grabbed at the woody stem of a bush and scrambled back up the incline. He didn't get far. Hands grasped him by the ankles so he couldn't kick out. As he slid backwards, Bert scrabbled in his pocket. He only had a few seconds. 'You won't get away with this,' he mumbled furiously as his stiff fingers closed on his glasses case.

Bert crashed onto the path where he lay at Cal's feet, groaning.

'No point yelling,' Cal pointed out cheerfully. 'No one's going to hear you.' With a last desperate effort, Bert clambered to his feet. With a sob, he launched himself at his adversary. Cal yelled. Beads of blood oozed down his left cheek from four deep scratches. 'You could've had my eye out, you bastard!' Cal yelled as he swung the weighted bag. Smiled at the crunch of bone. It only took a few seconds for him to tie the bag around the groaning man's neck.

A splash. The scummy surface of the canal rippled gently. Callum glanced up and down the deserted path before he loped away, smiling.

# CHAPTER 40

# CURRY HOUSE

'But could a woman have done that, do you think?' Peterson asked as they drove into the centre of town. Geraldine shrugged. 'Ray Barker's a strong guy,' he went on. 'Is it likely a woman could've overpowered him?'

'If it wasn't a woman, Barker's lying.'

'Or mistaken. Although he did seem genuinely embarrassed.' Peterson laughed. 'You'd think a guy like Ray Barker would want to be sure before admitting he was beaten up by a woman.'

'Unless he deliberately wanted to lead us off on the wrong tack.'

'You think he's protecting someone?'

'By someone you mean Callum Martin,' Geraldine said irritably. They were going round in circles. 'But Martin's got an alibi.'

They set about tracing John Squires' movements on Saturday evening. First on the scene, and drunk, with injuries to his face and hands, he had to be a suspect. They hadn't established a motive for him, but it was possible the attack had been a random drunken brawl between Barker and Squires. The police hadn't yet been able to contact the friend with whom John Squires claimed to have spent the evening.

John Squires said he and his friend had begun their evening in a pub in the centre of Harchester so Geraldine and Peterson began their enquiries there. No one in the pub remembered seeing Squires and his friend. The barmaid thought the photograph of John Squires might look familiar, but she wasn't sure.

Their next stop was The Curry House further along the High Street, where Squires claimed to have gone after the pub. The Indian restaurant was empty apart from a young woman waiting for a take away.

'Good evening, sir. Table for two?'

'No, thank you. We're looking for the manager.' Geraldine walked past the waiter to the bar. Peterson followed. He picked up a menu and studied it while they waited.

'Yes? Can I be of assistance?'

'Detective Inspector Steel and Detective Sergeant Peterson.' Geraldine held out her identity card. Peterson was still studying the menu. A young waiter brought out a tray of cutlery and started laying tables. Above the rattling, the manager told them he couldn't remember anyone coming to the restaurant on Saturday evening with cuts on his face. Nor could he specifically remember two men, possibly rather the worse for drink.

'We're always busy,' he apologised, glancing around the empty room. 'That is, the weekends

255

are always busy.' He checked his records and confirmed that John Squires had paid for two dinners by credit card at ten twenty five on Saturday night. They were able to identify him on the CCTV footage. His face was unscathed, as far as they could tell from the smudgy image.

'The time fits,' Peterson said as they left, 'and the manager doesn't recall Squires being injured when he came in here, so it looks like he got himself into a fight after he left.' John Squires had definitely been in the area of the assault some time after it had taken place. He could have been there when it happened. They needed to be more precise about the time he arrived on the scene if they were to eliminate him as a suspect.

They traced the cab driver who had picked up two men near the Indian restaurant on Saturday evening. He had dropped one of them round the corner from Squires' house before taking the other one on to the station.

He remembered the two men well. 'They were a bit pissed,' he said. 'Get a lot like that on a weekend. But they weren't kids so I took the fare. And the second geezer left a generous tip. Told me his firm were paying.'

'How would you describe them?'

'Just blokes, you know. Ordinary. I didn't look too closely but I remember they laughed so much I thought they were going to throw up.'

'Did one of them have cuts on his face?'

'I don't take punters who've been fighting.

They're the worst. Blood in my cab, no thank you,' he shuddered.

'And you're positive neither of them had cut his face or grazed his knuckles? It's very important.' Peterson asked. The cabbie was sure. Any injuries must have been incurred later, after Squires had left the taxi.

'Do you know the exact time you dropped the first man off?' Geraldine asked.

The driver scratched his head. 'It was about ten forty five when I picked them up. I dropped the first fare off about ten minutes later. That was a long ten minutes, I can tell you. They were laughing fit to bust. I thought they were going to throw up. You don't expect that from people their age. Then I took the second one to the station. It must've been around five to eleven. He said his train was due just after eleven. So it must've been before eleven, but not long before. He was in a hurry, kept asking me to step on it. Is that it or was there anything else?'

Geraldine paused, thinking. 'You said you didn't see any injuries when they entered the cab?' The cabbie nodded. 'What about when they left it? They weren't scrapping in the back were they? Or maybe one of them fell off his seat?'

'Funny you should mention that because one of them did fall over. The one I dropped off first. He was so pissed, he fell right out of the cab, tripped over his feet and slammed straight into a gate post. He must've given himself a bit of a bash.'

'Was he badly hurt?'

The driver shrugged. 'I didn't hang around to see. He was out of the cab by the time he tripped, nothing to do with me. Time's money and the other geezer was in a hurry. I only clocked it in my mirror. But he got up all right,' he added, suddenly anxious. 'He wasn't badly hurt.'

They ran over the times as they drove back to the station.

'The landlord said Barker left the pub around ten,' Peterson said. 'If he's right, Squires was still in the Indian when Barker was attacked.'

Geraldine frowned, wondering if they were wasting time on a random street crime fuelled by alcohol or drugs. 'If it was a mugging, why didn't they rob him?'

'Do you think someone was waiting for him?' the sergeant asked. 'Like Callum Martin?'

'I'll try and speak to Martin's girlfriend alone,' Geraldine said. She had the impression Peterson would be as pleased as her if they could pin Barker's injuries on Callum Martin.

He nodded. 'She's more likely to talk to you. I don't suppose she's got a very positive opinion of men. Martin's a brute if ever I saw one.'

# CHAPTER 41

# VISITOR

Behind the television, the curtain rippled as a chill draught blew across the room. Cal hadn't closed the sitting room door when he left. Ray swore. He picked up the remote control from the arm of his chair, knocking an empty beer can to the floor. It oozed a trickle of pale liquid on to the carpet.

Ray shivered. He wished Brenda would come down. She was never around when he wanted anything. A blanket would be nice, and another beer. He wriggled on his chair. If he shifted to the sofa he would be able to spread out, but he knew better than to move there. Cal had gone to the pub but his presence lingered. His BO hung in the air, mingled with Brenda's cheap perfume and the faint stink of vomit. Ray flicked through the channels, listened to a few minutes of a football game, caught the end of Top Gear and dozed off.

Ray jolted awake from an uneasy dream of bottles smashing and winced as his injured leg gave an involuntary twitch. With every breath his ribs stabbed at his chest. His eyes burned. Swearing, he fumbled for his pain killers. He remembered putting them on the arm of his chair but couldn't find them. He leaned forward, groaning softly, and felt on the seat of his chair. It would be typical of Cal to have moved them before he went out. He was a sick bastard. Or it could have been Brenda. Show her a packet of pills and she'd swallow the lot, no questions asked, and then lie about it. Messed up cow. He couldn't understand why Cal put up with her, how he could bring himself to touch her. Ray shuddered at the thought.

Cal was a vicious bastard, but Ray knew where he stood with him. In a way he was almost relieved when Cal lost his temper because, after that, he would be nice as pie for a while. It was worse looking over his shoulder all the time, waiting for Cal to blow up. Not that Ray ever fought back. Cal wasn't the sort of guy you'd want to hit. But there were ways of taking a beating. Unable to move, Ray would be a sitting duck right now, powerless to defend himself.

The filth were itching to give Cal a hard time. It had crossed Ray's mind he could drop Cal in it by accusing him of assault, but he didn't dare. If Cal found out, he would make Ray's life hell. And that was one thing Cal knew how to do. In the meantime all Ray could do was sit and stew. But one thing was sure, as soon as his eyes were sorted and his leg was better he would be off. It was driving him nuts living with Cal and his crazy girlfriend. When he had first moved in it had seemed like a brilliant idea. Together they were going to be rich. That optimism had soon faded. Cal wasn't going to lead Ray to untold wealth. He was more likely to knife him on a dark night. You just never knew with Cal.

He heard the door open.

'Is that you, Cal?' Ray asked. 'Thank God you're here. I'm in agony and I can't find my pills.' The figure in the doorway didn't move. Ray shifted awkwardly in his seat. 'Tell you what, I'm bursting. Give us a hand upstairs?' He held out his arm. There was no reply. 'What are you waiting for? I'm telling you, I need to go. I'm desperate.' Ray struggled to his feet. He gasped, more in surprise than pain, when someone pushed him back roughly on to the chair.

'Is that you, Cal?' Ray asked, licking his lips nervously. 'What are you doing?'

Hands grabbed Ray's arms. He felt rough rope looped around his wrists. The rope jerked tight. Ray yelped in surprise. He should have kicked out with his good leg, but he was too slow. He screamed as his ankles were secured with another length of rope, twisting his injured leg horribly.

'What are you playing at?' he demanded. Silence. 'What are you doing? This isn't funny.'

The stench of petrol hit him.

'What are you doing?' Ray cried out again. His voice rose in panic. He heard the rattle of a box of matches. Ray started forward in his chair, petrified. He couldn't stand up without falling. His ankles were tied together. He strained against the rope that bound his wrists. It cut into his flesh when he tried to move his hands.

'You can't do this. It's insane,' he protested hoarsely. 'What have I done to you? What about Bren? The house? You'll bust the TV.'

No one answered. The match box rattled.

'What the fuck are you doing? Stop it, mate. You've scared me good and proper.' Ray tried to laugh. 'Come and untie me before I wet myself.'

He heard the sound of a match being struck.

'Stop it, just stop it. You've had your fun. You've given me a fright. And this rope bloody hurts. Take it off. Now!' Ray was shouting, any vestige of self control gone, his jeans warm and wet between his legs. 'You're insane,' he whispered, sinking back on the chair.

'You'll never get away with it. Stop it right now. Stop it and we'll have a drink. Laugh about you giving me a good scare. Let me go now. Untie me. You've had your laugh.'

He heard another match being struck.

'I know who you are,' Ray was babbling in his terror. 'I know who you are. You won't get away with it.'

He heard a grunt. Feet thudded on the carpet. There was a rush of air. The front door slammed.

Then he heard hissing and crackling, and felt intense heat.

# CHAPTER 42

## SUPPER

'You coming for a drink, gov?' Peterson asked as they left the car in the station car park.

'OK. I'll see you over there.' First Geraldine wanted to call in to bring the duty sergeant up to date and find out if there had been any developments. There was nothing new.

The pub over the road was humid, packed with police officers and people calling in for a quick pint after work. The DCI was at the bar, talking to Bennett. The young constable, Polly, was standing very close to Peterson, laughing loudly. Feeling excluded, Geraldine wished she had gone straight home. She still had a report only half typed and she wanted to check through Bronxy's statement. She joined Ryder and Bennett. As she finished her half pint, the DCI announced he was off. Geraldine took the opportunity to leave.

'You want to watch him,' Bennett warned her with a sly grin as she passed by. Geraldine didn't reply. She already suspected there was gossip at the station about her and James Ryder. He often slipped into her office to mull things over. She had noticed curious glances once or twice when the two of them had left her office together. Dismissing the thought of James Ryder, she stepped outside, into the cold and dark.

When she arrived home, there were several missed calls and a terse message from Hannah on her answerphone. 'Geraldine, call me.' She pulled her laptop out of her bag, switched it on and went into the kitchen to make herself a pot of coffee before she phoned her friend.

'Hi Han, it's me.' Ready to voice her concerns about Craig, Geraldine was determined to avoid any reference to her mother. She wasn't ready to discuss that with anyone. She couldn't even think about it. Not yet.

Hannah interrupted her. 'Geraldine, at last. Where have you been? I need to see you.'

'OK, when do you want to meet up?'

'Now. I need to see you now.'

Fear struck Geraldine. 'What's wrong, Hannah? You're not ill?'

'No, nothing like that. I just need to see you.'

'Look, it's nearly eight o'clock. I do want to speak to you, but can't we talk on the phone? It can wait—'

'This isn't about you, for once,' Hannah butted in. Geraldine was taken aback. 'I need to see you now.'

'Is everything all right? Has something happened?'

'I don't want to talk on the phone,' Hannah insisted. She sounded as though she was crying. 'Just come over, please.'

Geraldine glanced helplessly at the file lying on the table beside her laptop. 'OK, I'm on my way.' This had better be important, she thought irritably as she closed her laptop down.

It took Geraldine just over an hour to reach Hannah's home. The children were in bed and the house was quiet.

'Where's Jeremy?' Geraldine asked as Hannah handed her a glass of wine. Hannah didn't answer. Geraldine took in the half empty glass beside a half empty bottle on the table. Hannah had been drinking alone. 'He hasn't . . . tell me he's not ill,' she amended her question. She knew it wasn't that. Hannah would have told her on the phone. 'You're going to tell me everything,' Geraldine said gently, 'but first, have you eaten anything this evening? Or are you just drinking? It won't help, you know.' Geraldine thought about her own private wine collection and blushed.

Twenty minutes later, Hannah sat weeping into a bowl of pasta. 'We've done nothing but row lately – when I've seen him, that is, which hasn't been often. He's been working all hours. Or so he said. Last night he came home late as usual and said we needed to talk.' She took a gulp of wine. 'He said he wants a break . . . I think he's seeing someone else. What can I do, Geraldine?' she wailed. 'I can't bear it. You've been through it. What can I do? I don't want to lose him. I don't want all this to end.' She waved her hands helplessly in the air. 'And what about the children? Tell me what to do, Geraldine?'

When they were younger, Geraldine had envied Hannah her looks. Geraldine watched her now, slightly overweight, her face puffy from crying, and sighed, remembering the girl she had met at school. Nothing had seemed to dent Hannah's high spirits back then. As best friends, they had gone around pretending to be sisters. A fierce longing threatened Geraldine's self possession; Hannah was the only person with whom she could share the terrible secret of her birth.

It was an effort to focus on her friend's problem. 'You have to talk to him, Han. You've come too far to let it all go. You have to talk.'

'I've tried. He won't.'

'Have you tried mediation?'

'He won't. I know he won't.'

'Have you tried? Have you asked him?'

Hannah shook her head. 'What if he's met someone else? Someone younger. Someone who isn't cluttered with children.'

'They're his children too. He's hardly going to think of them as clutter. Please, Han, stop crying. It won't help. It'll only make you feel worse. Now think about it. You don't know he's met someone else. It's hardly likely. And even if he has, even if he's going through some pathetic midlife crisis, you're still his wife. You've got children. Even if you're right, and it all turns out to be as bad as it could possibly be, life still goes on. He's not going to leave you.' She rambled on uncertainly, but it didn't matter what she said. Hannah wasn't listening.

Geraldine cleared the table, removed the wine glasses, and brewed coffee. When she returned from the kitchen, Hannah had calmed down. Geraldine's relief was short lived.

'Geraldine, I've got a plan.' Geraldine poured the coffee. 'You can help me.' Geraldine handed Hannah a cup and waited. 'I need you to find out if there's someone else.'

'Wouldn't it be better to ask him yourself? He's hardly going to tell me.'

'I don't mean ask him outright. I mean I want you to find out.'

'How am I supposed to do that?'

'I don't know. That's what you do, isn't it? Detective work. That's your job, finding out about people.'

Geraldine put her cup down. 'You expect me to spy on Jeremy?'

'Exactly. Who else can I ask? It's perfect. You're a detective—'

'Stop saying that,' Geraldine interrupted. 'You know I can't.'

'Why not? You're a detective, aren't you? That's what you do.'

'No, that's not what I do. I work in serious crime, Hannah, not checking on people who might or might not be cheating on their wives.'

'Geraldine, you've got to help me.'

It took Geraldine some time to convince Hannah that there was no way she could deploy police resources to set up round the clock surveillance on Jeremy.

'I was always there for you,' Hannah kept repeating. It was past midnight by the time Geraldine left, promising to call Hannah the next day.

'I'm sorry, I really do have to go. I've still got some reports I need to reread for tomorrow.'

'You always put work first.' Geraldine winced at the bitterness in Hannah's voice.

'You're tired and you need to get some sleep,' she answered gently. 'You'll have to be up for the kids in the morning.'

At the thought of her children, Hannah's face relaxed into a tearful smile. 'Ben's got a football party tomorrow. You're right, Gerry, life goes on, I suppose.'

'Life goes on,' Geraldine agreed. Mark had left her and she hadn't heard from Craig. 'Life goes on,' she repeated firmly. But not for everyone. Not for Evelyn Green, or Thomas Cliff, white faced in the mortuary. A memory of her mother's funeral whipped unexpectedly into her mind and she blinked. 'Reports to read,' she muttered to herself. 'Work to do.' Men might dump her but she could always rely on work to be waiting for her.

# CHAPTER 43

## FIRE

Brenda squirmed. The sheets smelled warm and sweaty. She didn't know how long she had been asleep. Downstairs she thought she heard a door close. Apart from that the house was quiet. She glanced up. It was a moonlit night. Through a gap between the curtain and the edge of the window she could see the rooftops over the road, sparkling in the rain. She pulled the duvet tight under her chin, snug and warm in bed. Too warm. She flung the covers off and wriggled her toes. Her legs were aching. A sudden cramp gripped her in the guts. She sat up clutching her stomach and gasping. The pain eased as quickly as it had started and she lay back down on the bed, relieved. Even without the covers she felt nice and warm, as though she was lying in a hot bath. There was a familiar smell she couldn't place.

'Cal?' she whispered. She called his name again, slightly louder this time. 'Cal?' He didn't answer. 'Why can't I go with you?' she asked out loud. It was too late. He had already gone. She remembered stumbling upstairs to get dressed so she could go with him. As she was searching for underwear, she had heard the front door slam. Cal had gone for a drink without her. He was always going out without her. 'He'll be back soon,' she told herself. 'He never stays away for long.' She half sat up and pummelled her pillow. 'He always comes back.'

She lay down and began to cry, snuffling into the duvet. She wiped her runny nose with the edge of her pillow case. Cal went out all the time. He hardly ever took her with him. It wasn't fair. Cal spent more time with Ray than he did with her. She was glad Ray couldn't walk. It served him right. She wished he would go back where he came from and leave her and Cal alone. They had been fine without him. They didn't need him in their house. He didn't belong there, not like her and Cal. 'We belong to each other,' she whispered.

Whenever she went downstairs Ray was there. And every time she and Cal went out, Ray was at Cal's side, his head hunched down as he hung on Cal's words. The pavement wasn't wide enough to walk three abreast so Brenda had to tag along behind them. It was as though she didn't exist.

'He can help out with the bills,' Cal had explained when he had first brought Ray home, but they didn't seem to have any more money now that Ray was sleeping in the spare bedroom. 'It makes sense,' Cal had told her. 'The room's empty, he needs somewhere to live, and he can pay us.' She had nodded. At the time it had seemed like a clever idea. Now she wasn't so sure.

'Where's the money, Cal?' she had asked him once.

'What money's that then? What are you talking about, you daft cow?'

'The money, Cal. You said there'd be more money for us, with Ray sleeping in the spare room.' Cal hadn't answered. 'Where's the money, Cal?' she had repeated.

He had turned on her then. 'What do you want with more money? I give you everything don't I? What more do you want? Ungrateful cow.'

She wasn't ungrateful. She pressed the back of her hand against her mouth, but she couldn't stop crying.

'Cal?' she called out again, as though saying his name would make him walk through the door. It was growing warmer. The smell was stronger. Like burnt toast. She wondered where Cal was and what he was doing. She opened her eyes and listened. From downstairs she thought she could hear someone calling. She pulled herself out of bed and hobbled to the top of the stairs.

'Cal?' she answered. 'Is that you, Cal?' Perhaps he had come home and wanted a cup of tea. 'Do you want a cup of tea, Cal?' She heard a voice. It didn't sound like Cal. 'Is that you, Cal?' There was no reply. She blinked. Her eyes were going funny. Everything looked misty, as though the hall was full of smoke. Brenda had wanted to get her eyes tested, but that cost money.

'Everything looks blurred,' she had complained.

Cal had told her not to fuss. 'Ignore it, it's just the dope, you silly cow.'

Brenda coughed. She didn't dare tell Cal she was scared of losing her eyesight. One of the girls at Bronxy's had gone blind. Cal would only laugh at her fears. Worse, if he believed she was going blind, he wouldn't want her any more. The best thing she could do was have a good sleep. When she woke up her eyes would be all right again.

'You're just tired,' she told herself. 'That's all. Just tired.' When you needed to sleep she knew it went to your eyes first. That was why her eyes were going funny.

'Look at you,' Bronxy had complained the last time she had seen Brenda. 'Your eyes are all blood-shot and you've got bags under there you could carry the shopping home in. You look like you haven't slept for a week. Go and get some rest for fuck's sake. I couldn't put you on the stage looking like that.' Bronxy called it a stage although it was more like a platform. Bronxy liked to talk about her show, as though the Lagoon was a proper theatre. Somewhere with a bit of class. Brenda smiled at the memory and then winced as she stretched out on the bed again.

She was feeling really hot now. Her eyes had gone funny again. She tried to go to sleep but her head hurt and the smell was bothering her. She wished Cal would come home. He had been gone for ages. She wondered where he was and what he was doing. She hoped he had only gone to the pub for a quick drink, and not out for the night on a job. In the distance she heard a siren wailing and shivered. She hoped they weren't out there looking for Cal.

# PART IV

*'I have sent to seek him and to find the body.*
*How dangerous is it that this man goes loose!'*

*Hamlet* – William Shakespeare

# PART IV

*'I have sent to seek him and to find the body.*
*How dangerous is it that this man goes loose!*

*Hamlet* – William Shakespeare

# CHAPTER 44

# ARSON

The Incident Room was bustling on Tuesday morning. The duty sergeant was rushing around, keeping everyone up to speed with developments. Geraldine arrived early and reread the latest reports before the briefing began.

'You're all aware by now of last night's incident in Garden Street,' the DCI said, looking round the room. 'The Fire Investigation Team have given us their initial report.' He paused. 'We're looking at arson.'

'Is that definite?' someone asked.

Ryder nodded. 'It seems there's no doubt about it.' He looked down at his notes. 'The fire started in the back room downstairs, used as a living room.' Geraldine and Peterson exchanged a glance. They had been in that room the previous afternoon, interviewing Raymond Barker just hours before the fire started. 'The Fire Investigation Team found traces of accelerant. The carpet was doused in petrol and set alight. This was deliberate.' Someone whistled. Ryder ran his hands through his hair. 'On Saturday there's a gas explosion and Thomas Cliff dies of smoke inhalation in the ensuing fire.' He glanced at the victim's picture on the Incident Board. 'Sophie Cliff believes Raymond Barker's responsible. The day after she sees him here, he's assaulted in the street by a woman, according to his statement. Of course he may be lying to protect someone.'

'By someone you mean Callum Martin,' Bennett said.

The DCI nodded before continuing. 'The hospital patched him up and sent him home and now, two days later, while he's unable to get about easily, someone sets fire to his house. He was lucky to survive. He's in hospital now, still unconscious. They've promised to call us as soon as he's fit to be questioned. That's two attacks on Barker in two days. I've put him under round the clock surveillance for the time being. The moment he comes round we need to see what he can tell us.'

He rifled through his notes. 'The Fire Officers found him in the back room where the fire started. He only survived because his armchair tipped over, trapping him underneath it. The chair offered him some protection from the heat and flames, and being on the floor he managed to escape the worst effects of the smoke, in a kind of air pocket beneath the chair. The chair crushed Barker's foot. He'll never walk properly again. But he survived. They're still examining the scene. In the meantime, while we're waiting for him to come round, we need to speak to the other person who was in the house at the time.'

'Someone else was in the house when the fire started?' Bennett sounded shocked.

'Brenda was upstairs. She escaped the worst of it. The other resident of the house, Callum Martin, claims to have been in the pub the whole time. So he was coincidentally out of the way, like when Barker was attacked the first time.'

'Convenient,' Peterson muttered.

Geraldine was at her desk when the DCI walked in. His face was already so familiar that Geraldine could hardly believe they had only been working together for a week. When he had first arrived at the station she had been taken aback by his habit of dropping into her office without knocking. She had grown used to his frequent visits and was flattered that he chose to bounce his ideas off her. He had given no indication that his interest in her was anything other than professional. Geraldine couldn't help speculating about what her life might become if that were to change. She had long since determined never to become involved with a colleague, but she had never been seriously attracted to another officer before. If James Ryder were to approach her, as a woman, she wasn't sure how she would react. She wished Craig had seemed more interested in her since their return from Dubrovnik.

The DCI looked worn out. Geraldine felt a sudden rush of sympathy for him. Not for the first time, she wondered if he had anyone waiting at home for him at the end of the day. There never seemed to be any talk about him, unlike some of the other officers. Peterson's name had already been linked with at least two of the young constables. Only the day before, Geraldine had come across one of them crying in the toilets. She had darted into a cubicle when Geraldine walked in.

Geraldine had waited for her to come out. 'Everything all right, Polly?'

'Yes, ma'am.' Geraldine had recognised the blonde DC she had seen hanging around Peterson. At the morning briefings, the constable's eyes kept wandering over to him. Geraldine had seen her in the pub, laughing too loudly at his jokes. Geraldine wasn't surprised. Peterson was cheerful and friendly, and certainly attractive, but Polly was a fool if she allowed herself to become emotionally involved with a colleague.

Geraldine reminded herself of that when the DCI entered her room. Nevertheless, the informality of his visits suggested a certain familiarity that she found exciting. The world seemed suddenly full of possibilities. In the shadow of James Ryder, Craig seemed pleasant but dull.

'What's your gut feeling?' James Ryder asked her. 'Is Martin our man?' Geraldine waited. She understood he had a theory he wanted to talk through. 'We can discount the alibi from Bronxy,' he went on, 'even though we can't disprove it. But what about the pub landlord? Why would he lie to protect Martin?' Geraldine shook her head and shrugged. There could be reasons. 'And wouldn't Martin have known Brenda was upstairs? But if it wasn't Martin, who else has got it in for Barker?'

'Sophie Cliff?' Geraldine suggested. 'Grief can do strange things to people, sir, and she believes Raymond Barker's responsible for her husband's death, and—' She paused.

'Go on.'

'It makes sense of the match, sir. Whoever attacked Barker on the street dropped a lighted match on his back.'

'And now someone's set fire to his house.'

'Thomas Cliff died in a fire.'

'It's a crazy idea,' Ryder said, his eyes alight with interest.

'But it makes sense, in a crazy kind of way.'

'Like you said, grief can make people do crazy things. Find her, Geraldine. Talk to her. See what she's got to say for herself. Let's see if she's got an alibi. Of course it doesn't prove anything if she hasn't, but . . .' He shrugged. 'Go and find Sophie Cliff when you're done with Martin and the girl-friend.' He turned and left the room as abruptly as he had entered it. Geraldine wished he had stayed longer.

'Would Martin have set fire to the house with Brenda upstairs?' Geraldine wondered as she and Peterson set off for the Blue Lagoon where Brenda and Callum Martin were staying.

The doorman gave them an ironic salute as he stood aside to admit them. 'Getting to be a bit of

281

a habit, sarge. You won't be the only police officer who's a regular of ours.' He gave Peterson a crude wink. Geraldine saw the sergeant's shoulders tense as he clenched his fists.

They made their way through the deserted club to Bronxy's office. She didn't look surprised to see them.

'We want to speak to Brenda.'

'Of course you do, Inspector.' On Bronxy's lips the quietly spoken title sounded like a taunt.

Brenda entered the room hesitantly and stared anxiously at Bronxy.

'You're all right, Brenda. Just answer the policewoman's questions and then you can go back upstairs.'

'Brenda, can you tell us exactly what happened last night?' Geraldine asked.

'Last night,' Brenda repeated flatly. She shrugged. Geraldine waited. 'Cal wouldn't take me,' Brenda mumbled at last. She was high as a kite. Her speech was slurred. She could barely manage to string two words together coherently.

'Last night, Brenda. What happened?' Geraldine persisted.

'Hot. It was hot,' she said, flapping her hands. Her eyes grew wide as she struggled to explain. 'Too hot. Roofs – in the rain!' She giggled unexpectedly. 'Rain in the moonlight.' She leaned forward and gazed intensely at Geraldine. Her pupils were unnaturally dilated. 'The roof is so pretty.'

'Brenda, there was a fire in your house. What happened? Who was there?'

Brenda was agitated now. 'Where's Cal?' She was crying. 'Where's Cal?'

Geraldine pressed on but it was a waste of time trying to get a sensible answer out of Brenda in her present state.

'She's in shock,' Bronxy explained.

'She's drugged up to her eyeballs,' Geraldine replied crossly. Bronxy's face twisted but she didn't bother to deny it.

Callum Martin must have been waiting outside because he walked in as soon as Peterson opened the door for Brenda to leave.

'Someone's made a nasty mess of your face,' Peterson said. Martin's left cheek was scored with four deep scratches.

'A cat,' Martin lied. 'I drowned it.' He trotted out his story before they had a chance to question him. 'I was in the pub last night. You can ask the landlord.'

'Don't worry, Mr Martin, we will.'

'My word not good enough for you?'

Geraldine was inclined to believe him. 'If he was lying, he'd have said he was at the Lagoon with Madam Bronxy,' she said to Peterson as they made their way back to the car.

'Should we check out the pub anyway?'

Geraldine nodded. 'No stone unturned,' she said. 'One way or another we're going to nail the bastard.'

'Are you as confident as you sound, gov?' Geraldine didn't answer. Peterson was growing to know her too well.

The pub was empty. Geraldine glanced around. 'Where's Bert?'

'He's not been in today.'

'I thought you said he's always here.'

'He's not here now.'

'Where can we find him?'

The landlord shrugged. 'He lives round here somewhere.'

Geraldine and Peterson had a coffee in the pub while they waited. At last a constable phoned back with Bert Cartwright's address.

'There's something else, gov,' the constable said. 'Bert Cartwright was a cop.'

'Run that by me again.'

'He was a detective sergeant when he left the force.'

'Are you sure?'

'There was an incident involving alcohol and he was forced to resign. He was a good DS, according to the records. Until he had to quit, that is. It was a long time ago.'

Before they left, Geraldine asked the pub landlord to let them know if the old man turned up. Bert lived in a rundown block of flats about five minutes' walk from the pub. There was no answer when they rang the bell. A neighbour let them into the building. They knocked on Bert's door. No answer. The lock was easy to open.

Inside they found stacks of old newspapers, a cupboard stuffed with moth eaten jumpers and stained underwear, and a stinking pair of boots with no laces. There was a small bottle of whiskey under the unmade bed and another one on a table in the filthy kitchen. Geraldine wrinkled her nose at the smell of damp. Bert wasn't there. They asked his neighbour to inform them when he returned. There was nothing else they could do.

Barker had been the subject of two sadistic attacks. He might not survive a third. 'Tell me, gov,' Peterson said, 'would you honestly care if Barker gets it? It's no worse than he deserves, and it'll be one less villain screwing things up for everyone.'

'The law's there to protect everyone. There can't be any exceptions.'

'I know,' he agreed. 'But even so—'

'We have a job to do, upholding the law. Once we lose our grip on that, everything slides into chaos.'

'I know that, but—'

'You can't choose who deserves the protection of the law. It's there for everyone.'

'I know. I just wondered.'

'Well don't.'

'You're that sure?'

'Have to be in this job. Otherwise—'

'I know, chaos. Do you ever get the feeling it's not far off, gov?'

'Don't go there, Ian. We've got to keep the devils at bay.'

'Is that the devils out there, or the devils within, gov?'

Geraldine didn't answer.

# CHAPTER 45

# HOTEL

Mrs Pettifer opened the door.

'Oh, it's you, Inspector. I'm sorry, this isn't a very good time. We're expecting visitors this evening so I'm afraid I'm rather busy. Can't this wait?'

'It's Mrs Cliff we want to speak to.'

'She moved out on Thursday.' Mrs Pettifer was unable to tell them where Sophie had gone. 'I think she was going to her parents. I think they live up North somewhere,' she added vaguely. 'Now, if you'll excuse me, I've got a lot on. I'd help you if I could.'

Geraldine hid her surprise on hearing that Sophie Cliff had left her neighbours' house. 'Thank you, Mrs Pettifer. Can you please contact me if you hear from Sophie. We need to speak to her urgently.'

It took the local police nearly an hour to confirm that Sophie Cliff hadn't returned to her parents' house. They had no idea where she was and hadn't heard from her since news of the fire had reached them. As Geraldine received the update, Ryder wandered into her office.

He studied Geraldine's expression as she put the

287

phone down. She felt herself blushing under his scrutiny. 'Where the hell is she?' he growled when she told him they had lost track of Sophie Cliff. 'Find her, Geraldine.' He stalked out again.

'I'm doing my best, sir,' Geraldine muttered crossly to the empty room. The DCI's dismay only increased her frustration. She passed a further anxious half hour before a constable came to tell her that Sophie Cliff had been traced. She was staying at a local motel.

Geraldine smiled in relief. 'How did you find her?'

'She finally answered her mobile phone, ma'am. We kept trying it, like you said.'

They found the rundown motel on the main bypass out of town. A man was lounging behind the counter watching a daytime chat show and stuffing a sugary doughnut into his mouth. He didn't look up when Geraldine and Peterson entered the grubby reception area.

Geraldine held out her identity card. 'We're looking for a Mrs Cliff.'

The man behind the desk shoved the end of his doughnut into his mouth and brushed his sticky hands together. He looked up at Geraldine, his cheeks swollen with the pastry, and clambered to his feet. 'We don't want any trouble,' he said, his eyes flicking to her card. Crumbs shot from his wet lips. 'She in some sort of trouble? We don't accommodate criminals. It's not that sort of establishment.'

'No. I'm sure it's not. And she's not a criminal, she's a victim.' The man tapped at his keyboard. 'Room 17. You're lucky. She only came back today.' He slumped in his chair and turned his attention back to the television. '17,' he repeated, flapping his hand towards a door at the far end of the reception room.

Geraldine led the way past a series of doors, to number 17. There was no response to her knock. She knocked again before trying the door. The handle turned and the door swung open. Sophie Cliff was sitting on the bed. She stared at the floor as Geraldine perched on a cheap plastic chair. Peterson slouched against the door. He gazed around the dirty room and straightened up suddenly.

'Mrs Cliff,' Geraldine began. Sophie didn't respond. 'Last night there was a second attack on Raymond Barker – the man you say you saw in your headlights on the night of the fire at your house. That's two attacks on Barker in three days. Mrs Cliff, we believe these incidents are linked. So, for the purpose of elimination, we need to know your whereabouts on both these occasions. Let's start with the first assault. Where were you on Saturday night?' No answer. 'Mrs Cliff, please answer the question.'

Sophie Cliff raised her head. 'Is he dead?'

'We need to know where you were on Saturday night.'

Sophie dropped her eyes. 'I went away.'

'Where did you go?'

'I went to the coast.'

'Where on the coast?'

Sophie looked up again. She spoke slowly, as though speaking in a foreign language. 'I went away. I had to get away from all this. You know, they won't allow me back in my own home. Not that I want to go back there. Not now. That's not what I meant. They're crawling all over the place. They've taken over my home. Firemen.' She let out a long shuddering sigh. 'My doctor told me I should go away. He suggested I went to my parents. I couldn't face their fussing, but I did go away. The doctor told me to.'

Geraldine glanced at a patch of damp on the wall. 'Where did you go?'

Sophie rummaged inside her handbag and handed Geraldine a receipt. 'Excelsior Hotel, Sandmouth,' Geraldine read aloud. The receipt showed a credit card payment dated that morning. 'May I keep this?' Geraldine asked. Sandmouth was about seventy miles away. The receipt indicated that Sophie Cliff had left the hotel that morning. 'When did you go to Sandmouth?'

There was a pause. Sophie seemed to be calculating. 'I went there on Saturday morning and came back this morning.'

'You stayed there for three nights?'

Sophie nodded. 'And then I came back here.'

Geraldine looked around the dismal room. 'Mrs Cliff, how long are you planning to stay here?'

Sophie didn't answer. She sat staring at the floor. 'If you leave here, will you go to your parents? Or is there somewhere else you might go?'

'There's nowhere.' Her voice was flat.

Geraldine stood up. 'Mrs Cliff, please don't go away again without letting us know where you are, in case we need to speak to you again. Do you understand? Please keep us informed of your whereabouts.'

Sophie looked up. 'Is he dead?' she asked again. 'The man that was attacked. The man I saw. Is he dead?'

'No, Mrs Cliff, he survived. He's in hospital, badly injured, but he's not dead. He's going to be all right.' Sophie Cliff's head fell forward, masking her expression.

As soon as they were back at the station, Geraldine contacted the police station in Sandmouth. 'I'd like this treated as a priority,' she said, 'and get back to me straight away. I need to know when she arrived and when she left. Dates and times please, as accurately as possible.' The credit card provider confirmed the transaction in Sandmouth on Sophie Cliff's credit card at nine thirty that morning. There was nothing else to do but wait to receive confirmation that Sophie Cliff had been in Sandmouth all weekend.

'If she's lying, that puts her right in the frame for the attacks on Raymond Barker,' Geraldine told Peterson. 'And if not—'

She didn't finish the sentence. Someone had

launched two vicious assaults on Raymond Barker and they had no other suspect.

'If not, then maybe Barker did lie to protect Callum Martin when he said he was attacked by a woman,' Peterson replied. 'That's two murders and two attempts on Barker's life. If you ask me, Martin's the one we should be going after. Let's hope Bert Cartwright has something concrete for us.'

Geraldine looked worried. They had contacted all the hospitals in the area but there was no sign of the old man. He had disappeared.

# CHAPTER 46

# SANDMOUTH

A call came through from Sandmouth station while Geraldine was in the canteen. She had been studying what Sophie Cliff had said. She knew most of the statements by heart and couldn't focus on them any longer. Her head was beginning to ache. While she was sitting quietly at a corner table, drinking a mug of tea, a couple of young constables came in. She recognised Polly, who had been crying in the toilets. The two constables glanced over at Geraldine. Choosing a table at the other side of the room, they sat with their backs to her, heads bent forward. Judging by the jerking of their two heads, they were both talking incessantly. As she left the room, Geraldine overheard a snippet of their conversation.

'He's not worth it,' the dark haired constable was saying.

'That's easy for you to say—' Geraldine heard Polly reply as she went out into the corridor.

She returned to her desk to find a new report waiting. A local sergeant had interviewed the manager of the Excelsior Hotel who confirmed that Sophie Cliff had arrived at reception at around eleven on Saturday morning. The manager said that room number 213 had been ready for her on arrival. She had stayed there for three nights, checking out at nine thirty that morning after having breakfast in the dining room. Their records showed she had eaten in the hotel, sitting down on each of the three evenings at seven o'clock when the dining room opened. She had signed in for breakfast at eight o'clock every morning. The local constable had been thorough. He had checked the CCTV from the hotel car park and was able to confirm that Sophie Cliff's car had not moved from the hotel car park throughout her stay.

Geraldine showed the report to James Ryder when he wandered into her office that afternoon.

'Summarise it,' he said, waving at the report in her hand. Geraldine was aware of him, perched on the corner of her desk, as she read. She tried to ignore his closeness.

'It's a bit convenient, isn't it, sir?' she asked when she had finished. 'Barker's attacked on Saturday evening on his way home from the pub, his house is torched on Monday evening and he's almost killed, and meanwhile our suspect is conveniently staying at a hotel nearly a hundred miles away at the time.'

Ryder sighed. 'Too much of a bloody coincidence,' he agreed, standing up. 'But Sophie Cliff couldn't have driven back here on Saturday and

Monday evening if her car was in the car park all the time.'

'The timing's possible, though, sir. She could've set all this up as an alibi—'

'And taken a cab—' Ryder interrupted.

'Or hired a car,' Geraldine added.

'Well, what are you waiting for?' he barked. 'Get moving on it. Check out every cab company and car hire firm. If Sophie Cliff travelled backwards and forwards between Harchester and Sandmouth on either of those two evenings – or both – we need to know. Check the trains and buses too. Any way she could've managed it. Go on then, get on with it.'

'Yes sir.' As the DCI closed the door Geraldine thought she overheard him say, 'Good thinking, Geraldine,' but she wasn't sure. She didn't know if she felt elated because the enquiry was opening up, or because James Ryder had expressed his approval of her.

It didn't take long to check the train schedules. There was no direct train from Harchester to Sandmouth. The last train on Saturday evening left Harchester at ten fifteen, ten forty on a Monday. Sophie Cliff couldn't have attacked Barker and reached the station in time to catch a train that would make the connection to Sandmouth that evening and it was impossible for anyone to have travelled from Harchester to Sandmouth by train on Monday or Tuesday morning and reached the hotel in time for breakfast at eight. Several constables set to work, checking taxi firms from all the interconnecting stations to see if a passenger had taken the last train from Harchester in the evening and completed the journey by taxi. Only one woman travelling on her own had taken a taxi from Lower Troughton to Sandmouth at eleven ten on Monday. Her destination turned out to be a private house three miles from the Excelsior Hotel. The passenger was traced. She wasn't Sophie Cliff.

It took longer to establish that Sophie couldn't have made the journeys entirely by car. Constables checked every taxi firm and cab hire company in Harchester and Sandmouth and every intervening town, village and train station. Only one journey had been booked from Harchester to Sandmouth on Saturday evening, at eleven o'clock, by a Mr George Kite. A constable traced Mr Kite who confirmed that he had made the journey in person.

Three hire cars had been taken out over the period. At the end of the day, the constable who had overseen the research handed Geraldine a list of names: Desmond James, Bobbie Geere, and Ellis Collamore.

They had drawn a blank. Sophie Cliff's car hadn't moved from the car park. With a car, she could have returned to Sandmouth overnight and appeared in the dining room again at eight on Tuesday morning. Without a car, it was impossible for her to have eaten in the dining room in the Excelsior Hotel in Sandmouth at seven on Monday

296

evening and been back in Harchester in time to set fire to Raymond Barker's house before nine o'clock. She couldn't have been responsible for the attack on Barker on Monday evening.

'Not unless she's superwoman,' Peterson joked. Geraldine didn't smile. It was past nine when Geraldine finally returned home to find a message from Hannah on her answer machine.

'Geraldine, call me.' With a twinge of guilt she deleted the message. It was too late to call back that evening.

# CHAPTER 47

# PANIC

'I told you before, you've got nothing to be scared of. It's always the same with you. What the hell have you got to be so scared about all the time? Don't I look after you? I keep you safe, don't I? Scared of your own bleeding shadow you are.' Cal sat down on the bed and lit a cigarette. He didn't offer Brenda one.

'What if they find out? What if they know it was you?' Brenda whimpered. She pressed herself against the back of a chair, legs bent, clutching her knees to her chest.

'What if they find out what was me? Do you have any idea how stupid you sound? I haven't got a clue what you're talking about. Talk sense for fuck's sake.' Cal flicked cigarette ash impatiently.

'I know where you and Ray went. I'm not stupid.' Brenda glanced fearfully at the glowing end of Cal's cigarette. 'I'm not stupid,' she repeated, raising her voice. Cal hooted with laughter. 'I know it was you, breaking into those houses. I know it was you topped that old woman.' Her eyes flicked nervously to the door, her hands fidgeted. 'Why did you do it, Cal? Why did you kill her? She was just an old woman. She never did you any harm. I saw her picture in the paper.'

'Would you mind telling me what the bleeding hell you're talking about.' Cal's voice was dangerously quiet. Brenda scrambled to her feet and moved behind the chair, out of reach. 'Who's this old woman you're talking about? What old woman?' He glanced at the door. There were other people sleeping upstairs at the Blue Lagoon where they were staying until the house was fixed up.

'And there was that fire,' Brenda went on, reckless now. 'I don't mean the one we had in our house. I mean the fire on Harchester Hill. The one where some guy died.'

'Cliff.'

'What?'

'That was his name. Cliff.'

'Whatever.'

'I'm telling you, that was his name. Thomas Cliff. It was all over the papers.'

'That was you, wasn't it?' Brenda pressed him.

'What was me? What are you on about?'

'That was you, started that fire, wasn't it?'

Cal stared at her. 'Mind your own business,' he said at length. 'What's it to you anyway? You think me and Ray are the only ones breaking into houses round here? Stupid cow. Could've been anyone. What makes you think that fire was anything to do with us? Don't you go blabbing your stupid ideas to anyone else. It's nobody else's business what me and Ray do in our own time. You keep your evil ideas to yourself, got it?' He raised his hand. 'No one knows anything about what we were doing, and that's how it's going to stay.' He stood up.

Brenda was too agitated to keep quiet. 'What if they find out, Cal? What if they're on to you?'

'Stop worrying, will you? You're doing my head in. I'm telling you, no one can put me in the frame. We're quite safe, as long as you keep your stupid trap shut.'

'They know, Cal.'

'Who knows what?' He stubbed his cigarette butt out on a dirty plate, watched it sizzle in a pool of vinegar, lit two more cigarettes, and threw one at her. She hesitated over whether to bend down to pick it up, and stamped it out on the floor instead. He had caught her out like that before. 'Suppose you tell me just what you've been blabbing about, you stupid bitch, and who exactly you've been blabbing it to.'

Brenda trembled at his tone. She kept her head lowered, unable to meet his eye. 'Not me, Cal,' she whispered. 'It wasn't me. I never said anything to anyone. I never breathed a word about anything to anyone. You know I wouldn't, Cal.'

'What then?' He took a long drag of his cigarette. 'Why don't you tell me exactly what you haven't been telling anyone.' He sat down again and crossed his legs. 'I'm listening.' He blew smoke at the ceiling and waited.

Brenda took a deep breath. She clutched the back of her chair. 'The filth were asking around the market about the bag Ray left behind at that old woman's house.' She lifted her head defiantly and stared at Cal. 'I knew he'd be no good for you, Cal. I said so, didn't I?'

He narrowed his eyes. 'You've been keeping your ears pinned back,' was all he said.

'I heard the girls from the market talking about it.' Her teeth were chattering so hard she could barely speak.

Cal stared at his cigarette. 'What girls? Tell me what you heard. Tell me everything, Brenda.'

'It was Maggie. The filth were round at her place, asking about a bag. A khaki bag. Like the one—'

'Yeah, yeah, I know. Like the one Ray left behind in the old woman's house that night. Bloody retard.' He spat out a thread of tobacco. 'What did she tell them?' Brenda was smiling to herself. Cal raised his voice and slapped his leg. Brenda jumped. 'I asked you, what did she tell them?'

'She never told them anything. They were just asking. Why would she tell them anything? They're filth, Cal. No one talks to filth. Maggie's all right.'

He grunted. 'Who is she?' Brenda shook her head. 'You're talking about the one who sells bags at the market? Who is she? Where can I find her?'

'Why do you want to know?' Brenda whispered. She was shaking.

Cal grinned at her. 'You tell me what I want to know, Bren, and I'll make it worth your while.

I know what you want. That's fair, isn't it? All you've got to do is tell me where the bag woman lives. Come on, Bren. I'm not going to hurt her.' He reached into his pocket and pulled out a small plastic bag. Brenda's eyes fixed on it as he waved it in the air.

'You won't hurt Maggie?' she said, starting forward.

Cal dropped his cigarette butt on the floor and ground it under his heel.

'You know I wouldn't do that. I only want to talk to her. Make sure we get our story straight, that's all.' He looked at Brenda and smiled, baring his teeth.

# CHAPTER 48

# HIT AND RUN

Maggie groaned as the alarm penetrated her dream. 'It's that dratted doorbell again,' her mother whined. Maggie kept her eyes closed. She knew there was no one at the door. Her poor mother had been dead for years. Reluctantly she reached out of her cocoon to hit the snooze button, the air chill on her naked arm. Resisting the urge to sink back into sleep she dragged herself out of bed and threw some clothes on. It was early but she was determined to be at the market before Geoffrey, if it meant getting up in the middle of the night. In her hurry she cricked her neck. Just when she thought her day couldn't get any worse, it began to drizzle. She reached the market, which was deserted, and started to set up.

'Blast this weather.' She hung small bags on hooks in front of the larger ones displayed beneath. When she had finished, she settled down on a crate in the corner of the stall and watched the market gradually take shape for the day.

'I'm freezing my tits off,' Alice on the next stall grumbled. 'Coming for a drink Friday?' Maggie nodded but she wasn't really listening. She was thinking she might leave early. It was a shame to waste all the effort of setting up but the market was dead and she was knackered. She looked around. No one else was packing up yet.

'What do you reckon?' she yawned. 'Is it worth sticking it out?'

'You're not thinking of clearing off already?' Alice glanced out from under her awning. 'The morning's hardly over. I'm going to wait a while. It might clear up.' After about half an hour the rain gave over. A weak sun glimmered through the clouds. Alice sauntered over to Maggie's stall. 'I reckon it might pick up at lunch time,' she said. 'Do you want a coffee?'

'Cheers.'

A few minutes later Alice handed Maggie a steaming polystyrene cup. 'I haven't seen anything of Brenda this morning, have you?'

'No. Maybe she's gone down with the flu.'

'Or picked up something nasty.'

'Someone nasty more like.'

'Couldn't be nastier than that fellow of hers. Colin?'

'Callum.'

'That's the one.'

'You heard any more from Geoffrey, then?' Maggie shook her head. 'It's a bloody disgrace. You ought to report him. Bastard.'

'Like the manager's going to take any notice. I'm bloody freezing.' Alice offered Maggie a cigarette. 'I'm trying to give up. Oh go on then,' she added quickly before Alice could put the packet away. They smoked companionably. Five minutes passed. Maggie was about to ask Alice if she still thought it was worth hanging around when suddenly the aisles were packed with shoppers.

By half past one, Maggie was exhausted from the effort of lifting bags down and hooking them up again, hauling banana boxes out of the back of the van to hunt for specific colours, and the effort to keep warm.

'Must be nice to work in a shop and not have to stand around freezing,' Maggie said. 'Got a fag?' Alice reached into her pocket but before she could oblige, a group of noisy girls stopped at Maggie's stall. They tugged bags off their hooks and dropped them, calling out, 'How much for this one? How much is that one?' None of them bought anything.

'Bloody time wasters.'

The market was heaving; women struggled with buggies, groups of girls shrieked and flapped, boys prowled or gathered in packs to fuss the girls, and determined women, handbags clutched against their chests, forged their way through crowds of loiterers. The noise rose, an ugly cacophony: laughter, music, babies crying, boys shouting, girls chattering and everyone calling out, 'How much? How much?'

By early afternoon a steady drizzle had set in again and the aisles had emptied. Maggie was fed up. She had hardly shifted anything all morning despite the bustle, and her shoulders were aching.

A few other stall holders began to clear away their stock. Maggie decided to pack up and had unhooked most of the bags when a man paused at her stall. His grey coat was too long for him and a cigarette smouldered at the corner of his mouth. He squinted at the bags still on display before picking up a khaki canvas one. He turned it over in gloved hands.

'Sell many like this?' he asked. He had a soft voice. Maggie gave him her patter. It was a popular line, top quality yet cheap. The man examined the bag, opened it up, peered inside, then raised his eyes and stared at Maggie until she began to feel uncomfortable.

'Do you want to take that one then?' she asked. He put the bag down and turned away. 'Please yourself,' she muttered.

'You know who that was?' Alice hissed at her.

'Who?'

'That bloke you were talking to just now.'

'What about him?'

'You know who he was?'

'He wasn't Johnny Depp, that's for sure.'

'That was Brenda's fellah.'

'What? The one that knocks her about?'

Alice nodded, wide eyed. 'I think so.'

'The one who did for poor Lily?' Alice nodded again. Maggie shrugged and finished packing away her bags. 'I'll be off then,' she said at last, straightening up and wincing at the stiffness in her muscles. 'What a lousy day.'

'Can only get better,' Alice answered.

'That's true.'

'You won't be wanting me to watch the kids after school today?'

'No, you're all right.'

Maggie was glad when she reached home. She was impatient to change out of her damp clothes. As she pushed open the gate and hurried up the path to the entrance of her block, a car pulled into the kerb across the road. The driver slouched in his seat. He watched her disappear into the building.

Maggie clomped upstairs to her flat where she changed out of her wet clothes and put her feet up. She dozed for a few minutes in front of the television until the children arrived home from school, noisy and irritable. It was time to make the tea.

'We're out of milk, ma,' Chloe said. 'Shall I get it?'

Maggie swore under her breath. 'I'll go,' she said. 'I need some cigarettes. You can start getting the tea on. There's some sausages left in the fridge.'

Maggie pulled her collar up as she stepped outside. At least it had stopped raining. She didn't notice a black car slip away from its parking space over the road. It dawdled behind her, pulling into the kerb a couple of times to allow other vehicles to overtake before it followed her round the corner into a deserted side street.

There was a screech of brakes and a squeal of tyres as the black car careered back on to the main road and drove at speed away from the centre of town towards the bypass.

A few moments later the urgent wail of a siren pierced the quiet of the evening.

# CHAPTER 49

# BODY

SOCOs were at work when Geraldine and Peterson arrived. Several uniformed officers were standing around guarding the scene which had been cordoned off. There was no sign of the DCI and no visible activity outside the forensic tent. A group of onlookers had already gathered. They watched Geraldine and the sergeant collect suits, masks, gloves and overshoes from the forensic van. Neither of them spoke as they entered the tent.

The victim lay flat on her back from the waist down. Her upper torso was twisted to one side, her arms flung out on either side of her body. The top of her skull was a mess of hair and splintered bone, the features beneath it splattered with blood but still intact. Geraldine recognised her at once. A navy canvas bag lay on the road beside her. It must have slipped off her shoulder when she fell, spewing its contents on to the tarmac: a well worn tan wallet, shattered mirror, cheap biro, loose tissues, mobile phone with the back fallen off and a bunch of keys.

'There's some cards in her purse,' a uniformed

officer announced, pulling them out of the wallet. 'We've got an identity.'

'Maggie Palmer, market trader, 27 Maple Court,' Geraldine replied. The dead woman's eyes were open, her mouth hung slack and one hand appeared to be clawing at the tarmac beneath her.

'Yes, ma'am,' the WPC said, holding out a market licence.

Geraldine looked up and nodded at Peterson. 'Another coincidence,' she muttered. He shrugged. It was only two days since they had visited Maggie Palmer at her home.

'She looks rather crushed,' a voice said lightly behind them.

Geraldine turned and acknowledged Dr Talbot. 'What can you tell us?' she asked.

The doctor knelt down beside Maggie Palmer and sat back on his heels. He studied the body for several minutes before he leaned forward. Deftly he unbuttoned the dead woman's jacket and cardigan to view her injuries. Maggie Palmer's white flesh was exposed to the air. Geraldine shivered as the doctor gently examined the body.

'There's remarkably little bruising on the chest, although she was hit here, and here,' he said quietly, pointing with long fingers. 'Smashed skull, cracked ribs, crushed pelvis . . .' Slowly he felt down the dead woman's legs. 'Traces of what looks like black paint in the lacerations around the left knee, which suggests an impact with a black vehicle.'

'Was it the head injury killed her?' Geraldine asked, gazing at a pool of blood around Maggie Palmer's head.

The doctor nodded slowly. 'The other injuries came after,' he said. 'Ribs, pelvis, legs, after the frontal bone.' He stood up, frowning, and met Geraldine's gaze. 'This doesn't look like an accident, Inspector.'

'Not an accident? You mean it wasn't a hit and run?' Peterson asked.

The doctor shook his head. 'These injuries are too extensive to be the result of a single impact. Someone ran over this body at least three times, forwards, backwards, then forwards again. As if they were . . .' he paused.

'Making sure?' Geraldine finished the sentence. 'We're looking at murder?'

'I'll need to take a proper look before I can give a view on that,' the doctor hedged.

'But you said it wasn't an accident,' Peterson said.

'That's my initial impression, yes, but don't quote me on it. I need to get the body to the mortuary and conduct a full examination before I can confirm it.'

Geraldine was in a hurry to hear the results of a full post mortem examination. In the meantime, SOCOs continued searching the road surface.

'What about skid marks?' Geraldine asked one of the SOCOs.

He shrugged. 'ABS is standard these days.'

The road had been closed off. Onlookers were questioning the uniformed officers on duty.

'I'm sorry, madam,' Geraldine overheard one of them say, 'we don't have any information for you.'

'But there was an accident. We know there was an accident. Someone was knocked down right here in the road.'

'And killed?' someone else asked.

'Bella saw the body!' another voice called out, hoarse with excitement.

'Of course there's a body. Why else would they have one of those tent things up?'

'Perhaps they're going camping.'

'For goodness' sake, show some respect!' a woman scolded.

'You tell him,' another voice chipped in.

Excitement rippled through the waiting crowd when powerful lights were set up to illuminate the road surface. Geraldine wished she could shed the weight of her responsibility and join them as a spectator, but she had seen Maggie Palmer's eyes staring out of her crushed head. She had heard the doctor's opinion that this was no accidental death. The growing throng of onlookers was chattering and calling out, as though the incident were an entertainment they were watching on a screen. A few of them grew restless, and began to drift away. Geraldine watched them leave with a pang of envy. She wished she could share their boredom, go home and forget all about the incident in the street.

SOCOs scoured the tarmac and found tyre marks near the body. When they finished scrutinising the road surface and photographing the tracks, the medical team were able to move the body. There was a suppressed sigh from the onlookers as a stretcher was carried from the tent, the body completely shrouded.

'Who is it?' the whisper went round. Geraldine wished she didn't know. She removed her protective clothing and dumped it in the bin. When she finished she turned round. The doctor had already gone. Only Peterson was waiting for her.

'What now, gov?'

'I wish I knew.'

The DI looked so woebegone that Ian Peterson felt an irresistible impulse to comfort her. 'Cheer up, gov,' he said lamely. 'It's only some woman. I mean,' he fumbled to find appropriate words, 'she's a stranger, is all I meant.'

'Yes,' Geraldine agreed, 'she's only a stranger.' To Ian's consternation, he saw her eyes glisten with tears as she turned away.

He took a step towards her. 'Are you sure you're all right, gov? You don't seem yourself . . . This wasn't our fault. We can't stop interviewing witnesses in case something happens to them. And in any case—'

The DI spun round to face him. 'Don't presume to know me, sergeant,' she hissed. If she hadn't been so angry, Ian would have laughed at her pompous words, but her face was dark with fury. Wisely, he said nothing. 'I don't even know myself,' she added enigmatically. Ian was surprised at the bitterness in her voice. He didn't dare ask what she meant. With a sigh, he turned and walked away.

# CHAPTER 50

# SCENE OF CRIME

Peterson set to work finding out as much as he could about the car involved in the fatal accident. Road Traffic Control had received no reports of a road traffic collision and had recorded the incident as a failure to stop. The SOCO team had found a few shards of glass which they thought came from a smashed headlight. There was evidence to suggest the vehicle was black, and Peterson was hoping the splinters of glass picked up at the scene would enable him to track down the model.

'Find it,' Geraldine said. 'Even if it's stolen—'

'Which it probably was—'

'It might have been driven away from a car park, somewhere with CCTV.'

The sergeant nodded. He turned back to the images on his screen. 'Once I've identified it, I'll check reports of vehicles stolen in the past day or two,' he went on. 'With luck, we might find the vehicle abandoned somewhere.'

Geraldine nodded. Dr Talbot was examining the body, Peterson was tracking down the vehicle. This time, with luck, not even Bronxy would be able to protect Callum Martin.

Geraldine looked up when James Ryder entered her office.

He didn't return her weary smile. 'Is it a coincidence, the old guy doing a vanishing act just now?' he asked. They were all frustrated that Bert Cartwright had not been found.

'The landlord said he's always there, day in day out. And he's not at home sick, sir.'

'And he's not in hospital,' Ryder said. 'What does he know about Martin, and where the hell is he?' Bert Cartwright's description had been circulated to every force in the country. 'I'm worried. Geraldine. I'm beginning to think something's happened to him.' He sighed. 'I'm thinking of organising a search of the woods near the old man's flat.' A neighbour thought she might have seen the old man walking towards the canal with an unidentified companion on Monday evening. It wasn't much to go on, but Geraldine thought the DCI was right to follow it up.

At two o'clock Geraldine went out for a coffee. She sat in Starbucks, trying to clear her head. Something had to break soon. Whatever else happened, they couldn't let Martin walk. But they had nothing to connect him to the hit and run. She considered the possibility that Maggie Palmer's death so soon after the police questioned her had been a coincidence. But the pathologist had reported that the car had driven backwards and forwards over the body several times. If it had been an accident, the driver would either have stopped, or else panicked and accelerated off in a hurry.

While Geraldine had been on a break, a report had been passed on about a stolen car. Geraldine and Peterson hurried off to speak to the owner. He was pacing in his front garden as they drew up.

'Has it been found yet?' he demanded as they approached.

'I'm afraid not, sir,' Peterson replied.

The car was a 2002 black Honda Accord. A quick email had confirmed that the tyre tread of the model matched a track they had found at the scene of the hit and run. The black paintwork was a further indication that the stolen vehicle could have been used to run over Maggie Palmer.

'Where did you leave the car?' Geraldine exchanged a glance with Peterson. If the car theft had been caught on CCTV, they might make a quick arrest. They could have it tied up before the local paper even went to print. She could feel her heart beating. Mr Ellis had left his Honda in an open air supermarket car park near the shopping centre in Harchester. 'Not the multi storey?' Mr Ellis shook his head. There were security cameras at the entrance and exit to the open air car park, and an attendant, but the main area wasn't overlooked.

'I was at the supermarket with the wife,' Mr Ellis said. 'What a nightmare. She had the kid in a buggy, I was pushing the trolley. A load of stuff. I take her once a week to stock up. It's not easy

317

for her, what with the kid and everything. She's not been well. So we come out with all the stuff and the car's not there. I thought I must've forgotten where I left it, you know how it is. We walked around for a bit, then I left Sarah waiting with the buggy and the trolley under the covered walkway because it started raining. I walked round the whole car park twice but it wasn't there. It wasn't anywhere. I told the manager and we put Sarah in a taxi home with the kid. The manager was great. They're delivering the stuff for us. He even stored the frozen stuff . . . He said they'd take care of everything . . .' He sighed. 'But he's not going to bring my car back, is he? They ought to have proper security, don't you think? Now what am I supposed to do?'

Geraldine went through the story again, making a note of the time the Ellis family had arrived at the car park, and the exact position of the car, which had been parked in a corner near the exit but out of sight of the car park attendant.

'And you're sure you locked the vehicle when you left it?'

'I think so. I always do.'

'An unlocked vehicle is a target for casual joy riders. If the car was locked, we may be looking for a professional thief.'

'I can't see why anyone would want to steal my car. It's not exactly a Ferrari.'

'Mr Ellis, we have reason to believe your vehicle, stolen between two thirty and three thirty, may have been used in a hit and run accident between four and four thirty this afternoon.'

'A hit and run? You mean someone was run over? You think my car was involved in an accident?'

'A woman was knocked down and killed, Mr Ellis. We don't yet know if it was an accident.'

Mr Ellis's mouth dropped open but he didn't say anything for a few seconds. Then he rallied. 'Don't tell my wife,' he said. 'Please don't tell my wife. She'd freak. And if the car turns up, I'm going to have to drive it again, aren't I?'

The car park was half empty when Geraldine drew into it. She had left Peterson at the station co-ordinating a search for the stolen Honda. A few people were pushing trolleys along the lanes between parked vehicles. Car boots were open. People were piling plastic bags inside. Daylight was beginning to fade when she approached the car park attendant's tiny hut. It was difficult to talk, with wind gusting through a row of trees that screened the car park from the road, and cars revving past the barrier every few minutes. Geraldine held up her warrant card. She had to raise her voice to gain his attention.

'Can't leave my post,' the attendant claimed.

'Call your manager.'

'What do you want me to say to him?'

'You can start by telling him you're obstructing the police.'

The little man hobbled out of his hut. He left the barrier up. Without a word he led the way into the store. The manager invited Geraldine into his office. She asked the car park attendant to accompany her.

'What's the problem?' the manager asked. He was sweating slightly. Geraldine reassured him that her enquiry had nothing to do with his store.

'We're investigating the theft of a vehicle from your car park this afternoon.'

The manager spoke rapidly, detailing the security measures in the car park. 'We do what we can,' he finished, 'but we can't watch all the vehicles all the time. Eddy here does a good job. Legally—'

'A very good job,' the car park attendant interrupted. Nodding his head above rounded shoulders, he looked like a tortoise.

'We're interested in tracing the driver and the vehicle,' Geraldine explained. She described the car. The manager wrote the registration number down.

'We'll look out for it. Do you remember seeing it, Eddy?'

'A black car? You've got to be kidding. I can't be everywhere. Would you remember every car that goes past?' He glared at Geraldine. 'Someone drives a car out, how do I know it's stolen? Long as they've got a ticket. That's my job, to check the tickets. I do a good job.'

'I'm sure you do, Eddy. No one's expecting you to remember all the cars you see. But can you remember anything about the driver of a black Honda that left the car park around three?' Eddy shook his head. It was hopeless. She turned to the manager and asked to see CCTV footage from that morning.

At two fifty a black Honda had driven out of the car park. The sun shield was down, concealing the driver's face. It was impossible to make out a face or the driver's stature, but digital enhancement confirmed the driver was wearing gloves. There was no point checking the used tickets for prints. A call to Mr Ellis confirmed that his car had a 'Baby on Board' sign in the rear window and a sticker from a local theme park, both of which were distinguishable as the car drew up at the barrier.

They knew the vehicle that had been used to kill Maggie Palmer. They had a shrewd idea who was behind the wheel. But they had no proof.

'Find the vehicle,' the DCI said in the pub that evening, 'and forensics will find something to prove Martin was driving it.'

'We don't know it wasn't a random joy rider who knocked her down by accident,' Bennett said, joining the discussion.

'And drove over the body three times?'

'To make sure she wouldn't be able to identify him, or the car,' Bennett suggested but even he didn't buy that for a moment.

'It's too much of a coincidence,' Geraldine insisted. 'We found a witness who could link Barker and Callum Martin to Thomas Cliff's death. Next thing we know, she's run over and killed. Barker's out of the frame. He can't walk, let alone drive right now. It must have been Martin. And now Cartwright's done a runner. Is it a coincidence or does he know something about Martin that he's frightened to tell us?' But though they might have grounds to believe Callum Martin had killed Maggie Palmer, they couldn't touch him.

'Whoever upsets him next, I wouldn't want to be in their shoes,' Peterson said.

Geraldine recalled a bloodless face staring blankly from beneath a shock of badly dyed blonde hair. 'We can't protect everyone,' she sighed. Callum Martin's girlfriend had denied several anonymous allegations of domestic violence although from her injuries it was clear that she was in an abusive relationship. If Callum Martin was capable of murder, Brenda might not live to regret her loyalty.

# CHAPTER 51

# GOSSIP

The DCI had sent a team of dog handlers into the woods beside the canal. They had found a pair of glasses they thought might belong to Bert Cartwright, but there was still no sign of the old man.

'Social Services are double checking their records,' Ryder said. 'There may be family members he could have gone to. We'll give it another day before we start dredging the canal.' He sighed. 'It's an expensive exercise. We have to be certain it's necessary.'

There was a flurry of excitement when a hire car that had been sighted on CCTV leaving Sandmouth on Saturday evening at seven thirty five was picked up by a camera in Harchester a couple of hours later. A phone call to the car hire firm confirmed it had been driven by someone called Bobbie Geere. A local constable was dispatched to follow it up. The manager looked flustered when asked about cars taken out the previous Saturday.

'It wasn't the lads' fault,' he explained. 'We had a problem with our computer system. Couldn't use the computers all day. According to head office, someone hacked in and caused the whole system to crash. A likely story!' As he spoke he rummaged through a drawer full of papers and pulled out a handwritten list of names with addresses and car numbers.

'The customer must've paid in cash. We get so many going through, and it being a Saturday, we had the boy in to help out.' He glared at the constable. 'We check their documents carefully. We've never had any trouble.'

'Do you get many punters paying cash?'

'You'd be surprised.'

The boy who had been on the desk on Saturday was equally vague. 'Nah,' he said, 'I can't remember.'

'Can you remember anything about the customer?'

'Nah.'

By narrowing down the time the car was taken, and studying the CCTV, a constable was able to report a blurred visual on the driver, a grey haired woman in steel rimmed NHS glasses who walked with a pronounced stoop. She wasn't Sophie Cliff.

Later that afternoon Geraldine went to the canteen. While she was waiting for her coffee she noticed Bennett sitting at a corner table laughing and chatting with a couple of local female constables. She went over to join them. They fell silent at her approach.

'How's things?' she asked. One of the constables put her hand over her mouth. 'Is something wrong?'

'Nothing, gov.' Bennett assured her. He frowned

at the giggling constable. After she had finished her day's work, Geraldine decided to call in at the pub over the road for a quick drink before setting off home. Peterson was at the bar with Bennett and one of the two female constables he had been having coffee with earlier on. The two senior officers were leaning forward listening to her.

'He was there again,' she was saying. 'If you ask me—' She glanced up, caught sight of Geraldine, and closed her mouth. A slow blush spread upwards from her neck to suffuse her whole face. Peterson and Bennett looked round. Peterson's face remained fixed, but his eyes opened a fraction more widely. He looked distinctly uncomfortable. Bennett looked down with a faint smirk.

Geraldine bought a round before asking casually, 'So who are you lot gossiping about?' As if she didn't know.

'It's nothing,' Peterson answered. They had obviously been talking about her. Geraldine left after one drink. She glanced over her shoulder on the doorstep. The inspector, sergeant and constable were leaning forward and they all appeared to be talking at once.

As if her day hadn't been bad enough, when she arrived home her phone was flashing with a message from Hannah.

Wearily, Geraldine picked up the phone and called her back. 'Han, I'd love to come over but—'

'Great. I'll put something in the oven.'

'I'm sorry, I can't—'

'Fish OK? And I've got a nice white wine already opened and in the fridge.'

'You're not listening. I can't make it—'

'I can put the fish on now so it'll be ready when you get here if you come now.'

'Hannah, I said I can't make it tonight.'

An hour later, Geraldine was sitting in Hannah's kitchen, dutifully eating. 'This is gorgeous.'

'Jeremy used to love my salmon teriyaki,' Hannah answered tearfully.

'I'm sure he still does.'

Hannah cleared away the plates and sat down. 'Geraldine, you've got to talk to him.'

'What?'

'You've got to go and see Jeremy. Talk to him.'

'Me? Hannah, he's your husband. We've hardly ever spoken to each other, apart from occasional small talk. I don't think he even likes me.' Geraldine did her best to dissuade her friend but Hannah was determined. 'Why me?'

'There's no one else I can ask. You're my oldest and my best friend, Geraldine. I'm asking you to talk to him.'

Geraldine sighed. It was an improvement on being asked to spy on him. 'What am I supposed to say? Accuse him of cheating on you?'

'Don't be silly.'

'What then?'

'You can start by telling him how worried you are.'

'What exactly am I supposed to be worried about?'

'Me, of course. Tell him you're afraid I might do something.' Geraldine shook her head, perplexed. 'Tell him you're worried I might kill myself.' Seeing the expression on Geraldine's face, Hannah added quickly, 'I'm not really about to top myself. The point is, you have to make him understand the consequences if he doesn't come back.'

'Suppose I agree to speak to him. I'm not saying I will, but let's say I agree. Do you know where I can find him?'

'He's staying with Colin and Nancy.'

'Colin and Nancy?'

'Colin. His brother.'

'Jeremy's staying with his brother?'

'Yes. That's what I said.'

'And you think he's run off with another woman?' Geraldine thought back to when her own boyfriend had walked out after they had been living together for six years. 'Where are you going to sleep tonight?' she had asked him. He had answered he was going to stay with a friend, admitting under pressure that his friend was a woman. She sighed. 'All right. What's the address?'

A woman opened the door to Geraldine. 'Yes?'

'You must be Nancy. I've come to see Jeremy.' Nancy hesitated. Geraldine had to stop herself reaching for her identity card.

'I'm sorry, what did you say your name was?' Nancy looked puzzled. She probably vaguely recognised Geraldine from the wedding.

Geraldine almost announced herself as DI Steel. She corrected herself just in time. 'Dee – Geraldine.'

'Dee?'

'Geraldine.'

Nancy looked even more confused. 'Geraldine?' Her eyes narrowed in sudden understanding. 'Are you a friend of Hannah's?' Geraldine nodded. 'Just a moment.' Nancy shut the door leaving Geraldine waiting on the doorstep. It was cold. At last the door opened again. 'Come in.'

Nancy led Geraldine into a small TV room on the ground floor.

Jeremy looked up, unsmiling. 'What do you want?' After his ungracious greeting, the conversation wasn't likely to go well.

Geraldine sat down. 'I want to talk to you about Hannah.'

'I hardly think my relationship with my wife is any concern of yours.'

He didn't refer to Hannah as his ex-wife. Geraldine relaxed slightly. 'Hannah's my oldest friend,' she said gently, 'and I'm worried about her, Jeremy. I don't think she's coping very well with your separation. I think you should talk to her. She may tell you she's fine, but . . . . I don't think she is. I'm worried about her.' She didn't pass on the message that Hannah was suicidal. 'Just talk to her, Jeremy. She's upset and very frightened.'

'Frightened?' Jeremy looked surprised. 'Look, it's

no big deal. I'll call her in my own time, OK? I just want some space, that's all. I'm so tired . . .'

Reaching home, Geraldine sat on her sofa and fell asleep. It was two o'clock in the morning when she woke up, too late to phone Hannah. She crawled into bed, exhausted, and drifted into an uneasy sleep. She dreamt she stumbled over a dead body with glittering blue eyes and tanned face.

'You can't kill me, I'm a doctor,' he said, although she knew he was already dead. His face changed and she saw her mother staring up at her. She was dead, but her arms reached out to Geraldine, pleading for a last cold embrace.

# CHAPTER 52

# INJURED

The absence of any adult relatives made the job harder. There was no one to make funeral arrangements, and probably no one to take care of Maggie Palmer's motherless children. An image of the old box file she had shoved to the back of her wardrobe slipped into Geraldine's thoughts. It occurred to her that she was treating the box in exactly the same way as her mother had, keeping it out of sight.

Maggie's neighbour, Alice Reynolds, came in to identify the body. 'Yes, that's Maggie. I've taken in the children for now,' she told Geraldine. 'Poor kids. They know me. I used to collect them from school every day when Maggie was working. She wasn't too happy about not being able to meet them herself, but needs must, Inspector. She was a good mother. She did what she could. I suppose they'll be taken into care now, poor little mites. I just dropped them off at school. Best to keep to their routine and the school's being very good about it all. They won't let me keep them, will they?' Recovered from her initial shock she had grown talkative. 'Will they let them stay at the school? I suppose I'll be able to see them, won't I?'

Geraldine said she wasn't sure. She recalled the small boy she had seen clinging to Maggie Palmer's skirt, and felt a sudden rage against the driver of the car that had killed her. 'Is there a father around?'

'There was, but he took off years ago, before I met her. I've no idea who he was. I think she mentioned his name. Jimmy, it might've been.'

'Jimmy?'

'That might've been it. Or was it? I'm sorry, I can't remember. I've known Maggie – I knew her, for three years and as far as I know the children's father never visited them or got in touch with her in all that time. I can tell you he left her just before – or was it just after? – her little boy was born, her second, and he's nearly eight.'

'No father then,' Geraldine said. 'Thank you for your help, Alice.'

After she had seen Alice Reynolds off, Geraldine returned to the mortuary where Dr Talbot was waiting. Maggie Palmer looked a lot smaller in death than she had in life. She lay on the slab like a broken doll, her injuries stark against the white of her flesh. Geraldine struggled to concentrate as Dr Talbot droned on about scalp lacerations, traumatic haematoma and depressed fractures.

'I thought you said there was only a little bruising,' Geraldine interrupted him. She gazed down at the dead woman, a pathetic heap of flesh

331

and bones that had once possessed the energy to work on a market stall. It was astonishing.

'She looks like she's been run over by a tank,' the doctor replied.

'A lot of injuries then?' Geraldine asked. The doctor nodded. 'Can you take us through them in order?'

'Right. Let's start from the top.'

'Is it possible to go through them in chronological order?'

The doctor frowned. 'There are severe contusions to the left temporal lobe, opposite the point of impact, which confirm a severe head injury resulting from a fall. In other words, she was knocked down from an upright position. The car hit here, on the knee. There are joint injuries, bone bruises and wedge shaped fractures, all caused by a high impact collision. Other indications of a bumper injury: soft tissue damage, bone bruising and glass fragment injuries, together with traces of blood and black paint on the outside of her left leg.'

'So, to clarify, she was hit on the leg by a car, injuring her knee. As a result of the collision she fell and hit her head on the road, and that's what killed her?'

'The fracture at the site of impact wasn't directly lethal when she fell but the ensuing traumatic intracerebral haemorrhage led to fatal cerebral oedema. The complication killed her almost immediately. But that wasn't the end of it. It looks as though the vehicle drove over her again, twice.'

'Tyre tracks indicate the car drove over her, reversed back over her and then drove forwards over her again,' Geraldine agreed.

'The second time it shattered her scapula, clavicle, sternum and ribs. The third and final time the car crushed her pelvis, sacrum and coccyx,' the doctor said, pointing at the various injuries as he named them. 'She also suffered injuries to three limbs: both femurs and patellas fractured, along with left radius and ulna. In addition the tarsals, metatarsals and phalanges on the right foot. In fact, almost every bone in her body's broken.'

Geraldine stared at the body. The doctor's commentary was beginning to sound like a lesson on the various bones in the human skeleton.

'I'd say the driver may have been worried she might survive and identify the vehicle,' the doctor went on.

'Or someone deliberately set out to kill her and made sure he finished the job,' she answered.

'It seems an odd way to kill someone. What if he was seen?'

Geraldine sighed. House to house calls in the quiet side street where Maggie Palmer had been killed had so far drawn a blank. No one who lived there had seen or heard anything.

Back at her desk, Geraldine was staring at the post mortem report when Ryder walked into her office. She smiled wearily up at him.

'Well?' he asked her.

'Nothing new.'

'You've seen the PM?' Geraldine held it up and he nodded. 'What do you think?' he asked. They talked it over but, whichever angle they approached the report from, the conclusion was the same. If this was an accidental hit and run, it was a very unusual one.

Two minutes into the morning briefing Geraldine's phone vibrated. At first she ignored it, then she slipped out of the room.

'Hannah, I can't talk now.'

Her friend ignored her. 'You saw Jeremy last night, didn't you? Why didn't you call me?'

'I would've called last night but I got back too late,' she fibbed. 'I only saw Jeremy for a few minutes. He didn't want to talk to me. But he didn't want you to be upset. He said he just needs some space. The best thing would be to talk to him. Give him a ring and tell him how you feel. Look, I have to go. I'm missing the briefing. Call him.' Without waiting for a response, she hung up and hurried back to the Incident Room. She felt wretched, as though she had let her friend down.

'We believe Maggie Palmer had information that connected Callum Martin to the recent burglaries. As soon as we spoke to her, she was killed,' the DCI was saying as she went back in. 'We need to put pressure on Martin, ask around some more. Do some door to doors with the neighbours. What about the witness in the pub? Has he turned up yet?'

'Bert Cartwright.'

'Yes. What was it he said?'

Geraldine checked her notes. 'He told us Martin and Barker had an argument on Saturday. He thought Martin was going to hit Barker. The landlord also told us Martin and Barker had a disagreement, but he's tight lipped. I don't think we'll get much out of him.'

'Well, let's see what we can find out,' Ryder said. He sounded worried.

The pub was empty when they walked in.

'You told us Raymond Barker and Callum Martin were arguing on Saturday,' Peterson said. The landlord didn't respond. 'Do you have any idea what they were arguing about?'

'It just looked as though they were angry. I could be mistaken.' Peterson pointed out the serious consequences of withholding information. 'I can't withhold information I haven't got, can I?'

'What about Monday night?' Geraldine asked.

'The night of the fire at Ray's place?'

'Yes. Was Callum Martin in here that night?'

'Yes.'

'What time did he leave?'

The landlord thought. 'I can't say for sure. Probably around nine. He left just after Bert.' He told them he hadn't seen Bert for a few days. 'Not since Monday. It looks like he's found somewhere else to drink.'

'He's not been seen by his neighbours since Monday.'

The landlord shrugged. 'That's nothing to do with me.'

'You're not concerned about him?'

'It's not my business. People come and go.'

'Do you have any idea where he might be? Has he talked about any family?' The landlord knew nothing about Bert but his name and his drinking habits.

Geraldine and Peterson checked at Bert's flat. He wasn't there. No one had seen him.

'I get a bad feeling about this,' Geraldine said as they left. 'First Maggie Palmer, now Bert.'

'Anyone who might have information about Callum Martin conveniently disappears,' Peterson agreed.

'If only we could find Bert,' Geraldine said. 'Where the hell is he?'

# CHAPTER 53

# CAR

A young constable, Ollie Letwick, spotted a vehicle abandoned off the Harchester bypass that morning. He noticed light reflected off the back of a car concealed in the bushes as he sped past.

'Done some damage there,' he said. 'Some bugger's driven off the road.'

Ted, the driver, slowed down. 'Best take a look. Could be someone still inside.'

'Looks like it was driven deliberately off the road through a gap in the bushes. I only noticed it because the sun caught it as we went past,' Ollie said. They circled the next roundabout and drove back.

'Keep your eyes peeled, Twicky. We don't want to go shooting past it.'

'It's not easy. These bushes all look the same.'

They went straight past and had to go round the next roundabout and return again.

'I hope this is going to be worth it,' Ted groused as he swung the wheel again. 'There it is!' Ollie shouted. They pulled up and jumped out of the car. 'Bloody hell. It's the stolen vehicle the DCI's been looking for.' He started talking rapidly into his radio, confirming the registration number. If it had been an accident, the car would most likely have crashed as soon as it veered off the road, but it had been manoeuvred neatly along a gap between the trees, smashing a path through outstretched twigs and brambles. It looked as though someone had been trying to conceal the vehicle in the vegetation only to crash into a tree trunk before it had been completely hidden from the road.

SOCOs arrived promptly. It wasn't easy for them to access the car but they wanted to examine it before moving it. DI Steel turned up and paced the pavement, talking to DS Peterson. Ollie tried to listen to what she was saying but was only able to catch snatches of conversation against the noise of passing traffic.

'They have to find something . . .' he heard her say.

The DS nodded. 'Found the vehicle . . .' he said.

Next time she passed, Ollie heard her mention a name, '. . . Martin . . .' Then she turned away, and the rest of her words were lost in the roar of a passing lorry.

The constable returned to the patrol car where his colleague sat patiently awaiting instructions.

'It must be a thrill,' Ollie said as he slipped back in the car, 'being a detective. I wouldn't want to work for her, though.'

'Why's that then?'

'She strikes me as the bossy type. You know.' His

companion shrugged. They watched DI Steel as she walked up and down, talking. Sergeant Peterson was bending down to listen to her. 'He's a good bloke, that DS,' Ollie went on. 'He's all right. What do you reckon to the DI then?' There was a pause as they both sat watching Geraldine.

'Reckon she gets the job done,' Ted replied at last. 'I reckon she's sharp as needles.' Ollie nodded. 'They say she's good,' Ted went on, voluble now that he had begun. 'I heard she once made an arrest before the DCI had even got going on the investigation. That's why they promoted her so quick. Bit of a know it all.'

'I heard that too,' Ollie agreed. 'I don't know that I'd like to work for her though,' he repeated.

'No. You're right there. Bossy women are the worst. She's quite a looker though.'

They paused, thinking. A call came through and the driver took it.

'Domestic in Garden Street,' he said and they pulled away. 'Neighbours called it in.'

'Never a dull moment,' Ollie said cheerfully. Ted grunted. Unlike his young companion, he had been on the job too long to feel anything but dejected about a domestic brawl.

SOCOs found nothing of interest when they examined the car among the trees. Despite the bright artificial lighting they had rigged up, the working conditions were awkward. In the end they decided to move the stolen car to the workshop. It was beginning to rain by the time they prepared to tow the car away. Geraldine watched them edge it backwards, away from a tree which had become unstable with the impact. A local tree surgeon was standing by to secure it. The car had been severely damaged when it crashed into the tree making it impossible to gather any information from the front of the vehicle to confirm whether it had been used to run over Maggie Palmer.

'They'll have to look again,' the DCI told Geraldine when she reported back to him.

'We'll keep looking until we find something, sir. There must be something, some thread from the victim's trousers, or a blood spot, something. They'll find it when they check again. They have to.'

'This isn't CSI,' James Ryder reminded her with a worried smile. 'More's the pity. We could do with a dramatic breakthrough. And a few glamorous women,' he added with an attempt at a light-hearted laugh. Geraldine forced a grin.

The forensic officers checked the car over again in the workshop, scrutinising the bent bumper, the radiator grill and the crumpled metal for any sign of a previous impact. The car was put up on ramps, and SOCOs began examining the underside.

'Found anything?' Geraldine asked when she visited the workshop.

A white coated figure looked up from the vehicle. 'We've only just started underneath,' he replied. He nodded at her. 'Don't touch anything,' he added unnecessarily. He flicked the bottom rim of a door and a fine cloud of rust flew from it. 'Give us a half hour or so. If you want to go back to the station, you can call us from there.'

'I'll wait here, if that's all right with you.' She walked away and leaned against the wall, waiting as the white coated figures conducted their painstaking scrutiny. She knew she wouldn't be able to relax at the station.

After half an hour, one of the team called out. 'Over here, sir.' Geraldine started forward. One of the team was shining a bright light on the underside of a back tyre. Geraldine walked round and squinted at it.

'Is it blood?' she asked as one of the men took a sample from the inner side of the tyre tread.

'Looks like blood. We'll need to confirm it. Why don't you get off now and we'll let you know the results as soon as.'

Geraldine returned to the station.

'Any news?' Peterson asked her as she hurried through the Incident Room.

'Maybe, nothing confirmed yet.'

'Well?'

'SOCOs think they've found a trace of blood on the back tyre of the Honda. They're testing it now and will send over their findings as soon as they can.' She waited at her desk, unable to focus on reading reports. At last her phone rang. The blood was human. It would take a while to match the DNA, but the blood type matched Maggie Palmer's.

SOCOs were all over the car checking the boot, the seats and flooring, crawling over every millimetre of it, inside and out.

James Ryder called the team together to bring everyone up to speed with the new developments. 'If they can find a cigarette butt, all our troubles will be over.' He tried to speak lightly, but his voice was taut. The tension in the Incident Room was almost tangible. Everyone spoke in hushed voices, as though making too much noise would interfere with the work of SOCOs in the workshop.

It was seven o'clock by the time Geraldine reached home to discover six missed calls on her phone, all from Hannah. Nothing from Celia. Her relief at Celia's silence had soured with disappointment. It seemed their shared past had meant nothing to her adopted sister. In the meantime, there was Hannah. Geraldine fortified herself with a glass of chilled white wine before she picked up the phone.

'At last,' Hannah said. 'Well? What happened? What did he say?' There was a pause. 'What did he say?' she repeated, sounding slightly hysterical.

'I'm thinking. All right. I went in and he asked me what I wanted. He didn't ask after you, just 'What do you want?', like that.' She took a sip of her wine. 'I told him I'm worried about you, said you were very upset and he ought to talk to you.'

'And? What did he say?'

'He said he just needed some space. He's tired, and that's all. He said he'd talk to you when he was ready and it was between the two of you and nothing to do with me. Which is fair enough,' she added recklessly. 'I mean, I don't know what you expected me to say.'

Hannah let out a wail. 'I told you. You were supposed to make him realise he can't just walk out like that.'

'He said he needs some time to think. Maybe you should just give him a bit of space. He'll come back when he's ready.'

'And if he doesn't?'

'I'm sure he will, Hannah. Why wouldn't he? I'm sure it'll work out fine in the end.'

'That's easy for you to say,' Hannah moaned. 'But what about the children? What happens to them if he doesn't come back? What happens then?'

'Then you'll just have to cope,' Geraldine replied. She regretted her harsh words as soon as she had spoken. 'I'm sorry, Hannah, I just don't know what you expect me to do. I can't make Jeremy do what you want. I have no influence over him at all. Now I really have to get back to work.'

'Your precious work,' Hannah snapped and hung up. Geraldine hesitated, uncertain what she could say to make Hannah feel better. She decided to give her friend time to calm down before calling her back. She pulled a report out of her bag, poured herself another glass of wine, and was just setting to work when the phone rang. With a sigh, Geraldine put down her file and prepared to listen to Hannah.

It was nearly midnight when she was finally able to settle down to her reading. There had to be some indication of intent in Callum Martin's statements, some slip that might help to crack the case. But if there was, she didn't find it. They still couldn't establish who had been driving the car that had run over Maggie Palmer.

Three times.

# CHAPTER 54

# HOSPITAL

Geraldine called in at the hospital on her way to work on Friday morning. The corridor was quiet, apart from an irritating hum from the lights. Geraldine approached the desk and waited until the nurse finished on the phone before showing her warrant card.

The nurse pointed her in the direction of Barker's room. 'Just for a minute, Inspector. The doctor said you mustn't disturb him. In any case, he's due his medication shortly. The doctor will be doing her rounds soon. You've just got time to catch him before she gets here.'

A young constable standing in the corridor opened the door and Geraldine saw that Barker was in a room on his own. One of his eyes was still hidden by bandages that swathed his head. The other was closed.

Geraldine approached the bed. 'Raymond Barker.'

He gave a faint groan. One bloodshot eye stared up at her with a flicker of recognition. 'I seen,' he croaked. His hoarse voice was barely audible. 'I seen.' Geraldine took another step forward. A faint whiff of burning mingled with the strong

345

smell of disinfectant. Barker's pale eye glared watery.

'You saw who did this?' she prompted him.

Behind her a nurse entered the room. 'Doctor's here on her morning rounds.'

'No,' Barker rasped. He tried to move his head and groaned again. 'I saw.'

'Time's up, Inspector,' the nurse interrupted. 'Raymond needs his rest.' She adjusted the drip and his eye closed.

'I saw,' he mumbled but his speech was slurred.

'Who did you see?' Geraldine asked urgently. 'Was it Callum Martin?'

'Inspector,' the nurse interrupted.

'Not him,' Barker whispered. Geraldine leaned over the bed to hear. 'Not him.' His lips quivered but he made no sound.

'Was it a man or a woman you saw?' The lips didn't move. 'Mr Barker, Ray, blink if it was a man.' He didn't respond.

The nurse turned to Geraldine and gestured for her to leave the room. 'The doctor's on her way.'

'When will I be able to speak to him again?'

'That's for the doctor to decide. Anyway, the patient's very confused at the moment. You won't get much sense out of him.'

'But—'

'I'm afraid he's going to be heavily sedated for a few days. He's not likely to be coherent for a while. Shock, compounded by medication.'

'How long until I can talk to him again?'

The nurse shrugged. 'I'm sure the hospital will be in touch.' She took Geraldine by the arm and ushered her out of the room. In the corridor, the young PC was chatting to a nurse. He stopped talking and straightened up as Geraldine passed.

'Call me as soon as he wakes up.'

'Yes, ma'am.'

The briefing was about to begin as Geraldine arrived at the station.

Ryder broke off what he was saying and looked expectantly at her. 'I was just saying you were at the hospital questioning Barker.'

Geraldine looked around the assembled faces. 'Barker told me he saw his attacker this time,' she began. The room was hushed. Footsteps echoed along the corridor outside. 'But that's about all he did say.' A barely audible groan seemed to rise from the floor. 'He was so heavily drugged he could barely speak. I asked him if it was Callum Martin who attacked him and he denied it. He tried to say something else, but I'm not sure what.'

'I hope he'll have something to say about Callum Martin when he's able to make a statement. In the meantime I've arranged frogmen to search the canal near where Cartwright's glasses were found.' The DCI paused. It was five days since the old man had disappeared. 'What about Sophie Cliff?' Ryder tapped Barker's picture on the Incident Board as he spoke. 'Sophie Cliff blames Barker for Thomas Cliff's death and when we fail to bring him to justice, as she sees

347

it, she takes matters into her own hands and goes after Barker herself.'

'She's got an alibi,' Geraldine reminded them. 'We've had confirmation from every taxi firm and car hire company in the South East. Unless she borrowed a car from someone she knew, there's no way she could've done the journey in time. Not on Saturday or Monday.'

'What about friends? Could someone have given her a lift? Lent her a car?'

'We've been asking around, her work colleagues, her mother-in-law, local CID have interviewed her parents again. Nothing. But there's something funny about it, isn't there? Why did she go to Sandmouth just then?'

'She probably needed to get away,' Polly piped up. 'Perhaps it all got too much for her, losing her husband like that.'

'Perhaps she hitchhiked?' Bennett suggested. They were clutching at straws.

'Too unreliable,' someone else answered. 'Not with such a tight schedule. And in any case, no one hitchhikes these days.'

The DCI shook his head. 'Too many bloody convenient alibis,' he said, not for the first time. He sounded angry. 'Forget Sophie Cliff for the moment. She wasn't involved in the hit and run—'

'As far as we know,' Geraldine pointed out.

The DCI ignored the interruption. 'Is there a connection between the attacks on Barker and Maggie Palmer's murder?'

348

'Someone's lying,' Geraldine said.

'Barker, Martin, Sophie Cliff, they could all be lying, the whole bloody lot of them,' Peterson added.

'What about the girlfriend?' someone asked. 'She's a woman.'

'Just about,' Bennett interjected.

'Brenda?' the DCI frowned. 'She was there in the house—'

'She's a complete fruit cake,' Peterson took over. 'If you ask me, she'd be capable of anything. She doesn't know what she's doing.'

'Let's talk to her again. If Martin's trying to cover his tracks, he could well have used Brenda as his accomplice. He kills the market trader who might be able to lead us to them. He attacks Barker on the way home from the pub, and when that fails, he gets Brenda to set fire to the house.'

'With her in it. She was upstairs when the fire started. If she was responsible, surely even she would have had the sense to leave the house, not go upstairs where she could well have burned to death,' Geraldine pointed out. 'We can try talking to her, sir, but it's almost impossible to get any sense out of her.'

The DCI frowned. 'OK, you can find out your schedules from the duty sergeant. I don't need to remind you we need to work fast on this, and we need to be thorough. Someone has made two unsuccessful attempts on Raymond Barker's life. Whoever it is, they might try again. We've got round the clock surveillance on Barker while he's in hospital, but he's not going to be there forever. Let's sort this mess out before he's discharged.'

No one spoke. They all knew the longer the case dragged on, the less chance they would have of finding Barker's assailant. And they were looking for someone intent on murder.

# PART V

*'then must you speak
Of one that loved not wisely but too well'*

*Othello* – William Shakespeare

# CHAPTER 55

# LAGOON

The Blue Lagoon looked very different without its mask of tawdry glamour. Curtains that appeared plush under red lamps showed threadbare in the light of day. The floor was streaked with a grimy concoction of cigarette ash and spilt booze. Small chairs stood in disarray where they had been left in the early hours of the morning beside tables littered with empty bottles and dirty glasses.

'Don't they clear up?' the sergeant asked. He wrinkled his nose in disgust. As if in answer to his question, a hunched woman appeared with a mop and bucket. She set them down with a clatter. Whipping a jay cloth from her overalls, she began scooping empty bottles and cans into a black bin liner, and smearing the tables with her rag.

'Sod those bloody girls.' She hobbled over to the bar for a tray. 'Never clean up their crap. Not my job to clear the glasses.' She eyed Geraldine and Peterson suspiciously. 'What's your game then?' She turned her back on them without waiting for an answer and busied herself filling the tray with dirty glasses, muttering as she shuffled between the tables.

'We're looking for Bronxy,' Geraldine announced. The cleaner ignored her. Geraldine nodded towards the back of the room. Peterson followed her to the office. Geraldine rapped once and turned the handle. The door opened.

Bronxy was sitting at her desk.

'We'd like to speak to Callum Martin. We'll speak to him alone.'

Bronxy smiled. 'I know, Inspector. You people don't like witnesses.'

'Just normal procedure.'

'When it suits you.'

Geraldine had spent the best part of a day researching Bronxy's past, looking for something to help them persuade Bronxy to retract the alibi she had given Callum Martin. Reluctantly, Geraldine had admitted defeat. It could take years to penetrate the smokescreen of aliases and false leads.

'Please tell Callum Martin we'd like to speak to him.'

Bronxy rose to her feet and walked to the door, moving like a cat in high heels. Geraldine promptly crossed the room and sat down behind the desk. 'We'll speak to him in here. If that's convenient.'

Bronxy glanced over her shoulder and shrugged. The door closed.

'You don't think he's done a runner, do you, gov?' Peterson voiced Geraldine's suspicion under his breath. She didn't answer. They waited. Finally the door opened. Callum Martin walked in. He was bleary eyed. Three of the scratches on his cheek looked scabby. The fourth glistened wetly.

'Mr Martin, we're investigating the fire at your home on Monday night. Can you go over your movements that evening for us?'

'I've told you where I was.'

Geraldine flipped open her notebook. 'We need to run through those times again.'

'Why? I already told you. It's nearly a week ago. I can't be expected to remember everything that happened a week ago, can I? I know your game. You think I was born yesterday. You've got it all written down, everything I told you last time, so if I don't tell you exactly the same you'll make out I'm telling lies, making it all up.' He shook his head. 'I'm not falling for that one. I'm not a bloody idiot. I can't remember anything except what I told you before. That's all I remember. So if that's it, I'll be off.'

'Mr Martin, someone set fire to your house. Surely you want to help us find out who did it?'

Martin scowled. 'Go on then. Ask your questions.'

'We're trying to pin down the time the fire started,' Geraldine lied. Peterson took out his note book. 'It must've been some time after you went out. You were alone, weren't you? What time was that?'

Callum lit a cigarette and blew the smoke

355

towards Geraldine. 'She was watching Coronation Street.' He took another drag of his cigarette. 'She likes Coronation Street, Brenda does. Load of rubbish. I must've fallen asleep. I woke up when it finished. So I went out for a jar. She asked to come with me, but she wasn't even dressed. At that time of night. Slut.' He paused to inhale. 'I wasn't going to wait for her to sort herself out, and as for Ray, he couldn't even walk, the sorry bastard. So I went out by myself.' He paused to inhale again. 'I went to the pub. I stayed for a while, just drinking, you know. I didn't talk to anyone. The landlord will tell you I was there. Why don't you ask him?'

'Mr Martin, you're not a suspect,' Geraldine lied again. 'We're merely interested in establishing the time the fire started. Are you sure you went straight to the pub?'

'Yes.'

'Did you see anyone loitering outside your house as you were leaving?'

'No.'

'And you were in the bar all the time?'

'Yes.'

'Drinking by youself all evening?'

Martin lit another cigarette before he answered. He spoke very slowly. 'I was in the bar for a while. By myself. Ask the landlord if you don't believe me.'

'Did you go straight home when you left?'

Martin considered. 'No. I took a walk to clear

my head. When I went home I saw flashing blue lights as I turned the corner. The fire had already started. It must've been about ten o'clock, when I got home.'

'Did anyone see you, out walking?'

Martin shrugged. 'How the hell would I know? It was dark.'

They interviewed Brenda next but it was pointless. She didn't even seem to remember the fire at her home.

'Fire?' she repeated, eyes vacant. 'What? Where's Cal?' Her hands trembled at her sides.

'That was a waste of time,' Geraldine complained as they left the Blue Lagoon. She took a deep breath, relieved to escape the stale air of the club.

'Where to now, gov?'

Geraldine hesitated. 'Let's take a trip to the seaside,' she said at last. Peterson gave a boyish whoop and Geraldine grinned.

It was a beautiful afternoon. They bowled along gentle inclines as the motorway led them through open countryside. It felt good to leave the confines of the town behind. Peterson drove at eighty down a wide sweep of tan coloured tarmac, golden in the sunlight. Many trees were still in leaf, russet, flaming orange and yellow with occasional evergreens, dark and dramatic. Although they were on a job, Geraldine felt an uplifting sensation of holiday. There was nothing for her to do but gaze out of the window. Too tired to think, she stared at fields rolling past, yellowing at the approach of winter.

'I've never been much of a one for the country-side,' Peterson commented after a while. 'Can't see what there is to get excited about.'

'It's not at its best this time of the year. It looks very different in the summer.'

'Yes, it must look very different in the summer. And the winter. Imagine all this, covered in snow. Funny when you think about it, how different things can look.'

Geraldine was thinking about the people who had hired cars in Sandmouth on 22nd November. CCTV footage of customers, and of cars driving out of Sandmouth in the direction of Harchester on the evenings of 22nd and 24th, had been scrutinised. Only one woman had made both journeys, Bobbie Geere. Geraldine thought about what the sergeant had said. Things didn't always look the same.

'What if?' she began.

'What's that, gov?'

'I was just thinking about the old woman who hired a car and drove from Sandmouth to Harchester . . . Could she have been Sophie Cliff?'

'In disguise, you mean?' Peterson sounded animated. 'With a false name?'

Geraldine called the station. 'We need to check if Sophie Cliff could have printed out a driving licence . . . a false one . . . she worked in IT . . . Yes . . . and any internet café in the area. Check in Sandmouth and Harchester and anywhere else within reach . . . And have another search for the

358

woman called Bobbie Geere.' She hung up. An atmosphere of excitement pervaded the air between them.

Geraldine stared ahead, impatient. 'Another half hour and we'll reach the top of a hill and be able to see the sea,' she said. Peterson shrugged. As though mirroring the sky, the road surface changed to grey. They passed a sign: SANDMOUTH 25.

'Another half an hour,' the sergeant agreed. 'Probably less. We're making good time. Should be there in twenty minutes – if the road's clear.' Geraldine wondered what they were going to discover when they reached Sandmouth. 'Let's hope it turns out to be worth the effort,' Peterson added, expressing Geraldine's misgivings. 'What's the betting they'll have Sophie Cliff on CCTV all Monday evening, and we'll be back to square one.'

Geraldine stared out of the window.

# CHAPTER 56

# EXCELSIOR

The Excelsior Hotel stood in its own grounds on the cliff top. It was opulently furnished in the style of a bygone era, with elegant cream and crimson flock wallpaper and dark red carpets and drapes. The modern chrome and black leather of the bar looked out of place beside the grandeur of the foyer and lounge. Geraldine and Peterson took a quick look around. A group of men in the bar were talking in loud voices. Geraldine listened, out of habit, as she walked by.

'. . . and then he hooked the ball into the rough.' Ubiquitous

music was playing, a beat without a tune. There was a faint clatter of cutlery in the background. Geraldine moved on, past a vase of tall yellow lilies. She turned away. Since her mother's funeral she had disliked the heavy scent of lilies.

A couple of women were chatting over coffee. 'It was perfect, but the only one in my size had a mark on it.'

'Oh, unlucky.'

Geraldine followed Peterson back to the foyer. The girl behind the desk was on the phone.

Geraldine thought that they must look like a couple waiting to check in. She wondered how it would feel, arriving at the hotel with Ian Peterson beside her, not as a colleague but as a companion. A boyfriend. She dismissed the thought with an involuntary shake of her head.

'You all right, gov?'

'Sorry to keep you waiting,' the receptionist said. Geraldine brushed past the sergeant and displayed her identity card.

'We're checking the arrival and departure dates for a Mrs Sophie Cliff who stayed here earlier in the week.'

The girl entered the name and scanned her screen. 'Yes,' she said, 'Mrs Cliff stayed here this week.' She checked her screen again. 'She arrived on Saturday morning and checked out on Tuesday after breakfast.' Although she had been on the desk that week she could tell them little about Mrs Cliff's movements. 'She stayed in room two hundred and thirteen. There's someone else in two hundred and thirteen now. I don't think you can go in.' She looked worried. 'But I do remember the woman from two thirteen, now I come to think of it, because she was a bit . . .'

'Yes?'

'Well, first of all when she arrived she said she had no idea how long she'd be staying. And she was – scruffy.' The girl hesitated and lowered her voice. Geraldine stepped closer. 'She looked – well, as though she needed a shower, if you know what I mean. And she had this vague look, as though she wasn't all there. To be honest, she gave me the creeps. I think she went out walking during the day,' she added, trying to be helpful.

'Walking?'

'Most of our guests play golf or walk on the cliff path.' She looked up as a group of men in golfing gear approached the desk. 'Excuse me, I'll just be—'

'I'd like to speak to the manager,' Geraldine interrupted her.

An earnest hotel manager took them into his office. He looked about twenty and seemed flustered by Geraldine's questions.

'We haven't had any problems with guests before,' he apologised, as though he was somehow responsible for the police enquiry.

The manager confirmed that Mrs Cliff had eaten breakfast in the dining room on Sunday, Monday and Tuesday mornings. She had eaten there on Saturday, Sunday and Monday at seven in the evening.

'Can you be sure about those times?'

The manager checked his database. 'Just a minute, yes, here it is. She checked into the dining room on Saturday, Sunday and,' he clicked the mouse, 'Monday evenings at seven exactly. Guests often eat early when they've been out walking all day. The views from the cliff tops here are spectacular.'

'Can you tell us how long she stayed in the dining room in the evenings?'

He shook his head. 'No. We sign guests into the dining room, for billing purposes, but we don't record what time they leave. I could ask the waiting staff, but I don't suppose they'd remember.'

'Where might she have gone after the dining room?' Peterson asked.

'She might have gone to the bar area, or to her room. Our rooms are very well appointed—'

'Do you have CCTV in the car park?' Geraldine interrupted his spiel. He nodded. 'Do you still have the footage from Saturday and Monday evenings?'

The manager drummed his fingers on his desk top. 'We keep it for thirty days, but your colleague's already asked about that. He took it away with him so I suppose it's still at the local police station. You could check with him.'

They took a statement from the manager. He sighed when they asked to be shown along the corridor on the second floor. He led the way, glancing at his watch but polite enough. Room two hundred and thirteen was situated at the end of a long corridor, opposite the lift.

'How easy would it be for a guest to leave the building without being seen?'

The manager told them it was impossible for anyone to enter or leave the building unobserved. 'Our security system is second to none.' The stairs and lift both led down to the entry hall, in full view of the reception desk and the porter, who doubled as a security guard. Access to the foyer and the entrance were covered by CCTV cameras.

'Is there any other means of access to the building, other than the lift or the stairs?'

'Only the staff lift, which is protected by a PIN code. All the fire exits are linked to the main alarm system, we have CCTV cameras at the back exit, and all the windows on the ground floor are kept locked. The insurance company insist on it,' he added. 'We're a very safe place to stay. We never have any problems with intruders. You can check our insurance records.'

'So there's no way anyone could leave or return to the building unseen?' Peterson asked again when they were back in the manager's office.

The manager shook his head. 'It's quite impossible. Unless . . .'

'Unless?'

'We do get busy when there's a function on.' He checked his screen again. 'Saturday was busy. It usually is. A wedding party. We had an influx of guests at around eight. The hall was heaving. But the ballroom's downstairs and we watch the stairs and lift carefully. No one could have gone up to the rooms without being seen. The porters do lift duty and check guests' room numbers, for security purposes.'

'But someone could have left the building unobserved in the melee?' Geraldine persisted.

'Of course. There's no reason why they couldn't have done so. It was a function. People are always free to go in and out downstairs. But no one can go up to the rooms without being seen.'

'But she'd have had to get back in again,' Peterson pointed out. 'We know she came downstairs to get to breakfast in the morning. How did she get back upstairs without being seen?'

'What time did the guests leave?'

'The function closed at midnight.'

'So the hall would've been busy then?'

The manager frowned. 'Look, Inspector, I'm not sure what you're getting at, but I can assure you our security measures are second to none,' he repeated.

'It's possible Sophie Cliff could have got in and out of the building on Saturday evening without being seen,' Peterson said as they went back to the foyer, 'but what about Monday night? Local CID checked the CCTV and they didn't see her or anyone like her using the lift or the stairs.'

On their way out, Geraldine stopped to speak to a porter. 'I wasn't on duty on Monday,' he said. 'That would've been Bern. He's not in today but he'll be on duty tomorrow.' Geraldine quizzed the old man for a while, but he couldn't help. She wandered outside to think.

Peterson went over to the desk and chatted to the receptionist. 'What about keys?' he asked. 'Can you check when a room's occupied through the electronic keys?'

'No. Some hotels have that facility but our system's not that sophisticated. We encourage guests to leave their keys at the desk when they go out, just in case we need to evacuate. The smoke alarms go off all the time. We had one go off only last week. We had to get everyone out, and of course it turned out to be a false alarm. We had to go along the corridors banging on doors in case anyone was in, because they don't always think to leave their keys when they go out so we don't know who's in and who's out. It happens all the time. Whenever a guest leaves the door of the shower room open, the steam sets off the smoke alarm. We put signs up in every room, please close the cubicle door, but they still do it. Some idiot leaves the door open and it's everybody out.' She pulled a face and smiled at the sergeant.

'Did you evacuate the hotel on Monday evening?'

'Yes, I think we did, but only for a few minutes. We only had half the guests out. The shower had been turned off and we sorted it out pretty quickly. Sometimes the guest's in the shower, and then they don't always hear the alarm—'

'Is it possible for you to tell us which room the alarm was set off from?'

The girl checked her screen, typing rapidly. 'Room two hundred and thirteen. It's on the second floor. Oh, that's where that woman you were asking about was staying. How's that for a funny coincidence.' She looked up, but the sergeant was already running out of the building, looking for Geraldine.

By now she had walked to the edge of the patio and was gazing out past the cliff top across a grey ocean, wondering what lay below the ruffled surface. The clouds broke, letting through a shaft of winter sunlight. Brilliant dots flickered on the water far below reminding Geraldine of the blue ocean she had seen in Dubrovnik.

# CHAPTER 57

# SUSPICION

Geraldine drove fast on the way back. It took just over an hour.

'At night you could do it in forty minutes,' she said as they reached the outskirts of Harchester. Peterson grunted. He had been unusually quiet on the journey back as though reluctant to return home. The closer they got, the more morose he became. Geraldine glanced across at him. 'Is everything all right?' He grunted again but didn't answer. 'Is it Bev?' she hazarded and was rewarded with a slightly more articulate noise. It could have been, 'Yes.'

'Do you want to talk about it?' she asked gently.

'Nothing to talk about,' he answered gruffly adding, after a pause, 'Bev's left me.'

'Are you all right?'

'I'm fine.'

'Is there anything I can do?' It was a clumsy question, but she didn't know what else to say. She liked Ian Peterson and felt genuine sympathy for his misery. At the same time, she was aware that her friendly impulse wasn't entirely unselfish. Peterson seemed to have no problem attracting women.

He would soon find another girlfriend. Geraldine was the one in need of friendship.

'She's left me. That's all there is to it.'

'Left you?'

'We had a row, she packed a bag. She left.' They drove on in silence. 'Tell you what, gov,' Peterson said as they pulled into the station car park. 'How about that drink?' Geraldine smiled, relieved. 'On one condition,' he added.

'What's that?'

'Two conditions, actually. We don't talk about the case and we don't mention Bev.'

'You're on.'

'And you did say the first round's on you?' They both laughed.

'So, I've got to watch what I say,' Geraldine grinned as she handed the sergeant a pint in the pub over the road to the police station. 'Here you are. Drown your sorrows.'

'I'll tell you what,' he said, 'I haven't had time to mope about Bev all day.' Geraldine smiled. Peterson finished his pint and stood up.

'Just a half,' Geraldine told him but he shook his head. 'I get it. Now you've had a pint off me, you're leaving,' she laughed. 'No time for—'

'Let's go somewhere else,' he interrupted her. 'They'll all be piling in here soon and . . . I just thought it might be nice to talk about something else for a change. Get away from . . .' he rolled his eyes around the bar, 'all this. Just for an hour or so.' Geraldine stood up and reached for her bag.

They found a quiet pub along the river on the other side of the motorway, past Ashford, where the river took a meander away from the railway line.

'This is nice,' Peterson said. He leaned on the rail and looked out over the water. It was a clear night. The river rippled faintly below them in the moonlight. Geraldine shivered. 'Want to go inside?' he asked. She smiled at his acuteness.

'I'm fine out here.' And she was.

After a while they went in. Cheered by the warmth of the pub, Geraldine relaxed. Their easy chat drifted back to their colleagues. Avoiding any mention of the case, they gossiped inconsequentially.

'Don't tell me you didn't know Polly's got a crush on you?'

Peterson turned away and coughed to hide his embarrassment. Geraldine laughed. 'And what about you and the DCI?' he asked. Although annoyed at being the subject of gossip, Geraldine didn't mind her name being linked with the DCI; she was flattered.

The evening passed pleasantly. Oddly enough, although the sergeant knew all about the case, Geraldine found she could forget about it when talking to him. He was an amusing companion, and she liked him.

'You gossip like a girl,' she told him and he grinned sheepishly. She could tell he was pleased. 'I don't usually,' he assured her. 'Only with you.'

'I'll take that as a compliment.'

After dropping the sergeant back at the station, Geraldine went home to type up her report. She poured herself a large glass of wine before sitting down to work. The image of an old man drinking alone in a corner of a pub crossed her mind. She hesitated before pouring her wine down the kitchen sink. The she brewed a pot of coffee.

Next morning she sat at her desk wondering if Sophie Cliff could have paid someone else to assault Barker but the bungled attacks weren't the work of a professional. As she tussled with possibilities, which grew more far fetched with each new thought, the duty sergeant tapped on her door. The DCI was on his way.

'We've found Bert Cartwright.' Ryder looked grim. 'He's been in the canal for about five days.'

'The body's been in the water all this time, without anyone seeing it?' someone asked.

'The divers brought him up with a bag of bricks tied round his neck. Whoever lifted it was strong. It seems unlikely Cartwright could have done that by himself.' There was a long pause.

'Bang goes any help Cartwright could have given us,' Peterson said. They had been hoping Cartwright had gone into hiding out of fear, because he had information on Martin. They had done their best to find the old man before Martin did. And all the while, he had been lying at the bottom of the canal.

'Maybe the PM will tell us something,' the DCI said. He didn't sound optimistic. 'Now, what else have we got?'

Geraldine sketched out her theory. 'Sophie Cliff booked into the Excelsior Hotel in Sandmouth for an open ended visit, stayed there until she'd achieved what she was there to do, then checked out on Tuesday morning, believing Raymond Barker had died in the fire she'd started in his house the previous evening. She could've slipped out under cover of a wedding party at around eight on Saturday evening, discovered Barker was in the pub, waited and attacked him on his way home at around eleven, returned to the hotel and slipped back in as all the guests were leaving.'

'A lucky coincidence,' the DCI remarked.

'Not really, sir. It would've been easy enough for her to have checked what time the function finished so she'd know what time to return. It just fell right that she found Barker alone. She could've been stalking him, waiting for her chance. Only he didn't die. She must've found out about that in the paper. Or she could have phoned the hospital. So she tried again. On Monday she set off an evacuation of guests from the hotel. She could've slipped up to her room after a quick dinner, set off the alarm at seven thirty, turned off the shower, and left the hotel in all the confusion of the alarm. Suppose she left at seven forty, she'd be back in Harchester at around eight twenty, just in time to see Martin arrive at the pub. Seeing Barker wasn't with him, she could have broken into the house, found Barker, started the fire and left at eight thirty, to arrive back in the hotel at around nine fifteen. I daresay if we examine the footage, we might see her go back in although it's impossible to identify some of the guests, all bundled up in hats and scarves. It's feasible she made the journeys, but we're still left with the question of how she managed to get hold of a false licence.'

'She could've used a stolen vehicle,' Bennett said.

'Or bought one,' someone else suggested. They discussed the possibilities.

'Perhaps she stole a car and it hasn't been reported yet.'

'The owner might be away.'

'She could have borrowed a car.'

'Or bought one. A cheap banger. A private sale.'

'There'd be no record.'

Geraldine was depressed by all the speculation. They were going round in circles. Sophie's movements might be almost impossible to trace. Geraldine put forward her theory that the suspect had hired a car under a false name, and travelled in disguise. Even she had to agree it sounded far fetched.

'Check out all reports of stolen vehicles,' the DCI said. He looked thoughtful. 'But if she was using a stolen vehicle . . .'

The briefing broke up in an atmosphere of frustration. The optimism at the beginning of the case had faded rapidly. They were no closer to arresting the person responsible for Evelyn Green and Thomas Cliff's deaths and since the investigation had opened Maggie Palmer and Bert Cartwright had been killed and someone had tried to murder Raymond Barker. All the records had been checked by constables, but Geraldine took copies of all the schedules from cab and car hire firms, stations and bus timetables, and known details of stolen vehicles, home with her. There were a lot of papers, but if there was anything to indicate how Sophie Cliff could have returned to Harchester undetected, she was determined to find it. There was always a possibility something had been overlooked.

Having drawn a blank with Sophie Cliff, Geraldine looked at Callum Martin again. The whole case seemed to be unravelling, going nowhere. She was absorbed in trying to work out how they might crack Martin's alibi when Craig phoned to discuss what they were going to do that evening. His cheerful voice jarred with her desperation. She answered more curtly than she had intended.

'Sorry, I can't spare the time right now.'

'It's Saturday night,' he protested.

'I'm sorry, my work's no respecter of weekends. I've got some reports I must get through. We're looking for a stolen car—'

'Can't it wait?'

'No. I'm sorry. It really can't.' She explained that there was a killer on the loose and lives could be at risk. Her words sounded melodramatic. Craig would think she was making excuses.

There was a brief pause before he offered to pick her up the next day for an early supper. Geraldine knew she would be working all day, but she agreed to spend the evening with him. Sunday was technically her day off. She had to see Craig if their relationship was to stand a chance. He already sounded as though he might be losing interest in her, if he had ever been seriously interested in her in the first place.

'What time shall I pick you up? Let's make it early. I know this really nice little pub by the river.'

'Sounds lovely,' Geraldine replied. She was already flicking through the next report she had pulled out of her bag.

Geraldine worked late into the night trying to trace stolen vehicles picked up on cameras between Harchester and Sandmouth on Saturday and Monday evenings. No evidence she found seemed to match the theory that Sophie Cliff had returned to Harchester in a stolen car. Her head was full of a jumble of names and times. She might as well have spent the evening with Craig, she thought angrily, as she climbed into a cold bed. And somewhere nearby, a killer was probably sleeping peacefully.

# CHAPTER 58

# MOVING ON

Sunday was frustrating. A couple of constables were taking phone calls, but the lines were relatively quiet. There wasn't much else going on. Bennett was around, somewhere. There was no sign of the DCI.

'It's so boring, sitting here waiting,' one of the constables complained as Geraldine walked past.

'Tell me about it,' Geraldine agreed. The waiting was the worst part.

She passed a dreary hour poring over statements, searching in vain for some detail that didn't fit. It was dull work. She had read them all before. Finding herself struggling to concentrate, she took a break to clear her head. It was raining so she went up to the canteen for a coffee.

'You any good at anagrams, Geraldine?' Bennett called to her as she went in. He had a newspaper open on the table and was doing the crossword.

'I'm afraid not.'

'Well, what about a clue then? Supports air, that's good luck.'

Geraldine shook her head. 'I haven't got the patience.' She sat down opposite him.

'Good luck,' Bennett muttered. 'Lucky . . . What's another word for good luck?'

'Serendipity. Fortune.'

'That's it! Of course. Good luck is fortune. For-tune. Don't you get it? When you support something, you're for it, and an air is another word for a tune. Well done.' Geraldine wondered if Bennett had ever been this animated about his work. 'What about this one?'

'Sorry, Les. It's all too clever for me.'

'It's really not difficult.' He put his pen down. 'It's just a question of substituting the right word for the clue.'

Geraldine smiled. 'I'm sorry but I can't get excited about crosswords. Playing with words just doesn't do it for me.'

'One more clue?'

Geraldine shook her head and sighed. That wasn't the sort of clue she needed right now. She finished her coffee and went back to her desk, leaving Bennett puzzling over his crossword.

Free from distraction, Geraldine should have been able to work her way through a great deal, but there was nothing demanding her attention apart from routine paperwork. Her thoughts kept wandering to Maggie Palmer. Presumably her children would miss her, but they were too young to deal with funeral arrangements and all the inconvenient paraphernalia of death.

She shied away from the memory of her own mother's funeral, and her thoughts led her to Celia.

It was a week since they had seen each other, at their mother's house. When she reached home, Geraldine picked up the phone and dialled Celia's number but before the connection was made she put the phone down. She didn't have the energy for an emotional scene right now. Craig would be picking her up in less than an hour. She had to get ready. Celia would have to wait. In any case, Celia hadn't called her. Perhaps Celia wasn't ready to meet either.

It was late afternoon, and cold, as Craig drove her out of town along country lanes lined with a bright carpet of fallen leaves. In the distant glare of sunset, trees blazed with a few remaining flickers of russet. Some had already lost all their foliage, their branches stark in the wintry sun. A Bob Dylan CD was playing. The melancholy strains suited the scenery.

Craig took her to a pub by the river. On a summer's day it would have been lovely to sit outside overlooking the water. Indoors it was an ordinary country pub with a restaurant. The car park was full and there was nowhere to park on the street outside. They had to leave the car round the corner and walk back in the rain. As they huddled together beneath his umbrella, Geraldine found herself wishing he would offer her more than protection from the rain.

'Pity we didn't come in your car,' Craig said as they stepped inside. 'We could've left it right outside.' Geraldine didn't answer. She knew some of her colleagues used their privilege as police officers to allow them to park anywhere. Others considered it an abuse of the system. Geraldine preferred not to pass judgement, but she never used her position to park in restricted zones.

'The food's not too bad,' Craig told her as he joined her from the bar. Geraldine tried to feel optimistic when he set a cheap bottle of wine on the table. Perhaps he didn't feel the need to try and impress her, but she remembered him splashing out on expensive wines on holiday. She watched him fill their large glasses.

'Geraldine, we need to talk.' She waited. He stared down at the glass in his hand. 'Geraldine,' he began again and hesitated. She stared at the dark liquid swilling in his glass. 'I'm a regular sort of guy.' He took a gulp of wine. 'While you were on your last case, I barely saw you. When we went away together, it was different. But now it seems it's starting all over again. I'm not blaming you. It's just the way it is. I do admire your dedication and I understand you feel you have to give a hundred per cent to your job. But I'm not sure I want a girlfriend who may be called away at a moment's notice to prioritise her work for weeks on end. I know it's not your fault—'

The food arrived and he stopped while they sorted out their plates. Geraldine picked miserably at her pasta, wondering how to respond.

When the waitress had gone, Craig resumed. He sounded more sure of himself. 'I think it would be best if we called it a day, before we start getting in too deep. Because I can see . . .' She waited. He wouldn't meet her eye. 'The thing is, Geraldine, I think I'm beginning to really fall for you and the trouble is I can't see it working out between us. Not in the long term.'

Geraldine put her fork down. She wanted to say she would change. Things were going to be different. She wanted to argue that it didn't make sense to end the relationship because he was beginning to have serious feelings for her. This was surely the time for them to agree to try and make it work. It had been a one off, her not being able to see him on Saturday night. It wouldn't happen again. It wasn't as if she had even found anything in the documents she had spent her evening studying. But she might have done. She knew she would make the same decision again.

Craig had sounded fine with her explanation the previous evening, happy to postpone meeting up until Sunday. 'At least I remembered to call and confirm this time,' he had laughed. And now this. Geraldine didn't say anything. There was no point. It was over. Her disappointment was so bitter, she could almost taste it, like vinegar on her tongue – or was that the cheap wine? Miserably she took another sip. And another. She wondered whether he had been planning to end the relationship on Saturday or if he had made his decision when she had put off seeing him. She opened her mouth to ask but was afraid she wouldn't be able to control her voice if she tried to speak. She drank some more wine instead.

'I don't want to play second fiddle to a corpse,' he added, with an attempt at humour.

Geraldine didn't smile. She stood suddenly and gathered up her coat and bag with quick nervous movements. She couldn't look at him. 'I'm not very hungry. If you don't mind, I think I'll ring for a taxi.'

Craig was taken aback. 'Nonsense. I'll drop you home. Finish your dinner. There's no rush.' He looked at her in genuine surprise. 'I hope you're not upset about this? I thought—'

She shook her head and forced a smile. 'Unless you've got work waiting for you when you get home?' he added.

'I've always got work waiting when I'm on a case.'

In the taxi Geraldine replayed the scene in her mind. What Craig had said reminded her of her ex Mark's words when he had left her. They had both accused her of putting her job first. Perhaps they were right and she was using her work to avoid intimacy in a relationship. Her misery was momentarily swept aside by anger but, by the time the taxi drew up outside her flat, she was resigned to her situation. She had her job. She didn't need anyone, least of all a man to mess with her mind. In her job it was vital to be able to think clearly. She was fine on her own, better off in fact. She didn't need the illusory security of a boyfriend. Love was no promise of happiness. Sophie Cliff had found love but it hadn't brought her happiness. Exhausted, Geraldine sat on the sofa with a glass of wine and closed her eyes, just for a moment.

The phone startled her from an uneasy doze.

'Geraldine, have you been drinking?' Celia asked. Geraldine was too tired to feel annoyed by the question, and too relieved. Celia was talking as though the estrangement over Geraldine's adoption had never happened. Perhaps it was better that way. Carry on as though nothing had happened. And what, after all, had happened between them? The situation was not of Celia's making, the shameful secret not hers to divulge. Geraldine and Celia had always been very different, and now Geraldine could understand why.

'No, well, yes.'

'I can always tell.'

'Well done you,' Geraldine said, but she spoke kindly. 'So how's my clever niece?' And just like that, Celia was chatting about Chloe, as though everything was back to normal. Geraldine sat, the phone to her ear, and listened to the gentle drone of Celia's voice.

'Geraldine, are you listening?'

'Yes.'

. . . . She was standing beside Sophie Cliff in the kitchen.

'This is where it happened,' Sophie said. 'He was lying here, in the dirt.'

'No,' Geraldine corrected her, 'he was found in the dining area.'

'How do you know?' Sophie asked. Her eyes glittered. 'Were you there?' She raised her hand and Geraldine saw she was holding a can of petrol. Sophie jerked forward and a spume of petrol arced out. Geraldine leapt back. Petrol sloshed on the floor, almost reaching her feet. Geraldine watched as Sophie pulled out a lighter. 'He's waiting for us,' Sophie said. Her eyes shone with a crazy fervour. She splashed more petrol out of the can . . .

Geraldine woke with a start to find she had spilt wine over her expensive trousers. She picked up the phone which had fallen from her grasp.

'Geraldine, are you there?' Celia was asking, plaintively.

'Yes, sorry, I just dropped the phone.'

'Where was I?'

'Back to normal,' Geraldine muttered gratefully.

'What's that?'

'I said I'm still here.'

'I know you're there. I wouldn't sit here talking to myself, would I?'

Geraldine stifled a giggle and reached for the bottle to refill her glass. She felt a rush of gratitude. An adopted sister was better than no sister at all.

'Geraldine, are you listening?'

'Yes. I'm here.'

# CHAPTER 59

# DANGER

The Monday morning briefing finished. Ian Peterson had just switched on his laptop, when Geraldine hurried up to his desk. Ian barely noticed the DCI standing behind her.

'Guess what?' she said. 'We just heard back from forensics.'

Ian started forward in his chair. 'The Honda?'

'Guess who's skin they've found?'

'Skin?'

'Flakes of skin, dandruff, on the back of the driving seat.' She was grinning now. He thought suddenly how young she looked. Her huge dark eyes shone like lamps.

'Callum Martin?' He was smiling too. He knew what she was going to say.

'Got it in one. They rushed the DNA sample through double quick. I gave them a kick, said we needed to nail the bastard before we lost him, and they had to give us something, and they did. They'd found it straight away, before the car was even moved, and sent if off for analysis, but hadn't told us.'

'They probably thought it belonged to the owner of the vehicle,' Ian said.

'They could have said something,' she insisted.

The DCI stepped forward. 'It doesn't matter now. Bring him in, Geraldine. Take Peterson with you, and take back up in case he tries to make a run for it. He's probably got a few bolt holes lined up, apart from the Blue Lagoon. Best not take any chances. We don't want to lose him now.'

'Yes, sir,' the DI replied, but Ryder had already left the room.

It didn't take long to arrange back up. They set off in convoy. Ian and the DI waited impatiently until the team were in position, front and back, before they approached the club. As he followed her, he caught a whiff of her familiar perfume and smiled. They made a formidable team.

The door was locked. There was no bell. Ian knocked loudly until his knuckles hurt, and shouted through the letter box. After a minute, they heard a voice inside. They couldn't distinguish what it said but the door creaked open and a doorman demanded to know their business. Ian hadn't seen him before. He brandished his identity card but the DI strode past and made her way straight to the office, taking no notice of the doorman's protests.

Bronxy glared at them when they barged through the door.

The DI spoke first. 'We'd like to see Callum Martin.'

'Well he's not here.'

'Where is he?'

'I don't know. But, like I said, he's not here.'

'You won't mind us having a look around then?'

Bronxy rose unsteadily to her feet, but her voice was even. 'Have you got a search warrant, Inspector?'

'A search warrant? We didn't come here to search your premises, but we will if that's what it takes to find Martin, in which case we'll require you to accompany us to the station while we wait for the warrant.'

'I don't have to agree to that.' Bronxy sat down and folded her arms. Ian could see she was agitated.

'So, what's it to be? We can do this any way you choose, only we're going to take a look around, whether you like it or not. And with the number of officers I've got in place round the building, no one's getting in or out while we're waiting for a search warrant. We can make ourselves comfortable if you want us to wait here.' The DI glanced round the room and pulled out her phone.

'Look here, Inspector, I've got a lot to do before we open—' Bronxy began.

'With uniformed officers surrounding the place?' The DI burst out laughing, genuinely amused. 'I don't think your customers are going to be queuing up, do you? So, what's it to be? It's your choice.' She turned to Ian. 'She's a brave woman, harbouring a murderer, wouldn't you say, Sarge?'

'Stupid, if you ask me.' Bronxy was silent. 'We'll

take a little look round then, shall we?' He opened the door.

Downstairs the club was deserted apart from a greasy haired young man stacking glasses behind the bar. The DI led the way upstairs, peering into rooms off the corridor. Ian had a confused impression of unmade beds, peeling wall paper and the stink of sweat as they checked each room, glanced behind doors, inside a wardrobe stuffed with glittering frocks, anywhere a man could be hiding. They saw a couple of women in bed asleep together, and a woman applying make up in front of a mirror.

Ian entered the end room first. Brenda was sitting directly in front of him, perched on the edge of a bed. She stared at him, glassy eyed. Callum Martin was standing by a window to the left, talking on his mobile. He half turned as the door opened. Seeing who it was, he tossed the phone on the bed.

'What the—' he began.

'Callum Martin, I'm arresting you on suspicion—' Ian broke off as Callum sprang on to the bed and knelt behind Brenda. Ian heard a sharp intake of breath at his shoulder. Callum had one arm across Brenda's throat, pulling her backwards against his chest. In his other hand he held a knife to the side of her neck.

'Mr Martin, put the knife down.' The DI's voice was low and even. Ian heard a rustle of movement behind him. He didn't dare take his eyes off the tableau on the bed.

'Don't move or she gets it,' Callum yelled. Ian nodded to show he understood. Callum looked wild. There was no knowing what he might do.

Brenda seemed dazed. 'Who is he, Cal?' she asked. He ignored the question, and pulled her head further back, her skin taut against the blade. Brenda gagged but she didn't struggle.

'What the fuck are you doing here?'

'We just want to talk to you, Callum.' Ian replied. He held his breath. No one moved. 'Put the knife down. You're not going to use it.' He hoped he was right.

'Fuck off.'

'Callum, look out of the window,' Ian went on quietly. 'There are police officers surrounding the building. You can't leave. Sooner or later you're going to have to come with us.' Callum stared at the sergeant, calculating.

'Cal, who is he?' Brenda asked.

'Shut up.' He tightened his grip on Brenda's neck. She began to choke. A siren pierced the air from outside and he stiffened.

'Callum, you're strangling her,' Ian said. He began to edge backwards to the door. He wasn't sure what else to do.

'Don't move!' Callum shouted. 'Come here.' Ian froze. 'Come over here or I'll—' He pointed the knife at Brenda's eye. 'I'll have her eye out.'

Suddenly Brenda became alert to the danger. 'Cal, what are you doing?' She stared at the point of the blade, centimetres from her eye. Callum drew the edge of the knife slowly down her cheek leaving a fine line, brilliant red against her pale skin. 'Cal? What are you doing?' Brenda's voice rose in a whine of fear.

'Sharp as a razor,' Callum said. 'Come here.' Ian took one small step forward. Callum placed the knife at Brenda's throat again. He leaned forward and whispered in her ear. Ian couldn't hear what he said. 'Come over here or she gets it,' Callum repeated. Ian inched closer. He considered taking a sudden leap to catch the bastard off guard, but it was too risky. The blade was pressing into Brenda's flesh.

Callum's head jerked up suddenly, staring past Ian's shoulder at the door. Ian hesitated and glanced in the mirror to his right, taking his eyes off the couple on the bed. In that instant, Callum released Brenda. 'Now!' he shouted. He flung himself off the bed towards the sergeant. At the same time Brenda launched herself at his legs.

Ian fell to the floor with a crash.

# CHAPTER 60

# HOME

There was a fire at Raymond Barker's house. He should have died. That would have been just. Tom had perished in fire but Raymond Barker had walked away, alive. The police detective had told Sophie about it. 'Raymond Barker's not dead. He's in hospital, badly injured, but he's not dead.'

In a frenzy, Sophie drove to the hospital. 'I'm here to see Raymond Barker,' she told the woman at reception. The woman didn't even look up. 'Raymond Barker,' Sophie repeated, wondering if the other woman had heard her. It was difficult to control her impatience. 'I'm here to see Raymond Barker. I need to speak to him.' She was entitled to that at least.

'Which ward is he in?'

'I don't know.'

The woman on reception tapped at her keyboard. 'Barker, you said?'

'Yes. Raymond Barker.'

The woman nodded at her screen. 'Raymond Barker. He's in Shannon Ward on the second floor. But he's—' Sophie didn't wait to hear the rest.

She followed the signs and made her way up a cold stone staircase to a landing on the second floor where swing doors led to Shannon Ward.

The corridor was empty. Sophie approached the nurse on the desk. 'I'm looking for Raymond Barker.' The nurse looked up. Sophie smiled at her. 'He's my nephew. I want to see him for myself. My mum's really upset.' She held her breath, waiting.

The nurse lowered her eyes. 'Third door along,' she said, adding, 'the one with a police guard on the door.' Sophie swung round and looked along the corridor. A young policeman in uniform was standing outside one of the rooms. She hesitated before slipping along the corridor, out of sight of the nurse's desk. She had come so close. The policeman ruined everything.

Sophie counted to a hundred before turning round to scurry back out of the ward. The nurse was talking on the phone and paid no attention to Sophie as she passed by the desk again.

Sophie knew she couldn't stay at the motel indefinitely, but she couldn't go home even if she had wanted to. The house was uninhabitable. The doctor had advised her to take a holiday. The police had told her not to go away without letting them know where she was going. It was all so confusing. She sat in her car outside the house that had once been her home, wondering what to do. She hardly recognised it. The windows were boarded up and there were ugly black streaks down the walls. She didn't dare think what it might look like inside. The key turned in the ignition. The engine revved. A sudden yearning wrenched at her guts. She switched the engine off and slipped out of the car.

Walking up the path, Sophie felt like an intruder. The house was unrecognisable. She had to remind herself it belonged to her. The key turned stiffly in the lock. Inside, she looked around, surprised. The hall was very dark. All the windows had been boarded up. She walked straight past the doorway that led to the dining room and kitchen. She tried not to look but her eyes were drawn to the gaping hole where the door had been. The dining room was smothered in feathery grey soot and ash. A horrible stench of burning assailed her, making her nauseous. She turned away quickly and hurried up the stairs, pinching her nose, trying to block out the smell. It was no use. The scent of death was everywhere.

The landing was a mess of ash and scorch marks. The upstairs of the house was otherwise relatively undamaged. A fine layer of soot lay everywhere but the rooms were familiar, furniture intact and in position, waiting for her and Tom to walk through the door. As if in a dream, she made her way to the bedroom. The room was dark.

Sophie turned on the light. Nothing happened. She sank down on the bed. It felt very soft after the hard mattress at the motel. She felt around for the switch on her bedside lamp. That didn't work either. The electricity must have been turned off after the fire. No one had thought to switch it on again. Perhaps it was down to her to contact the electricity board. There was no one else to do it. She sat quite still, thinking, for a long time. Then she seized her bag, and emptied it over the bed. Make up, purse, mirror, keys, diary and comb flew out.

Sophie picked up a large box of matches. She swept everything else on to the floor. With her eyes tightly shut, she lay down on the bed, clutching the box of matches to her chest.

# CHAPTER 61

# ARREST

Ian lay on his back, dazed. He was vaguely aware of Brenda kneeling on one of his legs. Her bony knees dug painfully into his shin. She was pummelling his other leg ineffectually with her fists. Tears streaked her cheeks, mingling with blood oozing from the cut on her cheek. She was gabbling loudly. Ian couldn't make any sense of her gibberish. He felt curiously calm. Brenda kept repeating the same words. It sounded like, 'Kill the snake, kill the snake.' Callum was holding one of Ian's arms down, and kneeling on the other. Ian couldn't see Callum's other hand. He could feel the point of a knife, pressing against his throat, the blade contaminated with Brenda's blood. He hoped it wouldn't pierce his skin.

The floor beneath them vibrated. Callum turned his head to look round at the door. Ian saw flecks of dandruff in his captor's hair and smiled. 'Gotcha,' he thought. Heavy footsteps pounded along the corridor outside. He heard the DI's voice barking orders. With a flash of relief, Ian regained full consciousness of where he was. He wasn't alone. Geraldine would release him from the madwoman whose knees were digging into his leg and the psychopath holding a knife at his throat. Ian swallowed nervously. Despite all his training, he was finding it hard to think clearly. He couldn't believe this was happening.

'Back!' Callum screamed. Ian saw thick white spittle gathered at the corners of his lips and smelt his stale breath. 'Back or he gets it.' Ian wrenched his head sharply to one side, away from Martin's stinking breath. A face was staring at him, cloudy in the mirror. Distracted by the pain in his leg, it hadn't occurred to him that he was about to die until that moment. He studied Geraldine's face, her eyes stretched wide in fear. For him. He felt a thrill of terror. Then Brenda's knee caught him in the groin, dangerously close to his balls. He winced. He twisted his head until he could see Geraldine's face in the doorway. She glanced at him then took a slow step forward, her eyes on Callum. Ian kept his gaze fixed on her.

'Think about what you're doing, Callum,' she said. Her voice was calm. Only her eyes betrayed her terror. 'You don't want to go down for murdering a police officer in cold blood. There's no way you could argue this was an accident.'

'What murder? Who's a murderer?' Brenda asked. She sounded panicky. She stopped punching Ian's legs and sat back on her heels. Ian breathed more freely. He concentrated on Geraldine.

'Shut it,' Callum told Brenda. 'Just shut up, you stupid cow, I need to think.'

'I need the toilet, Cal,' Brenda whined. Callum's eyes flicked at her in annoyance. In that instant, Geraldine shouted. 'Go!' Ian kicked out as hard as he could and jerked his head to avoid the knife. Martin's elbow caught Ian on the side of his head. Geraldine threw herself at Martin who fell across Ian's legs, pinning him to the floor. Brenda disappeared underneath Martin.

Two uniformed officers rushed in, yanked Callum to his feet and cuffed him, spitting and swearing. Ian pulled himself out from beneath Brenda and crawled to the bed where he hauled himself to his feet. His neck felt sore where he had twisted it violently, his legs were bruised and his shoulders ached from contact with the floor. Catching the expression on Geraldine's face he looked down. His shirt was soaked with blood. He frowned. Gingerly he felt his chest and abdomen before he registered that Brenda was lying on the floor. She wasn't moving.

'It's Brenda,' he gasped, 'Brenda's blood on my shirt.' He dropped to his knees beside the wounded woman. The front of Brenda's blouse was drenched in blood. One of the constables was already on the phone summoning urgent medical assistance. Ian explored Brenda's injury. Geraldine pulled a sheet from the bed and pressed it, bunched up and grubby, against Brenda's chest. The wounded woman moaned.

'You get your hands off her. Leave her alone,' Callum shouted.

'They're trying to save her life,' one of the constables told him.

'She's all right,' Callum told him. 'Brenda.' There was no answer. 'Bren!' Brenda stared up at him. Slowly her eyes fixed on him.

Her lips moved. 'Callum.' Blood frothed on her lips. 'Cal . . . what . . .'

'Sharp as a razor,' Ian said softly.

Geraldine pressed the makeshift wad of material against Brenda's chest. Ian straightened himself up, wincing at the stiffness in his shoulders. Cuffed and shaking, Callum Martin stood staring down at Brenda. 'Callum Martin, I'm arresting you on suspicion of the murders of Evelyn Green, Thomas Cliff, Margaret Palmer, Albert Cartwright and Brenda—' Ian paused, frowning. 'What's her other name?' Callum didn't reply. He watched as Geraldine tried to resuscitate Brenda.

'No pulse, she's in shock, she's lost a lot of blood. Where the hell's the medics?' Geraldine asked. 'I think we're losing her.'

'She was drugged up to her eyeballs,' Ian said helplessly. 'She wouldn't have felt a thing.'

'Bren . . .' Callum said. His voice broke.

'Oh take him away, for fuck's sake,' Geraldine snapped.

They drove back to the station in silence. Ian did his best not to limp as they entered the building. Embarrassed, he felt the desk sergeant's eyes on him as he crossed the lobby. He hurried to the toilet and was shocked at his appearance,

397

face streaked with dirt and sweat, hands and cheeks splattered with blood. Not his own. He washed himself thoroughly, wary of infection. With his face splashed clean with cold water and his hair combed, he didn't look so bad. He couldn't bear to put his shirt on again. In any case, it would be needed as evidence. He rummaged in his locker and found a jacket. He looked a mess but, apart from some nasty bruising, he was unhurt. He had suffered worse injuries on the football pitch.

Ryder was waiting for them in his office. His face was taut with anger. No attempt at explanation appeared to satisfy him that Ian hadn't been rash in exposing herself to Callum Martin's assault.

'You let him walk in there, alone—' he bellowed at Geraldine.

'I wasn't alone, sir. The DI was with me.'

'As I understand it,' Ryder glanced down at a statement on his desk, 'Geraldine was co-ordinating a rescue party to get you out of there.' Geraldine grinned as Ian's eyebrows shot up in indignation.

'Is something amusing you, Geraldine?'

'No, sir.'

'There is no possible excuse for your conduct,' the DCI continued. As he spoke, a terrible thought struck Ian. He was going to be disciplined. The DCI was going to recommend he be demoted to constable, or worse, put him back in uniform.

'Sir,' he interrupted. 'Would you at least read my report before reaching any conclusions about how you intend to proceed?'

'How I intend to proceed?' the DCI exploded.

'It's hardly fair to discipline me before you know what happened.'

'Discipline you? Why would I discipline you? You weren't the officer in charge.'

Ian took a deep breath. This was all going horribly wrong. He stepped forward. 'It was my decision, sir. I went in there on my own initiative. I wasn't . . .' he paused, 'I wasn't acting on instructions from the DI. If there's any blame . . .'

'I was responsible,' Geraldine interrupted him firmly.

The DCI's face went red. 'What the hell is this?' he demanded. 'I'm working with a pair of bloody lemmings. And what makes you think you don't both deserve to be disciplined for putting an officer at risk? As for how I intend to proceed, I'll tell you exactly what my intentions are, and I don't need to see your report, or anybody's bloody report, to help me make up my mind. I intend to see Callum Martin behind bars for the rest of his life and I will need your full reports on my desk before you do anything else, and certainly before you leave today, if it takes you all night. After which, I'm ordering you,' he pointed at Peterson, 'to take a week off, and get yourself to the doctor.' He paused before adding more quietly, 'on second thoughts, you'd better get those injuries seen to first, before you do anything else, Sergeant. That means now!'

'Yes sir.' With a quick glance at Geraldine, Peterson hobbled from the room.

# CHAPTER 62

# REALISATION

Over breakfast the following morning Geraldine tried to shut out the horror of the previous day by thinking about Craig. She told herself she wasn't disappointed about the end of their affair. He was right to call it a day before they became too seriously involved. She had been naïve, allowing herself to hope they might have a future together. She couldn't blame him for backing out – they'd had a good time, that was all. Craig was the wrong man. They had met at the wrong time. She just hoped she would meet the right man at the right time, whatever that meant. In the meantime, she had her work.

She poured herself a large mug of coffee and began to review the schedules she had brought home. She couldn't settle. Unwelcome images haunted her: Ian Peterson drenched in blood, Brenda calling for Callum Martin as she lay dying on the filthy floor. Resolutely Geraldine thought about Craig. She made a mental list of her reservations about him. His lax attitude towards the law could have been a problem. He had been eager to abuse her position to park in a restricted area.

Thinking back to their trip abroad, she recalled him laughingly offering to write in her passport. Admittedly the reason had been innocent, but even so it was the thin end of the wedge. It was easy to falsify official documents.

A thought struck her.

Hurriedly, she pulled a file out of her bag and leafed through it to find a list of people who had hired cars from Avis Rental in Sandmouth town centre the previous Saturday. She glanced down the short list of names.

## AVIS RENTAL UK

VW Gold automatic
   air conditioning     . . .    Desmond James
Renault Megane air
   conditioning     . . .    Jennifer Archer
Vauxhall Astra 1.6
   compact 5 door    . . .    Bobbie Geere

She turned to the next list and paused. Someone called Bobbie Geere had hired a car and driven from Sandmouth to Harchester on the night Raymond Barker had been attacked. Who was Bobbie Geere? So far they had been unable to trace the grey haired woman who had hired a car under that name. There was no evidence of a false driving licence printed in that name. All known forgers in the area had been interrogated, every computer Sophie Cliff could have accessed had been examined.

Geraldine picked up a black biro and began to doodle. She knew she was losing her focus, like Bennett, happily working out his crossword clues.

'It's really not difficult,' he had told her. 'Just a question of substituting the right word for the clue.'

The phrase repeated itself in her mind. It seemed to take on a new meaning: 'substituting the right word for the clue'. Craig had offered to write 'Dubrovnik' clearly over the faint imprint in her passport. It was easy to falsify official documents. Geraldine continued her doodling. Five seconds later, she knew how Sophie Cliff had driven from Sandmouth to Harchester and back again, undetected.

Sophie's doctor had recommended she take a short holiday while her house was out of bounds. Geraldine had checked the story herself. She turned the pages of her note book and found the right page.

'She's naturally very disturbed by her husband's sudden death. It's deeply shocking,' the GP had told her. 'I suggested she take a break. Go and stay with her parents for a while. It's not a good idea for her to spend too much time alone at a time like this.'

Geraldine wondered if the doctor's suggestion had given Sophie the idea to book into a hotel, and hire a car under a false name. She had probably planned to return to Harchester every evening to watch Barker and wait for a chance to exact her revenge. At the end of the evening she would park the hired car nearby and sneak back into the hotel ready to appear at breakfast the following morning.

On the first evening, Sophie Cliff had failed to set fire to Barker after assaulting him in the street. On the second evening Barker had spent the night in hospital. On her third outing, Sophie had broken into the house where Barker was apparently at home by himself. Prepared with a can of petrol and matches, she had attempted to burn Barker to death. Presumably she regarded this as just retribution for her husband's death. She must have believed she had succeeded because the next morning she had checked out of the hotel and returned to Harchester to wait for her husband's body to be released for burial. It was a desperate plot, and completely insane.

Geraldine drove to the station. She made her way to the DCI's office, ignoring the duty sergeant, and knocked firmly.

James Ryder looked up from his screen, surprised to see her. 'I thought you were off today—'

'It's Sophie Cliff, sir,' Geraldine interrupted. 'She's the one who attacked Barker.'

'She was in Sandmouth—'

'No sir. She drove to Harchester and back again on Saturday and Monday. And probably on Sunday too. I think she was determined to keep coming back, night after night, until she found her chance to attack Barker.'

'We've been through all this, Geraldine.' The DCI sounded tired. 'Unless we can find the car she stole, and prove she was using it for—'

'She didn't steal a car sir, she hired one using a false driving licence. She forged the name herself. It was easy enough to do. I can't believe we didn't spot it straight away, it's so obvious.'

'It's certainly likely. I agree it would've been easy for her. But we've checked all the computers she could have had access to, including all the internet cafes in Sandmouth, and—'

'It's simpler than that, sir. We were so sure she could have produced a false passport using her technological know how—'

'Which she could have done.'

'We overlooked something much simpler. And impossible to trace. Look.' Ryder frowned as Geraldine put her notebook down on his desk and opened it at a clean page. With a black biro she wrote the name SOPHIE CLIFF. 'It couldn't be done on a laminated photo driving licence, sir, but all it takes is a fine black biro, and the name on a standard green paper driving licence can be altered in seconds.' She changed some of the letters of the name she had written, S to B, P and H to Bs, C to G, L and I to E, F to R and F to E. The name changed in front of their eyes: BOBBIE GEERE. 'The second E of Geere is a bit squashed, changing the I to E, there isn't quite room, but the rest of it . . .'

'Pull her in. Now.'

404

Geraldine drove back to the motel. The manager barely looked up from his television. He shovelled a handful of peanuts into his mouth and shook his head. 'She's not been back since you were last here.' He chomped noisily, mouth open. 'People don't generally come back. We're more of a stop-over. People passing through. Ships passing in the night.' He seized another fistful of peanuts.

The local CID called on Sophie Cliff's parents but she wasn't there. They didn't know where she was.

Geraldine went to see Thomas Cliff's mother.

'Have you seen anything of Sophie since your son's death?'

'What would I want to see her for?'

'I'd like to speak to her—'

Mrs Cliff butted in. 'I knew it was her all along. I told you, didn't I?'

'I just want to ask her a few questions—'

'And now you don't know where she is. She's run off, hasn't she?' the old woman's eyes glittered. 'There's an admission of guilt, if ever I heard one. You should've listened to me. I told you it was her, didn't I?'

'And you have no idea where she might be?'

'How would I know? If you ask me, she's probably left the country. She knew I was on to her. It was only a matter of time before you lot caught up. Took you too long, didn't it? You should have listened.'

Geraldine returned to the police station but there

was no news. Sophie Cliff's description had been circulated to every train station and bus depot, airport and ferry operator, as well as every police station, but without any results.

The DCI walked into Geraldine's office, unannounced as usual. 'We'll find her,' he said, speaking more to himself than to her. She nodded. He didn't sound very sure and left as suddenly as he had entered. Geraldine turned to her computer and tried to focus on her report.

A few moments later her phone vibrated. Geraldine felt an irrational flicker of hope as she took the call but it wasn't Craig.

'At last. I've been trying to call you for ages. Guess what?' Hannah didn't wait for a reply. 'He's back.'

'What?'

'Jeremy. He's come back. Geraldine, how can I ever thank you?'

'Hannah, I'm really pleased for you, really I am, but it was nothing to do with me. I hardly said anything to him. I only saw him for a few seconds.'

'No, but you did go and see him. He said it made all the difference.'

'I can't think why.'

'He said it made him think what I might be like, all on my own, if he didn't come back.' There was a pause. Geraldine wondered about the conversations her friend must have had.

'I'd be like Geraldine if it wasn't for you,' she imagined Hannah saying to her husband. With an uncomfortable flash of insight she understood what they must think of her – pathetic, lonely Geraldine.

'Geraldine, are you all right?'

'Yes, of course. I'm really pleased for you, Han.'

'We're going away,' Hannah babbled, 'just the two of us. A romantic break. He says it's going to be a second honeymoon. My mum's taking the kids for a long weekend and guess what? We're going to Dubrovnik. Your recommendation.'

'That's great, Hannah.' Geraldine wedged the phone under her chin and resumed checking through the papers in her desk. 'Look, Han, I'd love to chat but—'

'I know, you've got to get back to work,' Hannah interrupted her, but she wasn't angry. She was laughing.

'Have a great time, and call me when you get back,' Geraldine said, but Hannah had already hung up.

# CHAPTER 63

# CANDLES

Driving home, Geraldine took a detour up Harchester Hill and turned into Harchester Close. The police cordon had been cleared away. A ribbon of blue and white tape fluttering from a gate post was the only evidence they had been there.

Geraldine parked outside number 17. The house was concealed from the road by high hedges. She paused at the gate and peered at the house front with its boarded up windows and black smudged brickwork. She crossed the empty drive and tried the garage door. It wouldn't open. The house looked deserted. She tried the bell. It didn't work. She knocked, loudly. No answer. A memory of blackened worktops above a floor littered with sooty debris flashed through her mind; a melted kettle, grotesquely misshapen, a congealed mess that had once been a phone, a coating of ash covering every surface. The stench of burning plastic seemed to fill her lungs and she turned away, breathing so deeply it made her light headed.

Halfway down the path Geraldine glanced back at the house. A glimmer of light flickered through a narrow gap in the boards over an upstairs window. Geraldine stared, but there was no further sign of life. She strode back up the path and rapped smartly on the front door. There was no answer. She examined each of the downstairs front windows but they were impenetrable. She rattled the side gate. It wasn't locked so she went through into the back garden. She couldn't see anything through the first four windows or the patio doors, but when she reached the final window at the back, she found a gap between two boards. Standing on tiptoe, she squinted through into the darkness, but couldn't see anything inside.

Summoning back up, she pulled off one shoe and hammered at the wood without making any impression on it. She turned and grabbed an ornamental tree growing in a terracotta pot, raised it above her head and hurled it at the path. The pot shattered. Seizing a long shard of clay she levered gently at the gap, prising the boards apart until she was able to work her fingers through the space and grab the edge of one plank in both hands. With a sudden effort, she shoved it and staggered as the wood gave way under the pressure. Splinters pierced her flesh and she scratched herself on a nail. She didn't stop to examine her injuries, but pushed at the planks, which had been nailed roughly across the window, until there was a gap wide enough for her to clamber through. She was careful to avoid contact with any remnants of glass left behind in the frame when the window had shattered in the explosion.

Climbing on to an upturned pot, she wriggled through the gap, landing awkwardly on her hands and knees on thick carpet. She pulled herself upright, swore under her breath as her knee hit a low table, and felt her way to the door. The stench of burning hung in the air. She wondered if she should have waited for back up, but couldn't turn back now. Someone was in the house. It could only be Sophie Cliff. If they waited, they might lose her. They might not find her again.

Moonlight shone through the window illuminating the study she was in. She stepped out of the room into darkness. The windows were boarded up. No lights were on. She felt in vain for her torch. It must have slipped out of her pocket when she fell in through the window. If she hadn't been inside the house before, it would have been impossible to negotiate her way around in the dark. As it was, she was going to find a few bruises on her upper arms and shins.

It was difficult to move around silently. At one point she thought she heard footsteps behind her. She spun round, squinting into the darkness, but couldn't make out any movement. All was quiet. She was making her way towards the front of the house when a slight noise made her stop. Above her head it sounded like someone had closed a door. In the faint light from her phone screen, she found her way to the stairs and began to climb, listening at every step.

Silence.

At the far end of the landing a line of light shone beneath a door. Shuffling towards it Geraldine felt, rather than heard, a presence behind her. She spun round. A heavy object clouted her on the shoulder. Startled, she lost her balance and staggered, disorientated in the darkness. Before she could recover, her assailant gave her legs a violent tug. She fell backwards to the floor. Something pressed down on her knees. Her hands were efficiently tied together and her ankles bound before her head began to clear. She was dimly aware of a shadowy figure above her as a rough cloth, like a towel, was wrapped around her head.

The darkness was impenetrable.

Firm hands gripped Geraldine under her arms and dragged her along the floor away from the stairs. She yelped as her shoulder hit a sharp ridge. She was being manoeuvred through a doorway. She waited, listening. Faint scratching sounds. The soft thud of feet on carpet.

As her blindfold was removed, lights flashed. It wasn't her eyesight playing tricks on her. The room was lit by flickering candles. They covered every surface: standing on cupboards, along a shelf above the radiator, on the ledge below the window.

'The electricity's off,' Sophie Cliff said casually, as though this was a normal power cut. 'They never put it on again. You have to do everything yourself.'

Geraldine looked down at her hands, straining uselessly against the cord. She turned her attention to her ankles which seemed to be more loosely secured. If she had enough time, she thought she could work them free. With difficulty she hoisted herself into a kneeling position so her feet were behind her, hidden from view.

'Sophie.' She was relieved her voice sounded calm. 'Untie me please. I want to help you.'

'You let him go.'

'What?'

'It was you. I remember. You found him and you let him go.' Sophie's voice rose in a shrill crescendo. 'He killed Tom and you let him walk away.'

'Sophie, I want to help you. Believe me, I want to see Tom's killer brought to justice as much as you do, but I have to work within the law.' She resisted the hysteria threatening her composure.

'Justice? Law?' Sophie shrieked, losing all vestige of control. 'There is no justice. Not in this world. But it'll all be over very soon. You and me, we're going to burn.' She seized a candle and held it high above her head.

'Sophie, put the candle down before there's an accident.' Geraldine rubbed her ankles together frantically. The cord was definitely loosening.

Sophie flung the candle on the bed, still attached to its saucer. Smothered by the folds of the duvet, the flame went out. She ran round the room, seizing candles and hurling them at the bed. 'For Tom!' she yelled. 'For Tom!' Only some of the candles went out. Geraldine watched, desperately trying to free her feet.

With a sudden rush the bed burst into flames. Geraldine groaned. Terror threatened to paralyse her. The pain in her ankles helped her remain alert. Scraping the skin off the top of one foot she broke free of the cord around her ankles and leapt to her feet. Flames flickered up the wall. The wooden slats of the headboard began to hiss above the blazing bed.

Geraldine forced her legs to carry her forwards. She found herself praying. 'God, get me out of this alive.' A voice was whimpering in fear. Her ankles stung from chafing. Her eyes were smarting. Instinctively she ducked her head as she walked forwards, step by step.

Sophie Cliff was staring, aghast. Flames licked the ceiling. She clutched at Geraldine's arm, as though she had just woken up to what was happening. 'Help me. Please. Help.' She swayed once then pitched forward, head first. Geraldine struggled to keep her balance as she stepped forward to break the other woman's fall.

Geraldine walked backwards to the door, dragging Sophie across the carpet. It wasn't easy, with her hands tied together. Smoke engulfed them. The heat was almost intolerable. The confusion of pain and terror threatened to overwhelm Geraldine, but she wasn't alone. She focused her mind on saving the unconscious woman in her charge.

As soon as she managed to haul Sophie through the bedroom door, Geraldine leaned her shoulder against it and pushed it closed. There wasn't much time. The room was about to reach flashpoint.

Sophie was so light, Geraldine was able to lean down and scoop her up, even with her hands tied. Holding Sophie across her outstretched forearms, she lurched along the landing and had nearly reached the stairs when her legs gave way. Behind her, she heard the roar of flames, accompanied by loud crackling sounds. The bedroom was ablaze. Spurred on by fear, Geraldine shuffled backwards on her elbows and knees, pulling Sophie along in her wake. When her feet reached the top step, she lost her grip on Sophie and fell, slithering down the stairs.

At the foot of the stairs she hesitated. She couldn't remember if this was the house with a double locked security front door. But first, she had to struggle back up for Sophie Cliff. She was half way up the stairs, crawling on her elbows and knees, when she heard crashing and shouting. Over her shoulder she saw a bright light and two uniformed officers burst in.

'Over here!' Geraldine shouted. The hoarse whisper that issued from her lips was barely audible above the hissing of the flames.

'I've got her,' a man's voice called out. 'A female. On the stairs. We need medical assistance here right away.'

'Fire!' a second voice bellowed. 'Any other doors or windows open?'

Geraldine tried to speak but at that moment the

414

wooden railings of the banister above them burst into flames, hissing. She screamed.

'Get her out of here!' another voice shouted. A man was leaning over her. Lifting her.

'There's a woman up there. At the top of the stairs. She's unconscious.'

'Up there! Anyone else in the building?' Two figures raced past her up the stairs.

Geraldine struggled to answer. 'No one. I'm all right. I can walk.' An officer ran down the stairs with Sophie Cliff across his shoulder. Geraldine followed and they hurried out of the building.

Outside, all seemed confusion, then uniformed constables had a cordon in place, a fire engine thundered up and was manoeuvred into position and a hose unfurled as the huge vehicle reversed slowly up the drive.

Geraldine waited by the gate. Her hands had been untied. She shivered inside a silver foil blanket someone had thrown over her shoulders. Fire officers brought the blaze under control.

'You're sure there's no one else inside?' a fire officer asked her, shouting above the noise.

'We were here a couple of weeks ago,' Geraldine heard a voice say as a small group of fire officers hurried past her. She watched as paramedics carried Sophie Cliff, still unconscious, into an ambulance.

'She was lucky. You were nearly too late to save her,' a fireman told Geraldine.

'Ten days too late.'

The officer opened his mouth to reply, but Geraldine turned and limped away past the police cordon, through the gathering crowd of onlookers shocked into silence by the second calamity to close their road in as many weeks. She started up her engine and drove round the corner where she pulled over and sat, shocked and trembling. Her hands stung as she clutched the steering wheel. She felt utterly alone and wished Peterson had been with her at the end.

# CHAPTER 64

# LIFE

Geraldine's spirits sank as she pulled into the hospital car park. It took a frustrating few minutes before she manoeuvred the car into a tight space. The mortuary never fazed her but she disliked everything about hospitals. Perhaps it was the idea of people in pain that upset her. Corpses suffered only indignity. Sophie Cliff was the third patient Geraldine had been to see in Harchester General in almost as many days. No one had yet thanked her for visiting. Somehow she doubted if Sophie Cliff would be any different. Passing the hospital shop, she bought a bunch of yellow chrysanthemums. As soon as she paid for them, she regretted her impulse. They were half dead before they left the shop.

Unlike Gordon and Barker, Sophie wasn't in a room by herself. Geraldine entered the ward and a strong smell of disinfectant hit her. A row of faces glanced up as she walked past. They wore a variety of hopeless expressions. Sophie Cliff lay at the far end of the ward, gazing listlessly up at the ceiling, white as the bed sheets. Geraldine almost didn't recognise her without her glasses.

417

She looked quite pretty in an ordinary kind of way.

'It was you, wasn't it?' Sophie greeted Geraldine as she approached. It sounded like an accusation. Geraldine clutched the weary bunch of chrysanthemums and wondered what to do with them. Sophie's brows drew together. 'What do you want?'

'I just came by to see how you are, that's all. I'm not here on an official visit.'

'Not come to interrogate me then.'

'No. Someone will be along to question you soon.'

Sophie turned her head away and Geraldine saw tears in her eyes. 'Why did you do it?' she whispered fiercely. 'They must all think you're a great heroine,' Sophie turned to face Geraldine, suddenly angry, 'rescuing me like that . . . I tried to kill you . . .'

'Well, I'm still here.' Geraldine tried to smile. 'And so are you.'

'You don't understand. I should have stayed there in the house, like he did. In the smoke. I meant to do it. Only I was scared. The fire . . . I wanted to run away. You shouldn't have been there. It shouldn't be like this.' She was crying in earnest now, her pale cheeks glistening. She made no attempt to wipe her face. 'You should have left me there. You had no right to be there.' Geraldine swallowed her meaningless platitudes. How could time heal Sophie Cliff's wounds? It wouldn't bring her husband back.

'Why did you do it?' Sophie asked again. She was staring at Geraldine now. 'They told me what happened. You risked your own life to save mine, after I tried to kill you. Why?' They gazed helplessly at one another for a moment. 'What's going to happen to me?'

Geraldine lay the flowers on the bed. 'The courts will be sympathetic.'

'I didn't mean that. I don't care what they do to me. But how am I going to manage for the rest of my life without him?'

Geraldine turned and walked out of the ward. She didn't look back.

'Don't worry, she'll soon be up and about, right as rain,' a sturdy nurse assured her. Geraldine hurried past without answering.

'What did you expect?' the DCI asked when Geraldine told him about the visit. He closed the door of her office, turned and raised his eyebrows at her.

'She made me feel as though I'd done the wrong thing.'

'That's ridiculous. You saved the woman's life. If you hadn't been there, she almost certainly wouldn't have made it. She has a chance now.'

'I don't think she wants a chance, sir.' Geraldine stared wretchedly at the floor. 'She chose to die and I prevented it.'

'Well, if that's what she wants, there's nothing stopping her. Unless you plan to stand guard over her for the rest of her life. She still has the option to kill herself. There's plenty that do. But she also has the option to live her life. And if it wasn't for you, she wouldn't have that choice. So please don't start bleating on about saving the poor woman when all she wanted was to die. Chances are in a few years' time she'll have remarried and be – oh, I don't know, raising a family, growing prize roses. Whatever it is people generally do when they choose to live their lives.'

'Once she's served her time.'

'Yes. There is that. Well, perhaps a spell behind bars will help salve her conscience. And she deserves to be punished for what she did. Being miserable doesn't give anyone the right to take the law into their own hands. Nothing sanctions that.'

'I know. And I daresay the courts will be lenient, under the circumstances. I reckon they'll find she was temporarily deranged after the death of her husband, don't you think, sir?'

Ryder let out a vexed sigh. 'Totally deranged, if you ask me. Round the bend and up the bloody wall.'

'She had just lost her husband, sir.'

'My point exactly. Anyone who gets married and wants to stay that way has to be completely barking.' With that enigmatic statement, the DCI left the room, leaving Geraldine to wonder, not for the first time, about his personal circumstances. She had been working closely with James Ryder for three weeks, but she knew nothing about him.

# CHAPTER 65

## FRIENDS

Geraldine spent the following day finishing off her final report and packing up her things. There was still paperwork to tie up, but the investigation was over. The flimsy internal wall of Geraldine's office shook as someone knocked. Before she could respond, the door opened and Peterson stuck his head in. 'Are you coming, gov? We're all off to the pub.'

'You're looking cheerful today.'

'We sorted it out.' He stepped into the office and closed the door.

'Sorted it out?'

'Me and Bev. It was this, funnily enough.' He pointed at his black eye. 'You'd think it would've put her off but soon as she saw it she was all over me. So we're back on. Till the next time.' He grinned. 'She said we belong together.'

Geraldine smiled back, wondering if anyone would ever say that to her. She didn't even belong in her own family. She turned away, suddenly brisk. 'That's great. Now, I must get packed up here—'

'Sure. Sorry, gov. See you over the road.' The wall

trembled as he closed the door. Geraldine sat down at her desk and opened a drawer stuffed with papers. She sighed and began rifling through them.

She had just about finished when James Ryder strode in.

'Still working, Geraldine?' He sounded put out but when she looked up she saw he was smiling. 'You coming for a drink?' Geraldine wished fleetingly it was a personal invitation from a man who wanted to spend time with a woman, not a DCI summoning his DI to a team drink at the end of a case.

'Yes, sir.'

'Is everything all right?' He hovered just inside the room.

'Yes, thank you sir.' She turned to collect her coat which she had thrown on the filing cabinet behind her.

She heard the door close but when she turned round, Ryder was inside the room. 'I always feel a bit low when a case ends,' he confessed. 'Once the adrenaline rush fades, and there's nothing left but paperwork.' Geraldine nodded, uncertain how to respond. 'But we've done a good job, so let's go drink to that. Come on, there's someone over the road who wants to see you.'

'Yes, sir.' For a second their eyes met, then he turned and left. The image of his tall figure lingered in her mind. With a sigh she pulled on her coat and left the room. It was no longer her office. There would be no more visits from James Ryder.

Geraldine wondered if they would work together again.

The pub was packed. Geraldine saw Kathryn Gordon at the bar, beaming, and made her way over. The DCI's face had lost its grey sheen. She looked more robust than ever. Geraldine wondered with a pang if she would work with James Ryder again, now that Kathryn Gordon was back. She looked around but couldn't see him. She turned to Kathryn Gordon.

'You look great, ma'am. You look as though you've just had a holiday.'

Kathryn Gordon was not so kind. 'I wish I could say the same for you, Geraldine. You look washed out. I hope you haven't been overdoing things? You're a valuable officer. You have to look after yourself.'

Geraldine bit back the obvious retort. She wasn't the one who had just suffered a coronary. Kathryn Gordon made no reference to Geraldine's visit to the hospital.

Leslie Bennett bought a round. They were all pleased that Callum Martin would go down, but five people had died and another had been crippled in the course of the investigation.

'So what's going to happen to Barker?' Polly wanted to know. 'Martin's arrested for the deaths of Evelyn Green, Thomas Cliff, Maggie Palmer and Brenda whatever her name is, and he's responsible for Sophie Cliff's suicide attempt too if you think about it. But it was the burglaries that started the whole thing off. Barker's to blame too.'

'That's Bennett's case,' Kathryn Gordon replied. There was a momentary lull in the conversation. They all waited to hear what Bennett had to say.

'We know Barker was in Deborah Mainwaring's property—' he began.

'He admitted as much,' Peterson said.

'But as for the Cliff house,' Bennett paused and took a swig of his pint. 'Not a lot we can do without any evidence. We got a warrant to search their house, but there was no sign of the stolen goods, and we couldn't find any glass cutters. We'll keep on at Barker though.'

'An ongoing investigation,' Kathryn Gordon said and a low groan went round the gathered officers.

'Exactly,' Bennett agreed. 'We know he was involved, along with Martin, but there's no way of proving it. Martin'll go down for murder, one way or another. There's too much on him. He'll be going down for a long time.'

'Can't be too long,' Peterson interjected.

'But we can't touch Barker for now. We'll keep watching him though. Sooner or later he'll slip up. And when he does, we'll be waiting.' Bennett didn't sound very dynamic.

'But they were responsible for the whole thing,' Polly insisted. 'We can't let them get away with it.'

'Martin's not getting away,' Peterson said.

'Has he made a statement?' Kathryn Gordon asked.

'He denies everything,' the sergeant told her. 'But he killed the woman, Brenda, and we've got him driving the stolen vehicle used to run over Maggie Palmer. That's two murders, and assaulting a police officer.'

'We don't know Barker's a murderer,' Geraldine pointed out. 'He was with Martin on the burglaries but, for all we know, as far as he's concerned, it all went wrong and he never intended for anyone to get hurt. He certainly seems pretty clueless about what happened. And he hasn't exactly got off scot free. He was assaulted and almost burned to death.'

'He won't be able to walk properly again,' Bennett added. 'And he'll be disfigured for life.'

'Lost his good looks,' a constable said and a few people laughed.

'At least we've got Martin,' someone said.

Kathryn Gordon looked uneasy. 'From what I've heard, Martin killed his girlfriend, Brenda, in a struggle. He can plead manslaughter. As for the other victim, Maggie Palmer, we can prove he drove the car that was used to kill her, but can we prove beyond all doubt he was driving it at the time of the accident?' No one answered. The celebratory mood fell flat.

At that moment, James Ryder burst into the pub, beaming. 'I've just heard from forensics. Sample tissue has been retrieved from under the finger nails on Cartwright's right hand.'

425

'The scratches on Callum Martin's face,' Geraldine said with sudden excitement.

'We'll have to wait for DNA confirmation,' Ryder added, 'but they've found a fragment of someone else's hair under one of Cartwright's nails. It matches Martin's stubble.'

'Do you think Cartwright did it deliberately?' Geraldine asked. 'Realising Martin was about to kill him, he dropped his glasses hoping they'd be found and lead us to him, and scratched Martin's face knowing it would incriminate Martin if we found the body.'

'More likely he lost his glasses in the scuffle and hit out at Martin in a desperate attempt to defend himself. I like your theory, but it sounds a bit far fetched. He was an old man frightened for his life,' Ryder replied. Someone handed him a pint.

'He was a detective sergeant,' Geraldine protested. Her voice was drowned out by cheering as the DCI held up his glass.

'Whatever happened, we've nailed Martin for murder,' he said. There was another cheer. 'I couldn't have asked for a better team. And, as you all know, partnership is what this job is all about.'

'Yes,' Geraldine agreed, 'we're a good team.' No one was listening to her. She raised her glass and drank to the memory of a solitary old man sitting in the corner of a pub.

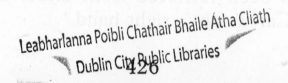